COUNT ON ME

Lauren Dane

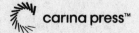 carina press™

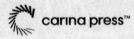

ISBN-13: 978-1-335-21582-6

Count on Me

This is the revised text of the work first published by
Samhain Publishing, 2014

This edition published by Carina Press, 2019

COUNT ON ME

LAUREN DANE

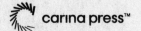

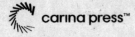

carina press™

ISBN-13: 978-1-335-21582-6

Recycling programs for this product may not exist in your area.

Count on Me

This is the revised text of the work first published by Samhain Publishing, 2014

This edition published by Carina Press, 2019

Copyright © 2019 by Lauren Dane

www.CarinaPress.com

Printed in U.S.A.

COUNT ON ME

Author Note

Dear wonderful readers,

I'm so thrilled to say all my Chase Brothers and their friends and loved ones in Petal, Georgia, are all available to you once more! Aside from some basic, clean up edits of my terrible grammatical crimes, the stories are the same.

These families and characters have a special place in my heart and I'm so pleased you all love them too.

Welcome back to Petal!
Lauren

Playlist

Some of you enjoy it when I talk about the music on my track list for my books. For *Count on Me*, Luke Bryan was sort of this book's patron musical muse!

Play It Again—Luke Bryan
Blue Ocean Floor—Justin Timberlake
Oklahoma Sky—Miranda Lambert
Dreams—The Kills
The Long Way Around—Dixie Chicks
Shut It Down—Luke Bryan
Wait for Me—Kings of Leon
Fall into Me—Brantley Gilbert
Somebody to Love—Valerie June
It Is What It Is—Kacey Musgraves
Temple—Kings of Leon
Take It Outside—Brantley Gilbert
Back on the Map—Kacey Musgraves
Crash My Party—Luke Bryan
Rain—Patty Griffin
I Found You—Alabama Shakes
Dixie Cups and Jars—Waxahatchee
Beautiful War—Kings of Leon
Roller Coaster—Luke Bryan

Supersoaker—Kings of Leon
I See You—Luke Bryan
That's My Kind of Night—Luke Bryan
Safe—Miranda Lambert

Royal and Caroline's song: Crash My Party—Luke Bryan
Caroline's song: Back on the Map—Kacey Musgraves
Royal's song: Out Like That—Luke Bryan

Chapter One

Caroline adjusted the front of her blouse as she waited in the elegantly appointed reception area of the Law Offices of Chase and Chase.

She'd prepared for the interview much the same way a general might prepare for war. Every contingency had been planned for. Every possible question she might be asked needed to have an answer.

All the research and preparation kept her mind off being back in Petal for good instead of one of her usual visits, which tended to last just a few days.

The receptionist, as pretty and elegant as the walnut furniture and framed black-and-white photographs of Petal over the last century plus, spoke quietly over the phone and then turned her attention to Caroline.

"They're ready for you now."

She led Caroline into a small conference room where three men, all clearly related, stood upon her entrance.

"Ms. Mendoza, it's a pleasure to meet you." One of the men she recognized from the pictures on the website—the younger of the Chase brothers who ran the firm—held out a hand. "Peter Chase."

She took it. "Nice to meet you as well. Caroline Mendoza."

The silver fox she knew was Edward Chase smiled at her, warm and open, as he held his hand out. "Edward Chase."

She shook his hand and objectified him. In her head of course, she wasn't a savage.

"Justin Chase."

He was the next generation, she knew. Peter's youngest son.

Edward indicated a chair. "Please sit. Would you like some tea or some coffee?"

"No, thank you."

Clearly Edward was in charge as he conducted the interview. He led her through the interview basics. Asked her what drove her.

Finally, Peter Chase broke in. "Why then? Why make the move from a city where you'd built a successful practice, where you could bill nearly four hundred dollars an hour, to Petal where you'll be lucky to make half that? And not even a third of that on those two or three cases we take on from the county?"

"Some things have happened recently that led me to reevaluate my life and my future. I was born and raised here. Lived here until I was sixteen. My sister and brother live here with my maternal grandparents. My brother is about to graduate high school and head off to college. I just want to be around them more than a few times a year. Life is too short to be halfway across the country. I've missed enough of their lives."

"We're the only firm in town. What would you do if we said no?"

"Well, I could hang out my own shingle. But that's a lot of work, and though I've done it before, I don't really want that at this stage in my life. I've got my resume in at firms between here and Atlanta. I sat for the bar here a few years back, just to have it in case I ever wanted to move to Georgia again, so I'm good to go. No matter where I end up."

"You're ambitious and accomplished. You aren't averse to going down to the jail or out to the prison. We'd be fools to say no. We already have a client list that encompasses a fifty-mile radius or so. I do most of the criminal-defense work now, but with you on board, we could do a lot better. You have the appellate experience we'd like as well. You're a hometown girl. You're incredibly qualified and we'd like to offer you a job here. Partnership track if that's what you're looking for." Edward pushed a piece of paper her way detailing salary, bonus structure, benefits and the steps to partnership.

She looked it over. It was exceptionally fair. She already had a nest egg from selling her share of her firm in Seattle. Most of it she wanted to hold aside for college for her siblings so this would enable her to live a comfortable life and not have to touch that other money.

"Before you accept though, I'd like to address the elephant in the room," Peter said.

Ah. There it was.

"My father."

All three Chases nodded.

"My father's arrest, trial and incarceration are what sent me to law school to start with. I've spent the last fifteen years of my life in one way or another trying to prove his innocence. Despite his death, I plan to continue to search for my mother's killer and to exonerate my father."

Edward drew in a slow breath, probably trying to find

the right words to bring up the other elephant in the room. "Your grandparents aren't going to like that."

"I love my grandparents, but we *don't* agree about who was responsible for my mother's murder. Regardless, the person who killed my mother is walking free, maybe even here in Petal, and I will not allow that to continue unchecked. My mother is dead. My siblings and I grew up without our parents. My father spent fourteen years in prison slowly dying. It's offensive to me that the real killer has been free all this time. I'll be careful to keep my actions separate from Chase and Chase, but it isn't something I'm prepared to stop pursuing."

"We've discussed this, Peter, Justin and I. I'm of the opinion that if I were in your place, I'd do the same. You understand the difference between your personal search for justice and what we do as a firm. That's the only issue we have any business caring about. You keep that distance and we're just fine. Can you start next week?"

She agreed and found herself with a job.

Chapter Two

Caroline took a stroll along the sidewalk to peek in the various storefronts on her way to the grocery store.

Some of the places she remembered remained. The Honey Bear with its bright red tabletops and black-and-white striped booths and chairs. Her dad would bring them home blond brownies as treats sometimes. She warmed at the memory.

"Caroline!"

A tiny woman in towering heels and equally towering hair hurtled in her direction. Caroline smiled even before she recognized Polly Chase, Edward's wife and something of a town matriarch.

"Mrs. Chase, hello." Caroline took the hands Polly held out, squeezing them. She'd always liked the older woman who'd often volunteered in the school and library as Caroline had grown up. Her sons were several years older, but they were each so ridiculously handsome and well mannered it had been impossible for any young woman to have not known who they were.

Polly Chase was lovely. The kind of Southern woman Caroline had always admired. Mrs. Chase wasn't just old school in her appearance, Caroline bet the other woman never left her house without being done up. She'd certainly never go to the market in pajama bottoms.

At the same time, she managed to pull it off without being judgmental or uptight. She owned herself in ways Caroline found herself admiring greatly.

"You look pretty today." And Polly did. She wore a blue scarf that brought out the green in her eyes and the gold-blond in her hair too. Her nails were done up nice and she smelled really good.

"Thank you, sweetheart. I was just out visiting a friend of ours recovering from surgery." She paused a moment. "I am so glad I ran into you today. Are you too busy to have a cup of cocoa and something sweet with me at the Honey Bear?"

This was the boss's wife and someone she admired. There was no drawback to saying yes.

"That would be wonderful."

They headed back the other way and into the Honey Bear, which was warm and smelled like the best thing on Earth.

The woman behind the counter erupted into a sunny smile when she saw Polly. "Hey there, Mrs. Chase!"

Then she turned to Caroline. "I'm so glad you came in. I've been on the lookout for you."

Melissa Gallardo had been an acquaintance back in school but over the last several years they'd become social-media friends. It had been nice to come to Petal and have a friend already.

"I told you yesterday I was finally finishing up with emptying all my boxes and I'd call you."

"You two know each other? I came in here and planned to introduce Caroline to you, Melissa." Polly grinned.

"We knew each other in school and reconnected on-line three or four years back. I'm concerned about the impact on my wallet now that someone who loves bags as much as I do lives in the same town." Melissa winked.

"Well then, I assume you two would like a table?"

Polly nodded. "Oh yes, a table would be good, thank you, honey."

Melissa grabbed two menus and took them to a booth with a great view of the sidewalk. "This way you can people watch."

"Can you start us off with two hot chocolates? I'm pretty sure we're going to order something to eat too, but I want to look at the menu first."

Melissa patted Polly's arm. "You bet."

Once they'd gotten their hot chocolates and Polly had ordered vegetable soup for both of them along with some cinnamon buns, she turned back to Caroline.

"Edward is so pleased you're joining the firm. He's been talking about you so much it makes me laugh. I think my husband has a crush on your career."

Caroline laughed and then wondered if she should feel bad. Was that a warning? Was Polly mad?

Polly patted her hand with a chuckle. "Justin—that's my nephew—anyway, he's been pushing his dad and Edward to hire some new blood to expand what they do. He came over to the house with your resume when it arrived in the mail a few weeks back. He and Edward talked about you for hours at the table that night.

"And it means Edward can take a step back more often and spend time at home. We have an anniversary trip coming up and lots of grandbabies to love up on, so you help him do that more often."

"Well, I'm happy to hear that. Sometimes it's easy to

get caught up in your job, especially when it's your firm. When Edward gave me a tour of the place, he showed me all the pictures in his office of your growing family. He was so proud of each and every one of them."

"I would have had ten kids if I could have. Having grandchildren is the best of both worlds because I get to see them all the time and spoil them and hand them over to their parents. It's funny, I've been in love with Edward since I was seventeen years old and I didn't think it was possible to find new things about him to adore. But watching him with our children and their families, well, it's something special."

Caroline smiled but the realization that she'd never have that settled into her stomach like lead. Her mother was dead. Her father was dead.

Polly's smile fell away. "Oh, dear. I'm sorry, I didn't even think."

Caroline shook her head. "You have every right to be happy about things like that. They're good things."

"I knew your parents. I liked them both a great deal, and I have never believed that your daddy could have done it."

Relief washed through Caroline at Polly's words.

"He looked at her like the sun rose and set with her. And she looked at him right back that way. It just never made sense to me the way the whole thing was handled. I just want you to know that. It's going to be difficult here in town sometimes. People judge you based on what they've heard, not always what they know. But you hold your head up."

Caroline blinked back tears. "Thank you for that. Truly."

Their food came, and Melissa tipped her chin to indicate the heaping plate of french fries she'd also delivered. "Fries because why not? They were hot and crispy." She winked at Caroline.

Caroline popped one in her mouth, wincing at the heat, but they were so good. "So awesome. Thank you. I'll call you tonight. I need to go grocery shopping first because I have peanut butter and a box of stuffing. I did maybe eat pie for breakfast."

The Proffits, the people who'd owned and run the Honey Bear for near thirty years, wanted to retire. Their son was an architect and didn't want the business. Melissa and her fiancé had owned and run a cooking school. Something bad had happened, and Melissa, who was Maryellen Proffit's niece, had moved to Petal seven months before to take over and run the Honey Bear and seemed to be happy she had.

"Okay. We close up at five thirty so any time after six or so." Melissa hustled off to help some customers while Caroline and Polly chatted an hour more or so before Caroline needed to get going or she'd never get her grocery shopping done.

On the sidewalk, after Polly had bussed her cheek and click-clacked away in her heels, Caroline could only smile and shake her head at what a total force of nature Polly Chase was. Edward was a really lucky man.

Chapter Three

Caroline stared up to the box she needed.

On the top shelf.

Naturally.

Sighing, she looked through her cart to for something to use to tip it down. Nothing that would work.

Muttering a curse, she stretched and just barely missed it. She'd totally climb the shelves if she had to but the last time she'd tried it, she'd ended up knocking a bunch of jars down and they broke and it was pretty embarrassing. Heaven knew she had enough to work against as it was without an incident on aisle ten with cereal.

"Lemme get that for you."

She looked to the side at the very tall cowboy who'd sidled up to use all his height to retrieve her box of cereal.

"This here?" He pointed at the natural cereal she liked.

"Yes, thanks."

He grabbed it.

"Can you please get two? I figure I may as well just have a backup now, you know in case you aren't around the next time I'm here."

He pulled one more down and turned to drop them in her cart. That's when she realized it was Royal Watson. All grown up.

He faced her and all her parts stood up and cheered. Like a full-stadium wave.

"Hey, it's Caroline Mendoza."

Oh. That accent. All Southern charm. Sexy and slow, like he tasted every word, savoring it before he let it go. She did love a Southern drawl coming from a man who used words like *ma'am* when they opened doors and retrieved things from high shelves. She knew it was pretty old school of her, but damn she didn't even care.

"Hey, it's Royal Watson. Thanks again for the assist."

His grin made her want to moan.

Back in high school, he'd been two grades ahead. He'd been that super cute older boy who probably never noticed her existence. And of course by the time she'd grown into her body, he'd grown into his *everything* and she'd left town.

He had great hands. She tore her gaze away from them and her brain from imagining them on her because *hello*, grocery store, in front of people and all.

As if he knew what she was thinking, he got just a smidge closer. "It's good to see you. You're in town. For a visit or?"

She laughed, putting a hand at her hip. "Come on now. Are we pretending you haven't already heard I moved back to Petal? I may have forgotten my share of things about living in small towns, but your business is everyone's business." And her past had so much meat for the gossip table, she knew tongues had been wagging ever since she signed the lease on her apartment three weeks before.

"All right. Well, my aunt Denver is famous for two things. First, she makes the best coconut cake in a hundred-mile radius. Maybe even the whole state of

Georgia, but there's some serious old-lady cake competition out there so I can't be totally sure. Second, she's got a nose for gossip that is, as my uncle says, unparalleled. I was just being neighborly and was gonna let you divulge all the details to me yourself."

She pushed her cart and he followed. "Yes, I'm back for good."

He loped along at her side. "I may as well come with you. You're what they call size challenged. In case you need something else from the top shelf, I'll come in handy."

"Oh you're not going to use the S word? Go on then. Short. I'm short."

"Why, Ms. Mendoza, I do believe you're yanking my chain. I think you're more fun sized than short."

She blushed. "I don't know why they have to have shelves that are so high to start with. How do all the little old ladies get their cereal anyway?"

"Darlin', they eat Cheerios and mother's oats. All that fancy organic stuff is on the high shelf 'cause it's just you city girls who eat it. I'd check the sell-by date on it, just in case it went bad in 2010 or something."

"There's not a darned thing wrong with wanting healthy options."

He grinned again. "I'm teasing. Well, I'm telling the truth, but also teasing. Heck, we converted the farm into an organic operation three years ago. I'm always happy when people want the healthier option."

"You did? That's awesome."

Before she could ask more questions, they had to skirt around a gaggle of women who gave him the once-over twice.

"I see it'd be impossible to take you anywhere." Caroline gave him a raised brow.

He held his hands out all innocent-like. "You, sweet thing, can take me anywhere you like. In any case, I can't be blamed for being so handsome and charming."

She laughed. Good Lord he was adorable.

"So you're working with Edward Chase then?"

"I bet the gossip already knows what color my sheets are too. Yes. My first day is Monday."

"Makes sense you're a lawyer now. You did love to argue back in school."

As if he'd ever noticed her! Had he?

She managed to pretend she was cool and not giddy. Probably worked. "My uncle says it's a wonderful thing when you can make a living off your most annoying trait."

She paused to put some soup in her cart. "Can you?" She pointed toward the chicken broth.

"There's cans of it right there," he said as he pulled the carton down.

"I have to buy three of the cans to make one of those cartons. And I can use the carton more than once. It has a screw-on top."

"Ah."

Back toward the front of the store he paused, turning to her so she was caged in by the buggy and his body.

Her heart sped as he seemed to block out everything but him.

He lowered his voice, getting just a little closer. "You grew up gorgeous, Caroline."

She licked her lips, his gaze locked on her mouth. A blush crept up her neck, and she tightened her hold on the buggy before she grabbed him by the front of his shirt and hauled him close for a kiss.

So close she could see the gold flecks in his green eyes. The shadow of the dent in his chin even through the scruff of his beard. His skin was sun kissed, his body one of a man who worked outside a lot.

The heat of his body washed over her as the scent of him—of the cold air outside, the detergent from his shirt—reached her nose. It turned out to be pretty difficult not to lean in and sniff him. She bet he smelled really good where his neck met his shoulder.

"Whatever can you be thinking? I hope it's really dirty."

He was without a doubt ridiculously sexy. There was chemistry between them, for damn sure.

It was…sweaty palms, dry mouth, slow-dance-in-a-high-school-gym chemistry. He made her giddy and silly even as he made her tingly and super hot for him. All in the freezer section of the local grocery store in Petal. That took some major testosterone.

"I'm pretty sure the frozen peas don't need to hear my dirty thoughts. As for your compliment? Uh, my genes, thank you. Except the ones that made me short. Though I sort of think fun sized is a good descriptor."

"I bet the peas would be as excited to hear you talk dirty as I am. You should give me your phone number so I can call you and ask you out."

Lord he made her smile. "I should?"

"Oh yeah. I give really good date. How long's it been since you've been dancing, Caroline?"

"Too long apparently." She cocked her head and looked up at him. "Well, Royal, I'll make you a deal."

"Oh yeah? Let me hear it then. I'm sort of easy for big brown eyes."

It had been years since she'd flirted like this. It felt really good.

"You find me in town, and the next time I see you, I might just give you my number. Until then thank you for your assistance with the high shelves."

She winked and moved past him. "It was very nice to see you again. And for the record? You grew up awful sexy."

Royal watched her go, a grin on his face. Caroline Mendoza was fucking beautiful. Oh sure, she'd been pretty enough all those years ago when she'd been a younger girl. But the grown-up Caroline, damn did he want a taste of that.

He went back to get the stuff on his own shopping list, and when he went through the checkout, that damned Melanie Deeds was working the register. The woman was like the clap. She kept showing up no matter how hard you wished she'd just go away.

"Hey, Royal."

He nodded. "Melanie." He didn't want to engage, but he wasn't raised to be rude either. He busied himself getting his wallet out and swiping his card to pay for the groceries, hoping she'd get the hint.

"I saw you talking with Caroline Mendoza."

So the answer to that getting-the-hint thing was clearly a no.

He nodded, not wanting to say anything to encourage her. Not that it made one bit of difference.

"You know her daddy done kilt her momma. Trash. Her brother and sister, they're okay. They stayed back here to live with the Lassiters, but *she* went on out to Los Angeles." Melanie wrinkled her nose. "With *his* people. Look at her back here like she never up and left Petal in the first place."

He knew it would do no good at all to go down this

road with her. And if he took the bait it would be all over
town in ten minutes. Better to give her as little ammu-
nition as possible.

Still, he wasn't just going to remain silent. "Lucky for
her she looks darned good doing it." He looked to the register and repeated his earlier question. "That the total?"

"You don't want to go and tar yourself with that brush,
Royal. You got free of them Murphys at long last, why
do you go and get involved with trash like a Mendoza?
Everyone knows what she is."

He narrowed his gaze. "*Them Murphys?* You mean
my best friends? And Caroline isn't trash, though certainly there are *some* who'd say so. Guess I can't blame
'em, seeing how beautiful and accomplished she is and
all. Now, *is that my total*, because I'd like to pay for my
groceries and get away from you as soon as I can."

Charlie Perkins was behind Royal in line and snorted
a laugh he tried to cover up with a cough.

"I'm just trying to warn you. Folks around here—the
decent ones—aren't going to associate with a person like
that. A murderer."

"I'll let you know when I'm speaking to a decent one."
He pulled some twenties from his wallet, tossed them
down, cancelled his card and put it away before grabbing
his grocery bags. "You ought to try being decent, Melanie. It does your heart good." He strolled out, annoyed.

He'd gone out with Anne Murphy for several years so
he was more than familiar with the stupidity of those in
Petal like Melanie. It wasn't that he didn't know Caroline would be judged by some. Her mother's murder had
been a horrible event in Petal history, and the trial and
subsequent conviction of her father had the town splitting up into camps.

Royal had been young, a senior in high school when the whole thing had gone down. He wasn't sure what to think other than to know Caroline was not to blame for what her father did or didn't do.

He loaded the bags into his truck and headed home. He'd had some major tingles for Caroline Mendoza. She made him laugh. Called him sexy.

It had been eighteen months since he and Anne had broken up for good. He'd wanted something permanent, and she never would accept it so he finally had to walk away.

Eighteen months of licking wounds and then moving on. Dating a lot. Having some great sex too. But nothing like he'd had with Anne, because he'd been in love with her. It was old fashioned, he knew, but fucking was a hell of a lot better when you were connected with the person you were in bed with.

Caroline was someone he'd known peripherally, but there was something new about her too. Unusual. He liked it.

He planned to make it his goal to find her around town to get that number. He could have gotten it on his own, but he rather liked the idea of letting it all play out slow. Enjoy it.

She'd give in eventually. She was pretty clear about that, so why not let it play out and see what happened?

This was the best thing that had happened to him in a grocery store pretty much ever. He snorted and started home.

Edward Chase was mighty glad the pastor must have been hungry and finally closed out the sermon so Edward could head home with his wife and have lunch.

Polly gave him a look, a hint of amusement on those

pretty lips of hers. She knew him inside and out. Hell she probably had a snack for him in that giant handbag.

"Shane and Cassie are coming over with Ward. I think Maggie and Kyle are bringing the boys by as well. Good thing I started that ham before we left." She was talking about their two oldest sons, their wives and their grandsons.

He grinned, knowing how much noise and energy his boys and their families came with. Knowing his wife was in raptures when she got to love all over their grandchildren.

"Hummingbird cake for dessert and I've got potatoes in the slow cooker too." She winked and he squeezed her to his side.

"I'm a very lucky man." He brushed a kiss over her mouth. "Even luckier when everyone goes home," he whispered as he straightened.

Her delighted laugh sped his heart. There wasn't another person on the whole of the planet who made him feel like the one he'd cleaved his life to.

He might even be able to squeeze a little time with her in bed before everyone arrived if they could get out of church fast enough.

He steered her toward the doors but before they got there, Abigail and James Lassiter stepped into their path.

Abigail extended her hands, and he took them, squeezing before letting go to shake James's hand.

"We won't keep you long." Abigail's accent was old-school Georgia. She'd been third runner-up for Miss Georgia in her day. Even in her eighties she was still striking. She was a powerful person with very set opinions on everything. She'd grown up in Atlanta, where her people owned and ran one of the oldest and largest building companies in the Southern US. She'd met and married James, a Petal boy born and raised, and they'd settled just a few blocks from where Edward had grown up.

There was history there. James was fifteen years older than Edward. He'd been the quarterback, the most popular this or that. His family and the Chase family had been tight as James's father had been a judge in the county for forty years. James Lassiter was sort of like an older cousin in Edward's extended family.

Abigail smiled Edward's way. "We wanted to thank you for giving Caroline a job at the firm. She needs some roots here and with you she has them."

Edward shook his head. "Believe me when I tell you it was no imposition or even a favor on our part. Your granddaughter is a coup for us. She's incredibly accomplished. For her to have so much experience at her age is stellar. We're thrilled to have her on board."

Polly shifted, sliding her arm through Edward's. "Caroline is so intelligent and successful. You and James must be so proud."

Edward knew she had taken a shine to Caroline, but this was more. Polly had just planted a flag with that declaration. Caroline Mendoza was under her protection. Woe to anyone who lobbed anything at the girl now.

Abigail though, she smiled, a genuine flush of pleasure that reached her eyes. "We're very proud. James's daddy would have been so thrilled to see his great-granddaughter go into law and do so well."

But then the smile faltered. "Now that she's back, James and I are hoping she'll finally let go of her fool notions about *that man*."

Edward had known it would only be a matter of time before it came up, but even he was surprised by the venue.

They walked out to the church steps and down toward the parking lot. He aimed for the car, preferring to avoid the topic.

But Abigail wasn't having it. She planted herself in their path. "Heaven knows we've tried over the years. Tried to force her to see the error of her ways. She has no call to go stirring up painful memories for a lark. She needs to grow up and get serious."

Edward shook his head. "She's a grown woman, Abigail. It's not my place to get in the middle of this." Nor was it theirs. But he'd been blessed enough to have never lost a child so he had a difficult time saying that part aloud.

"She's shaming this family by siding with his people."

Polly's pretty green eyes narrowed and her grip on his arm tightened. "Now, Mrs. Lassiter, I surely do hope you don't really feel that way. Why your Caroline is such a beautiful, successful young woman. Family minded. Sometimes our loved ones have opinions we don't agree with, but we love them just the same."

Abigail took Polly's measure. Polly was no slouch herself though, and gave Abigail a similar look. Abigail broke her gaze first as she sniffed. "She should show her love by not demeaning the murder of her mother. You and Edward are good influences on her. I'm simply asking him to exert some of that in the right direction so she can have a home in this town."

"We're glad to have her on board at the firm. And most assuredly happy to have her in town. She's an asset to us and I hope we can be one to her as well. It was very nice to chat with you both, but Polly and I need to get home. We've got kids and grandkids coming over for lunch." Edward kissed Abigail's cheek and squeezed

James's shoulder and firmly stepped away, guiding his wife toward the car.

He had some thinking to do because this situation wasn't going away. He liked Caroline, and he knew she'd be in for a bumpy road as she settled back into Petal.

Chapter Four

"Ready to head to the courthouse?" Edward paused in her doorway. She'd been there since about seven and had already put the cases and files in order and begun to get her schedule organized.

She stood, grabbing her suit jacket and sliding it on before hoisting the strap of her bag onto a shoulder. "Yes. Thank you."

Edward, Peter and Justin had all offered to let her come along as they went to the courthouse, and she'd eagerly accepted. It was good to get to know what their schedules looked like when they were working and to be introduced to people that way. They tended to see you as a colleague that way instead of perpetually the new girl.

Edward was the only one in the firm who currently practiced criminal law so he also offered to take her to the jail. Given the firm's location and the types of cases she'd most likely get, she'd end up at one of the local county lockups and some of the outlying city jails. Occasionally she'd need to go to one of the over thirty prisons in the state. But she knew a few of them pretty well already, especially the Georgia Diagnostic Classification State Prison where her father had been on death row for fourteen years.

As they walked, Edward motioned across the street. "How about you let me take you to lunch afterward? It's meatloaf sandwich day at the Sands, and chances are better than even that there'll be cherry pie."

"I haven't been there in ages." The diner had dominated Main Street in Petal since before her parents had been born. It had also been the chief competition to her parents' family-style diner and café out on the main highway.

So many memories greeted her every single day she woke up back home in Petal. Which seemed stupid when she'd been back to visit at least twice a year since she left. It wasn't like she'd totally left it behind.

Edward's eyes went kind. "We can go elsewhere if you like."

"No. No I'm fine. It's not like I can avoid going to diners my whole life. Anyway, diners are the best source for gravy and gravy-related products. Like I'm giving that up?"

At the end of the block, they paused at a hail for Edward.

Edward smiled as he turned to face the living incarnation of every single hot-cop fantasy she'd ever had.

"Hey, son."

Edward hugged his oldest son and turned to Caroline. "Caroline Mendoza, this is my son Shane. He was recently elected police chief here after running the sheriff's office for years. Shane, this is Caroline, though you might know her from school."

He shook her hand as he gave her a once-over with cop eyes. Albeit gorgeous ones. She was used to cops looking at her like that, especially if they were just meeting her in her official capacity. Over time she'd made friends with a lot of the cops she dealt with after they got to know her and realized she wanted justice just as much as they did. She was fair, though, without vanity she could say she was damned good at her job. But she didn't cheat or lie to win, and despite its failings, she did believe in the system.

Shane Chase was a cop, and she was not only a defense attorney, but new to his town and to his dad's firm. He'd suspect her until she proved she was worthy of his trust, and she was all right with that.

"I think I was too far ahead of her in school to have been there at the same time." Shane turned his attention back to Caroline, and while it was clear he was still going to keep an eye on her, his expression was friendly. "Welcome back to Petal, Caroline. How are my dad and uncle treating you?"

"It's only been a few hours, but so far I've gotten a lunch invitation out of it so I can't complain."

"We're on our way to the courthouse. I figured I'd toss Caroline into the deep end and let her handle some bail hearings."

Which was news to her, but okay then. She'd done bail hearings so many times that even in a new jurisdiction she should have no problems.

They headed up the front steps and into the large foyer of the courthouse. "We're on the second floor. That's where they bring over the non-flight risks from the jail. We'll have hearings on the three cases I put on your desk this morning."

This had been a test of her preparedness. She'd read those case files before he'd even arrived at the office. It was easy to forget that Edward Chase was an incredibly accomplished man because he was charming and jovial.

But beneath that exterior he was a little bit of a shark. It made her like him even more.

"Depending on the judge I think Reggie Miller and Marvin Wilson should be fine. Abel Carson though, this is his third arrest on receiving stolen goods. From what I understand of this judge, she doesn't take too kindly to repeat offenders. Even when their daddy owns the car lot and the feed store in town."

Edward grinned like she'd just won first prize.

She dived in and handled the hearings. Edward didn't say much after he introduced her to the judge. She met with her clients, and maybe two of the three wouldn't be back for a repeat performance if she could get them out of trouble.

After wrapping things up at the courthouse, they'd headed over to the Sands for lunch. Once they'd put in their orders and two tall glasses of iced tea had been set before them, Edward raised his in Caroline's direction. "You did a good job today. Glad to have you on board."

She snorted but raised her glass back. "Thanks."

"So, tell me something, Caroline."

"What's that?"

"Your daddy was found guilty and he lost three appeals. Why do you still think he's innocent?"

She preferred direct people in her life and Edward Chase was no exception. Better he ask than she try to figure out what she could talk about and in how much detail.

"Where was the motive? Why would a happily married man with no criminal history and not a single whisper of trouble in his marriage suddenly violently murder his wife? They had nothing. The only physical evidence was paper thin. His DNA at the scene? A diner he was in

daily? He had no defensive wounds. If he'd have stabbed
her forty-two times, how did he not nick himself a single one? Where was the murder weapon? There was so
much evidence they just never followed up on. There
were footprints outside the back door. Three sizes bigger than my father's. There was blood, three drops of it,
from my mother's body to the back door. Not the same
type as my father's. They never even ran a DNA test."

"So why arrest your daddy then? Why put him on
trial? Why find him guilty?"

"Sure, because you and I both know people never ever
get railroaded for stuff they didn't do."

"No shortcuts, Ms. Mendoza." He wagged his finger.

"Look, here's this guy, an outsider in a small town.
The beautiful blonde former cheerleader and homecoming queen is horribly murdered." Her jaw hardened for
a moment as she thought about her mother, about how
truly lovely her mom had been. Caroline had seen the
crime-scene photos, the ones her father's family had refused to let her look at until she'd turned eighteen and
gotten the case file herself.

Her mother had been broken. Stabbed and bloodied.
Hanks of her hair had been cut off with a knife, probably the same one that had killed her.

"They come in, she's been horribly killed. My father
is holding her and he's in a fugue state. He can't answer
their questions. He's covered in her blood. It's a neat
package, and while the sheriff you have *now* is certainly
no slouch, the one Petal had then wasn't going to turn
away from an easy answer. A Mexican guy comes in,
takes their golden beauty and kills her. He told the court
during my dad's trial that that's what *people like Enrique
do*. I'll never forget that as long as I live.

"My father made an easy target. Add lazy police work and an overloaded system, and you got a conviction. He had a decent defense. Hell, his attorney even helped me appeal on inadequate defense. The other procedural stuff?" She shrugged her shoulders. "I used to think all I had to say was *he didn't do it* and they'd let him go. It's what drove me to law school. And then I learned that wasn't enough. I have a sense that some evidence was withheld but not enough to actually build a case. I know for sure there's evidence missing. Phone log pages from the days following the murder for one."

Edward nodded as they paused when their lunch arrived.

"He didn't do it. I knew my parents better than anyone else who testified. They argued, sure, but not in an abnormal way. She spoiled us and he spoiled her and they were good. My dad was a gentle person. And no one was more damaged by her murder than he was. He used to weep all the time that the real killer was out there. He worried over me and my siblings, for our safety."

She shook her head. "This is a man who never even spanked us, how is that guy going to stab his wife forty-two times and hack off her hair? And why? Where did the hair go? Where did the weapon go? Whose blood was it at the scene? There was not enough to overcome reasonable doubt. At all."

"How long has this been your personal project?"

"I left here and moved in with my uncle in Long Beach. I was sixteen. I spent the next year or so fighting counseling, but my uncle and my dad's parents pushed until I went. Every time I came back here, I'd sort of lose my way and it took me a few months to get back on track again. But right before I graduated from high school, I

read a piece in a magazine about the Innocence Project
and a man they'd just freed from prison after a DNA test
proved he wasn't the murderer. I was eighteen."

"You never doubted? Not even once?"

"They arrested him that night and he never came
home. We all moved in with my grandparents here. They
were convinced from that moment and we were never
allowed to speak otherwise. But I just…" She shrugged.
"It never occurred to me that he was capable of such a
thing. He just wasn't. And my mom was really smart.
Strong. She wouldn't have stayed if he was the monster
they said he was at trial. If for no other reason than us.
She would have died to protect us. If he'd been abusive,
she'd have left him."

"How do your grandparents feel about this whole thing?"

"It's complicated." She snorted. "I mean, you know
them. I know the Lassiters and Chases have been friends
for a few generations now. They believe what they believe, which is their right. I don't think they were ever
going to hear anything else other than my father's guilt."

"I've known your grandparents a long time, yes. And
your grandmother is…well, you're a lot like her. She's
very sure of her opinions. But unlike you, I'm not sure
she's looked into any other explanations of the murder."

"Most people don't. I understand that. Their daughter
was killed. The authorities told them who did it and that
was enough. It is for most people and it's that way for a
reason. But they see my leaving Petal as a betrayal. To
them, I chose a side. We don't talk about it. But when
it comes up, as things people try to bury with resent-
ment always do, it's ugly and judgmental. They loved
my mother and there's no room for me to love both my

parents. They see my belief in my father's innocence as a betrayal of my mother."

He didn't speak for a long time, but it wasn't an uncomfortable silence so Caroline made a serious dent in her meatloaf.

Edward liked Caroline Mendoza a great deal. It took courage to believe things others didn't. Especially when he knew it had estranged her from her mother's people as well as her siblings.

After his chat with Abigail and James at church the day before, he'd come home and spent the rest of the afternoon and evening with his family. But Caroline had been in the back of his mind.

Caroline and her father's case.

On the way home in the car, Polly had said, "The way they talk about that girl bothers me. Abigail has no right at all to make it out that Caroline is selfish. Imagine, Edward, what it must have been like for her growing up after her momma was killed. Her brother and sister always had Abigail and James there for them. But they talk about Caroline like she's that uncle who keeps going to jail for stuff no one wants to talk about. I don't like it one bit."

His wife was clever, and she had a heart bigger than anyone else he'd ever known. He could see right then that Caroline would be pulled into their family if Polly had any say. And he'd never seen a single person who could resist his wife when she set her mind to something.

"What do you think, Edward?" Polly had asked.

"About what, lamb?"

"Did Enrique Mendoza kill Bianca?"

"I didn't go to the trial. I've read the articles about

it. I've never been entirely comfortable that reasonable doubt was overcome."

"People are going to be hostile to her. She's going to need folks in her corner."

"You proposing us?" He grinned.

"I never get in your work business. That's your world and it's not my place. But, if you ever thought maybe he was innocent, that she was right, well I imagine that would sway more than a few folks in town. She's alone. I know the Lassiters have suffered, but they're wrong to shut Caroline out the way they do. You can't put conditions on love that way."

Again, Polly had been right and he'd been thinking about it since then. He'd thought about it ever since Caroline's resume had shown up in the office. Had even before that, on and off over the years.

He'd decided when he'd gotten up that morning to get some answers of his own, and what he discovered would help him decide what to do next.

"I wager you have a file. On your father I mean."

Caroline nodded. "I do."

"Can I see it?"

Hope lit her gaze but it was wary at the edges. "Why?"

"I'm going to be honest with you because I'm not very good at lying and I respect you too much to play games. I have never entirely felt convinced of your father's guilt. I'd like to see what you've gathered up."

"All right. And then what?"

"It's not going to be totally easy, you know, coming back here and pursuing this. People feel threatened when you start hacking away at the foundations of the things they believe keep them safe. If I read what you've got and I am convinced of his innocence, you'll have another person to help. Another person in your corner. But if I read it and I'm not, well, I'll tell you that too. But I won't ever make you stop trying to prove his innocence either way. That's your business and your right."

"You've got yourself a deal." Her smile was a little weak but it was there.

Chapter Five

Royal had come to town pretty much daily since he'd seen Caroline in the grocery store. He hoped he managed to bump into her soon or daily trips to town might be seen as more stalkery and less *hey I hope I can bump into Caroline today.*

He'd tried the courthouse and some of the restaurants near her office. A girl had to eat. He knew she was around. Petal was Petal after all and the gossip machine was in full swing. Word was all over the place about her return.

She was beautiful so that was mentioned a lot in positive and negative terms. A lawyer, also mentioned a lot. Frowned on, though less so, because she'd started with Edward Chase's firm. Whispers about her father had made him uncomfortable on many levels.

So he'd come to town. First to grab his aunt's prescription and to drop off some invoices, and now to stroll by the offices of Chase and Chase to see if he could engineer bumping into a fun-sized brunette with big brown eyes and a fantastic rack.

It was after six, but he figured she wasn't one for leaving right at five.

And like he'd dreamed her up, she pushed out of the

doors and settled the strap of her bag on a very well-dressed shoulder.

Damn her mouth was gorgeous. She wore the ghost of a smile as she turned on the sidewalk and headed in his direction.

Royal raised his hand and waved, and when she noticed him, her attention settled like a physical thing.

"Hey now, it's Caroline Mendoza."

That ghost of a smile bloomed into a genuine one. An expression that told him how happy she was to see him.

"Why hello, Royal."

He tipped his chin in her direction. "You're even better than Friday."

One of her brows went up. "You're pretty good with the flattery."

He hadn't been entirely sure about the Friday line so he was glad she'd liked it. "I do believe you said if I bumped into you around town you'd have a drink with me."

"I think I said I'd probably give you my number if you bumped into me around town. However I'm thirsty and it's been a long week, so let's pretend I totally did." She held up a coat and some files. "I need to drop this all off and to change. Because nothing about stockings says relaxation."

He gulped. "Stockings, huh? Well I don't know if it says relaxation, but it sure does say all sorts of positive things to me."

She grinned.

"Did you drive?"

"I only live four blocks away so I walked."

He took her files and coat. "I'll carry them for you. How about we do dinner *and* a beer? I'm starving."

She shrugged and took up walking next to him. "All righty."

For a short person, she moved surprisingly fast. Sort of headfirst. She seemed so very sure about everything she did, right down to walking.

She led him up a set of back stairs to her apartment, and he barked a laugh. "One of my friends used to live here. A bachelor pad of sorts."

She unlocked and waved him in, but he held the door for her. "Really? I guess I should be glad the walls can't talk."

Considering the life Marc Chase had lived before he'd ended up with his wife, probably not. Unless Caroline liked dirty-talking walls.

She looked back at him as she hung her coat up. "You can drop those files on the table. Where are we going to dinner?"

"Huh?" He'd been staring at her ass and only caught a word or two.

"Dinner? Jeans okay or do I need to dress up?"

He panicked for a moment. He'd planned on the Pumphouse. They had a great menu and plenty of beers on tap, but should he take her somewhere nicer?

"That wasn't a trick question, Royal."

"Go on, laugh at my confusion."

"I would if I knew what you were confused about. How about this? I would very much like to relax. A pitcher of beer, a burger, tacos, pizza, you know, casual stuff."

"Sounds perfect. The Pumphouse then. So jeans are just fine."

"I'll be out in a few."

He cruised around her apartment, looking at the pictures on the walls. He paused at the wedding photograph. Her mother and father so very young. Hell, younger than he was right then.

Love was stamped all over them. He knew at that moment, without a single doubt, that Caroline saw them just like this. Her memories of her parents were of these two people. And he understood it. These two people could not have ended the way they had with Bianca Mendoza's broken body in her husband's arms. Not with Enrique as the man who killed her.

Royal didn't know the truth of it, but he knew what she saw, what Caroline believed.

"They were eighteen. She was pregnant with me but you can't even tell."

She'd come out and he hadn't even heard.

"You ready?"

He turned and the breath was knocked from his lungs at the sight of her. "Good Lord above you're beautiful."

She smiled and there was shyness in it. He hadn't seen even a hint of shyness about her, and it sent a wave of tenderness through his gut.

He tipped his head toward the picture of her parents. "I recognize the church. My parents were married there too. She was pregnant as well." He winked and Caroline swallowed hard and the smile she gave him this time was different. Not flirty or sweet, there was…gratitude maybe? He wasn't sure what it was, but for a brief moment she was vulnerable.

It was gone after a breath or two, though, replaced with her take-charge expression. "Come on then. I'm really hungry, and one of my clients was such a pain in the ass this week I need at least two beers."

He took her hand once they'd reached the sidewalk,

and the shock of it sang up his arm. She fit there with him, her hand in his.

She didn't attempt to pull away as she adjusted her pace to his.

The Pumphouse wasn't at full capacity just yet, so they grabbed a small booth near the front windows. He wanted to slide in next to her but he refrained. Across from her he could look his fill, that'd be fine too. The next time, or maybe the time after, he'd claim that space next to her in a booth.

"Beer me." She winked and he liked it.

He ordered a pitcher of a local brew they'd started serving recently.

"I've never eaten in here. What's good?"

"You haven't? It's not like you never came back to town, right? I know you visited a few times a year."

"Do you, now? Have you been keeping tabs on me?"

He started to explain and noted her smirk.

"Lord amighty, woman, I thought you were serious for a minute there."

Caroline snickered as she looked over the menu. "You've met my grandparents, right? Do they strike you as the type to eat in a place like this? My grandmother might keel over at the mere sight of paper napkins, Royal. She's not eating nachos and having three-buck pitchers." She burst out laughing. "Though, oh my God, I'd love to see the look on her face if she did."

"Well, her loss then. The burgers are good. Nachos too. Wings. Bar and grill food."

She put her menu down when their server brought the beer, and she ordered a cheeseburger and rings. He'd been planning on wings, but her order sounded so good he went with that too.

"So tell me then at the end of your first week at work, how's Petal treating you?"

"It's been pretty good. Polly Chase brings me casseroles and cakes. Just for existing. She's freaking amazing, that woman. Tiny woman, huge presence. Oh and her hair. Big hair. She smells good. I've decided I'd like to be her when I grow up."

He snorted. "Polly Chase is a force of nature. Edward is so laid-back and mellow, and she's so chatty and nosy but in the best way. I mean, well you know what I mean."

"Edward's been wonderful. He did sort of just toss me in the deep end with some clients, but that's fine. Partly I think he was testing me, which I'd do in his place. Hell I did it when we hired new people at my old firm. You have to know if people can handle their shit." She clapped a hand over her mouth. "Sorry. Stuff."

His brows flew up and then he snickered. "You worried about offending me or something? I've heard bad words. I say them sometimes too."

"I'm trying to readjust my speed for Petal. Things are different here. I'm already different enough, I'm trying not to make it harder. I have a swearing problem."

His laughter died to a snort. "I get it. But between you and me, I'm not going to be offended. Also, I get the feeling you sort of enjoy being tossed into the deep end. You seem to be the type who thrives on a challenge."

She shrugged. "Makes me happy to keep busy. I like to work hard and play hard. There are plenty of attorneys who hate the courtroom and are happy to write motions and briefs. Me? I love the courtroom. I love the constant and varied challenges with trial. It's a person's life, so I always take it seriously. But there's an art to it as well as skill. I'm weird, what can I say."

"That's not weird at all." In fact it was totally sexy. But he'd wait to share that until they'd been around each other more. He also bet that intensity translated to how she'd be in bed. And he really wanted to know that firsthand.

"Anyway, so to recap, busy work week. Free cake and chicken casserole. I'm having a beer with a handsome man I used to crush on hard back in school. Not a bad first week at all."

"You had a crush on me?" Pleasure swamped him.

"Duh. Who didn't have a crush on you? You have that smile, the slow, sexy one that makes all the girls tingly. You're pretty to look at. You have an extremely fantastic rear end."

She paused when their meal arrived.

"You were saying about my ass?"

"Hush you. You know you have a nice butt. Anyway how was *your* week?"

"Dealing with a root-worm problem with the cabbage. Lost about half the crop. My aunt has been helpfully gathering bits of gossip about you. She's pleased you have a good job and says I could do a lot worse than a gal with some gumption even if she is related to Abigail Lassiter. I probably shouldn't have said that last bit out loud."

Caroline laughed and drank her beer. "It comes as absolutely no surprise to anyone who knows my grandmother that she can be off-putting. Bossy. Annoying. Judgmental. She's very sure of herself. It's just everyone else who disappoints her."

Royal was very glad he'd been raised by his aunt and uncle after his dad had died and his mom had pretty much given up on parenting. They'd always been so good to him. They were solid, committed to family and community. The Lassiters were of that class who tended to look down on half of Petal. Oh sure they did things for the disadvantaged but while Polly did it with an open heart and love, Abigail did it because it was expected and with a barely withheld put-upon sigh.

Frankly, he was surprised Caroline had turned out as normal as she had under the circumstances.

"Right now you're asking yourself, *how did she turn out the way she has when her grandmother is so prissy and uptight.*"

He blushed. "I'm told I can be rude sometimes. But in my defense, I did keep it in my head. I can't help it if you go and snatch it from my thoughts."

She shrugged. "You're not rude. I love my grandparents, but I wasn't raised by them. I was raised by my parents and later by my dad's people. Different philosophy. They did okay by my brother and sister."

Mindy Lassiter was sort of prissy too, but Royal kept that to himself.

"Anyway, root worms? That sounds gross and not fun in any way. And you said your farm was organic now, so how do you deal with that when you can't use chemicals?"

"There are some natural ways to deal with it. I spent most of the week pulling out the diseased plants. Had to burn those and hope the rest are not affected. There's this stuff, you sprinkle it around the plant on the dirt and it cuts up any bug, worm, whatever, that tries to get past. Try not to be mesmerized by my job. I know it's incredibly exciting."

"It *is* interesting! Why did you switch over to the organics?"

"We had a bigger spread but it was increasingly harder to compete against the big factory-farm industry." He shrugged. "My uncle wanted to retire and give me the operation, so I had to figure out what I wanted to do." It had happened at a point in his life when he was at a low. In love with a woman who loved him back, just not enough. So he'd sort of leapt. Seeking something totally new. While it had taken him another year and a half to break things off with Anne for good, the shift to an organic operation had been easier to accept.

Traditional farming had been the family business, but he and his uncle spent all their time trying to stay afloat and ahead of loan payments. He'd read a number of pieces about organic farming and had done a lot of research into all sorts of ways to go about it. When he'd presented a business plan to his uncle, the old man had grinned, slapped his back and thrown all his confidence and support Royal's way.

"I proposed that we sell off all but fifty acres and move from two major crops to several smaller organic crops to sell to restaurants, start a CSA box, and to distribute to local farmer's markets and grocery stores who carried organic produce.

"It took a while. You can't just not use pesticides and call yourself organic. There's a process. Lots of hoops to go through. About two years from the day I decided to give it a go, we planted the first crops. Last year we added the CSA box. We work with several small farms and have three hundred subscribers in this area. Next year we might work with one in the Atlanta metro area, but I don't want to expand so fast we screw up our balance. We hit the local farmer's markets, and many grocery stores within a sixty-mile radius stock our stuff. We're going step by step at this point. Some stuff works, other stuff not so much. I *like* being a farmer, you know?

This land has been in my family for generations so it means something to me to continue on with my own stamp on the place."

"Wow, this is awesome. Congratulations, Royal. I'd really love a tour. I used to get a produce box back in Seattle. I was just thinking I needed to look around for one here."

She wasn't just saying it, wasn't flattering to fill the silence. Her eyes were warm, her smile open, and something about that appealed to him a great deal.

"I think I can hook you up with both a tour and a subscription."

She talked with her hands. Animated. Her face open and full of emotion. Having a conversation with Caroline Mendoza was a full-speed race one minute and a slow drive through the country at sunset the next.

She exhilarated him. She was interesting. Fascinating really. Beautiful. Funny. Smart too.

"So why did you come back?" He held up a hand. "Feel free to skip that question if it's too personal."

"I came back because"—she took a bracing gulp of beer—"I don't like not handling things."

He sat back, patient enough to let her speak at her own pace.

"I like having my shit under control. I like facing things that make me worried or sad. I know my grandparents on my dad's side. My *abuela* is still alive and raising Cain. I've got a big, close-knit family in Los Angeles and Portland. My uncle and his partner live in Long Beach. I have three other uncles, two of which also live in Southern California, the third in Portland. They're married and have kids. I've got great-aunts and great-uncles, cousins and second cousins. I know them.

They know me. I can show up on any of their doorsteps and not have to knock before going inside."

Royal nodded. "That's a good feeling."

She smiled, feeling understood. "It is. They keep me grounded and loved. I never had to…" She sighed. "I never have to hide my whole self when I'm with them. It's comfortable and good, and I miss them all very much.

"But there's this space." She pressed the heel of her hand over her heart. "My sister and brother should be part of that in my life. I love them both so much. But I'm closer to my cousins than I am to my own siblings. I knock when I visit my grandparents. I schedule time to spend with my sister and brother. My brother who calls himself Shep like half of himself doesn't exist."

She nodded her thanks when he poured her some more beer.

"I hate that I don't have that ease with my mom's people. I hate that I feel like an outsider in the town I was born and raised in. I hate that my brother and sister have shut the door on all that love I just talked about, and I hate that my mom's parents have made it that way."

He nodded. "I get that. So Mindy and Shep, they don't see or have contact with your dad's people at all?"

"Since the day my mother died, they've refused. My grandparents, the Lassiters I mean, have consistently stood in the way. At first the Mendozas tried via the courts, but my dad's parents didn't want to make things harder. Mindy and Shep were a lot younger than I was, they had it…different than I did. By the time they got older, it was painful for my dad's side of the family just to try to get access. In the end, it would have hurt my siblings so the Mendozas backed off."

"So you came back to smooth the way between your daddy's people and your siblings?"

She shook her head. "When my dad died in prison, everything I'd sort of compartmentalized fell apart. All the spaces in my life where I'd neatly stored people and relationships just sort of dissolved into a messy heap. I realized I couldn't deal with this distance between me and my siblings. That I couldn't just walk away from this place, which is as much a part of me and who I am as it is my siblings'. I can't make them want to have a relationship with our dad's family. But I'm their sister and they should know me. More than just a few times a year. My dad would want that. My mom would want that."

He leaned forward and slid his fingers through hers, tangling them. "I think they're lucky to have you as a big sister."

"I'm not sure they think that way. As much as I want it to be so, we're not close." She raised a shoulder. "They suspect my motives. I end up being so careful all the time to not upset anyone that I'm not totally me. It's artificial and that's not something you can build a real foundation on."

His mouth flattened out. Angry on her behalf. She warmed at that defense, even so subtle. "Why are you being careful? Mindy is an adult, Shep is nearly so, they don't need you to tiptoe around who you are."

What could she say? That when she was twenty her grandmother hauled her into a side room and threatened to never let her see her brother and sister again if she ever spoke of her father or his innocence? That she'd reminded Caroline just how easy it would be to poison Mindy and Shep against her so they'd refuse to see her like they did their father's family?

She took a deep breath. "I have to skirt the elephant in the room to keep the peace. We—that is my siblings and I—experienced the death of our mother very differently. I was far older than they were so I had a more developed relationship with our parents. And their families too. We're very different and my grandparents… Well I suppose I believe they've used that to their advantage to keep that gulf between me and the rest of them."

"Why do you think that?" Not a judgmental question.

"Look, I'm not knocking their grief. I lost her too. But my grandmother is every bit of the control freak I am now. She was given a story of what happened and that is that. To even question it is to choose a side in her mind. Feeding Mindy and Shep an absolute is a way to keep them on my grandmother's correct side of things. It makes it easy to control them, where they go to school, who they see. What they believe. I'm a wild card. I'm a messy bed and unfolded laundry, and as you might imagine, Abigail Lassiter doesn't like either of those things. I wanted to see my sister and brother. I wanted to keep this part of my life alive, even if strained. So I danced to her tune."

"But you're going to change the record now?" One corner of his mouth quirked up.

"I guess you should know this up front, before we go out again or anything like that. I have spent a huge portion of my life, especially the last fourteen or so years, trying to prove my father's innocence. I don't push it in my siblings' faces, but if it comes up, I speak the truth. The truth as I see it. The truth as I've pieced it together after combing through every little piece of evidence I come across over and over. He's dead now. That he lost his wife, his children and his freedom and ultimately his life to the acts of a person who is still out there is something I cannot remain silent about. They kept saying I should move here, my grandparents I mean, so I have. But I'm not Mindy. I'm not easily controlled. And my sibs are old enough to deal with me as adults now." She shrugged.

"First things first. There will most definitely be more dates and *things like that*." He snagged one of the last onion rings off her plate, and she snorted. "I like the way you smell. I like that you're up front with what you want and how you feel. You have no idea how fucking refreshing that is. Sexy too. As for the rest? I don't know the whole story, and as we get to know one another, I'd like to hear your side, what you know. Whatever the reasons you're back, I'm glad of it."

That easy acceptance of her—of the way she felt and her right to feel it—should have been commonplace but it wasn't. She was Caroline Mendoza, the daughter of a convicted murderer.

Back in Petal, there was a thin line, the sharpest she'd ever walked. While she'd been able to build relationships in her life in Los Angeles and Seattle, they hadn't experienced the events surrounding her mother's murder and the trial in the same way people in Petal had. They had an ownership over the history, up close and personal that others didn't.

She'd been pitied and reviled. Humored and ignored. But being believed, or at the very least given the space to have her own feelings and beliefs, well that was rare and it made her appreciate Royal even more.

"Thank you for that. If you have questions, ask them. I'll answer them the best I can."

He kissed her fingertips. "I think we need to finish our

beer and food, blow out of here, grab something sweet and maybe smooch awhile."

"I'm totally on board with that plan."

After they'd finished, the sheer volume in the room had risen as it had gotten past nine on a Friday night. People played pool in the back, servers shuttled through the room with pitchers of beer, and there was a lot of laughter, shit talking and curious looks her way.

A bunch of people came in and shouted his name. He tore his gaze away from her—a thing she liked a whole lot—and grinned, waving. "Hey!"

She recognized a few of the Chases in the throng of handsome men. Some other faces looked vaguely familiar, but they'd all grown up in the time she'd been away.

"You gonna play tonight?" they called out.

Royal looked back her way and she rolled her eyes. "Depends," she said quietly with a smirk. "I won't be insulted if you want to play pool either."

"I was about to introduce you. I have no desire to play pool with my reprobate friends when I'm on a date with you. But I surely do like the sound of that depends."

He tossed down money to pay the bill and slid out from the booth, holding a hand she took and let him haul her to her feet.

He wrapped an arm around her shoulders, and they strolled over to his friends with her snugged up to his side. And she totally pretended to miss the way some of his friends' eyes widened momentarily.

"Y'all, this is Caroline Mendoza. I think several of you may have known her at school, though most of us were older except for Trey and Jacob, who were probably still in middle school when she was in high school." He'd told most of them about her. Hell, he saw most of them at least three times any given week anyway.

He pointed. "That's Nathan Murphy." Nathan shot her a smile and a wave. Though Nathan was his ex's older brother, he was one of Royal's closest friends and he'd been the one to urge Royal to finally end things or settle for what Anne was willing to give him. "He's a high school teacher." He went down the line. "Trey Rosario and Jacob Murphy, who also used to be my housemates. Marc Chase and his older brother Kyle."

"Oh! Marc as in the walls talking?"

He burst out laughing and nodded. "Yes, one and the same." He turned his attention to Marc. "She's renting your old apartment."

"Ah! Well it's a great location. Safe, well lit. You're the same Caroline who came to work with our father, right? Welcome home." He shook her hand and gave her a handsome, genuine smile, and it made Royal glad to see.

The others followed suit, though Nathan gave him a brow rise when Caroline's attention was elsewhere.

They all chatted awhile before Royal stole her away, done with sharing her for the night. Of course that's when Anne walked in with a passel of Chase and Murphy women. She saw him and came over to give him a big hug and kiss smack on the lips.

She was still one of his closest friends so it wasn't like it meant anything romantic. But Caroline stiffened a little so he put his arm around her shoulders again. Anne, however, remained at his other side, her arm around his waist.

Not awkward at all. He rolled his eyes inwardly.

"Anne, this is the woman I told you about. Caroline Mendoza, this is Anne Murphy. Anne is one of my oldest and dearest friends."

Anne raised her brow his way. "Um and we were seriously dating for six years. He must have forgotten that part."

He tried not to goggle at Anne's words. There was an edge to them, which wasn't usual for her at all. But Caroline held her hand out to shake Anne's. "I think we were in school around the same time. Your sister Beth was in my year."

Anne looked slightly abashed when her rudeness was not reciprocated. Caroline was so confident and well mannered it made Anne's words seem even more petty.

Anne nodded and looked back to Royal. "You guys hanging out here to play pool and drink beer?"

"Nope. We had dinner, and I am about to squire Caroline out for some pie and coffee. See y'all later."

They waved but Royal held her close to his side as they headed back out.

"I'm sorry about that. She didn't mean to sound rude."

Caroline stifled her snort of disbelief. "Of course she did. Now, you said pie and coffee?"

He struggled with his desire to follow up on what Caroline had said and wanting to push it away so they could enjoy their time together. Anne had never looked even mildly miffed when he'd gone out with other women. She'd moved on, dating around, and he most assuredly had. There'd been no post-break-up sex, as there had been all the times before. Their last break had been final and for real. Their shift into a very close friendship had been for the best, and it worked for them both.

Why she'd be snippy now he didn't know.

He pushed it aside as they settled in at the Sands for two big slices of apple pie with ice cream and large mugs of milky coffee. There was an ease with Caroline he'd shared with very few people. Added to the chemistry building between them, and he was filled with all sorts of feel good by the time they wound up on the sidewalk again.

He wasn't ready for the date to end, but it was nearly eleven and he'd been up since four thirty and she had probably been up nearly as long.

"What are you doing tomorrow night?" he asked.

"I have plans."

Oh. Well that was unexpected. He did *not* approve of any other men who thought they could get in his way with this woman. "Mind if I ask what you're doing?" He failed at sounding casual by about five miles.

Her brows flew up as she got his meaning. "Oh! No. It's not a date. I mean, you're the only person I'm seeing. I'm going over to my friend Melissa's tomorrow. I'm meeting her at her place, and then we're off to Atlanta for lunch, shopping and a movie." She smiled brightly, and he spun her neatly and pulled her in close.

She looked up at him as he backed her to the steps leading to her apartment. When she'd gone up a few, they were eye to eye and that's when he kissed her.

He'd wanted to kiss her since he'd caught sight of those beautiful breasts of hers in the cereal aisle at the market the weekend before. Had thought about this very moment over and over. Had wondered how her body would feel against his, what she'd taste like.

None of it was anything close to the reality of those tits pressed against his chest as her mouth opened on a sigh, her taste, a little coffee and cream, the sweetness of vanilla from the ice cream, filling him until there was nothing but the way she felt, soft and real and her lips against his.

* * *

She pushed closer, winding her arms around his neck, sliding her fingers into his hair, tugging at the curl at his nape.

Royal Watson knew his way around a kiss, and boy was that Anne Murphy a total idiot for letting this go.

His tongue didn't slide into her mouth, it seemed to flow, a sensuous dance with hers, stroking, teasing, tasting until she was spineless, offering herself up to whatever he had to offer.

She sucked that very talented tongue, and he groaned, pulling her impossibly closer, and she knew he was as into that moment as she was. Oh yes he was. When they tumbled into bed, it was going to be hot, hot, hot.

He nipped her bottom lip just right. Not gently at all. Barely shy of pain, and then he licked the sting away, making her the one who groaned this time.

It went on like that for long minutes, making out on her back steps, the cold air not even bothering her because her skin was on fire for him.

He'd reached up to undo her ponytail at some point, wrapping her hair around his fist to guide her exactly where he wanted, and damn if that didn't make fireworks explode all points south of her belly button.

At the end of the block, a car door slammed and an alarm double honk sounded, and he breathed out, breaking the kiss.

"You and me. A week from tonight?"

She nodded.

"Good. I'll pick you up at seven and make you dinner. Then we'll head to the Tonk. I'm gonna hold on to you all night long on the dance floor."

"How could I refuse? I can drive to your house, though. You don't need to pick me up."

"I know you can. I'll see you at seven next Friday." He caught up with her on the stairs, heading to her door. "I'm also going to go inside right now, make sure everything is all right, and then I'm leaving because if I don't, I'm going to want to do a hell of a lot more than kiss you, and I get the very strong sense that the fantasizing I'll be doing will only add spice when it finally does happen." He gave her a look that stole her breath as heat flooded her belly. "And it will happen."

In the years since she'd left Petal, she'd dated a lot of men. Most of them she'd enjoyed. They were well mannered, and the ones she'd had sex with had shown her a good time. She loved beards and flannel and a nice tailored suit too.

But none of them were even in Royal's neighborhood. That sweet-talking, courtly mannered, good old boy, disguising a big heart and a serious amount of sex-appeal neighborhood.

She rarely denied herself things she really wanted. She wanted Royal Watson and had zero problem admitting it. And most definitely enjoying it while she had it.

Who knew if it would last more than a few weeks or months? But she did know she planned to savor every minute.

"Good night, Royal. Thank you for dinner and beer and pie and coffee and most definitely for that kiss. I'll see you next Friday."

He grinned and her body did the wave for him again. Bending, he stole another quick kiss and stepped back. "You bet you will. Good night, Caro."

Chapter Six

"I'm so glad you found the place all right." Melissa opened the door with a big smile.

Her house was a secondary, far smaller building behind another on the outskirts of town. "This is a seriously cute place." Caroline spun slowly as she took it all in. It wasn't very big but it was an explosion of color, nearly like a cartoon, but in a good way.

The little house was a golden yellow with red and white trim. It was bold and bright and it totally worked.

Melissa waved her inside. "Come in!"

Inside it was one big, open space. A bed on one wall with bright orange sheets and teal blankets was the sort of thing Caroline saw in magazines and loved, but it never looked right when she did it.

A kitchen to one side and a living area on the other. Big windows looked over a back deck.

"Come spring, we'll have dinner out there." Melissa indicated the deck. "You can see parts of town so at night there are pretty lights. Farmland to the west."

"Nice! This is so adorable. I'm jealous."

"This used to be a sort of artist's studio for the man who built the house originally. They moved away, and my brother Danny and his wife bought the big house so the rent is cheap, I see my nieces a lot, but it's private and no one bugs me."

"Sounds like heaven."

"Let's get on the road. I'm already starving so lunch needs to be in my life and soon."

They headed out, with Melissa driving as she knew where she was headed.

Once they'd cleared town, Caroline settled back.

"Right now I'm in an apartment. It's convenient. Walking distance to work. Five minutes from the grocery store. I really like Main Street. It's pretty and festive so it's a great view. But it's not a home. It's a temporary place to sleep while I figure out where to truly put down roots. Seeing your house today makes me underline the *figure out where to live* item on my to-do list."

"My sister-in-law is a real estate agent so remind me when I'm not driving to get you her card. I'll introduce you. She's great, and I'm sure she can find you something you really like."

"Much appreciated. I'm month-to-month with my place but now that I have a job and I'm settling in to town, I need to walk around more to get a feel of all the neighborhoods and then find—hopefully—the perfect place."

"Smart. So tell me about your date."

She told Melissa about how Royal had showed up after work and how they'd gone out for dinner and drinks. "And okay, so are you friends with Anne Murphy?"

"Oh, girl. I know the Murphys. We grew up not too far from each other. I also know she and Royal were together for many years, but he broke things off for good about a year and a half ago. They're still close though, so I think she comes with the mile-long legs and the very nice butt."

"I know. She wasn't totally rude last night, but she made sure to mention to me that they'd dated and she kept her arm around his waist. I'm not in any position to be jealous really. It was a first date and they have something far deeper than that."

Melissa blew raspberries. "Whatever. She had her chance. More than once. He sounded like he was embarrassed."

Caroline thought over his reaction again. "He seemed surprised at first. I got the feeling she'd been okay around women he'd dated before or at the very least that her reaction was unusual. He said she didn't mean to be rude. I was like, dude, duh of course she did. But he skirted around it in a mainly charming guy way, and I certainly didn't want to argue about it. She's probably being protective."

After a beat Caroline guffawed. "Look at me being charitable."

Melissa snickered. "Maybe. But it's over in any case so *too bad so sad*. I say we can put her on probation. She can be on the *we don't like her* list until she proves herself."

"Ha! I'm so glad I know you."

They laughed as they pulled into the lot of what could only generously be called a hole in the wall.

Once Melissa parked she turned to Caroline and put a hand up. "Okay, so I know it looks bad. But once on the way back to Petal after seeing a concert in Atlanta, this was the only place open and we were starving. I promise you'll be thanking me in about an hour."

"Okay then." They headed inside where Melissa proved to be telling the truth about how good the food was.

Caroline raised her glass of tea before finishing it.

"You have no idea how much I needed that today. So thank you."

"I'm so glad you're in Petal. I know it's hard. And I know you're feeling alone. But I'm your friend so don't forget that."

Caroline hadn't forgotten it, but it had been really nice to hear anyway.

"The next order of business is to find something to wear for my date next week. He's making me dinner, and then we're going dancing at the Tonk. I've never gone dancing at the Tonk. I was sixteen when I moved away. Do I wear jeans? A skirt? What sort of shoes?"

As they left the restaurant, Melissa linked her arm with Caroline's. "We've got this, Caroline. You're going to knock his socks off."

She looked up at the tap on her door and smiled when she caught sight of Edward.

"Do you have a few minutes?"

"Like two maybe?" Caroline looked at her watch. "I have an appointment with an investigator regarding my father's case at ten thirty."

Edward nodded. "Ah! Perfect." He held up the folder she'd provided when he'd asked about the case.

She waved at the little seating area in her office. "Sit, please."

They settled and she pretended she didn't notice the file folder in his hands as he placed it on the table. "So I read all this over."

After he'd asked for everything she had about her father's case, she'd handed it over the following afternoon. A little over a week had passed and she'd gotten more nervous every day.

"Your talents are wasted doing this job, Caroline. You need to be one of those crusading investigative attorneys who free people all over the country."

She made herself remain silent, but she blushed at the compliment.

He flipped the file open, and she saw he'd made notes on a separate page. "The level of dogged research, of triple and quadruple checking and interviewing you've done is meticulous. I had my doubts, as I told you, of his guilt. After reading everything you've gathered, I'm absolutely convinced your father wasn't guilty."

Relief rushed through her at his words. Vindication followed, as it did every single time she was able to show people the evidence and they saw it like she did.

"I hope you don't mind, but I spoke with Peter and Justin about this as well. I want to help. Justin wants to help too. This is pretty out of Peter's specialty area, but he's totally in support of Justin and me helping and giving some of the firm's time and money to the effort."

She blinked back tears. "I didn't expect any of this. I just… I just want to prove his innocence. I don't want his death to mean nothing. I don't want people to keep on thinking he was capable of such a thing. And I don't want the real killer out here living a life that was stolen from my dad and me and my siblings too. I don't expect the firm to take on my cause."

He grinned, reaching out to pat her hand. "I know you don't. Which makes it easier to offer, I suppose. You're not alone, Caroline. Let us help you. *Justice delayed is justice denied.*" He indicated the Gladstone quote she had on her wall. "I think this has been delayed long enough. You're back in Petal to dig for the truth. Let's do it."

Edward stayed for her meeting with her investigator.

She'd worked with Ron Rogers before on her dad's case when they'd needed things done for the appeals. She was an attorney. A really good one she could admit, but this sort of investigation work wasn't her strong point and Ron had the time, skill and contacts to handle it.

When she ducked out to grab some lunch, it was with a huge smile on her face and a weight lifted from her shoulders.

She dashed into the Honey Bear, craving something warm and hearty. A big bowl of soup and a sandwich would hit the spot perfectly.

There was a counter on the bakery side that snugged up against the window with barstools so she took her lunch there, settling in to watch the people outside as she ate.

She'd sort of stared off into the middle distance as she chewed when someone tapped on the window, and she nearly fell off the stool.

It was Royal.

He held his hands up and came inside. "Sorry! Didn't mean to startle you." He gave her a hug and she hugged him right back, so totally pleased by the way her day was turning.

And then he kissed her. Right there in the Honey Bear. In front of the windows. It wasn't a full-on tongue-kiss seduction like they'd shared at her door the weekend before. They were in public after all. But it was definitely not a kiss you'd give a friend. Nope, this was a *hey everyone I'm dating this person* kiss.

"It's good to see you too." She managed to stop herself from grabbing the front of his shirt and hauling him in for another kiss. Barely.

"You here for a while? Like long enough to have lunch with me?"

Lunch with Royal would be a really nice thing indeed. "Yes. I just sat down five minutes ago."

"Be right back."

She watched—because yeah, great ass. He joked with Mrs. Proffit, who worked the register, and shouted out a greeting to William, another Murphy, this one the head baker.

Royal was comfortable in his skin. Easy. People always smiled as they talked to him.

Within a few minutes he was back, sitting close as he spooned up his chili.

"What brings you to downtown Petal today?" She bumped his shoulder once he'd taken a bite.

"I was at city hall. I had to file some permits. We have a roadside stand, at the farm I mean. I have to fill out the paperwork once a quarter. Anyway. I knew it was chili day so I figured I'd get some to go. Then I was rewarded by the sight of a gorgeous woman sitting inside, and my day got *way* better. How are you?"

"I am having a really awesome day, as it happens. Even better now."

"All this mutual admiration is making me blush."

They both laughed and continued to eat.

They had a rhythm. Easy. There was energy too. Just being with him made her sort of intoxicated with all those feel-good chemicals.

He told her he'd gone bowling the night before with his friends. It was clear Anne had been there, but truthfully Caroline was pleased he wasn't making a big deal out of it. She didn't want it to be weird, and she'd have to find a way to deal with Anne because Caroline really liked Royal.

"What are you doing today?" he asked as he reached out to brush her hair back from her shoulder. It pleased her to have him touch her. Simple and warm. This man made her feel good.

Royal had been operating on very little sleep after a late night bowling and then darts at the Pumphouse along with drinks.

On top of that mild hangover, one of the irrigation hoses had gone out on him, and he'd spent two hours in the mud in the cold getting it replaced. And then he'd had to run that permit to city hall so he was not having such a great day.

He'd planned to grab lunch to go and head back to the farm to get stuff done. But Caroline had been in the window, so lush. And then once you focused on her, you saw the edge her intensity gave her. She gave off so much personal charisma and energy it seemed to hum around her.

It was like that frequency snagged him. He wanted to touch her and smell her and listen to her laugh, and he was harder than he should have been in public but Caroline Mendoza had a lot of stuff he wanted to roll around in.

She *looked* at him when he spoke. And she listened to him as well. She was pretty much the most brilliant person he'd ever met. It was so fucking sexy that she was intelligent and powerful.

And she had a really foul mouth. She reined it in mainly in public, but sometimes she got her rant on. Also. Really. Hot.

And funny.

"I think I should tell you I have a big crush on you right now," he said, leaning in and kissing her forehead.

Pleasure seemed to light her. She didn't try to hide it or play some sort of game. She liked what she liked, and she didn't apologize for it. There was such a ferocious verve in her.

She touched her forehead to his briefly. "That's very nice to hear."

"That so?" He shifted back to drink some of his soda and look all he wanted at her.

She nodded. "You made my stomach get a little fluttery."

It was his turn to be pleased.

"Aside from the permit—it's never fun to deal with that stuff—how's your day been?"

He found himself telling her all about the hose breaking and nearly freezing to death—though he skipped the hangover part. He also told her about his night with his friends. He'd made a conscious decision not to make any big deal of seeing Anne. She was his friend, one of his closest, and she was part of his life. He came with his crazy aunt and uncle and his friends. He wanted Caroline to be one of his friends too.

She didn't seem upset when he'd talked about an event that included Anne either, which he'd been relieved about.

After about an hour she began to pack her stuff up. "I've got a hearing. I need to head over there."

"Can I walk you over? I have to get back home to finish all the stuff I had to put off earlier. Plus I need a good night's sleep since I'm taking you out tomorrow."

"I'll be sure to eat a hearty breakfast. I have a new outfit."

"Score. I can't wait." He took her trash and threw it out with his and opened the door. It was cold as they headed up the block to her office. The cold was a good excuse to put an arm around her shoulders and pull her closer. She moved into that spot against his side like she was meant to be there.

As they neared the corner where they'd veer left, he gave her a quick kiss. "I know you need to look badass and all businesslike when we turn this corner and you put your job back on. So I wanted to steal a kiss from you now."

"Thanks for that."

They turned the corner and while he kept an arm around her, he didn't kiss her when they parted ways. He took her hands, squeezing them briefly. "I'll see you tomorrow night."

"Yeah. You will. Have a good rest of your day, Royal."

"You've pretty much made that part happen already." He waved as he stepped away, and she put a hand on the door to go inside.

"I'm in *so* much trouble with you, aren't I?"

He laughed. "Oh, yes."

Chapter Seven

Royal knocked on her door and whistled when she opened up. She wore a pale blue button-down shirt—with the right amount of buttons undone at the throat. Her belt was wide and it emphasized that va-va-va-voom shape of hers. Damn her curves made his mouth water, and suddenly he questioned his choice to take her out instead of keeping her all to himself.

He made a circling motion with his finger, and she rolled her eyes, spinning slowly so he could appreciate the way her jeans cupped that butt of hers just right.

He paused at the footwear. "Wow. Those are some boots."

"I bought them last weekend. I have to admit I've been wearing them all the time except when I was at work."

They had little skulls embroidered all over them, but the way they were constructed, at a distance, it looked like lace. "Darlin', they say Caro. Like in big bold letters. I like 'em."

"Yeah? They even look awesome when I'm in my pajamas." She blushed a little and he got close enough to take a sniff.

"I do like your perfume." He kissed her throat, just below her ear.

She had him all revved up just from her smell.

"Now all I'm going to be able to think about is you in those little sleep shorts and a tank top with those boots. Don't know if you sleep in those or not, it's just what my fantasy brain cooked up."

Surprised laughter bubbled from her. "Thank you." She slid her arms around his waist, and he shifted closer, bending his knees to kiss that mouth.

She was delicious. Soft and sweet against him. She hummed, snuggling into him, and a deep sort of tenderness and protectiveness bloomed through his gut, so unexpected it made him pause a moment.

"Well come on then. I have a big dinner cooking right now, and then I plan to show you off on the dance floor."

"I hope you're not expecting me to know any fancy dances. I'm a fail in that department."

"Sugar, you just follow my lead and everything will be just fine."

She locked up and strolled with him down to the street where his truck was parked. He opened her door and helped her up.

"Maybe I need one of those extra steps that extends down from the running board."

"Hush up."

He kissed her again and jogged around to the driver's side.

"How'd your day go with your friend? I forgot to ask you yesterday at lunch."

"It was a really good day. Melissa Gallardo, you might remember her?"

"Ah, yes. She's taking over for the Proffits, right? She was younger, your age I'm guessing."

"Yes. She and I went to school together but never really became friends until just a few years ago when we reconnected online. Anyway, I spent too much money on clothes, ate a lot of great food and caught an action flick."

"If you bought what you're wearing now, I'd say it was worth the price."

A reflection of her flattered grin greeted her as she gazed out the window once he'd left the main road.

Her breath caught as they turned off the main road and hit the drive leading up to the house.

Royal's house. A place he'd built along with several of his friends, sat up on a rise so it looked over all fifty acres of what was now Watson Organics.

"I bet you have some pretty great sunrise-watching from your place."

"I do. Sunsets too, from the front of the house." He hoped she'd be around a lot. Enough to see exactly what he meant. Sunrise from his bed was one of his favorite things about the house. He bet it looked marvelous on her naked skin.

He parked and helped her down, liking the excuse to touch her. "Come on in. I'll give you the tour. Watch out for Spike, he likes to get under your feet."

"Spike?"

"Spike is my cat. He'll be at the door. He knows when the truck pulls up, and he'll be annoyed I locked him out of the back of the house where the kitchen is."

When he unlocked the front door, there was indeed a pretty, fat tortoiseshell cat waiting there.

The cat chattered at Royal, who bent to scoop it up and scritch under the chin. "I know. But you're a stone-cold chicken thief and you can't be trusted with my dinner."

This was given a snort and a purry sort of last chiding sound before two different colored eyes shifted to Caroline.

"Caro, this is Spike."

Caroline moved slowly, giving the cat enough time to register his displeasure, before she stroked her fingertips over the cat's head and then scratched him behind the ears.

"Hey, Spike, what's up?"

There was something very charming and utterly disarming about the way Royal reacted to his cat. It was sweet and funny, and that he was good with animals wasn't that much of a surprise to her. But it was sexy anyway.

Royal gave her a grin before putting the cat on his feet. "Now that the introductions have been given, would you like a tour of the house?"

She nodded. He took her coat and hung it in a closet just off the entry, along with her bag. Then he slid his hand into hers and drew her down three steps and into a large, open room. Slate tile in varying shades of earthy red lined the floor and a large, cream-colored rug was the base of a seating arrangement. Two couches faced one another with a low table between. A fireplace framed the far wall.

"Wow, the blue of those couches is fantastic."

"Thank you. I wasn't convinced it would work with the tile in here. But a friend pushed me on it and I'm glad I listened."

There was a slight pause before he said *friend*, and she knew he meant Anne. She wanted to sigh. She wanted to not think about this woman who clearly was a big part of his life even now. She wished it didn't matter. Wished she was mature enough not to be bothered.

For the moment though, she'd sweep it under the rug. Her feelings or not, it was too early to discuss it.

He led her to the left. "This is my office."

Wow, if only her home office was this nice. Large windows fronted it, leading out to a big, wraparound porch. A big, L-shaped workspace dominated the room, with a computer on one part and a flat desk/worktable taking up the rest. File cabinets were neatly built into the far wall along with bookshelves filled with binders and books about farming techniques.

At that moment she realized, truly understood, just what this land and farm meant to Royal. And how big a job it was. Cowboy boots and wranglers or not, this man was a CEO in his own right.

"I'm out in the earlier part of the day. In the fields I mean. But I come back here in the afternoons to escape the heat and the noise. Always work to be done, but this room gives me a perfect view over the hoop tunnels and the orchard."

"This is a great workspace. I have workspace envy right now."

He grinned. "I just finished that worktable a few weeks ago."

"You made that?" Good gracious, he did woodworking too?

"I did. I like to be busy I guess. The table I wanted was ungodly expensive so I was able to do it exactly how I wanted for like a third of the price."

"I'm super impressed."

"Good. Come on."

He took her hand again and led her through a set of doors he'd closed off. "These are great at keeping the house cooler and also locking Spike out of the kitchen if I'm cooking in the slow cooker and not around."

Spike wound through their legs and then shot into the hall when the doors opened up.

"This is what I think of as the heart of the house. When I'm done working, I come back here."

More windows, these took up pretty much the entirety of the back of the house. An open space, the large kitchen flowed into the dining area to one side and a living room with a television and media center on the other.

"It smells really good in here."

"I'm a pretty good cook. I'm roasting a chicken. I have a barter going on with some of the other organic operations in the area. The chicken is free range, fed organic feed. It's fresh, which makes such a difference. I didn't make the bread though. Picked that up at the Honey Bear."

She grinned. "I'm addicted to their sourdough twists. Also did you know they had cinnamon rolls without the raisins if you ask?"

He barked a laugh. "I'm going to have to introduce you to Lily Murphy. Nathan's wife. She hates raisins but ordered the rolls with the raisins and picked them out because they had more frosting on them. Now William makes the raisin-free ones with just as much icing."

"Clearly she's got good taste." In men too, because Nathan Murphy was gorgeous. "Raisins are a blight. Gross. They're an offense to grapes, which are wonderful."

"Note to self, no raisins in anything I make for Caroline. *I* like raisins. I eat them by the handful."

"Ew. Well, I knew you had flaws. You were too perfect otherwise. The plus is, now I can get trail mix and pick around the raisins and not feel bad. You can have all mine."

He sidled closer. "Too perfect, huh?"

He made her laugh. It had been a long time since a new romance had made her so giddy. "Stop that. You know what you look like. Plus this house? Wow."

"I built it. Well, not all of it. That's when Trey and Jacob lived here. Jacob and his older brother helped me with the plumbing. Trey did a lot of the electrical along with another friend of ours. I knew what I wanted. This piece of land had a house on it, but it was small and didn't have much of a view. It was a waste. So I lived there while we built this one."

"How long did it take? I can't imagine. I mean, I like to be active, but painting a room is as DIY as I've ever managed to get. I'm super impressed. This place is fantastic."

"All told, from start to finish, it took three years. I'm still not completely done. Some of the bedrooms upstairs don't have furniture yet. I fill spots as I can afford it and when I find the perfect pieces."

She strolled to the French doors leading to the back porch, which was a little wider than the front. There was patio furniture out there and a huge gas grill as well.

"I'm still working on the landscaping. We razed the old house so I'm pulling that land into a large garden. I've been hitting garden shows to get ideas."

She'd underestimated him.

Oh sure she'd thought he was smart and funny and handsome. The way he'd told her about the organic operation had impressed her. But there was a whole other side to Royal she hadn't even suspected. Creative. Artistic. He was the kind of person who got an idea and then made it happen.

That was amazing.

"Just for your information, I love gardening. I mean, I'm no landscaper, but I had a big back garden in Seattle with raised beds for my veggies. If you ever need help or company to go to a garden show, I'm totally up for it."

Surprise flitted over his features and then he smiled. "I'll be taking you up on that, Caro. You can bet." He pulled out a chair. "I'm going to pull the chicken out of the oven to rest a bit. Want a beer or some wine?"

"Why don't I get that? I'll set the table while you deal with the food? A fair distribution of labor."

He pointed. "Plates are in the cabinet there. Silverware in that drawer."

"You want wine or beer?"

"There's a nice bottle of red over there on the sideboard. Glasses on the rack."

They worked to get the food ready and it was an easy, natural flow. They had a good rhythm, and she found the space natural for entertaining and having multiple people moving around at once.

He was also a really good cook. All the more reason to keep him around.

He clinked his glass to hers. "To new beginnings."

She heartily agreed.

Royal hadn't expected her to pitch in the way she had. She'd told him he'd cooked so she'd clean up. So he perched on the counter and watched her move around his kitchen as she rinsed and put things away, loaded the dishwasher and all that stuff.

As they worked they talked. An easy back and forth.

He'd learned she loved action movies and historical romance novels, as well as going to the batting cages and ice skating.

She carefully edged around the subject of her father, though he knew, as she'd told him the Friday before, it was an important part of her life. On one hand, he liked that she respected him enough to not shove it in his face, but on the other hand, he found himself wanting her to open up and share her struggles with him.

Once they'd finished up, they headed out.

By the time they walked through the front doors at the Tonk, things were in full swing. The dance floor was packed, tables full of laughing, drinking people. He loved the place on a Friday, so full of energy.

He also wanted to show her off, he couldn't deny it to himself.

Plenty of men looked at her and then to him as he kept an arm around her shoulders. It was the way of things round those parts. Caroline was perfectly capable of taking care of herself, obviously, but there was no harm in letting folks know she was with him.

He wanted her comfortable in town. First, because he liked her. He liked her, and he wanted her to feel positively about her new home so she'd stay. And because he knew there were rumblings about the whole case and her trying to prove her father's innocence. He didn't like that one bit. Mindy and Shep got a free pass, but somehow Caroline was going to get shit on because she believed differently? Because she'd done the work to look into the situation, which he knew damned good and well 99 percent of the shit talkers in town didn't bother to do?

He wanted his friends to like her. He hung out with them all the time and knew if they gave her a chance—

and that night was a step in the right direction—she'd find her place in their group as well.

He saw Jacob and Trey first, along with Cassie and Shane Chase, and Joe and Beth. Trey waved when he caught sight of them and the others turned.

"Do you mind if we sit with my friends?"

She shook her head. "Nope."

He kept a hand at the small of her back as they wound through the crowd to get to the table.

He pulled her chair out and sat close, his arm around the back of her chair. "Hey, all. Caroline, you know Jacob and Trey."

She waved.

"I bumped into Caroline and my dad last week on their way to the courthouse." Shane turned to his wife. "This is Cassie."

Cassie raised her glass. "Nice to meet you. My mother-in-law adores you. She's a good judge of character."

"Thank you for saying that. I've decided I want to be Polly Chase when I grow up."

Beth had been frowning until Caroline said that and her expression softened.

Cassie laughed. "Right? She's incredible. You should see her with a group of small children. She's like the baby whisperer."

Shane's smile widened at the interplay between the women. "Just give her a wide berth if you see her on the road."

"Well that's how Shane and I met. Polly rear-ended my car on my first day here in town. So it's not *all* bad that she's a menace behind the wheel."

"And this is Joe Harris and Beth Murphy."

Caroline tensed ever so slightly. He wouldn't have

even known if his forearm hadn't been touching the back of her neck.

"We were in the same class, Beth. Nice to see you again."

Beth nodded. "I remember. Welcome back to Petal." Joe also murmured a hello.

"There's a pitcher on the way. Do you want anything else?" Trey asked them.

"Beer is just fine with me. I'm still stuffed from dinner."

One of Royal's favorite songs came on, and he stood, holding a hand out to Caroline. "Darlin', you said you liked to dance so I hope you were serious."

She took his hand and he brought her to her feet. "I'm totally serious. Just remember what I said about the fancy stuff."

He bent to her ear. "Remember what I said about letting me lead."

"I get the feeling it would be impossible not to." He heard the amusement in her tone and it made him smile.

Though they were surrounded by people on all sides, it was just him and Caro out on the floor. Despite the difference in their size, she fit him easily. "You were so full of it to even pretend you can't dance." He spun her easily and drew her back to him.

She tipped her head back, laughing, exposing the line of her throat and thrusting her cleavage up just right. He bent and kissed her chin before he spun her again.

They were out a few more songs before they made it back to the table to cool off and drink a beer or two.

"I am seriously going to steal your boots," Cassie said when they settled in.

"Thank you." There was not really a higher compli-

ment in Caroline's book than a woman compliment-
ing another woman's shoes. "I just got them. I'm sort of
bummed I can't wear them to work."

Shane laughed. "I'll give you twenty dollars to wear
them on Monday. I need to stop in to see my father's
face."

"I have a hearing Monday morning. I don't think
Judge Herndon would be so happy to see them. Your father probably wouldn't bat an eye if I wore them. He's
pretty laid-back. Your uncle though? He might not be
so easygoing."

"Ha, that's true. My aunt jokes that she irons his pajama pants."

"He's brilliant. He could totally teach a master class
on brief writing. I wish so much that I'd learned how
from him."

"My dad often says the same thing. About my uncle
being brilliant, I mean."

"He should know. Your dad is no slouch himself."

"Thanks. I think so, but I'm obviously biased."

The conversation touched on all sorts of stuff, some
serious, most of it just fun lighthearted stuff. It was nice
to not have anything heavy to deal with so she could totally relax and enjoy a night out.

"So, Cassie, I hear you own the bookstore?"

Talk turned to books and the bookstore and adjust-
ing to life in a small town after living in a big city. She
and Cassie compared some of their favorite places to eat
in Los Angeles, and out of the corner of her eye, Caroline noted that Beth relaxed a little as the conversation
progressed.

Cassie was warm and funny, and as Caroline came to
find out, had been a surgeon before suffering a debili-

tating injury. She'd come to Petal to flee an abusive ex who'd nearly killed her. She'd clearly found her prince charming though, in the shape of Shane Chase and the town she'd adopted as her home.

Polly was the common denominator, which was no real surprise. Polly who'd opened up her family and her heart.

Caroline said as much and Cassie nodded eagerly. "I couldn't ask for a better mother-in-law or grandmother to my son."

Beth chimed in. "My sister Tate is married to Shane's brother Matt. Polly sort of pulled us all into the Chase family like she did Tate. My nieces and nephews are treated like her grandchildren. We go to their house for the holidays. She's a far better mom to us than the one we were born with."

Caroline couldn't help but soften toward Beth. She remembered just how awful their parents had been back in the day.

"Seriously, your mother is awesome," Caroline said to Shane.

"Scary sometimes. She won't even play when she gets mad. But yeah, she's pretty awesome."

Things mellowed as Beth opened up with her, telling her about the salon she owned with her sisters—Anne included—and Joe's mechanic shop. They all laughed at the stories Trey and Jacob told about Royal and the others, and by the time they headed out, Caroline realized she really liked Royal's circle of friends.

On their way out though…

Royal had been walking out with Caroline and the rest of their friends when Benji Ahern stepped in front of her, bringing her up short enough that Royal stumbled, his arm circling her waist to keep her from falling.

He hadn't had much interaction with the youngest Ahern boy. Enough to know he had trouble keeping his act together when he drank, and from the looks of it, he'd been in the bottle for a while already.

Benji gave Caroline a look that brought Royal's hackles up. He straightened and prepared for whatever was about to happen.

Benji wiped his mouth with the back of his hand and sneered at Caroline. "I heard you was back in town. I hoped like true trash, you'd float your ass away though."

Caroline's expression shuttered. "I'm sure you're quite the expert on trash."

Trey laughed and moved up to flank them. Royal appreciated the support. Royal attempted to get in front of Caroline but she pushed a little to hold in him place. As if he'd leave her standing between a drunk aiming to start a fight and Royal, instead of getting himself in a place to protect her better. In the end, he stepped firmly into Benji's line of sight and Caroline.

With an annoyed snort, Caroline took Royal's hand, craning her neck to see his face.

Her features were earnest and he saw the embarrassment in her gaze. "Don't get into it. Not over this. He's not worth it." She kept her voice low and calm, but he still wanted to punch Benji.

"I think you'd best be moving along, Benji. You're drunk as well as an asshole. I'd say something like how I'd hate to have to punch you, but I'd really like that. I'm not twenty and I don't want to brawl like an animal. Unless you push, then I'm happy to. It's up to you."

Shane rumbled behind Royal, enough to get Benji's

attention and give him the opportunity to back off and shut up before trouble got started.

"What are you doing, Royal? What could this...this—"

"Don't. I'm not joking now. I'm not going to allow you to disrespect Caroline. You've said more than enough about something that is none of your damned business."

"Course it's my business. This is *my* town. We don't need any more criminals in it."

Caroline stepped from behind him, but Royal slipped an arm around her shoulders to keep her next to him and out of Benji's reach.

Royal should have known she wasn't going to let herself get pushed around though. "Criminals?" Caroline looked to either side of where she stood. "Who are you talking about? Last I checked, having an opinion didn't make you a criminal. Though in your case it makes you stupid. Now run along. I'll give your opinion the weight it deserves." She turned her back to look up at Royal. He pulled her closer, splitting his attention between her and Benji. "You ready to go?"

"I can't punch him even just a little?"

The real smile he got in response was his reward.

"Nah. He's not worth it."

"Petal PD agrees with that statement." Shane stepped even with Royal, keeping Cassie behind him. "Get going, Benji. You're embarrassing yourself by threatening a woman half your size."

Benji sneered, but moved along with one backward glance.

Caroline breathed a sigh of relief.

"Come on then." Royal kept her close and dared anyone to step up to them at that point. No one else did. But when they finally got outside, she stopped as they got to the dirt parking lot.

"I'm really sorry to have ruined everyone's night with that."

It was Beth who replied to Caroline. "Fuck that guy. No, really. No one gets to judge you for what someone else did or didn't do. Fuck him for using his size to try to embarrass you and to threaten you that way."

Surprise flitted over Caroline's features briefly, and Royal wanted to give Beth a kiss smack-dab on the lips.

"Thank you."

"He's a dung bag. Shane, you should have let Royal punch him." Cassie grinned.

Caroline shook her head. "You get into a fight with a guy like that, and you're giving him what he wants. He's a little man who needs to use other people to be relevant. You're better than he is, Royal."

He didn't want her to feel exposed and it was clear she was. She wore her confidence easily, but right then it was more like a shield. He clenched and unclenched his fists, still angry at Benji's bullshit.

But he needed to focus for her sake. Because she was uncomfortable and upset, and if he couldn't plant his fist in Benji's face, he'd make her feel better another way.

He brushed a lock of her hair from her face, tucking it behind her ear.

"See y'all later." He nodded to his friends.

Cassie hugged Caroline and so did Beth. He gave Trey and Jacob the stink eye which automatically meant Trey kissed Caroline on the cheek and winked at Royal over her shoulder.

"Okay, you, let's get out of here."

Chapter Eight

She barely met his gaze once they were inside at her place. "I'm really sorry about tonight."

"Sit down and I'll get your boots off." He pointed at the couch and she complied. He pulled the boots off, placing them in a corner.

Before she could get up again, he moved back to her, kneeling between her legs, his palms sliding up her calves to rest on her thighs.

"I do not accept your apology because it's dumb."

Her brows flew up so he leaned in to kiss each one.

"It's not dumb." Her bottom lip jutted out just a smidge and he nipped it.

"It *is* dumb because Benji was a fool and you don't need to be sorry for dumbasses unless you're the dumbass. And you're not."

"This isn't the first time and it won't be the last. It's exhausting enough for me, but I'm used to it. You and your friends aren't, and I'm sorry you had to deal with it."

He frowned. "Girl, you don't even know. This is a small town. Full of petty little asshats like Benji who have no shame about getting up in people's business. Doesn't matter that they don't know what the hell they're talking about. Beth has seen her family attacked time and again by small-minded jerks who judged those kids for the sins of their parents. For growing up how they did. Before Matt Chase married Tate, he punched someone in the face at the homecoming game after the guy was talking shit. People change as the times do, but some people are born jerks and they'll be jerks until they die. Benji falls into that camp, and there's no way I'm going to let you apologize for his bad manners."

She wrapped her calves around him, pulling him closer.

He brushed his lips over her mouth and she slid her fingertips through his hair. She wrapped herself around him, and he liked the way she felt, soft where she was supposed to be but strong too.

She tasted good so he settled in for a long slow kiss, pressing her back into the couch, leaning into her as she received him.

"Don't your knees hurt?" she murmured against his mouth just before he shifted to her jaw at her ear. She exhaled on a shiver as he licked against her pulse there.

Not as much as his dick hurt, but he wasn't going to say that. Still, now that she'd mentioned it, his knees did hurt.

"But I'll have to stop kissing you to move." He nibbled the lobe of her ear and she sighed.

"Make it quick." She yanked her head away from his mouth and he managed to get up on the couch. Which was even better when she spun, straddling his lap to face him.

"Damn, girl, you're trouble. I like it."

Her laugh made him shiver. Low and throaty and full of all sorts of dirty plans, he liked it. "Looks like I have you exactly where I want you."

"I shouldn't tell you because then you'll know how easy I am for you, but you can put me wherever you like and have me any way you want me. I'm game for whatever you have in mind."

One corner of her delicious fucking mouth tipped up. "Did you take your vitamins this morning?"

He grabbed that sweet behind of hers and pulled her close. "I think I can manage to muddle through."

"I'll be bringing my A game."

"That might kill me. But I'll die with a smile on my mouth."

She undulated then, brushing the heat of her center against the line of his cock, and he groaned, his fingers digging into the ass in his grip.

Her hands slid into his hair, and she held his head as she kissed him, taking over, and damn he let her because she was sweet and hot and on fire in his lap.

It had been at least ten years since Caroline had just kissed and kissed a man for hours. The memory of it paled in comparison to how Royal made her feel. This long slow seduction was new for her. She wasn't one to delay when she felt a sexual attraction to someone.

But he was different. This whatever-it-was between them was different, and despite her horror over the situation earlier that evening at the Tonk, letting him draw her in at such a delightful pace was thrilling.

His hands slid up to her waist, heating her skin through the material of her shirt, and she willed them higher and higher. But the vibrating coming from his pocket kept interrupting.

Finally with an annoyed groan, he broke the kiss. "I'm sorry. I can't tell if it's texts or a call."

She snuck a look at the clock as he pulled the phone out of his pocket. It was two in the morning. Who was texting him that late? She chided herself for that. It wasn't her business, and sometimes her friends texted her late too.

He mumbled something and typed quickly before he slid the phone back into his pocket.

"Everything all right?"

He kissed her again and sighed happily. "Yes. It was just Anne texting. She heard about what happened and was asking about it."

"Oh." She said this with what she considered her court face. No real emotion, just a recitation of a word.

She must have failed though because he blushed. "There's no reason to be jealous."

That made her laugh, and then she poked his side extra hard, his yelp making her feel better. "I'm not jealous, Royal. I don't have cause to be. We've gone on two dates. I've been in your life for what? A few weeks?"

"Anne Murphy is one of my best friends. That's it."

Caroline rolled her eyes. "That's stunningly male. *That's it.* There's no *that's it* when it comes to a best friend. And certainly not when it comes to a best friend you used to love in a romantic sense. But as I said, it's fine."

It totally wasn't but she'd look like a clingy psycho otherwise. It didn't take a genius to see what Anne was doing, and right then she looked like one of those exes who didn't really want the guy but didn't want anyone else to have him.

Which was probably totally unfair to think because if he liked her, and everyone else seemed to, Anne was probably a nice person. But it was internal dialogue so she could be as catty and unfair as she wanted to be.

He opened his mouth to argue, she could tell he was going to, so she leaned down to kiss him and he grinned and let her, meeting her mouth with his own.

"Now that I've satisfied my need to smooch you for the moment, let's revisit this whole thing about Anne."

She groaned and got up. "Ugh, let's not. It's over. Why are you trying to revive it?"

He unfolded himself to stand—damn he was tall—and headed to her. "There's no such thing as *fine* with a woman. It's fine means *I'll kill you in your sleep*."

"Ha. No it doesn't." Not that time anyway. She sighed. "Look, this is not a winning conversation for me. I'm not mad, I promise."

He looked her over carefully and then pulled her close. She tiptoed up to kiss him and he bent his knees to meet her halfway.

She wanted him. Pretty badly, but if they had sex right then she'd be thinking of Anne the whole time. Well, not the whole time. Clearly that was an exaggeration because whatever he was bringing to the table behind his zipper was more than enough to get her total attention.

She pulled back and smiled. "I want to be the only woman in the room when we fuck."

He paused and sucked in a breath. "You got some mouth on you, Caroline. It's sexy. I like that you say what you feel and don't play around. But there's no one here but me and you. And trust me, when we fuck? It'll be me and you. For hours."

"Oh, I know." She grabbed his cock through his jeans, squeezing lightly. "You wouldn't be here in my living room if that weren't the case."

"I am not holding feelings for Anne."

Caroline wasn't sure if she believed that. But it didn't matter. She didn't have the right either way. "That's not what I mean. I mean, we have some sizzling hot potential between us. It'll happen, yes it will." And when it did, she would be the only woman in the room or there'd be no sex at all.

"But it's late and I just stopped kissing you to take a text from another woman and even though we're not together anymore and haven't been for a year and a half, it's weird and she's here between us no matter what."

"You're really smart as well as sexy."

He sighed. "I have to work tomorrow. A long, long day. I'd ask you over or out to do something but I'll be busy until like eleven or so and then I'm passing out. *But*, I take Sundays off, my one day a week where I sleep in and have breakfast out and play all day. What are you doing?"

"I'm having brunch with my grandparents and siblings after church. I mean after they go. I'm a Quaker and my grandmother informed me that was just pretend faith. So I'm sleeping in and having a bloody mary before I meet them over at their house. Want to come?"

He looked panicked and she laughed. "Teasing. I promise. I wouldn't do that to someone I hated, much less someone I liked."

"Come over Sunday when you finish up with them. I'm going to stay in and have a fire, read and watch movies. I'll leave my door unlocked. Next week will be hectic. I've got a harvest and then a new planting will start. I may not be around much. Why don't you go on and agree so I won't have to be a whole week without seeing you."

"You're going to get tired of me and then what?"

He laughed, but it was quiet and thoughtful. "I'm not sure that's possible. And it sure isn't right now. Come over Sunday. Bring a bag if you want to give me a trial run." He brushed his lips over hers and she followed him to the door.

"I don't know how long it's going to take."

"Like I said. I'm sleeping in until at least noon. Then I'm staying in my pajama bottoms and a T-shirt and hanging out all day. Come when you can. I'll be there for any sort of stress release you might need after several hours with your grandparents."

He went onto the small landing outside her door. She leaned against it and called out softly. "Hey, Royal?"

"Hmm?"

"Thanks for defending my honor tonight. At the Tonk I mean."

He shook his head. "Of course I did. See you Sunday, Caro. Sweet dreams."

Two days later, Caroline stood on her grandparents' front porch and knocked. Shep answered with a grin and then he pulled her into a hug. "Hiya!"

She hugged him back, smiling. "Hey yourself."

He kissed her cheek. "Come on in. You know you don't have to knock."

"Well actually I do. You guys lock the door."

He paused, surprise on his face. "You don't have a key?"

It took every bit of her self-control but she managed not to snort. "Nope."

He frowned.

She fished in her pocket and handed him one though.

"This is to my apartment. If you ever need to come in for whatever reason."

"Thanks. I'll knock though. Just in case you have a gentleman caller."

She laughed, unable not to at his teasing tone. "Okay then."

"Come on back. Gran's in the kitchen and Mindy should be back shortly." He leaned in closer. "She went to church with Garrett and his family."

"Oh no. Is he a Baptist?"

Shep laughed. "Yes!"

Their grandmother must have had kittens over that.

"What are you two up to?" Her grandfather smiled as they entered the kitchen and dining room at the back of the house.

"Nothing much." She squeezed her brother's arm and then moved to kiss her grandfather's cheek. "Morning."

"You mean afternoon, don't you? Church was nice today. The pastor gave a great sermon. Too bad you missed it." Her grandmother jutted her chin out, both to chide and demand a kiss.

Caroline gave a kiss but wasn't going to allow the chide to bother her. Her faith was her business, as was how she spent her Sunday mornings.

"Glad you had a good morning at church. Can I help with anything?"

Her mother would have wanted her to try her hardest so she did. And damn it, they were close to Shep and Mindy so why not her?

She wished it didn't matter. Wished she had the confidence that it didn't make her feel small and unimportant.

But she'd be damned if she gave in to it, even if she craved that ease they seemed to have with her siblings.

"Why don't I set the table?"

"Mindy usually does."

"She's not here, Gran," Shep interrupted. "I'll do it. Sit down, Caroline. Want some coffee? I was just about to make some with that fancy K Cup thing you gave me for my birthday."

"Oh! I'll do it. You do the dishes, I'll make the coffee."

"He's too young for coffee," their grandmother said. Caroline and Shep ignored it.

Caroline looked through the spinner with all the cups and chose one for herself. "What kind do you want?"

"I want the macadamia nut kind."

She wrinkled her nose. "Gross."

He laughed as he put out silverware.

She made them both coffee. Her grandfather was drinking tea, and her grandmother shook her head when Caroline asked her if she wanted coffee and muttered about how they had a perfectly good coffeemaker already.

"Y'all need to get Caroline a key. Did you know she didn't have one?" Shep asked his grandfather once he'd finished putting milk in his coffee.

"Oh. You're right. I'm sorry, sweetheart. I'll go down to the hardware store this week and get you one."

"Thanks, Grandpa. It's not urgent or anything."

"Hush. It's silly to make you knock on the door the way you did this morning. It just slipped my mind." Her grandfather patted her hand.

Mindy came in all laughter and chatter with her boyfriend, Garrett, in her wake. "Sorry we're late. We needed to get Garrett's aunt back home." Her sister caught sight of Caroline at the table and smiled. "You're here."

Caroline got up to hug her sister. Garrett nodded at

her, keeping his reserve. One he only had with her apparently as everyone else got a hug and a big smile.

It was early days. She hadn't been around him much while the others had known him for years. It would take time. She just had to be patient.

They sat down to eat, and after a while of trying to draw people out and get to know them better, she just let it go. Mindy was wrapped up in Garrett, who loved the sound of his own voice and maybe her sister. Her grandparents approved of this, despite his apparently Baptist leanings. Her grandmother probably already had plans for how she'd convert him to Lutheranism once they got married.

At least Shep appeared to want to interact with her, answering her questions about school.

"I want to go to law school," he said with a grin.

Pride warmed her. It ran in the family after all, but it meant something to her personally too.

"Yeah? Awesome. Hard work, but it's worth it if you love the job."

"You do then?"

"I do. Weird as it sounds, I love the courtroom. Not everyone does, but it's my favorite part of the job. There are other legal jobs out there. When the time comes, if you still want to pursue law school, I can hook you up with folks I know so you can see what their jobs are like. Get a perspective that way."

"As long as he doesn't defend the guilty," Garrett said.

Caroline cocked her head, trying to figure out if the comment was about her or defense lawyers in general or what.

"Everyone's innocent until proven guilty, so that's

easy enough." She smiled, not wanting to argue and ruin everyone's brunch.

"But what about once they're proven guilty? What then about the people who keep trying to free them?"

Oh. *No.* No fucking wet-behind-the-ears near-stranger was going to lecture her about what she'd spent fifteen years learning. He never knew her father.

The table went still.

"We talking about me in particular, Garrett?" Years in the courtroom had given her pretty excellent control. She wasn't going to lose it there in her grandparents' home, but she did let her feelings flash in her gaze—just briefly—and was satisfied when he flinched. She'd eat this little punk for breakfast.

"No. Of course he isn't." Mindy elbowed Garrett.

"Why pretend she's not making a mess?" Garrett asked. "She's back a few weeks and already she's starting fights all over town."

"I'm losing track of your point, Garrett. Is it that I'm a defense attorney? Or that I believe in the innocence of my father or that some piece of trash got in my face when I didn't even know he existed until that very moment? Or really how any of it is your business in any way."

"You can't come back here and tear this family down more than your father already did."

"This is not appropriate dinner-table conversation," her grandmother said severely.

"She needs to be taken in hand, Abigail. She's wearing her welcome thin already. If you two feel like you can't say it, I will."

Caroline spoke before anyone else could. "Let me make myself really clear. I've known you for about ten minutes. I don't need your advice and I certainly don't need your censure."

"You need to be told."

Caroline smirked. "You need to gain about twenty years' worth of experience and wisdom before you'd be ready to even imagine yourself capable of doing that for me."

"Garrett, that's enough." Mindy's distress was clear in her voice, which is why Caroline kept her swear words to herself.

"I agree. Garrett, this is my house and I'm telling you to stop this immediately, young man." Her grandfather had his serious face on and even her grandmother calmed down when he used it.

"I apologize, James. You know I love your family. I just hate to see it get torn apart." He shot her a look. This little shit had no idea what he was poking with his stick. But she wasn't going to do this at her grandparents' kitchen table like an animal. Not if she could help it.

Petal was small enough they'd cross paths again when he wouldn't be able to count on her manners. And then he'd understand just who he thought he could push around. And he'd know how very wrong he was.

She let him see all of that in her gaze, and when he blinked and shifted away from her, she knew she'd gotten her point across.

Caroline finished up, and after helping her grandmother clear and clean the dishes and get the area tidied, she kissed her grandmother's cheek. "I'm going to go now."

Abigail sighed. "He thought he was protecting us."

Well and that it was *us* and didn't include *her* was part of the problem.

"We'll have to agree to disagree about that. But I'm tired and I'm done for today. It was nice to see you though, and you know how much I love your roast chicken."

Shep rolled into the room as she dried her hands and moved to grab her bag.

"You're leaving already?"

"I've been here three hours. It's time for me to go."

"Let me walk you out." He cast a glare at Garrett as they passed through the living room.

Caroline paused to kiss her grandfather. "I'll see you soon."

"You're leaving already?"

"I said the same thing. Guess she can't feel comfortable in her own grandparents' home because some people have bad manners." Shep looked pointedly in Garrett's direction.

Caroline rolled her eyes. "I'll see you later, Mindy. Call me if you want to get together this week sometime for a movie or something."

Her sister got up, clearly caught between Caroline and Garrett. Whatever. There's no way she'd have ever tolerated any man talking to her sister that way, but they were different people.

"You don't have to go."

Caroline hugged Mindy. "Yes, I do. I'll talk to you soon."

Garrett got up but she turned her back on him. If he thought for even one second that she would pretend he hadn't been unconscionably rude, he had another thing coming.

Shep walked her out.

"He's a jerk. You don't have to go because of that crap he said."

"Yes he is. But he's Mindy's boyfriend and that was

Grandma and Grandpa's house. I'm a grown-ass woman, and I'm not getting into a slap fight with a dumbass like I'm in middle school. I know what I am, Shep. I know what I believe and I am not ashamed of it. My beliefs don't do a damned thing to you, or your grandparents or Mindy. Especially not to Garrett Moseby."

He licked his lips but didn't speak like she thought he wanted to. Instead he leaned in and hugged her tight. "I'm so glad you're back here for good. I missed you and it's nice to have you around."

She grinned. "Ditto. You too. I mean, you call me if you get some free time. I know you have school, but after school one day this week or next, let me take you out for pizza or something. Away from here."

"You got a deal. Love you, Caroline."

That softened her annoyance at Garrett.

Shep waggled his brows. "You can tell me about Royal Watson when you take me to pizza."

"How'd you know? Jeez this town and gossip."

Shep laughed. "Just wait until you two do it. I bet I'll know within eight hours."

"Ew. No you won't because he's not the type to talk about that stuff."

She hugged him one last time before getting into the car. "Behave and don't forget to call me."

She drove away, but she was smiling. She'd take that as a partial win.

Chapter Nine

Royal, true to his words to Caroline two days before, had slept in late and done nothing more taxing than shuffling to his kitchen to turn on the coffeemaker and make himself an egg sandwich.

The day before had been a long one. From five to just past midnight when he stumbled to bed. But as he looked out over his land, he saw new things growing, freshly turned earth in some spots, covered beds elsewhere.

His world, and he was making it work.

Once the coffee was ready, he headed to his living room. Spike curled around his feet when Royal situated himself on the lounge chair to watch some stuff he had waiting on his DVR. He glanced at the clock as he sipped his coffee. Brunch with her grandparents should take a few hours. It was noon so perhaps he'd see her by four or so.

He hoped.

They'd left each other under some weird circumstances, but he couldn't get the sound of her saying she wanted to be the only woman in the room when they fucked out of his head. He'd heard *fuck* over and over and over in her voice.

Caroline was like no one else, and he liked that a lot.

What he liked most though, which surprised him so much, was the way she was also vulnerable and soft at times. Her confidence blew him away. Made him hot. She barreled into the room, her energy attracted attention. Not just his. It wasn't that she was pretty, though she sure was. It wasn't her body, which was also stunning. She was just one of those people who seemed to have her own gravity and people moved around her.

He enjoyed that. Enjoyed being with her and having her choose him to focus on instead of all the other stuff she could. Admired her focus.

But it was the way she reacted over Anne that he found himself marveling over.

It wasn't the jealous thing. Though, truth be told who didn't like it when someone got a little jealous over an ex? Anne was gorgeous in her own right and they were close. The other women he'd gone out with hadn't really said much about it. Anne came with the Royal package. She was one of his chosen family. Though he didn't love her in a romantic sense anymore, he'd always love her. Always have her in his heart because she was someone in his life. Had been part of his life history for longer than she hadn't been.

He'd expected a woman like Caroline to at the very least pretend she wasn't bothered. That she was up front about her discomfort, while being rational about whether or not she had a right to be, fascinated him. She was a big girl. A woman in charge of her shit, and damn if that wasn't incredibly attractive.

In the meantime he had to figure out how to deal with the Anne situation. Her text had been about the scene with Benji at the Tonk. She'd heard about it from Beth and wanted to know the details. It had been a text like thousands of others they sent back and forth, but it felt differently in some ways because if he was correct, Anne was jealous of Caroline too.

Maybe a year ago he'd have given it a different kind of thought. He might have gone to Anne and said, *hey do you see? This is a woman I can see myself with a year from now.* Two, five. This is the kind of woman a man can build a life with. He might have given Anne the chance to come to her goddamn senses and marry him.

But that had passed. He could finally say—and mean—he was over her. Yes, she was important to him and always would be. But he didn't ache for her. Didn't dream about a life together or kids with her. He'd let go, and it felt normal after a lot of heartache.

Caroline consumed his thoughts. It had been a short period of time and he was smart enough to take it slow. But after years of fruitless love with a woman who couldn't ever give him what he truly wanted, feeling so intensely for someone else was liberating. Exciting.

He watched a movie and fast-forwarded through a football game, pausing at the highlights before Anne came in.

"Yo," she called out.

"Hey."

She handed him a cup. "Brought coffee."

"You're awesome." He lifted his cup in her direction.

Spike defected, abandoning Royal for Anne, hopping up into her lap and butting her hand until she laughed, scratching behind his ears. "You're so easy."

"What brings you out here today?" Sundays were usually days the entire Murphy clan congregated to eat and hang out. Sometimes with huge swaths of Chases.

"You didn't call me back yesterday."

"I didn't call anyone yesterday. I'm tired as hell after yesterday."

"Ah. So I wanted to get the scoop on the scene at the Tonk. Where's your girlfriend?"

He didn't argue with her tossed-out word. She'd meant it to needle him, but he found he liked it enough to roll it around his head and smile at the thought. "She'll be over later. She's having brunch with her grandparents."

"I heard she started some shit over at the Tonk. That's a record, your what, first date, and you're already having to punch people to defend her?"

"Now come on, did you hear *that* or did you hear what actually happened?"

"Stop being like that."

"Like what?"

"Making excuses with a lovesick smirk. Don't get all gone for this girl. She's not one of us. She's not your type."

"She's not? Please explain how you're so sure about that."

"She's got shoes that cost more than the chair you're sitting in. Her grandparents drive a new car and go to church with Edward and Polly. She's an outsider and she's bringing a suitcase of trouble straight into town."

"Your sister is married to a Chase. She probably goes to church with them too."

She waved it away.

"You jealous, Anne?" He softened his tone and she narrowed her gaze.

"I'm trying to protect you from heartache! She's not your type. She's just slumming."

He put a hand up. "Whoa. Look, I get it. You're protective and I appreciate that. But you don't know Caroline. And I'm insulted on so many levels I can't decide where to start so I'm just going to skip it because you and I both know you're full of shit."

Anne frowned. "She's a lawyer and you're a farmer."

"I totally am. And she respects what I do, as it happens. And she didn't start that shit at the Tonk. Benji did. Benji was out of line, just like Dolly and half those girls are when they talk shit about you and your siblings because you're Murphys. I didn't stand for that then and I won't take it now. No one deserves to get judged for what their parents do and you know that. Hell, if you gave her half a chance you'd actually like her."

"Christ, Royal, you're a lovesick idiot. I'm trying to help you."

"I don't need your help, Anne. I'm dating someone. I like her. She likes me." He shrugged.

"She comes back here after being gone for years."

"Is that illegal now? She was a kid! Jesus. *After her mother was murdered*, Caroline, at sixteen, went to live with her uncle. You act like she went on TV and denounced Petal as not good enough for her. You of all people ought to understand what it means to be marked by what your parents have done."

"She's defending a murderer! People are going to start thinking you're like her if you keep on this way."

"I'm not so sure he was really a murderer. I've read up a little. Some of the stuff she's written, some articles about it and her struggle to prove his innocence. But in any case, I can make my own mind up. If people judge me for what someone else thinks, that's their problem."

"So if she was a Nazi and you dated her that would be fine?"

He snorted. "It's a pretty big leap to take from going

through the legal system to try to prove someone's innocence and find the real killer to Nazism. Isn't there some internet rule about bringing Hitler into an argument?"

She laughed. "Her boobs have entranced you."

"They're pretty awesome boobs."

Things eased between them and he breathed easier. He didn't want Anne to feel bad. He cared about her. But this silly tantrum over Caro was just that and he wasn't about to give in.

"I should go. I'm supposed to stop by and get fresh eggs to bring over to Tate's."

"You know, she's going to be here in a while. You could stay and get to know her a little."

Anne rolled her eyes. "No thanks. I don't want to elbow in on your action. I'll see you later." She bent to drop the cat in his lap and give him a quick kiss.

"Just…be careful, please. People get worked up about this stuff. It tore the town in half before, and this sort of thing doesn't just die away. Everyone in her family thinks he did it. Doesn't that tell you something?"

Carrying Spike draped over his forearm, he followed her to the door. "Yes, it tells me that when she truly believes something she believes it to her heart. She's not going to pretend to think or feel something she doesn't. That's an important quality in a person."

"Ugh. You're totally smitten." She sighed and slapped his butt before she bent to smooch the cat's head and scoot out the door. "Later."

"Later. Say hey to everyone for me."

Caroline told herself she was going home, but she stopped at the Honey Bear, bought pie and sandwiches anyway. Her car aimed itself in Royal's direction and she went

with it. Heading away from the heart of town to the outskirts, where the houses and businesses dropped away,
replaced by rolling hills of farmland and orchards.

Familiar dread warred with the happy memories of
it all. This was the way to E and B Family Style Diner
and Kitchen. The diner had been a second home. The
back room had a desk where Caroline had done homework after school.

She'd learned how to drive a stick shift on this long,
straight piece of road, her dad beside her in the cab of
his truck. She had no idea how he'd remained so calm
as she'd ground his gears over and over. But he never
lost his cool.

There it was.

She paused and then pulled over across from the place
that used to hold the diner. Patty Griffin's "Rain" came
on the radio. Tears blurred her vision of the empty lot.
They'd razed the building to the ground ten years before.
No one wanted to buy it, no one wanted to rent it and run
a business from it, much less eat there.

Weeds were the only thing left other than the cracked
asphalt. She and her siblings owned it now. An empty lot
where her mother was murdered and her father had found
her. Caroline rested her forehead on the steering wheel.

Even her tears were contraband. In Petal, her grief
for her mother had been questioned. Every tear she shed
was examined. That she grieved her father too had been
some sort of proof she hadn't cared about her mother.

She never felt this way anywhere else. But it was there
in Petal where she ached to be able to talk about her
mother with the people who knew her and not have *that*
look come into their eyes. They either thought about how

she believed her father or how she left town, or that her mother had been so brutally killed.

It left her feeling examined so closely it was impossible to grieve freely.

But Caroline missed the way her mother had brushed and braided her hair. No one had been able to duplicate those elaborate fishtails and the French braids at her temple that had swept back into a ponytail at the back.

She'd had a crown that day. Her mother had done it before Caroline had left for school. Because there'd been a boy. Caroline couldn't even remember who the boy was at that point. Only that her mother had been rushing to feed Quique and Mindy, and Caroline had asked at the last minute.

But her mother had sucked in a breath and smiled, asking Caroline for details about the boy as she'd brushed and divided her hair, spraying it with water from a purple spray bottle to make it easier to braid.

The last time Caroline had ever seen her mother alive was when Bianca had called out an I love you from the porch as Caroline ran out on her way to catch the bus.

The police had come to their house with their grandfather. Caroline would never forget what his face had looked like. As if he'd crumple at any moment. Caroline had refused to let them take her hair from that braid for three days until her grandmother had done it when Caroline had finally passed out, exhausted from not sleeping.

From asking over and over when her father was coming home.

In truth, she'd never really come home since then either.

She pulled away from the side of the road, wiping her face on her sleeve and heading to Royal's.

* * *

She knocked on his door, and he opened with a smile, his gaze raking over her and pausing at her eyes. "What's wrong?"

He drew her inside.

"Nothing. I brought pie and sandwiches." The cat swayed into the room, saw it was her and after a quick wind around her legs, swayed out.

Royal took the bags in her hand.

"Come on through. I was just getting hungry so your timing is perfect. I have coffee, iced tea, beer, root beer, Coke." He waved at his kitchen, and for whatever reason, him not treating her like a guest made her feel better.

"I got a few sandwiches because I wasn't sure what you'd want." She grabbed a mug and poured coffee.

"A few? There are ten sandwiches in here, girl."

"Well now you have some for tomorrow when you're out all day."

He turned and pulled her close. "That's nice. I get so busy and I put lunch off and then I rush home and eat a bunch of junk because it's easy and fast."

She frowned. "You work awfully hard not to treat yourself better. I'm going to be getting on you about that. Just be warned."

He kissed her and her sorrow flitted away.

"You taste like tears, Caro. What happened today?"

"Ugh. Let's eat sandwiches and make out instead."

He barked a laugh. "We can definitely do that, but I want to know what's wrong too."

She paused and wondered if she could let go of it enough to tell him. If she could trust him not to push her away, and if he did it was best to know it early on because she came with all this junk in her life.

"Don't make me withhold kisses until you share. That only hurts us both."

She groaned. "It's just been one of those days."

"Come on then. Get some food, and we'll go into my living room and snuggle while you tell me."

Caroline chose a ham and swiss on rye and her cup of coffee and followed him into his living room. He had a fire going and a blanket he'd clearly been using on his recliner chair. He grabbed it and tipped his chin toward the couch.

Bossy.

She settled but he took her plate away and put it on the coffee table. "Take your shoes off, darlin'. I'll be right back with some thick socks."

She started to argue, but he left and she realized how dumb it was. Her feet were cold and the idea of his socks sort of made her happy.

As she dropped her boots near the front door, Caroline paused to look at the pictures on the nearby table.

"My mom and my uncle when they were kids." He grinned as he handed over the socks. "Honey, you need to wear thick socks on a day as cold as this one. Not that I begrudge you a pair of mine, but I don't like thinking of you with cold toes."

She followed him back into the living room to put the socks on and get tucked up on the couch next to him. "I had on super-cute boots that I'd normally wear with a skirt. I'm wearing socks. Just not thick ones."

He rolled his eyes and took a bite of the sandwich. "Thanks for this. So, I take it the brunch sucked."

She sighed. "My sister's boyfriend is a self-righteous little prick. He thought he'd school me on embarrassing my family. Apparently the word in town is that I started a fight with Benji instead of the other way around."

"Who is she dating?"

"Garrett Moseby."

Royal sneered. "Mindy can do better than him."

Caroline shrugged. "I can't give her advice. One, she doesn't ask for it and two, my grandmother seems to like him. Maybe Mindy can't do better. Maybe I *am* embarrassing them. I don't know. But I do know I won't let a punk like Garrett give me a lecture about anything but being a punk."

"Did you punch him in the nose?"

She laughed, leaning over to rest her head on his shoulder a moment. "I'll have you know I tried very hard not to fight with him at my grandparents' dinner table. But if I see him in town, he better run."

"You gonna take him to school? I think that would be a mighty sexy sight so you'd need to do it when you were with me."

His humor broke that knot of anger loose and she felt a little better. She tried not to smile but she failed. "If I did I'd whip him with a ruler. Who does he think he is anyway? Like I'd stoop to the level of the likes of Benji and randomly start a fight at a bar? I don't even know the guy."

It was Royal's turn to sigh. "Enough people saw what truly happened Friday night that any time someone says you started it, the truth will out."

"Maybe. People get offended when you won't believe what they think you should."

He turned. "I don't like that he made you cry. Makes *me* want to punch him in the nose."

She shook her head. "He didn't make me cry. It made

me mad. The tears." She paused a moment before deciding to take a leap and trust him. "Do you know that empty lot off the highway near the farm supply store? That was where my family's diner was."

He pressed a kiss against the top of her head. "And you have to pass it to get here. They bulldozed the building ten years ago. I'm just so used to traveling that road that I don't think about it. I'm sorry."

"This is not your fault in any way. I'm not saying this right. Let's eat and watch movies and spend time together."

"Nope. I mean, yes do eat and we will definitely spend time together, but if ever someone needed to get some stuff off their mind, it's you. I'm an excellent listener."

"You should know me awhile, maybe even touch my boobs before I show you just how crazy my baggage is."

He reached out and totally felt her up! It was so fast and unexpected she wasn't offended. Not that she wasn't absolutely fine with him touching her breasts in the first place.

His pleased laugh made her shake her head. He was so amused with himself. "Oh my God, you're such a handful."

"I feel like a Lost Boy, but come with me." He waggled his brows before he got serious again. "Well, now that I've rounded second base, and let me tell you, your tits are fucking spectacular, you can share your crazy baggage. Caro, I'm not going anywhere."

She took a deep breath. "I should have gotten a beer."

He got up, went to get them both one and returned. He clinked his bottle against hers. "I know you haven't always been able to count on people in your life, Caro. But I'm not them."

"I feel like I can't express my grief here. In Petal I mean." She cleared her throat and took a few gulps of her beer. "It's suffocating. Sometimes the walls feel too close. Like everything I do is under inspection, and I tell myself *fuck that, this is my life and I am not ashamed.* I try to ignore all that attention, but in doing so I'm sort of hyperaware of it instead."

He nodded, listening. And it felt good to let go of the words she'd been holding back. "I'm just very careful in my life when I'm here. Hyper conscious of appearances. It's lonely sometimes and I want to reach out to these people—all of whom were such a huge part of my life until I was sixteen—and I can't. I want to have that ease Mindy and Shep do with my grandparents. I tell myself that it was my choice and it was. I left Petal, and when I did, I left them. So then I tell myself that I have to show them what they need to see."

"Essentially the parts of you utterly removed from your parents and the murder at all. You turn it all off to protect them but they have no right to demand it. That's not fair, Caroline. It's not fair of them to expect you not to have feelings. You're still their granddaughter. They need to love you for who you are, for *all* parts of you."

She shrugged. "I argue this point with myself all the time. And maybe sometimes I don't know where that ends. Whatever it is, I'm walking such a fine line. Constantly measuring my reactions to everything, and then I think, *oh my God I can't do this for the rest of my life.*

"I'm the oldest, my parents would want me to hold our family together. Anyway, I sat there and looked across the road, and I let go of it. It felt good. I was lightened and I processed some stuff. I'm seeing Petal differently now that I'm living here than when I did when I only came back a few times a year. This is my hometown, and ugh, it's complicated! And then I feel guilty for being angry over how much I'm having to give up. And I don't mean my firm or my house or my car, those things. But the ability to truly relax enough to be a whole person. I don't feel safe enough to do that here."

He started to speak but she held a hand up. "*But* I just realized right now that this little moment is sort of a root. A root to building a community, my safe place here. You're part of that."

"Contraband grief. Wow, that's a powerful concept. I'm sorry. I've lost my father, and my mother, well I've had to give her up little by little as she's declined over the years. Grief is important. It'll eat you up if you can't express it in your own way. You do what you need to. Feel what you need to. Don't let anyone else police that."

"Which is easier said than done."

He snorted. "Yes, that's true. You're tough though. And when you need an ear, I'm around. I'm happy you feel like I'm part of what makes you feel safe in Petal. That's a really nice compliment. One of my all-time favorites, I think. Just know that with me, you can cry or whatever anytime."

She smiled up at him. "We should change the subject now. How was your Sunday?"

He let her.

"So far so good. I slept until ten. I wanted to sleep later, but you know how it goes. Your body is used to five so I think my days of sleeping until noon are past. But I slept in, and then I read in bed for a while before wandering out to make coffee and some food. Caught up on my stuff on DVR. Nothing at all taxing. And now you're here so it's a pretty damned good day all around."

"And did you get everything you needed done yesterday?"

"I've yet to actually get everything I needed done when I needed it done. But I came close. Which I'm counting as a win."

"Tell me about your day yesterday."

She leaned against him as he recounted his day, embellishing here and there to entertain her better.

"You really should have sex with me." She blurted this in one of their quiet moments.

He paused a moment and then put his beer down. "Should I?"

She nodded. "Yes. I mean, unless you don't want to. If you don't want to, then no you shouldn't."

He took her face in his palms, kissing her softly. "I really want to."

This made her laugh and he pulled her into his lap. "I also seem to recall this particular position for kissing being a favorite of mine. I wasn't wrong."

She undulated, stroking the heat of her pussy against his cock, sending shockwaves of pleasure through him.

"Yeah, that's it. I remember now."

He put his hands at her hips, and she dipped her mouth down and breathed a kiss onto his lips.

This was good. Damn she tasted so sweet. He kissed from her lips to her ear just to hear that little whimper she gave. The weight of her in his lap was so perfect he was nearly afraid of it. Maybe he should be. She made him feel things he wasn't sure he could.

She reached up and pulled her hair from the chignon at the base of the back of her neck. The material of her shirt pulled up, and his hands landed on the warm, soft bare skin of her belly and he groaned, sliding his palms up her back, skin to skin.

The backyard lights came up as the twilight slid away into full dark. With a muffled curse, he managed to stand with her legs wrapped around his waist. "Come on."

"Where else could I go?"

He laughed as he headed to his bedroom, kicking the door closed or they'd have a furry visitor.

He tossed her to the bed, and she fell back with a laugh, the spill of all that dark hair framing her face. He moved to turn on some music, trying to find a thread of patience because damn he wanted her right then and there.

But when he shifted in her direction, it was to find her having reached the bottom button on her shirt and then shimmying from it.

"Holy shit."

He got to his knees on the bed to face her, kissing her bare shoulder. Her breath hitched, which sent her cleavage closer to his face, and he gave in, turning to brush his lips against the curve of each breast.

"No front catch?" he murmured as he slid his hands around to her back to unfasten all that lace and underwire.

"They're too big for that stuff. I can't afford to go busting out of a bra while I'm delivering a closing argument."

He laughed, pushing her back, his hands going to the waist of her pants.

Gaze latched on to her face to gauge her willingness, he slid the button out of the hole and unzipped. She lifted her ass as he drew the pants, and a scrap of dark blue silk that was her panties, down her legs.

All that skin bared to his gaze and his gaze only.

Damn.

He took her in from the tousle of glorious hair, the hard, dark nipples capping breasts that made his mouth water, the dip at her waist, the flare of her hips, the curve of her thighs sliding into toned calves and then feet painted with the same pale pink she had on her fingers.

So feminine and sexy and in his bed.

One corner of her mouth lifted. "Come on then, Watson."

He pulled his shirt up and off and was out of his pants and shorts in record time as he resumed his place on his knees, staring at her body again.

He whistled low. "Jesus. I can't believe all this lives underneath your clothes. I mean, I was impressed before, but this? Wow."

She reared up enough to grab his cock in her fist, squeezing just right. "Show me, don't tell me."

It was his turn to laugh as he bent down to take her mouth again. She nipped his bottom lip and slowly moved her fist up and down.

Then she rolled him over and kissed his neck as she straddled his body. She paused, listening to the music for long moments before she locked her attention back on him. "I love this song."

"Is this what you do when your favorite song comes on?" He gave her a dubious look.

"Only with a chosen few people. I don't even know who it is though. My country-music muscles are sadly pretty weak."

He took her breasts into his hands, testing their weight before sliding his thumbs back and forth over her nipples until they went tight. "This is Kacey Musgraves. 'Back on the Map' is the name of the song."

She wriggled free and kissed down his belly, and her gaze locked with his, licked up the line of his cock until he lost all words.

All he had was feeling. It washed through him as he watched her. Those lips wrapped around the head of his cock, the way her tongue swirled around him before she sucked him back into her mouth again and again and again until he nearly reeled with it.

He touched her shoulder. "Wait. Wait. Not yet. Want to be in you when I come."

She paused, pulling off, that mouth of hers all swollen and glossy. "No. But you'll have plenty of time for that too."

The gentleman in him warred with the man who wanted to take and mark and ravage. He dug his fingers into the blanket trying to hold on to the former.

She pulled back again. "Problem?"

He shook his head, nearly frantic.

She cupped his sac, scoring it gently with her nails. "You're hesitating."

"Manners!" His voice broke halfway through the word.

She laughed, and while keeping his gaze, she licked over the slit like every single fantasy he'd ever had made into flesh. He swallowed his words.

"You made sure I consented. You'll obviously make me come. So fuck manners, Royal. Let go. It's just me and you here."

Then she took him so hard and deep, he let go of his manners and thrust his hips. His fingers slid into her hair.

She took him into her mouth over and over and over until the pleasure was so sharp he had no other choice but to fall into a climax so hard he saw lights behind his closed eyelids. His skin went hypersensitive, shivers covering him when she kissed his hip.

"Give me a moment. I don't have feeling above my toes yet."

She laughed, moving to rest her head on his biceps as he stroked a hand through her hair.

He took a deep breath and stretched before turning and pinning her beneath him. She grinned. Damn he loved that grin of hers.

"Hi."

"Hi."

"I'm going to lick you now. Pretty much everywhere I've been fantasizing about since that first night in the grocery store."

"You wanted to lick me even after I made you get cereal off the top shelf?"

"I like doing things for you. Plus, when you reach up your tits push forward and your ass arches back. It's like the perfect position for your body."

She laughed as he slid his tongue down her neck, pausing to lave the hollow of her throat. "You taste good."

"I do?"

"Like the cold air outside. A little bit of your perfume I think. Your skin. Damn your skin is addictive."

She arched back as he kissed his way down the middle of her chest and headed first to her left nipple and then her right.

"You're really good with your mouth," she breathed out.

He drew the edge of his teeth against her nipple before he continued down her body, kissing and licking as he went. "I haven't even reached my final destination yet."

"I'm on the edge of my seat."

"Good, that's where you need to be so I can eat your pussy."

She gasped, and he paused, wondering if he'd gone too far. But she slid her fingers through his hair and tugged.

Guess not.

He pulled her open using his thumbs to part her to his mouth and his gaze. And when he took that first long lick, they both sighed happily.

He licked slowly, getting to know her, what she liked, what made her gasp and arch. She wasn't shy about expressing herself, which was as hot as everything else about her.

Her thigh muscles trembled a little as he licked and nuzzled, drawing her closer to orgasm as her body readied for it. Her taste on his lips drove him. He needed to make her feel good, as good as she made him feel.

And when she came, she tightened her grip in his hair and that only added to the experience. To her taste flooding him as she climaxed against his lips.

"Yes."

She sighed happily as he kissed his way back up her body and to her mouth.

"I think we need a break for a beer, and then we start round two of this party."

"I'm all for that plan."

She watched as he left the room. Spike burst through the door like they'd been hoarding bacon in the bedroom. He looked around, and satisfied there was no unclaimed bacon, he hopped up on the bed and put his paw on her exposed foot.

When she didn't move quickly enough to pet him,

Spike gave a little demonstration with his nails that had her sitting up.

"You're bossy, cat. I sort of like that in a person." Caroline scratched under his chin, and he flopped to his back to give her better access.

"He's easy for women." Royal came in and handed her a beer. She took several gulps.

Caroline needed to come over here for this exact sort of stress relief because even after the day she'd had, she was really relaxed.

"Apple doesn't far fall from the tree?" she teased.

Royal laughed, coming in to kiss her long and slow. "I'm only easy for a very few women. Lucky for me, you're right here in my bed."

She pushed him to his belly and straddled his butt.

"You like being on top," he said into his pillow. This morphed into a groan when she began to knead the muscles at his shoulders and neck.

"I figured you might be a little knotted up after all that physical work you've done and with all the deadlines you're facing."

His skin was warm against her fingertips, pliant beneath her palms.

"Dear God. Just so you know, I don't plan on giving you up. You're smart, funny, gorgeous, your mouth is a deadly weapon and you give massages too. The perfect woman."

She kept working, massaging the knots from his muscles until he'd loosened up into a warm mass of hot man flesh.

She dropped to the side, and he turned, seeing so much more than what was on the outside. Which she liked, but it scared her as well. No matter how much she imagined she'd be able to keep it light with this man, she was so wrong.

"Thank you." Because the things he just said about her had made her happy and she wanted him to know it.

He stretched his arms up over his head and got bulgy and sinuous, and it made her a little breathless. He tipped his chin at her. "And thank *you* for that."

"What? For what?"

Grinning, he got close enough to kiss her. "For the massage and for the way you just looked at me."

"Oh. Well. I mean. Look at yourself."

He rolled her over, pausing to kiss her again. "I'd rather look at you. Though looking at you does affect me." He rolled his hips, grinding his cock into her thigh to underline his point.

"Well, thank goodness for that. How else could you fuck me otherwise?"

He nipped her bottom lip. "Damn I love your mouth."

He leaned across her as he dug around in a drawer in his bedside table and pulled out a shiny foil packet.

"Thank God." She'd only realized about five minutes before that she might not have any condoms. She was sure they could have figured out something else to do with their time without them, but she was glad they didn't have to now.

"Since you like being on top, I'm going to stay with that theme." He flopped to his back and tore the packet open, rolling it over his totally revived dick.

She hopped over him, adding a little wiggle just to see the way his attention shot straight to her boobs.

Slowly—ever so slowly—she took him into her body. She wanted it hard and fast. Wanted him to maybe even leave a mark. But that first time she knew they were learning one another. Drawing closer and more intimate. It was hot without a doubt. But also tender, which she liked.

He hissed when she had him inside her fully. She sat, letting her body stretch around him. It had been a while and he...well he was pretty talented in the size game.

"Yeah, this is the fuckin' way to spend a Sunday. Hands down. You're so hot and tight I'm having to do math to keep this from ending before it even starts."

She laughed, bending down to kiss him. "I'll take this over brunch at my grandparents' any day."

He growled a little, all protective and stuff, and it sent a shiver of delight through her. No one had growled over her before.

And she found herself on her back, Royal looming over her as he stretched her legs, putting her heels at his shoulders.

"I like that you're very flexible."

She wasn't in a place where she could form too many words. But she sure did like this being-overpowered thing. She liked the way he put her how he wanted, but even though it was a little rough and abrupt, he didn't hurt her—not in a bad way anyway—as he did.

He was big inside her. Big and thick as he slid in deep over and over. As he thrust, he petted covetous hands all over her skin, every part he could reach.

"I'm torn. I want to come so bad I can feel it in my teeth." He used those teeth, turning his head to give her ankle a nip. "But this. Caro, this is so good I never want it to end."

"We can do it again, you know," she managed to get the words out before he made her writhe once more.

"We can. And we will. I suppose now would be an important time to let you know how much I like sex."

She tightened herself around him. "Good. I like it too. So get to it."

He laughed, and slowly but surely, the force and depth of his strokes intensified until her boobs bounced. Not much else, given the way he had her positioned, but it left her open to his touch, which he provided.

He walked up her thigh with his fingers and circled her clit with just the right pressure. Slow but not so slow it frustrated. No, this was a seduction. A tease of what was to come. Of what *he'd* give her.

As he got closer, he brought her along, playing her body like a sex genius or something. And when she flew apart, arching, her eyes sliding closed as she rode her orgasm, her body tightening and convulsing around his, she heard his muffled curse and knew he was right there with her.

Long moments later he put her back on the mattress gently before disappearing and returning quickly.

He jumped into the bed beside her, pulling her close, and she was too relaxed and swamped with feel-good chemicals to protest at all. She nuzzled his throat, her nose buried there in all that muscle.

"Will you sleep over? I get up early, but then again, I bet you do as well. I'll even make you breakfast."

It wasn't like she had the muscle control to drive a car just then anyway.

"Yeah. I need to be up at five thirty. I like to use the treadmill as I warm up for my day."

"You can ride me instead."

Laughing, she flopped onto her back, still in the circle of his arms. "That sounds way more fun."

Chapter Ten

"You should come out to my place tonight after work."

"I should?" She smiled even though he wouldn't be able to see her expression over the phone.

"You totally should. I've been marinating these ribs all day. They're going to be really good and I think you need that in your life today. With me."

"You're right. I'll bring something sweet and beer."

"Perfect."

She paused and then forged ahead. "So I was thinking of leaving for the day." She'd been planning on something like a manicure, several glossy fashion magazines and some time in her bathtub. But she'd far rather spend the time with him.

"I'm going to ride out and check some crops. Want to come along with me?"

"Yeah! I'll go home to change and get beer and cake. Or maybe a pie. I'm not sure which way I'm swinging right now. I'll know when I see it."

"The way you view baked goods makes me hot."

"That's good as it's an essential part of my makeup as a human being." She saved and closed the document she'd been working on. "I should be there within an hour."

"I'll meet you at my house in an hour."

She hung up and got her tail out of there before anything else hit her desk and needed her attention right then.

At her apartment she also packed a quick overnight bag. She'd leave it in the car just in case spending the night wasn't looking like a reality.

The beer she already had so she put it in her trunk along with her overnight bag and a file she'd need if she was running late and headed straight to court rather than being in the office early. She had every intention of being at work early, but stuff happened and it paid to cover all your bases.

At the Honey Bear she waved at Maryellen Proffit. Since Caroline and Melissa had built their friendship, Mrs. Proffit was warmer, happy to see her. The Honey Bear, over the three weeks she'd been working at Chase and Chase, had become a safe spot for her, and she often took some of her work down in the afternoons after the lunch rush, to grab a booth and work while she had some coffee or tea and a snack.

It was a trophy of sorts. Her first official Caroline spot. Back in Seattle she'd had many of them. But each small inch of ground she gained in Petal was ridiculously hard fought. It meant a lot that she could come in and feel like they were happy to see her.

After making all her choices, Caroline paid and Maryellen bagged her order up. With a wink, she filled a little white bakery box with chocolate chip cookies. "With walnuts."

"You're a bad influence! I love that about you."

Maryellen blushed. "Oh you. Now go on and have a nice time with Royal. If you see Melissa before I do, give her a hug from me."

Caroline squeezed Maryellen's hand before scooping her bag up. "See you soon, Mrs. Proffit."

Maryellen had told her to call her Maryellen instead of Mrs. Proffit but Caroline hadn't been able to do it regularly yet.

As Caroline pushed her way out, Beth and Anne stood just outside.

Beth smiled and Anne's mouth faked one but didn't bother to hide the lack of genuine feeling behind it.

"Hey there."

"You here getting an afternoon snack?" Beth asked.

"Yeah and for after dinner too." She could have said what exactly she was getting it for, but this tension between her and Anne was so stupid and such a big time-suck she just didn't.

She wanted things to be civil with Anne. It made Royal upset otherwise. Angry and sort of embarrassed, and Caroline hated that Anne was making him feel that way. But at the same time she knew how much Royal cared for Anne and her family. She liked him way too much to not at least try to fit into his world with his friends, and it was clear that even though they liked Caroline they would line up with Anne.

And she understood it. But it sucked and it made her tired.

"You?" Caroline asked, meaning *hey, now you share this personal thing about your life and that's how you make friends*.

"Joe has a late night at the garage and I need to go grocery shopping so I figured I'd just come in here and get him and Buck something to eat instead."

"Buck's the dog, right?"

Beth warmed, her smile sitting more naturally on her

face. "Yes. He could come home with me and hang out and wait for his dad to get off work. But he believes he's an integral part of the repair process."

"Ah. So he's Joe's Patronus?"

Even Anne thought that was funny.

"That's exactly it. I'm going to have to share that one with Joe."

Caroline stepped away from the door. "Sorry for blocking your way. I'll see y'all around."

"Wow, that y'all sounded almost Southern," Anne said.

Beth gave Anne a look and pushed her sister inside. "I'd say it *totally* sounded Southern. I guess it's like riding a bike. Before long you're going to start saying *bless your heart* when you're being insulting."

"Is that when my transformation is complete?"

Beth snorted. "Georgia is like the mafia. You can't ever really leave." She winked. "Have a good afternoon off."

"Thanks." Caroline waved before she headed to her car.

Caroline and Royal had been dating three weeks. Long enough for Caroline to be even more certain she really liked Royal Watson in her life. She *could* be the better woman and step aside to give Anne one last crack at Royal. But fuck that. Royal would have gone after Anne if that's what he'd wanted.

That should have settled it and everyone could move on.

But damn, she hated feeling like everyone around them was just waiting for Anne to get the hell over her pissy behavior so they could open up to Caroline fully.

Which was bullshit. She *wanted* to get to know his friends better. They'd gone out on group things a time or two. But she knew they hung out regularly, and other

than those few times they all went out, there had been
no real movement toward her by any of them.

She never wanted Royal to feel like he had to choose.
But if they kept closed off to her, she and Royal probably wouldn't last. She wasn't interested in being made
to feel like an outsider as entertainment for other people.

She headed out of town, toward his house and tried to
put it all away.

He waited for her on his porch, sitting on a rocker,
one booted foot on the railing. But when she got out, he
was up and moving to her, taking the bags from her arms
before leaning down to kiss her.

"Mmm. You taste good."

"If you think I taste like maybe I ate one or two of
the chocolate chip walnut cookies, you'd be totally lying.
To yourself."

He grinned. "Sugar, you can eat all the cookies you
want." He then noted her overnight bag. "Yeah? You
want to stay over?"

"I mean if you want me to. Don't feel obligated. I
wanted to be prepared. Just in case."

"Do you want to stay over?" he repeated.

She nodded, and he kissed her on his way to grab the
handles on her bag and hefted it from the trunk.

"We'll put this in the house and then head out."

She followed him in.

He handed her the bag. "Put it in the bedroom and
meet me back out here."

Spike didn't do much more than open an eye to be sure
she wasn't a serial killer before he went back to napping
in a patch of afternoon sun slanting across the bed. She

dropped her bag next to what she thought of as her side of the bed and turned to leave.

Spike made a huffed sound. Outraged she didn't pause to pet him.

She shook her head, moving to obey the demand in that feline gaze. "Sorry. I thought you were sleeping and didn't want to disturb you."

He snorted, getting some snot on her and then giving her a look that said she deserved said treatment.

"You're a rogue, Spike." She gave him one last scratch before she headed into the bathroom to scrub cat snot off her arm and hand.

When she came back out she stared at Royal for long moments. He was on his phone. One hand on the glass, the other holding the phone to his ear. His gaze was far off. Probably thinking in numbers as he apparently tended to do like the crazy smart man he was.

He spoke awhile and then turned to her after he hung up. "Sorry about that."

"You're working. It's fine."

"Good." He plunked a cowboy hat on her head. "You need to have some protection from the elements. Rain, sun, whatever. Also you look really sexy wearing a cowboy hat."

Reaching out, she grabbed him by the belt and the waist of his jeans and pulled him close. "How can I argue when I happen to think *you* look really sexy in a cowboy hat too? Also, I am a big fan of the new trend in facial hair."

"You mentioned last week that you liked facial hair on a man." He shrugged.

"It's bone-meltingly hot." Both the way it made him look and that he'd done it for her. She kissed a spot where he had some gray. "I can't even tell you how many truly dirty things you make me feel when I look at this salt and pepper."

He tipped her head back and her hat fell as he moved in for a kiss. He caught it, gripping the hat against her butt.

He held her fast against his body, sending a thrill through her. His mouth wandered from her lips to her ear until she hissed at how good it was and tugged his hair.

"Okay, okay. Come on." He groaned as he broke away from the kiss. "I need to do this, and after I'm done it'll be just me and you."

"You have a deal."

"Are you okay to ride on your own ATV or on mine?"

"I'm fine on an ATV. I promise not to four wheel all over your vegetables."

He grinned. "All right then. Follow me."

He led her out along the northern edge of the property. He liked this part of the land. His house was on a similar rise down to the south. But back here he could see out over the lake in the distance, some of the smaller rivers and creeks. It was still wild, and now that it was late March, life had burst up over the landscape as far as the eye could see.

Wanting to share it with her, he pulled over and parked.

She did the same, and when he got off his four-wheeler and turned to speak to her, he had to pause, stunned into silence at the sight of her on an ATV. She still wore the hat and goggles, but it was her smile that made him go weak.

So much joy on her face. *He* made her feel this way. She felt that with him and around him, and damn it felt good.

"I figured you might want to look."

He tipped his chin at the view.

She hung the goggles on the handlebars and headed to where he stood. Suddenly he felt shy. Maybe she wouldn't care about that. He was already dragging her down to look at carrots.

But her smile remained at what seemed like ten thousand watts. "Wow. What a view."

"You should see it at the change of the seasons. Scratch that. I mean, I can't wait to show you what it looks like as the seasons change."

She nodded. "Yeah, that was better."

They headed down to his carrots and she got her hands in the dirt. She wasn't afraid to put her back into something, and damn if she didn't fill out her T-shirt just right. He spun her, pulling her close. "Thanks for helping out. I didn't intend inviting you out here to put you to work. Got some mud on your shirt and jeans."

She blushed. "I'm washable. So are my clothes. Anyway, I liked it. Like I'm part of your everyday life."

He liked that too.

"Come on back to the house. Dinner and some beer too, I think."

She nodded and followed him.

He guided her to his bedroom. "Get changed. I'll get cleaned up quickly so I can throw the ribs on the grill."

She put on a new shirt and soft yoga pants before padding out to the kitchen, dodging Spike as she went.

She hadn't been in the kitchen since he'd put the food she'd brought away. She paused as she took in all the flowers.

"I was down at the flower market. I saw them and thought you might like them."

"Thank you. I do, and I love cornflowers most of all."
She brushed her fingertips over the lush blue/purple pet-
als. "So much pretty blue." She pointed to the iris. "The
creamy white of the magnolia, it's the perfect combo of
color in here."

"The cornflowers remind me of you." He stepped
closer, his thumb sliding over her bottom lip. He smelled
like the castile soap he used. Clean and simple.

"Me?"

He nodded. "They're wispy and lacy in parts they
can look nearly delicate, but overall they're strong. A
little sharp edge here and there, but none of that detracts
from the total beauty of the flower itself. You have sharp
edges. You have spots that look so strong and unbreak-
able from a distance, but when I focus I can see how
hard you're working to keep it together and build something here."

"I come with baggage. Death-row-shaped baggage."
She tried to shrug it off but he stopped her.

"Don't belittle it. This isn't a fad for you. You're doing
what you absolutely believe is the right thing, and you do
it without apology, even when you catch shit from people
who don't know a damned thing."

"Okay. I won't belittle it. But it is what it is. It's not
easy. But it's worth doing either way. All I can do is live
the way my parents taught me. I'm sorry it's been weird
for you with your friends and people in town."

"I don't give a fuck about that."

"You don't?"

"Nope. I'm all in, Caroline. You get me? Those idi-
ots who cause a fuss don't mean a thing to me. Because
they don't know you. But I know you."

She pulled him down for a kiss. "I think you might, yeah."

"I'm going to boil the ribs first and then barbecue them."

"Works for me. Want a beer?"

After dinner and kitchen cleanup, they settled in his bed to watch a little television. It had been a really long time since she'd cuddled up to someone in bed and caught up on shows.

Her secret joy was that she and Royal had two shows they watched together. It was silly she knew. Shallow too. But it made her happy. It was normal and fun.

Spike was pretending to be sleeping instead of waiting for one of them to accidentally move a toe so he could repel the alien scum trying to get into our universe through a space-time rift in the bed.

Royal, the big goofball, kept jiggling his foot and then cursing when the cat bit his toe or caught it on some claws.

"Good Lord, between the two of you." She shook her head, neatly avoiding a lazy swipe from a furry paw.

"We're cute." He picked the cat up to cuddle and smooch Spike's head. But Spike growled at him and glared until Royal put him down. "Fine. Some people love me!"

Yeah, some people did.

Spike jumped from the bed and left the room in a huff so she took that opportunity to shut the door.

Royal snorted. "He's gonna take his ire out on me, you know."

She remained leaning against his door for a while, just watching him. Then she pushed to stand and whipped her shirt off.

"That's what I'm talking about."

He went to his knees and got rid of his clothes as she quickly finished undressing. She took a running leap into bed and into his arms as he laughed, pulling her close to kiss her senseless.

Soon enough he'd levered her so she was on her back. "You're so good at that. My God I can't even imagine what you were like in high school. It was probably a good thing you never noticed me. I'd have turned to cinder if you'd kissed me like this back then. And you're far too good at your romance moves, mister. You've been working on it since you were a teen, haven't you?"

One of her brows rose and he winced.

"I suppose," she said, wrapping her legs around his thighs, "it's a good thing I like how smoothly efficient you are at getting me on my back and naked within mere minutes of being alone with one another. I love how hot you are for me all the time."

"Oh. You do?"

She rolled her hips, brushing her pussy against his cock. Knowing he'd feel how wet she was just from kissing.

"Yes I totally do. I love it when you're staring off into space when we're out in public and you get some look and I *know* you're thinking about fucking me. It's pretty hot. I like it."

"Good, because I do it pretty much every three minutes or so. Imagine fucking you, I mean. Or your mouth wrapped around my cock. Or my lips on your pussy. Your taste." He kissed her, slow and drugging until she'd relaxed beneath him utterly. Her fingers were twisted in his hair, holding on, keeping him close.

The knowing of it settled in. He'd be in her. On her or

under her. He'd make her feel good. His hands all over her, his taste in her mouth as he kissed past her mouth and down her throat.

He was so good at this whole sex thing. He touched her with a kind of naked greed, watching her reactions as he licked, bit, pinched and sucked on all parts of her. Learning her.

And he was a really good learner.

They had major *click*, that shockwave of physical and chemical reaction that seemed to heat them both up just when they were around one another.

Another knowing had begun to form in her belly. A deep sort of connection to Royal that astonished her. Filled her with joy and anticipation but fear too. He was the real deal. The kind of man who'd be not just a boyfriend but a mate. He was a man she could see herself with in a year, five, ten.

His mouth found her nipple, and she sighed, arching her back, her nails digging into his shoulders.

"*Oh!* Stubble." She gasped at the rasp of it against her nipple. The kiss had been hot enough but the feel of his beard against the sensitive skin of her breasts and nipples was beyond description.

"Should I go shave?" He paused, the tip of his tongue flicking her nipple.

"No. It's hot." It nearly hurt but not quite, so she let herself enjoy it. Enjoy him.

"Gotta admit I like the idea of you having some beard burn underneath all your work clothes."

He kissed down her belly, and she luxuriated in the feel of him, so sure, so long and lean, his hands large and strong. His mouth was full, most usually turned up into a smile. He could be very serious too, but his mouth wanted to smile. His mouth totally deserved to be that cocky.

He kissed over her hipbones and down her thighs, making his way to her pussy. Her body tightened with anticipation, and when he blew over her labia she nearly came up off the bed.

He nipped the inside of her thigh and then pushed her thighs open wide, holding them in those palms of his.

He took a lick, and she sighed, feeling as if she melted into the mattress. The man knew what to do, that much was blatantly clear. He had just the right pressure of lips and tongue, keeping her on the edge but not making her wince.

She'd had some pretty decent oral sex in her life. There had only been two men who'd hemmed and hawed about going down on her, and they didn't last long after that. But she'd had some master-class-level head and some bargain-basement head, and Royal was in the former camp. Like at the top of the class or maybe the graduate program was named after him because holy hell did he know what to do with his tongue and her clit.

She came hard. So hard her jaw ached a little from clenching it to keep from yelling.

"That's more like it. I missed seeing that."

"It's only been four days," she mumbled.

And then he was pressing into her body. Slow. Inexorable. Filling her up. He was on his side, behind her, holding her thigh where he wanted it as he thrust into her.

"You may not realize this, but you are so damned beautiful when you come. Like a perfect sunset. It builds slow and smolders until you just full-on dazzle and then fade slowly."

"I'll be adding that one to my all-time-favorite Royal compliments folder."

He laughed, kissing her shoulder and getting even closer. He braced his foot against the footboard of his bed and pressed in hard. So deep it stole her breath. And pulled out slowly only to do it again, a little harder the next time.

Caroline reached back, the tips of her fingers grazing his temple and the softness of his hair.

He slid his hand from her hip to her lips. "Lick them for me."

Holy. Crap.

She breathed out in a shudder of sensation at the tone of his rough words. It worked. Hell yes it worked. She licked his fingers, reveling in the way he gasped, feeling all the right kinds of dirty.

When those slick fingers moved again, it was to her clit where he slowly squeezed it in time with his thrusts.

This time climax slammed into her, sharp and hard. Nearly painful, but then the pleasure bloomed super hot over her, and she moaned.

"Jesus," he muttered, never losing his rhythm until he held her still with the press of his palm right below her belly button. Just a few more harsh breaths and he came, his teeth grazing her ear as he leaned forward. "So. Good."

He rolled from bed as she flopped onto the pillows, catching her breath.

On his way back from the bathroom, she called out. "You may as well open that door or he'll pout."

Royal laughed as he opened up, and Spike raced into the room, making sure he hadn't missed anything really good.

He jumped up, chittering at her in his purry tone.

"I know. It's comfortable in here and we're always handy to pet you when you want love and I shooed you out. I'm sorry."

He headbutted her lips, and she gave him the kind of brisk petting he liked. Until he didn't and got up to stalk off.

"I'm getting used to this," Royal said as he got into bed and pulled Caroline close. "You here with me. Your stuff around. Waking up to you in my bed all warm and amenable to morning sex as long as I make coffee."

"It's an important quality in a person, right?"

He kissed her soundly. "It's a very important quality in a person. It's up there along with *will help move irrigation hoses* and *not afraid to get dirty.*"

That was a great compliment. She knew she was pretty enough, and men loved boobs so she was good in that department. Knew she was smart. But that he knew she'd chip in and work alongside him if he needed it, well that meant a lot.

Chapter Eleven

Caroline indicated Ron take a seat as she smiled at both him and the police officer from nearby Millersburg.

Elliot Charles was a police officer there and had gotten in contact after Ron had made a visit.

No shadows in his gaze or hard lines at his mouth. His grip was strong but not sweaty or too hard.

"I just made a pot of tea. Would either of you like a cup?"

"Tea would be good, thanks. It's wet out there today. Goes straight to my joints."

Caroline didn't say it out loud, but Officer Charles's joints looked just fine to her. Mighty fine, in fact, he was quite the uber masculine looker.

She raised her brow his way. "You can't possibly be old enough to have sore joints."

She poured him and Rob both a cup before nodding in the direction of the milk and sugar if they wanted.

"Thanks for making the time to see us, Caroline," Ron said as he stirred sugar into his tea. "I figured you should hear Elliot's story so I brought him over."

"I'm all ears."

Elliot sipped and then put his cup back down on the table. "I'm a friend of Shane's. And of Edward and Polly.

Polly is actually my fourth cousin on my dad's side. Anyway. So I was over visiting with them last weekend and your situation with your father came up."

Her defenses rose.

"I believe he's innocent and I'd like to help."

Ron sat forward. "I'm going to speak to the department there. See what we can root out. Some of the cops in that house are old-timers with great memories."

She nodded and turned to Elliot. "How do you come by your belief? About my father's innocence, I mean."

"I was your age. When your mother died. Now too I guess." He smiled and it made her relax a little. "My grandfather did a syndicated column about law and justice issues. When your mother was killed and they put your father on trial, my grandfather was absolutely convinced he was innocent. Because he was in the press, he got a pass and went to the trial. Every single day. And he was utterly convinced your father was wrongfully convicted. I studied the case through him, I guess. At the start and then I became a police officer and I studied the case from a different perspective, and yet, I agree with my grandfather and with you."

"Wow." She smiled at him, raising her mug in salute. "Well I gotta say I'm totally floored and pleased. Thank you for extending your help."

Ron went over what he planned to speak to Elliot's co-workers about before leaving. Elliot gave her a card and invited her to come along with Ron if she liked.

She headed off to her client meeting feeling much better than she had since she'd arrived in Petal. Things were...surprisingly good.

She and Royal had officially been dating a month.

Not a long time really, but enough that she was getting used to him in her life. That she turned to him when she had something funny to say, or to relate some weird happening in her day. She liked Royal a lot and he liked her right back and that was pretty freaking nice.

And the sex was outrageously good.

More than the very positive direction in her romantic life, she had the help—and guidance—of Edward Chase, along with the skills and efforts of Justin Chase. Edward had sort of taken on a mentor role since she'd arrived in Petal, and she appreciated it very much.

And, she ended up winning two of the four motions she made, which was a pretty nice thing indeed.

Royal knocked on Nathan and Lily's front door, and Lily, now seven months pregnant, answered with a smile. "Hey, hon, come on in."

He kissed her cheek and headed inside. "He's in the living room with a passel of Chases and his brothers. But before you go, tell me about her."

Lily was best friends with Beth, who was Anne's sister. They all formed a big clique of smart, tough, beautiful women who had each other's backs. He liked them all, including Anne. While Beth had been with them on a group date sort of thing twice more since their date at the Tonk, she'd warmed to Caroline, but there was still a reserve that flustered him. Caroline was a nice person. She was fun to be around, and that his friends were playing games over some long-dead relationship he'd ended because Anne wanted totally different things really pissed him off.

He was trying to let it work out without any interference, but Lily was asking and it clearly was some sort of weird thing so he might as well answer.

"I'm sure you've heard already." He gave her a raised brow.

She shrugged, a smile still on her face. "Sure I have. From everyone else who's met her, which doesn't include me. I want to hear from you."

"I can't help it if you and Nathan never go anywhere because he's grading papers and you're looking beautiful and making a baby and all. Her name is Caroline Mendoza."

"I was in her year. I remember her. Dark hair and big brown eyes. Pretty. I can't imagine how hard it was for her after her momma was killed. She works with Edward now. Polly surely does like her."

"I do too. You will as well. She's easy to like." And she was. They'd done tequila shots one night, and he'd let her talk him into riding that stupid bull at Flannery's over in Riverton.

"She's a kick-ass mechanical-bull rider." He laughed.

Lily paused a moment and then smiled. "That's sort of awesome. I take it you rode over to Riverton?"

He nodded. "She agreed to the mechanical bull *before* we took any shots."

"She does seem to be one of our people." Her grin smoothed out. "Nathan said you looked at her differently than you look at other women you've dated."

Honestly this was like the suckiest version of *Groundhog Day* ever. "Again? Is this about Anne?"

"Well sure it is."

"I've been with Caroline a month on Monday. In the year and a half before this, since Anne and I really broke up, I went out with countless other women countless other times. How the hell is it about Anne *now*?"

"You dallying around is one thing. Pfft. But Caroline is different apparently. Your one-month anniversary is Monday? How do you even know that?"

"I just do. Even if she is different—which yeah, she is—Anne and I have been *done* for a long time. She moved on. I'm moving on with someone I really freaking like. I'm full-on having a thing with a woman who is intelligent, confident, ambitious, beautiful, and yet she's funny and doesn't complain about getting dirty out at the farm or the cat hair Spike leaves on her stuff."

"Beth likes her." And since the two were tight, it would probably weigh in Caroline's favor. Then again, to a Murphy, family trumped all else, so if Anne wanted them to ice Caroline out they would. They'd feel bad, but they'd never choose an outsider over one of their own.

"Beth is pretty smart. And she's apparently making her own mind up like you *all* should. I don't think you're the kind of person who'd judge someone they haven't even met."

Lily waved a hand. "Please. I'd *totally* do that for a friend. Hell, I *have* done that for friends. But Polly Chase can't say enough about Caroline. And Beth says she's okay. Trey and Jake seem to like her. Nathan said she's kinda gorgeous. Joe agreed by the way."

Nathan came down the hall, taking in his wife, his gaze lingering at her belly. "Oh my Lord, Lily, you have to leave the man alone." He turned to Royal. "Come on back. There's food and beer and everything you could need while sitting in front of a huge television."

"Why don't you guys come over for dinner this Saturday night?"

Nathan sighed heavily. "Stop meddling."

She rolled her eyes at her husband. "I'm not meddling! I swear. I want to meet her. Is that so bad? I'm a nice person, Nathan Murphy. Did you think I'd invite her over and then stare at her without speaking all night? You said yourself that this was serious so all right. Royal is like family so I'm checking her out."

They'd been standing in the front hallway for about ten minutes, and any time now someone else would come out to look to see where everyone had gone. He didn't want to have this discussion anymore. Caroline would be embarrassed at being the center of this discussion. He needed to wrap it up.

"I'd be happy to accept that invite, but not if it's going to be weird for her. It's hard enough for her around Petal at times, I'm not doing it to her on purpose."

Lily snorted. "Such a low opinion of me." Her face softened. "I can't imagine how hard it must be to constantly be the focus and for something so awful."

"Sometimes the stuff people say to her, hell the stuff her grandparents say to her, makes me so angry." He needed to be with her more. She needed the fucking backup when she was out or with her family. He hated that she had to deal with so much hostility at times and that her family wasn't a safe place for her no matter how much she wanted it to be all right. "She's worth knowing, Lily."

Lily kissed his cheek. "All right. I believe you. It looks nice on you, by the way."

"What?"

"You care about her. I like to see it."

She went back toward the room where everyone else was.

"I just don't see why it has to be weird," he muttered to Nathan.

"You and Anne were together or about to be getting back together or just having broken up pretty much for six years. We all hoped she'd come to her senses and let you love her. But she didn't. And I don't know if Anne will ever be able to see a truly long-term romantic commitment as anything but a terrible trap."

Royal sighed heavily. "No. Not even for me. It used to make me sad in a different way. I wanted her to love me like I loved her. And she just never did and I just couldn't deal with that anymore. But I'm not angry at this point. I'm glad we broke things off. We're much better as friends. I can count on Anne as a friend. I can trust her to put me first. But I am full of this…depth of feeling for the first time in years, and, Nate, she looks at me the way I know *I'm* looking at her. This is good. I'm fucking happy. So I'm sad Anne doesn't have it. And that she'd never have had it with me anyway. One of these days I hope she opens herself up to love with a guy who gets to her in a way no one else can. At one time I wished it would have been me. But I know better now."

What he had with Caroline was already deep, more intense by the day as they got to know one another better. The difference of being with someone who was as into you as you were them, with a partner who wanted more from him.

Nathan nodded. "That's fair. I've only met her once, but she seemed nice and you like her so that's fucking fine, okay? You don't need to apologize to anyone for moving on and for really liking this woman." Nathan looked back over his shoulder to be sure they were still alone. "Look, Anne sees it's different. You let go and have truly moved on. She has to let go once and for all.

It's hard for her and she's not being herself. But she'll get there eventually. Letting go is hard."

"She never really held on." And that was the damned truth. She'd never fought for him or their relationship, and in the end, after years of hoping it would change, he accepted it never would and he'd truly broken away from her.

"Doesn't matter. You know that. You were good to my sister during the time you were with her. You walked away, and in that, you respected her wishes and accepted her choice. I know it sucked, but very few people would have done that. Anne trusts you and she's going to have to share you. You've given her all your attention for all these years." One shoulder rose before Nathan reached over to pat his back a few times. "She'll come around."

The *she* in question showed up an hour later, and they all hung out for several hours before he headed out. He needed to be up early, and he hadn't seen Caroline in several days between her schedule and his. He wanted to try calling her or making enough time to take her to lunch the next day.

"Jeez, hang on a second." Anne came out of the house, his coat in her hands. "Your coat. Oh and this." She handed him a bag. "Tate made cookies today so you're one of the lucky recipients."

"Nice. I'll call her tomorrow to thank her." He hugged Anne and she kissed his cheek. "I'll see you later."

"Why didn't you bring her tonight?"

"Caroline?"

Anne nodded.

"She had court all afternoon and had to work late." He'd been there hours, and this was the first time she'd even spoken about Caroline and now that he thought about it, it pissed him off.

"So you're not avoiding us when you're with her?"

"Annie, what the fuck is going on?" He leaned back against his truck.

"What do you mean?"

"Really?"

She shrugged and looked at a spot just over his right shoulder.

Royal rubbed his palms down the front of his jeans. "I'm not avoiding anyone, but everyone is tiptoeing around and it's so stupid I could spit."

She put a hand on one hip. "Ooh. When spitting comes up, you really do get all twitchy. Why let her, this, get between us?"

His anger wisped away as he snorted. "You were friendly with several of the women I dated since we split. But now all the sudden there's tension and everyone is stepping carefully and damn it. I'm falling in love with this woman and it fills me with so much fucking joy I can't begin to describe it accurately. You're my friend and I want to share that with you because I share all the other things that make me happy or piss me off or whatever. I miss you."

"No one is telling you not to date this chick."

"Your opinion is important to me."

"You know my opinion. I think she's bad news."

"You're still the worst liar ever. Oh my God." He shoved a hand through his hair.

Anne Murphy winced because he could still read her so well. A little embarrassed at how obvious she'd been, she went for a lazy shrug. "Calm down for heaven's sake. I don't actually think she's bad news in general. She's all right I guess if you like her type."

He burst out laughing. "Her type, huh? What type do you mean? Successful? Independent? Intelligent? Beautiful? Financially secure?"

Oh. My. God. She was in hell. Why couldn't Caroline be dumb? Or unattractive? None of the others he'd dated meant anything to him. Oh sure he was a nice guy, and he was friendly and courteous and all that junk. But Caroline had been different since that very first time Anne had laid eyes on her at the Pumphouse.

Royal Watson was truly moving on. No, he'd moved on before Caroline came to town, but before Ms. Perfect Hair blew into town Anne had all of Royal's attention.

And now he was *falling in love* with someone. That someone wasn't her.

"Enough already. No, I mean pushy. She's very… strident. It rubs people the wrong way."

"If people are rubbed the wrong way when another human being is powerful and doesn't apologize for wanting to be successful, then they need to find a way to deal with it. The problem isn't Caroline's for being intense."

"All this stuff about her dad is messed up."

"It is. Which is why she's trying to clear his name and find the real killer."

"Oh. So you believe all that now?"

"Do you want me back? Is that it?"

"And if I did?" She couldn't seem to stop speaking.

He looked at her for a while without speaking. "I told you a year and a half ago what I needed. I'd been telling you for years before that, and you said you didn't want what I needed. We talked about that shit for days and days and it was awful and I was bummed out for a long time because I missed you and I loved you. I loved you after that too."

His perceptive gaze took her in as he spoke. "But I have stumbled on this thing with Caroline. I didn't expect it to be her. In fact I had a hard time imagining it would be anyone but you in the wake of our breakup. But it *is* her. This woman who I really like to be around, and I don't appreciate that you'd fuck with me and pretend you want me back when you don't. You just don't want anyone else to have me. That's shitty, Anne. I'd never do that to you."

He gave her a hug. "I'm going to go now before I get any angrier. You need to get your shit straight. I'm with Caroline. That's how it worked out. Don't be destructive with my trust. She's my girlfriend, and if you keep this up and continue to make this a problem, it drives her away. Even though she doesn't say anything about it, it's obvious there's some sort of tension. It's hard enough for her right now as it is, I'm not going to let her be in a situation where she's uncomfortable. Which means it's you making me choose, Anne. It's not fair."

She rolled her eyes but let him go because he was totally right and she had to face it. Maybe. Or maybe she needed a grand gesture.

Out in his truck he texted to see if Caroline was up but when he didn't hear back after five minutes or so, drove away from the curb and headed home.

As he pulled up his driveway, his phone pinged, letting him know he had a text. On the way into his house, he opened the screen to see her text.

But he loved to hear her voice and before he could text, seeing if she was up for a call she typed in: call me, silly.

Spike came bounding up but wandered away when he
ascertained Royal wasn't carrying any bacon or cheese.

So he called her.

"Hey."

Her laughter made him grin. "I was sure you were
going to make a joke like *hello, silly.*"

"Damn, you're good at this girlfriend thing." He toed
his boots off and left them in the front room near the
door.

"Aw."

"Aw?"

"I'm your girlfriend?"

"Well yeah. You think I cook waffles and let my cat
lay all over just anyone?"

"I was so tired when I got home. I took a long shower
and I felt better, but your voice makes me far less tired."

"Can I tell you how much I love how hardcore you are
in your job and what a badass you are over your mission
to prove your dad's innocence? You're big and bold and
beautiful and smart, and it's sort of overwhelming, the
whole you, I mean. But then sometimes you say something to me, and it's honest and a little vulnerable and
it blows me away. I dig that I see a side of you probably
not that many people get to see."

"Well it seems sort of dumb not to just, you know,
tell you how I feel."

"Speaking of that, it's our one-month anniversary on
Monday. I figured I'd just say up front I know this, and
so I thought you could come over for dinner after work
tomorrow. Sleep over and you can leave for work Friday
morning from here. And of course Friday night we're
going out. I was thinking something totally old school

like dinner and a movie. More staying over. Because I
like you nearby."

"You're pretty good at this boyfriend business. I'll
come over after work tomorrow and spend the night. I'll
even sleep over Friday night because hello, I like you at
my disposal for all my wicked desires. I do have to work
a little though. And I'm expected at Lassiter Central for
lunch on Saturday. Ugh."

"We'll both go."

"Oh we already established that I like you. Why would
you believe I'd do that to you? I'm just maybe going to
take a Benadryl and then drink a glass of wine."

"No. I mean it. I hate that you line up for this every
week. But if you're going to do it, you don't have to do it
alone. Let me go with you. Let me get your back."

"We'll talk about it tomorrow night. You sound exhausted. How was everyone?"

"Long day at work, but we finished up a planting
and so I can breathe for a day or two without panic. But
I ate a lot of sliders. Like, I don't know how many, but
that could just be my conscience kicking in and being
ashamed I ate eight of them."

She laughed. "We'll say it's self-care."

"Speaking of Saturday, Lily and Nathan invited us
over for dinner Saturday night."

"Um. Okay. Sure."

"Lily specifically told me she was looking forward to
getting to know you. I know it's hard."

"Ugh, convo for another time."

"Fine. I'm counting on it. Now, I'm going to take a
shower and go to bed. I'll see you tomorrow night. Just
text me to let me know what you think your schedule
will look like."

"How about I bring something?"

"Like takeout? That works."

"No, silly. I'll make dinner. In your kitchen obviously. I'll bring the fixings over tomorrow."

"Yes, that would be very good. I like you cooking in my kitchen."

"Sleep well, Royal. I'll see you tomorrow night."

The problem was, she thought the next day as she looked at herself in the mirror, she needed a haircut. Caroline dialed Melissa. "Do you have any recommendations for hair?"

"I assume you mean in a non-Murphy-run shop?"

"After yet another negative encounter with Anne, I'm not trusting her anywhere near my hair. I don't *think* she'd do anything. She doesn't seem cruel, just unhappy that I'm around. But I don't have a horrible haircut death wish, so I'll be taking care of my hair-coloring-and-cutting needs elsewhere."

"Good point. There's a place in Riverton. Hang on a second." She heard some rustling, and then Melissa was back with a few names and numbers.

"Thank you. It's my one-month anniversary. As Royal reminded me last night. We're hanging out pretty much from tonight through the weekend. Or through to Sunday at least."

"Well then Sunday come over for a barbecue. You and Royal, I mean. Clint should be back in town. It'll be good. We'll sit on the back deck and eat too much." Clint was Melissa's rebound after whatever went down with her fiancé. Clint was a menswear buyer for a large department store chain. He lived outside Atlanta but spent a lot of time traveling.

Caroline wasn't sure if Clint would be around for long, but he was fun and he made Melissa happy and that was sort of all either of them seemed to want just then. "Sounds good. I'll talk to Royal about it. He's so social, I'm sure he'll be up for it if he's free."

Caroline paused and finally the words burst from her. "Okay so I have to vent. I think if Anne wasn't such a bitch over Royal—*who is not hers anymore* and she doesn't really want him, for God's sake—anyway, I think if she was a normal person around me, I'd actually like her. My patience at letting her work through her shit is dwindling. I get it, they're her friends and so they all hold back, but that feels like shit. Maybe this dinner over at Lily and Nathan's on Saturday will be a step in the right direction. They're his friends! I want to be part of that. They don't all have to be my best friend, but at this point every time I end up in any group situation, even when I have a good time, it's never totally comfortable, you know?"

"I do and I'm sorry. I hope this thing Saturday is good too. Maybe you need to take Anne aside and talk to her. Clear the air."

"I've thought about it. I've wanted to give her the space and time to get past this thing and then we could just sort of act like we were okay to be around one another. But she's trying so hard not to like me. It's exhausting, I tell you. If there weren't all these other people around who Royal loved so much, I'd give her a reason to hate me. But I can't lie, if I lost Royal I'd be totally bummed out too."

"Do you think…he'd go back?"

"I thought about it. For the first few weeks, I told myself if he was going to go back it wasn't my concern be-

cause it had only been a short time. And then I started to
tell myself that if he'd wanted to go back, he would have.
And that's where I am now. Royal just isn't the game-
playing type. If he wanted Anne, he'd have gone back
to her. And it's clear she's fishing in those waters. But
he's not biting. Which okay now, knock it off. He's not
interested, you're truly over and fuck you, he's mine."

Melissa laughed and laughed. "Girl, you are gone for
Royal. Also, your sense of confidence here is off-the-
charts awesome. My God. I'm in awe."

"There may be a lot of things in my life I'm unsure
about, but I just… I'm falling for him. And it's awesome,
and if his ex could just really let him go, things would
be so much easier. For him way more than me. These
are his friends, he obviously wants to be around them."

"I say the next time she pulls some sort of shenanigans
you need to have a little heart-to-heart with her and lay it
all out. Sister Murphy needs a little truth in her life. You
might have to be the one to give it to her."

"Maybe. Which is lame. But whatever. Okay, I need
to get back to work. Thanks for the info. I'll text you
about Sunday."

"Got it. Have fun tonight."

"I will! Talk to you soon." Caroline ended the call,
tucking her phone into her front jacket pocket. She had
another meeting and some work to finish up, and then
she was out of there.

After that meeting and wrapping up all her loose ends,
she headed out, at long last. But she was brought up short
when she rolled into the reception area and ran into her
grandmother, and then Royal came in as well, pausing
when he caught sight of Abigail.

Her grandmother had a look, a tightness around her eyes and spine. Caroline had seen it enough in the past that she knew a blow up and lecture was coming. Also enough to not want to introduce Royal right that moment. "Grandma, I wasn't expecting you. Is everything all right?"

"I just got a call from my friend Susan. Her nephew is a police officer in Millersburg, and she told me you were going to do a presentation about *his* innocence."

Good Lord, right there in her workplace? Holly had gone home an hour before so it was empty, but anyone could walk in at any time.

With a sigh, Caroline waved her hand in the direction of her office. "Why don't you come back? We can continue this in private."

"Private? Girl, you have no idea what it means to be quiet or private. I forbid you to go over to that police station and shame this family once again by defending your mother's murderer."

Anger began to simmer in her belly. The words used and the way they'd been delivered only made it worse.

"I think we started off wrong here. I understand your feelings on this issue. I respect your right to believe whatever you believe. But I expect the same. I won't be called to heel like a dog on a leash. My investigator was invited by the police in Millersburg, and he will speak to them. They're law enforcement, and of course as such should care about a murderer on the loose."

"The real murderer died in prison like the garbage he was."

Royal took a step forward but Caroline shook her head. Her grandmother knew he was there. She was playing to an audience.

Count on Me

But Caroline, though not as big a drama pro as her grandmother, still had a degree in theatrics and a belly full of this nonsense from her grandmother. "That man was my father. And he's Shep and Mindy's father and he was my mother's husband as well. Do you know his regrets were never about himself? I'd go see him, and he'd be broken up imagining my mother's last minutes. Or that my sister and brother were growing up without a mother. He missed them, and it broke his heart that they could ever believe he was guilty."

"He was guilty!" Her grandmother's eyes glittered with hatred. "She never should have gotten together with him to start with but she had to." Abigail gave her a pointed look, reminding her *she* was the reason they got married.

Royal stepped up then, putting himself between Caroline and her grandmother. Like a shield against all the hurtful words her grandmother used like a weapon. "I'm afraid I'm going to have to stop you. You're going to say something else you regret and can't take back. Mrs. Lassiter, I surely am sorry for the loss of your daughter. Caroline loves you and came back here, in large part, to mend some fences and work on her relationship with you and her brother and sister. But it seems to me she's got a right to feel how she does about her father."

Royal eased back to stand next to Caroline, reaching out to take her hand. Everything was suddenly so much better because he'd reached out and defended her.

Abigail Lassiter gave him a long, measuring look. "There will be lunch at our home on Saturday. Eleven thirty. Don't be late." Abigail turned her attention back to Caroline. "See you then."

With that, her grandmother kissed her cheek, turned and swept from the room.

"Run."

He looked at her, amused. "What?"

"Run. She's got your scent now, but I can keep her busy while you escape. Sorry you'll need to leave the state."

"Caroline, I hate that she talks to you that way."

She wanted to lean into him and let his energy calm her. But they were in public and her freaking associates could come out at any moment and it was bad enough her grandmother had pulled that shit while they could have been overheard. Caroline didn't want to make it worse.

"I came to get you. I was in town already so I adjusted my schedule to pick you up."

"I have to drive in to work tomorrow."

He opened the door after it was clear Abigail had truly gone and left the building.

"I can drive you in. I like taking care of you. It's not like I don't need to be up anyway. Then I can stop at the Honey Bear for coffee on my way out too."

"All right. I just need to run home to get my stuff."

They walked and various people called out hellos here and there. He opened her door, and she got up and in.

At her place he ran the food for dinner and her garment bag and overnight case to his truck, but when he got back she was waiting, smiling.

"Okay, so I've got a little something for you."

He grinned. "A present?"

"It's not a big deal."

She handed over a small ice chest with some bungee cord and the cold inserts for it. "Inside there are all the little containers you might need. I mean. You said you went out and were gone all day and forgot to break to eat or what have you. You can strap this to your ATV and have stuff to snack on and eat and drink."

He pulled her into a hug. "That's a really thoughtful present. Thank you. I've been meaning to do something like this."

He kept that in one hand while she closed and locked her door, and they headed back to his truck so he could drive them to his house.

"In case I was mistaken, I was invited to lunch Saturday."

"That was a command, not an invitation. Abigail Lassiter doesn't ask permission."

"She's out of line."

Caroline sighed heavily. "Doesn't matter."

"Yes it damn well does matter. Why do you spend all your time advocating for other people and their rights, but you just let her steamroll you the way she does?"

"They're all I have left."

"That's bullshit. You have lots of people who care about you in your life who don't try to cut you down and make you feel like dirt all because you freaking believe your father. Are you really going to talk to the cops over in Millersburg?"

"Well Ron is and I might swing by to listen in. He and Elliot Charles, a cop from Millersburg, came to my office on Monday. Ron is going over there to talk to the cops in the department and see what he can find. He— Elliot, I mean—told me he believes my dad was innocent. His grandfather was a local crime and justice reporter. I think I have a couple of his pieces about my father's case in the master file. Anyway it's a good way to introduce myself to these guys. The old-timers always have so much great info on old cases."

"Charles. They're related in some way to the Chases, right?"

"Yes. Polly is Elliot's cousin like four times removed or something like that. He was with them over the weekend and contacted Ron. They both came to see me Monday. I think he'll prove to be handy when I talk to his cops."

"Good that you have an ally."

"She looks a lot like my mother." Caroline hadn't intended on saying that, but with him it all seemed to come out anyway.

He sighed. "Your grandmother?"

"Yeah. My mother was pretty much the opposite of Abigail Lassiter. My mom was open and funny, and she loved learning new stuff and trying new things. If you met my mom she'd know all about you in fifteen minutes because people just talked to her. She always did front-of-the-house stuff at the diner because people loved her. She'd come over to their table and ask them how things were and end up holding babies or looking through someone's vacation pictures. She was the kind of person who gave off a light and you wanted to be around it. My grandmother looks a lot like her and sometimes that makes it worse. Because I need my mom, you know? I have aunts who absolutely love me. Uncles. Cousins. My paternal grandmother. I have people I can turn to but it's not the same. And none of them are near."

"My dad died about nine months after your mom got killed. I was pretty much raised by my aunt and uncle, even though we all lived on the same farm for most of my childhood. My mom has always been sort of dreamy. My dad shielded her, did everything for her. She just didn't know how to do much and no one ever expected her to learn so there's a sense of helplessness about her. My aunt Denver? Now she's the opposite. Steadfast. Hardworking, and I've yet to see something she can't do immediately or master within half an hour of practice. She's a farmer through and through. And she's my mother. She didn't give birth to me, but she is my mother in every way that is important. She was sturdy when my mother was... *not*. My uncle is old school. He's sort of stoic, but he's always been there for me like a dad when my biological one gave my mother every bit of his love and attention."

He hadn't spoken in this sort of detail about his life. It pleased her he trusted her enough to reveal these parts of himself.

"And then he died and she got into a car accident about two years later. She was injured pretty bad. Was in a coma for six days. In the hospital for five weeks. Like I said, my mother isn't strong. She's gone through a series of surgeries and she's never really recovered."

Her heart ached for him. "I'm so sorry."

"She lives in an assisted-living facility near Atlanta. She likes it there. Likes being coddled and cared for, and that's where she'll die. I hate that this is reality, but it is. My aunt and uncle are the parents the ones I was born to never managed to be. I don't know what I would do without them and their advice. So I know what you mean when you say it's not the same."

She took his hand, saying nothing else until they'd reached his house and she'd turned on the oven to put the lasagna she'd put together that morning in to bake. Spike scampered around, chasing a balled-up piece of paper he kept bringing back to Royal to throw.

* * *

"It's totally all right for you to find yourself *oops sorry busy* on Saturday afternoon, you know."

He handed her a glass of wine. "I'm going with you." He clinked it. "I seem to recall you liked this one." He turned music on, and Kacey Musgraves's "Back on the Map" came over the speakers. Caroline smiled, putting her glass down to get close enough for a kiss.

Instead he got *her* close enough to haul to his body and then into a slow dance with some grinding and heavy petting thrown in and *oh wow* it worked.

Her head rested against his chest, her pulse a slow, warm throb. Her breath was full of his scent, the heat of his body radiating against her face.

The hands he slid up her back kept her pressed to him. He was a really good dancer. Slow and sexy. He moved… oh my God the way he moved. He loped, but with intensity, and such a thing shouldn't even be possible but it was and he was really good at it.

When she imagined herself in his eyes, she felt beautiful. Sexy. "Coming back here would be so much harder without you. You make me happy, Royal."

He pulled her tighter, his heart beating resolutely against her ear on his chest.

"I thought I knew so many things before you came here. I thought I knew what it meant to be undone by someone. But I didn't. I didn't know it at all. Not until you filled my vision and I fell in love with you. You undo me, Caroline. It's terrifying and awesome all at once. Like a thrill ride."

He'd just told her he was in love with her.

She tipped her head back to look up into his face. "Do I have loop de loops?"

"Oh fuck yes you do. You're swoops and swirls and dizzying turns. You turn me upside down all the time. Sometimes you smile a certain way and *damn*. I'm hit by something new about you."

She stared at him, swallowing hard.

"Wow."

The song ended and Luke Bryan's "Shut It Down" came on.

"I don't think I've ever undone anyone before. I really like it."

He laughed and kissed her, diving into her taste until he was nearly drunk with her. "I hadn't welcomed you to my house yet. Terrible breach of manners on my part."

"You're a really good host that way. Thanks for sticking up for me. With my grandmother. Thanks for sharing that stuff about your mom with me. Thanks for slow dancing in the kitchen and wow, I…thanks for loving me."

There was a pause and he felt her energy shift and he waited, hoping like hell whatever she said next was good.

And it was. "I've been falling in love with you since you fetched cereal for me off the top shelf. You backed me against something then too."

He did very much enjoy backing her against things or getting her prone on the bed or the couch. He did it right then, backing her to his kitchen counter gripping the smooth edge at her back. "It's pretty much my favorite pastime." He kissed her again.

The oven dinged that it had finished preheating.

"Okay, woman, let's get this dinner started. Tell me what you want me to do."

She put the lasagna in the oven. She made a salad,

and he put out some garlic twists she'd picked up at the Honey Bear.

"In a few weeks it'll be warm enough to be outside. I have one of those deck heater things. I also have a new piece of outdoor furniture on order. It's a covered chaise for two. I'm thinking ahead."

"Awesome. I don't have any outdoor space at my place. Yours is so lovely. It'll be nice to use it."

"Interesting thing that. Want to help me plant some pots for the deck? I traded some kale for groundcover and flowers, and I have the box planters out there anyway."

Her smile—Christ, she was pretty—brightened. "I'd love to help you plant. But one thing."

He set the table. "What?"

"Melissa invited us over Sunday afternoon for a barbecue. Clint is back in town so you can meet him too. Plus you can see her adorable little house."

Caroline had been trying damned hard with his friends so of course he'd do things with her friends and get to know them.

"Sounds good."

They settled at the table and filled their plates.

"So, do you have like a basic talk when you discuss your father's case? Like the case in an outline or gif-formed answer?"

She ate and watched him for a while. "Why?"

"I've been thinking a lot about this. I've read some on the internet. This is important to you. A part of who you are, and I think I'm at the point I should know about this and have an opinion."

"Are you sure?"

"At first I thought I'd let it sit awhile to see how you and I worked out, what our relationship was, before I pushed it. Then I panicked thinking, *oh my God what if I ask her and I don't believe her?* So I read stuff online. Some of the pieces you've written and those written after your father lost his appeals. I want to hear your explanation. Your intro to the case. I know you have one. I want to understand it better. Please."

And over the next two hours she laid it all out. The same things he'd already been bothered by, like the lack of any real motive and the way the DNA at the scene that didn't match her father's had never been followed up on. She explained how each time they had something new they couldn't just automatically take it to court, that there had to be a basis for each thing that she could bring up to the court and new evidence wasn't always enough.

And when she'd finished, he began to take notes and ask follow-up questions.

They sat in his hot tub, breath misting in the night air. "Jesus."

She looked up at the sky.

"I believe you. Your father is innocent."

"You don't have to say that."

"I don't. But I believe it anyway. How freaking aggravating. All that legal stuff, the hoops. I had no idea it was so complicated. And now I have even more admiration for you. You've done all this?"

"It started when I was eighteen. I went to college at UCLA, and I had the ability and resources to start digging. So I did. I didn't have much of anything. I started teaching myself how to do stuff. I saved up and paid for legal help when I could. In time I was able to get some low-cost help. I only had to pay filing fees in some cases. But I knew if I went to law school, I could arm myself better. Be more able to free him finally. And I got involved with the Innocence Project and started speaking nationally, and my grandmother would call and yell at me about how I was betraying my mother. I've tried to tell them, tried to get them to allow me to show them all the evidence but they refused.

"I had my own money then, and I was able to hire appellate attorneys who were far better than me to do that work. We had some significant movement and then he got sick. We put aside most of our main work with his case and began petitioning the court to commute his sentence or transfer him to a prison with a hospital better suited to his particular cancer."

She drank, silent awhile before she continued. "And during that time I came to my grandparents and begged them to at least let me tell them what I knew so they could better make up their minds. I only asked for a chance to talk to them. I begged for his life. But they refused."

"Have you ever tried to talk to your siblings? Away from your grandparents I mean."

"I was twenty and was just starting my junior year at UCLA. I came back here for Mindy's birthday, and my grandmother came in as I was answering a question about our parents. She grabbed my shoulder and hauled me into my grandfather's home office. She was so angry at me she vibrated with it. She told me how easy it would be to influence my siblings to not want to see me. And she said it with such icy calm. She slapped me. Right as I was speaking she just hauled off and slapped me so hard my lip split."

Rage shot through him. He didn't like Abigail Lassiter one damn bit. From then on he'd be there to get Caroline's back when she dealt with them. He wasn't going to allow them to rip her apart anymore.

"She's hardcore. And totally fucked up. God, I'm so sorry, Caro."

"She's doing what she thinks is best."

"She's being mean and spiteful. Come on. That's such a crappy thing to do to someone. She's emotionally manipulative and abusive. She hit you? With her hand and with a threat to stop you from seeing Mindy and Shep."

"Well the problem is that I gave in to it, and if they were hardwired into her worldview a decade ago? Shep, well he's more curious about the world. But Mindy, she's so wrapped up in trying to make our grandmother proud and be the girl who chose the *right* future. The most rebellious thing she's done is date a Baptist."

He laughed, kissing her temple.

"So I gave in and never mentioned it, and there's this unspoken thing going on. Like I'm hiding it. But now? I'm feeling so much less inclined to let anyone make me feel ashamed of knowing what I know after I actually did some research. I know this case backward and forward. That they just won't listen and realize the truth of this tears me apart."

She blew out a breath.

"Caro, you can't make things better all on your own. You're making all the sacrifices here. I just don't know how you could claim to love someone all the while reinforcing a divide keeping them at a distance."

"I'm trying to give it time. So they can see I'm back for good. I want them to be able to count on me, and that sort of trust needs to be earned."

"You came back here for them. For birthdays and holidays and you gave up a life in Seattle. For them."

"It's working with Shep. I mean over the past several weeks he's been more comfortable with me. He texted me a few times this week. Mindy? Well since that brunch I've seen her once. The other times I was supposed to see her she cancelled. And now when I suggest we do stuff, she wants Garrett along but when I say oh double date, let me see what Royal is up to, she insists it's more a girls'-night thing. Only with Garrett. I'm weak, but I can't. No, I won't. If she wants me out of her life, okay. But she doesn't. But she's also letting this guy control her and it's gross and I can't pretend my way past that. So we had an argument about it, and I know it makes things worse but I only have so much patience with this dumb crap."

"As you should. Because Garrett isn't policing what she does, he's policing what you do. That's creepy and gross and makes me want to punch him in the nose."

"I'm officially calling an end to this discussion so we can move on to something much nicer to talk about. Like sex or your ass. Or how you're a really dirty guy when you're dancing."

He picked her up and deposited her in his lap. "You got the special, super-deluxe dance package. With extra dirty."

She laughed, leaning down to kiss him.

She had a bathing suit on. Not that he was complaining because she looked fantastic in it and he'd be seeing her naked by the end anyway. He reached up and untied the top, freeing her breasts.

"Hey!"

He nuzzled her nipples at the water line. He'd need to take this party inside soon. The condoms were in there, and it was a cold-enough night that doing anything seriously sexual outside was inadvisable.

"Hey what?"

"You're just randomly untying bathing suits now?"

"Nope. Not randomly. Only yours. And for a very good reason. I like your nipples."

He managed to stand and help her out even though he was so hard he was sure 90 percent of his blood was currently in his cock.

She got out, toweling off as he did the same, shooing her toward the door. And then down the hall to the master bathroom. "Strip off your suit. Rinse off when you finish." Royal shoved his trunks down and off, dropping them into the mesh basket in the bathtub, and bent to grab her suit as she finished stepping from it. "We'll toss them in the wash later."

"Was this just a reason for you to get me naked?"

"Naked and in a situation where it'd be normal for me to rub my hands all over your naked, wet body." He popped the cap on her body wash and drizzled it over her skin in ridiculous quantities.

He rubbed slick hands all over her skin. "You're very inspired this evening."

"You're apparently my muse." He knelt, looking up the line of her body. "Man. I'm in big, big trouble," Caroline whispered.

"I'm afraid that's the truth." He stood, sliding his body against hers as water pelted them. "There's no cure for that. And the only treatment is lots of time with me."

She massaged shampoo into her hair and then used conditioner, and though he kept her within reach, left her alone enough to finish up and get out, drying off as he did the same.

"It's late and we both have to be up early. I vote we get right to sex."

She laughed as he pulled her toward his bedroom.

Chapter Twelve

"That's some smile you got going on there," the server said as they sat down.

Royal shrugged. "Look at her. What's not to smile about?"

The server nodded. "You do have a point."

"Four Friday nights ago I took this gorgeous creature out for the first time."

"Wow. That's awesome. Congratulations."

Royal winked at Caroline. "Thank you. Naturally a pitcher of margaritas will be necessary."

Caroline looked at her menu again quickly. "Yes that. And guacamole, please."

"Good idea," Royal agreed.

Their server left and Caroline looked up to find Royal grinning at her. "What's that face for?"

"I just like looking at you."

The margaritas arrived and they put in their food order before settling again.

He clinked his glass to hers. "I have to be up at six or so tomorrow, but I'll be done by ten so I can get back and cleaned up for lunch. Feel free to use my office to work in. You know where everything is."

"I still can't believe you're willing to do this after the way she was yesterday."

"I told you, I'm not having you go over there and expose yourself to attack. Not alone. I'm going to be there to get your back. After a certain point though, I'm going to ask you why you do it at all."

"Because it's only been six weeks since I came back. I can't erase fifteen years of absence with a month. I'll revisit this later on if things don't improve. I don't give up on stuff. Not that easily."

"I've been told by my aunt that we're to stop by their place Saturday before we head over to your family's. She and my uncle want to meet you."

"Awesome!"

"I stressed several times that we were going to be eating a meal in about an hour so we didn't need snacks. But you really never know with my aunt. She's one of those people who bakes hams and turkeys just in case company comes by or you get a little puckish and only a turkey leg can satisfy."

She laughed. "All right. I'll let you take the lead on that."

Dinner was leisurely. The food was awesome, and the margarita buzz would serve her well during the movie playing at the Orpheum that promised lots of explosions and gunfire and pretty heroes and heroines who ran in slow motion.

Perfect.

Of course once they arrived, he was already thinking about snacks.

"Dude, where do you even put it all? Seriously, it's so unfair that you eat the way you do and stay so lean. Makes me want to bite you."

He put an arm around her waist, pulling her close. "Feel free to bite me anytime you like."

"Incorrigible. Oooh, Red Vines." She put a box on the counter. "Just water, please."

"It's like four dollars for a dollar fifty bottle of water. Tap water most likely."

"Life's full of little tragedies."

He snorted and gave her a grumpy face when she started to pull out money. "What? Let me pay for the snacks. You paid for dinner and the tickets."

"We talked about this already." He paid and she allowed it so they could move away from the counter, and when they finally got settled and she helped herself to some popcorn, she was back on the topic.

"The thing is, we didn't talk about this at all. You went all he-man and declared the person inviting pays, but you won't let me pay then either. It's silly not to let me pay for stuff."

"You just relocated and gave up a way better paying job to move here. I didn't."

"Well that's dumb. Not even credibly connected to this situation. This isn't a vacation to a luxury resort in the Bahamas."

He sighed. "If I agree will you let it go?"

"If by letting it go you mean will I win graciously and not crow about it? Yes I'll let it go that way."

He kissed her quick and hard.

"It's a good thing I find independence sexy."

"Only because I also have a really good sense of humor."

She leaned her head against his shoulder as they shared popcorn. Then a bunch of people came in, including Beth Murphy and her fiancé, Joe, and a woman

Caroline bet was Lily Murphy holding hands with Nathan Murphy.

They saw him and waved, making their way over.

"I should have asked you first. Sorry about that," he said quietly.

"I'm just going to say *I'm* not the source of that particular problem, Royal. You know who is though, so take it up with her."

"You're right. Okay? You're right."

She smiled at everyone as they approached before she said to Royal, "Of course I'm right."

They had to stop at her place for a few minutes after the movie and were on the road back to his place shortly after that.

"I have flourless chocolate cake, chocolate, chocolate chip ice cream and those salted caramels you love."

"Wow. You should step on it. I may have to eat it when you're having your way with me."

Laughing, he pulled into the garage and they went into the house that way. She put her stuff down and allowed him to pull her into the bedroom.

He flipped on the light. "Goddamn, I need to see you naked."

That's when Caroline realized they weren't alone.

Anne Murphy was in Royal's bed.

Naked.

"What the fuck are you doing, Anne?" Royal asked.

A very good question and one *Caroline* intended to ask. Caroline turned to face Royal, placing her hand on his chest. "You need to go."

He started and then shook his head. "Let—"

"Get out, Royal." Caroline cut him off before he could

say anything else. Firmly, she pushed him from the room and into the hallway.

"Sweetheart," Royal said in that sweet cajoling tone he often used to get her naked.

Caroline held up a hand for a moment to stay him. "Don't. Right here and right now, what's it going to be? Is this a Royal and Caroline type thing or are you going back to her? I need to know."

"*You.* Fuck. I choose you. Over and over. She'll get dressed, and I'll walk her to her car and get this straightened out."

Caroline stepped back into the bedroom. "Oh, yes, this will get straightened out. But I'll be doing the straightening. If you come into this room before I say come in, I will walk out of here and out on you. This has gone on too long. It needs to be clear."

He nodded. "All right."

She turned back, kicking the door closed and taking in Anne, who was quickly getting dressed.

Anne kept her head down, her hair covering her face. "I'm sorry. Jesus. I knew this was a mistake. I knew it before I came over here."

Caroline leaned back, blocking Anne's only exit from the room.

"If you knew it was a mistake, why are you in my boyfriend's bed naked?"

"I was here long before you were."

"Yeah, and you were gone long before I was here too. Don't you have any pride?"

"What the heck are you talking about?"

"You've been a dreadful bitch the whole time I've been back in town and dating Royal. I get it. He's awesome. Smart and handsome. Funny. Sexy. He opens doors and uses his manners and brings me coffee in the morning because he wants to take care of me. I get it. You don't have that in your life and it sucks. I got it. It sucks because you had him. He loved you and wanted forever from you, and *you* didn't want that back. To your credit though, you were finally honest and put your foot down and let go so he could find what he wanted and needed with someone who wanted those things too. Not you, if you recall."

Anne zipped her pants up and sat to put her socks on. "You're mad and you should be. He's with you. I knew it was a bad idea before I even came over here."

"So why did you? He's gone. You let him go. You can't undo that."

"Why not?"

Caroline huffed. "A few reasons. To start with, because I'm not going to let you, silly. Royal is a fantastic catch. But he's mine. You know it too. He's moved on. Which is another big one. Like before I'd even come to town." Caroline raised a shoulder. "Lastly, you don't even want him.

"See the first few reasons are fine. I mean, they suck for you, but not for me. But it's the last that pisses me off so much. You come in here with this half-assed plan that Lucy Ricardo could be proud of *and you don't even want him*. You just don't want to lose him in your life. And I've been trying to give you the time and space to get yourself together. But I have to tell you, between you and me? You're being a selfish bitch."

Anne gasped.

"What? Do you have something to say? Because you know I'm right. He's a good guy. The best I've met and he's a good friend to you. He cares about you and puts you first, and I'm over here waiting for you to finally get yourself handled so you don't keep pushing him away. *He's* miserable when you do that. I'm staying out of the way, but this is where I will step in and say no. This is not a game I'll be playing. He's not yours anymore. Not this way. You have essentially had a platonic marriage since you two broke up. No sex, but he's been your husband. Flirting and helping you out and still putting you first, even when you two dated other people. No more.

"But he's your friend. He loves you and as far as I can tell, being loved by Royal Watson is pretty fucking awesome. He's not a toy you discard and then suddenly want back when someone else recognizes his value. But you're playing with him and that's gross."

Anne crossed her arms over her chest. "Who are you to judge? You don't know any of us."

"I'm someone who loves Royal. And if you loved him you wouldn't be yanking on his chain this way. You don't want him. Not really. Don't keep this up.

"I don't have an issue with anyone else in your group. Though there again you're being a selfish bitch. I'm inclined to be forgiving because I know what it means to feel alone, or that you're losing someone who understands you so well. I know what that feels like. But you don't have to lose him. I'm not standing in between you in any other way but this one." Caroline pointed at the bed. "I haven't gotten in between you and Royal, and I don't care to. But I will absolutely get in between you when you're in his bed. You get me?"

"You want to be around the group? You never come to any of our events."

"No. I'm rarely invited because you are there, and everyone is tiptoeing around you and how you feel. If freezing me out is what you're aiming at, you're pretty good at it. Your friends are always nice to me, but the only times I'm around them is when you aren't around. And you generally are. So yeah, you don't get to use that one."

"You're a super bitch."

"I should have a big B on every sweater and shirt I own." Caroline nodded.

"I'm a super bitch too."

"Yeah, I've heard. I've only seen the unpleasant side of that though. That's the lazy bitch game. Easy enough if you substitute meanness for bitchiness."

Anne sighed. "I've been a dick to you."

"Yeah, you have."

"I'm sorry. I haven't given you a chance and I've cock-blocked you with my friends and family too. But for Christ's sake, do you have to be so perfect?"

"What?"

"Look at you! You're petite and gorgeous and super smart and accomplished. I can't compete with that."

"But you *aren't* competing with that. Royal already loves you. There's no competition there. Also, yeah, this from a nearly five-eight Amazon with great hair."

Anne did a decent hair flip. "I do have great hair. So do you, but you need a trim."

"Yes, I have an appointment early next week with a new stylist."

"Not at my salon you don't. I have the new client roster and you're not on it for next week."

"As if I'd let you near me with scissors. Are you fucking insane?"

"You have a foul mouth."

"I do."

"Great, add it to the face and the body and the letters behind your name."

"Wow, I'm really a great catch." Caroline snickered.

"Everything okay?" Royal called out from the hall.

Anne spoke up first. "Your girlfriend and I are having a discussion, Royal. No one is bleeding. But a beer when she's finished with me would be good."

"Are you okay, Caro?"

Nicely played, Caroline thought. She called back, "Right as rain."

"He really digs you." Anne snorted. "Also, even if I hated you, I'd never butcher hair. That shit gets out quick in a town like Petal. I have a reputation to protect at the very least. Cancel your other appointment. I'll get you in with Tate. She's almost as good as I am with scissors."

"I'll need to think on that. But for the rest, do we understand one another?"

"Look, you don't know me, and that's my fault. But I'm actually an okay person. I think we could sort of be friends, maybe."

"Don't flatter me so."

Anne laughed. "I do like that you're bitchy. At first you were so nice and avoided being crass and stuff. I wondered if you were strong or cowed. I should have known Royal wouldn't have gone for anyone who was the latter."

"Partly I did it because it made you even more aggravated. When I didn't rise to the bait and respond back in kind. Really, I just come off looking nice while you look like you ate a whole bowl of sour grapes."

"That's brilliantly devious. Since it appears you're a long-run sort of addition to our group, I suppose you should hang out with us more. On Sunday we do a big meal at my sister's house. You should come with Royal."

   "We have plans, but in the future? I'd love to be included."

   "All right. Well you should come along on Wednesday night. No bowling this coming week, but we get together, drink beer and eat too much while we talk over movies to agitate my brother Nathan."

   "All right. I think I can do that. Thanks."

   "So, you're in love with him."

   Caroline nodded. "I am."

   "All right. Well, be careful with him."

   "Yeah, I can manage that."

Royal, feeling very smug about how smart the comment about the chocolate cake was, and then all sorts of itchy to watch her eat it while he fucked her, keyed off the truck, and they headed inside.

   He allowed her to pause to put her stuff down before he began to tug her toward his bedroom. First he'd get her naked and then he'd make her come. Then he could relax, they could have cake and champagne and way more sex.

   Only to walk into his bedroom and find his ex naked in his bed.

   Caroline was *pissed off.* He got off, just a little, okay a lot, with the way she'd taken control and staked her claim on him.

   Spike remained at the far end of the hallway. He didn't blame the cat at all. Royal wanted to run and hide too. But he stayed close. Pretending he wasn't eavesdropping when he totally was.

   Caroline could have ripped Anne to shreds. It was her job, after all, and one she was obviously very good at. But she didn't.

   Oh she didn't exactly go easy on Anne. No, Caroline

held a mirror right up to her and made her take a long, honest look at herself.

She wasn't petty, or cruel.

But she marked her territory in no uncertain terms, and he liked that a whole lot. He planned to tell her exactly that as soon as he got the chance. Caroline had told Anne he was Caroline's man.

And then she'd given Anne just the smallest of openings, and thank goodness Anne had come to her senses and taken it, making a genuine overture of friendship.

It would take Caroline a while before she truly trusted Anne. Or hell, maybe everyone else too because of how everyone had been holding their breath to see what Anne was going to do.

Finally Caroline opened the door and he didn't spare a glance for Anne, instead moving to Caroline. "Everything all right?"

"Yeah. I think so. How about I go get beers while you two talk."

He pulled Caroline up to her tiptoes to kiss her before she moved down the hall, talking to Spike, who followed her.

Anne put a hand out to stay his words. "Before you say anything, let me first tell you I am so sorry. I was such a dick to Caroline, who probably needed a friend more than she needed me to be a bitch."

He leaned against the doorjamb. Things had shifted between them, but he still cared about her.

"And I was a dick to you too. Putting you between us all the time. Playing with your feelings about me. I'm truly sorry for that too. Because you were never anything but honest and forthright with me. You still are.

Maybe I was testing to see if you'd choose me because I just wanted someone to look at me like that. But the thing is, it's so special because she looks back at you the same way. You two click, and I got scared and sad and mean. I felt like she was stealing you away. That's not the case, I know."

"You're important to me. I love you. I always will. But she's someone to me now. My future, I think. It's early days yet, yes. But whatever anyone thinks, it's different. I know it. She knows it. I don't want anyone getting hurt. Her feelings matter and I'm putting them first. You had no right to do this tonight. I'm really angry you'd try to cause a rift between me and Caroline. It's fucking shitty. I didn't resent you. All those years when I worked so hard to make you love me and you just never quite could. Not enough. And I *never* resented you. I understood what it was. And when we finally broke up, and you said, essentially, that you couldn't commit yourself to me permanently. And at last I was like, *okay then, so this is never going to happen.* Our relationship didn't change that much except the sex we were having was with other people. We stayed friends. We stayed connected to one another's lives and I truly appreciate that. But this was so rude of you. Cruel and hurtful. Imagine if I had said, *oh my God, I love Anne, it's over, Caroline.* Huh? Imagine I'd said that and how she would have felt. And for what? The outcome of this stunt could have done her damage, and I don't know, it makes me feel like I have to be extra protective around you now. She didn't change how I felt about you. But *you* changed the way I feel about you."

"Ouch."

"I know your parents were shit at being parents. And they're shit at being married. And they're shit at being human beings too. I know growing up like that gave you some pretty strong ideas about marriage, and I respect that. But I want a wife and I want kids and I want to go camping and go to daddy-daughter dances and all that stuff. I wanted that with you once. But then I didn't. And fine, you didn't want that. I respect your opinion and your choice not to commit to anyone. I need reciprocity here. I let go. Because that's what you wanted. And now I've found someone who might be the person I make babies and go camping with. I need you to understand that. And I need you to respect and accept that."

She nodded. "You're right. I was mean and she didn't deserve it. You didn't deserve it either. I'm sorry."

"All right. So, we good in the Caroline department?"

Anne nodded. "I think I could actually like her. Though you know, Royal, it would be easier on a girl if the woman you fell for wasn't so freaking ridiculous. Not even an overbite or a zit. And she totally uses bad words. Like a boss. I'm unwillingly and yet quite frankly impressed."

"Sorry not sorry about that part. She's pretty fun. Plus when she gets tipsy she makes up the best nicknames for things and people. It's the best party trick ever. Come on. There's beer. You can probably stay an hour or so. But then, scram. Because I have plans of an extremely graphic nature to concoct with my lady friend."

Anne wrinkled her nose.

Out in the kitchen, Caroline had opened three beers, and a cat sat on her shoulder as they both looked out the windows.

"I can't believe he's taken to doing that." Royal grinned at the sight.

"He essentially steers me with a helpful prick of his claws." She looked at him carefully. "We all straight now?"

He moved to Caroline, grabbing the cat and setting him down so he could get close. "All straight. Thank you for being so awesome."

"Not that awesome. But you're welcome."

"What do you have to eat?" Anne started to poke around in the fridge.

Caroline rolled her eyes but picked up her beer. She didn't seem angry or even upset. But she was wary, he could see that much.

"Are you two hungry? I can make sandwiches."

"No thanks. We just had dinner at El Cid. I am stuffed full of carbs and margaritas."

To her credit, Anne didn't stay more than her allotted hour. By the time she left, there was a little more ease between her and Caroline, and Royal was beyond happy about that.

Chapter Thirteen

Royal came back to the house after he'd been working all morning. She watched as he pulled off his work boots in the mudroom off the back porch. He dropped his pants and tossed them into the washing machine, along with his shirt and socks and underwear.

He looked up then to catch her staring. And grinned.

"I'm going to shower so I'm respectable when we go to your grandparents' for lunch. On the way out, we'll stop by my aunt and uncle's place."

"Okay. But all the soap in the world isn't going to clean you up, dirty man."

He waggled his brows as he sashayed his cute naked ass past where she was sitting at the kitchen table getting work done.

She'd already gotten dressed and put on makeup while he was out working. She'd taken over not his bathroom, but one attached to the guest room across the hall. He was so messy and used to living alone that his stuff spilled across every surface.

She briefly considered jumping into the shower with him but realized that would cut it too close because she'd have to get ready all over again, and she didn't want to have to rush out on his aunt and uncle.

And it was important. She wanted to meet them and was glad they wanted to meet her too. She finished up her work as Royal got ready, finishing about five minutes after the water turned off in the master bath.

Spike hopped up so he could walk over her files and notes, plopping his butt onto her keyboard. He meowed and gave her a *you may pet me now* face so she gave in to his terroristic threats and even kissed his head because the crazy cat was as charming as his person was.

"Just toss his butt down if he gets in your way."

Spike snorted and moved to her shoulder, which had become his favorite perch. He rode around on her shoulder all the time.

Caroline turned to tease Royal and ended up struck totally silent as she took him in from his black trousers to the pale blue oxford shirt.

But the belt. *Well.* She stood. "Your cat is an extortionist so I have to be careful with how much I deny him. Also he's cute and furry. You, however, look good enough to thoroughly muss up. Is that a new belt?"

Pleasure washed over his face. "Thank you, sweetheart. Please feel free to muss me up for hours and hours anytime you wish. Belt isn't new, but I haven't worn it in a while."

"I really like it." She didn't even know why. But it made her hot. Wide, honey-tanned leather leading to a big-ass belt buckle. She slid her fingertips over the metal of the buckle.

"I have this fantasy." Royal shook his head. "Never mind. We don't have the time, and if I think about it too much, I'll be hard and useless for hours."

She was flushed all over. She grabbed a file folder

and used it to fan her face. "Be sure to revisit this topic with me. It's relevant to my interests."

"Who knew you'd have a belt-buckle fetish?"

"I don't think I did until just right now. It's the whole look. You're so long and lean, and that belt sort of makes your shoulders look wider and accentuates your waist. I don't know exactly, cowboy, but I'll gladly take it."

He grabbed his keys. "I'm driving. So you can have wine."

"That just *isn't done*. They don't drink in the daytime. That's what layabouts do, don't you know? Oh and me and my friends when we go on our annual vacation. But Abigail would frown at every single detail of those vacations, so."

"Are there pillow fights or pudding wrestling?"

She barked a laugh. "Sure. Day-drinking while on vacation with your girlfriends clearly paves the road to dancing until four in the morning, or skinny-dipping. Though to be totally fair, I'm fine blaming skinny-dipping on four margaritas by two in the afternoon."

"I think I need to go with you on this vacation. Keep an eye on all this action."

"Ha. Nope."

She freshened her lipstick after kissing him quickly. Her hair was held back with a headband. Her grandmother approved of headbands rather than her hair being loose. She also liked to put it in a bun, but Caroline had a love bite at the back of her neck. Right at her hairline.

"Should I bring something for your aunt? I can run to town and come right back."

He rolled his eyes. "No. This is just us stopping by on our way out. Fifteen minutes at the most."

Their house was on the other side of the land the farm

sat on. A big, pale yellow farmhouse. His grandfather had built the house for his grandmother. Then his uncle had taken over when his brother—the day drinker and layabout—got married to Royal's mother and it was clear the older Watson boy was too wrapped up in his bride to get anything done.

Uncle Bob painted it pale yellow because Denver loved yellow. They'd made that big yellow house a home for Royal. His parents had lived in the original building Royal's grandparents had used while the house was being built. One of the two bedrooms there was Royal's.

But he'd slept in the big yellow house. In a room that was his. Where he'd kept his books and his clothes. Denver and Bob's table he sat at four days a week or more.

It was home.

He pulled up and got her door, taking her hand as they headed in.

"Don't slam that screen door," a woman called out.

"I haven't let it slam since I was fourteen or so. She still says it," Royal said in an undertone as they went inside.

"Seems to me it works then. Her telling you not to do it." Caroline shrugged. "That's a success story right there, Royal."

"Oh, I like her. She's smart." A woman Caroline's size came into view as they walked into the kitchen. "Royal, you were telling the truth. You're short like me. Which is nice because now I'm not alone."

Caroline held her hands out. "I'm Caroline. It's wonderful to meet you."

Denver grinned. "Nice to meet you too. I've been pestering Royal for weeks now to bring you by so we can meet you. I'm glad he finally obeyed. You hungry?"

"Aunt Denver, I told you, we're going to lunch at the Lassiters'."

Denver did this thing with her mouth that made Caroline snicker.

"Aunt Denver, can we not?"

Caroline waved a hand. "Oh it's fine. She didn't actually say anything. Her expression, I probably wouldn't have even caught it if I wasn't trained to judge people's facial expressions all the time."

"Your grandmother has a good heart. She's always a huge contributor when we do the food drives in the spring and winter. She just has a very specific idea of how things should work and an audacity to believe she should be able to set rules for *everyone* else based on her ideas. She's great at brainstorming fundraising ideas, for instance."

"But maybe no one likes to work with her because she's not much of a team player."

Denver thought that was hilarious. "Yes." She sobered. "But she loved your mother. And she loves your siblings too. She brags about you. She's not all bad."

"You're a straight shooter, aren't you?"

"Hell yes, I am. What on earth is the point of pussyfooting around stuff?"

"My grandparents are good people. I love them and I respect them. What happened to them when my mother was murdered, well, it changed them, all of us, forever."

"Sure. And I feel for her. Losing a child is a terrible thing to bear. But wrongs on top of wrongs doesn't make the pile smaller, does it?"

Royal grabbed control and changed the subject. "And on that note. Where's Uncle Bob?"

"He's in his shop. Go get him so he can meet Caroline. She'll stay here with me while you go."

Royal rolled his eyes, but he said his *yes, ma'am* and moved to do as she'd asked.

"Lord above I thought he'd never go and I'd have to keep on pretending I have good manners." Denver snorted. "Want some hot tea? Water's still hot."

"Yes, please."

"Sit. I'll bring it over." Denver waved Caroline over to the table so she went.

"We have about five minutes, maybe seven, before Royal and Bob come back. Bob's in the middle of some woodworking project. It's his new hobby since Royal fully took over. Which is fine with me because it keeps him out from under my feet. Anyway he'll draw Royal into some long conversation about how great this or that whatsit he's making is. So, I hear Garrett Mosby gave you some trouble. He was in my Sunday school class when he was in middle school. I can't imagine he's improved much. Handsome though. I guess he and your sister will have pretty babies."

"He's...can I be direct with you?"

"I'd dislike you otherwise."

"He's one of those men who isn't very strong or bright or even that nice. He's handsome enough. He finds women like my sister and my grandmother, and he latches on. You know like he's protecting them when really he's just building himself a little bully pulpit so he can keep his women in line. As far as he's concerned, *everything* women get upset over is an overreaction. No issues women face are as important as what men do. He's the guy at the next table over at a restaurant who will explain to you how you feel about something he's overheard you talking about."

"That's just not how a gentleman acts. He doesn't get it from his daddy, who is as nice and mannerly as they come. But Garrett, he's the baby. Some parents do just spoil the baby rotten. I think that's the case here." Denver pinned Caroline with her gaze. "Royal wasn't born to me. But he's my son sure as if he was. So if you're wondering if he shares things with me, he does. Nothing that would be a betrayal of your trust. But he's thoughtful, Royal. So he told me about this Garrett thing, and I've also heard there's some trouble with Anne."

"I think at least that part is smoothed out." Caroline remained very careful. If Anne had been around for six years, chances were Denver liked her. Or she wouldn't have been around long.

"Well, that's good. I love Anne. She's a good girl. But she and Royal are far better off as being close friends. She needs a different sort of man, and he needed a woman who saw things the way he does. Wanted the same things. Anne…well I'd tell you she hasn't had an easy life. That she regards Royal as hers and would have a difficult time loosening up when he finally met a woman and truly fell for her. I'd tell you that, but it seems to me, you have had your share of traumatic childhood stuff."

"We worked it out yesterday. Who knows, we might even end up friends." She didn't want to give any more detail than that.

"Good." Denver paused. "I just want to tell you that I knew your parents. Your mother was gorgeous. Inside and out. We often stopped in at the diner on the way home after church on Sundays. There's no way anyone could ever make me believe he had anything to do with harming your mother. Petal is talking. It's what Petal does. Sometimes it might feel like everyone is out to get you or thinks you're bad or wrong for continuing to try to prove your dad's innocence. But that's far from true."

Bob came in with Royal, who nervously checked her over to see if his aunt had done any damage. It was sort of cute. They stayed another few minutes and then got back on the road to town.

"Should I be apologizing?" Royal asked as they made it out to the main road.

"Nah. I like her. She's plucky. She told me she knew my dad."

"Yeah. I remember something about it. At the time they were upset. But you know the whole damned town was upset. I was seventeen, nearly eighteen years old. I'm ashamed to say I didn't pay attention much back then."

"If it hadn't been my family or a friend, I probably would have too. Sometimes it's like this whole thing happened in someone else's life, and then I remember. Anyway, she said nice things and that I wasn't alone."

"She's pretty amazing. Once back in grade school there was this teacher who I swear no matter what I did she just hated me more. My grade kept getting worse until she showed up over there at the school and demanded to see any paperwork that supported such a low grade. Then the teacher tried to say she wouldn't talk to Denver because she wasn't my legal guardian."

Caroline gasped, just imagining how Denver would have reacted to being told such a thing.

Royal cackled with glee. "Exactly. You understand. I mean, they didn't have my official guardianship, but it was well known who really raised me. So yeah. I ended up with a very respectable B minus in that class after all. She's little, but she packs a wallop."

"Denver Watson, defender of the weak. I like it."

They drove and laughed, but she got more and more quiet the closer they got.

"Last chance," she said as they pulled off Walnut and onto 35th. The thirties were considered the "nice" part of town.

"I can slow down right here. Even if she's peeking out the front windows—which she'd never do, you understand, how crass—and she won't see."

"I already told you, I'm not going anywhere. I'm here for the look on Garrett's face when I show up. Asshole thinks he can treat my woman like crap?"

"Are you my defender now?"

"I know you're totally capable of doing this yourself. But I want to be there." He pulled up at the curb and keyed the truck off. "I'll park here instead of the drive."

"Quick escape. Smart."

He walked with her up to the front door.

She knocked and opened up, calling out. She had a key. She needed to use it and one day it wouldn't be awkward.

"Hey all! Royal and I are here." She hung up their stuff and stashed her stuff in a hall closet.

Shep came out, tipping his chin in that dudespeak thing with Royal. "S'up?" Royal asked as he tipped his chin back.

She gave her brother a hug and kissed his cheek. "Hey you. We're still on for Thursday, right?"

Shep nodded. "Totally. I'll meet you at your place at five thirty with a pizza and the next *Buffy the Vampire Slayer* DVD."

She turned to Royal. "Shep and I are stone-cold addicted to binge-watching television series. We just finished up *Farscape*. Oh my God I'd forgotten how much I loved that show. Anyway. So we finished up *Farscape* and now we're on to *Buffy*. We also eat pizza and ice cream and drink root beer." And over those times he'd been in her apartment, they'd gotten a lot closer. He talked to her about his life in ways Mindy and her grandparents didn't. She didn't hide away her pictures when he visited, though she did generally keep her stuff regarding the case in her spare room that doubled as her home office.

He just used the key she gave him. He knocked, used the key and called out. The sheer normalcy, the intimacy of it was simple and absolutely positive.

"Awesome. Such great shows."

Shep nodded. "They're all in the kitchen and dining room. Just so you know, if Garrett acts like a jerk again today I'm saying something."

Caroline smiled, touched. "Aw man, that's pretty sweet of you. But I don't want a scene. I just want to have a pleasant lunch."

Shep and Royal looked at her and then at each other, and she knew they'd do whatever they wanted.

And maybe that sort of felt awesome.

They moved to the kitchen. Her grandmother was at the stove with Mindy, but when her sister saw her, she put down the spoon she'd been holding and came over to hug her.

Royal waved before turning to her grandmother. "I didn't officially introduce you before. Royal, this is Abigail Lassiter, my grandmother. Grandma, Royal Watson."

He took her hand, shaking it gently. "Nice to meet you."

Garrett came over to where they all stood in the kitchen. "Let's hope today goes better than the last time she was around her grandmother."

"Stop it, Garrett," Mindy warned.

Caroline ignored Garrett and indicated her grandfather. "My grandfather, James Lassiter. Grandpa, this is Royal Watson."

"You her boyfriend?"

Caroline smiled tightly. This was starting way earlier than she figured it would.

Royal nodded with a grin as he shook her grandfather's hand. "I am, yes, sir."

"You're a smart boy then." Her grandfather rarely made such pronouncements, so it was really nice to hear. Even nicer when Royal blushed a little.

"My sister, Mindy."

Royal nodded. "Hey, Mindy."

Caroline found it odd how he'd gotten so very cool. He wasn't unfriendly or hostile, but Royal was a big flirt. Didn't matter if they were babies or old ladies in walkers, he was just one of those men who were charming. But he'd dialed himself back by half.

Royal didn't make her introduce the last person. Instead he turned and took Garrett in. "And Garrett Moseby. We've met before a time or two."

If Royal had been distantly polite to Mindy, he was glacially cold to Garrett. That comment he'd made hadn't done him any favors in Royal's book, that was clear. And super flattering. And so nice it made her chest tighten a little.

Still, he was in her grandparents' house so he was polite, but at the angle she stood she saw the look that passed between the two men.

"Thank you for having me today," Royal said to her grandparents, dismissing Garrett totally.

"Your name does tend to come up more and more frequently these days, so we thought it would be good to meet you." Her grandfather patted his arm.

"Can I help?" Caroline asked her grandmother even though she knew the answer.

"You can take the glasses and the tea to the table."

It was silly. Nothing exciting but damn it, it felt huge.

They all settled at the table and began to pass platters of food around. "I'm pretty excited, Grandma. Your pork chops are my absolute favorite in the world. Royal, you're going to be so happy you came along."

Her grandmother smiled. "Thank you. Royal, Caroline tells us you're the face behind Watson Organics."

Royal did what Royal did so well. He was funny and charming. He listened. He had great manners. He got along with people. He even made it look effortless. She wondered if this was real, if he just dug chillin' here at her grandparents' house with Garrett, who kept making what he thought were super cutting remarks but he was such an amateur she sort of pitied him.

Until he decided to toss a live one her way.

"Can we just address the issue of Caroline giving talks about her mother's murderer and dragging up painful memories for everyone?" Garrett asked.

"I told you we'd do this on my schedule, Garrett." Her grandmother sighed. "You only make things worse so hush up."

Caroline, her voice very cool and careful asked, "And what is it you want to address?"

Royal shifted his body, draping his arm over the back of Caroline's chair. He wanted her to know he was there for her, and he wanted them to see it and know he would protect her.

"You need to call this thing with Millersburg police off, Caroline. I forbid it." Her grandmother drank some tea before continuing. "This will only cause more pain."

"I am not doing this *for* you. Or *against* you. Or *around* you. Or *because* of you. Or *in spite* of you. In fact, you have nothing at all to do with this. I respect your opinions and your pain. But you do not tell me what I can and cannot do. You do not tell me how it is appropriate to express my beliefs."

And her grief. For God's sake this was messed up. Royal wanted to toss her over a shoulder and run from the room.

But she kept calm. So much that he saw it at the edges, how that control was keeping her together. And that made him even angrier.

"That man killed your mother. Every time you go out there and say otherwise is a slap in the face to her memory. I am simply putting my foot down on this. You're being selfish and rude."

"You don't own the market on grief!" Caroline's voice rose for a moment before she found her calm again. "She was my mother, and it's the worst thing I can imagine to *know* the person who killed her also killed my family when they let my father go down for murder. He did not kill her. I lived with them. You didn't. I saw them in just about every type of circumstance. *He didn't do it.* There is no motive. He was murdered by the same person and I will not remain silent. Not until the person who murdered my mother and tore my family up is in prison."

"Leave her be!" Shep slammed his fist on the table. Quiet descended as everyone stared at the family member least likely to pound his fist on a table. "She's trying to build a life here. Every time you do this, you push her away. I've had it. I want her around. Stop chasing her off."

"What about what she's doing?" Garrett spoke.

"Why are *you* speaking at all?" Caroline turned to Garrett. "This is not your business."

"I'm one of the men of this family. You need to defer to better judgment. No offense, Royal. Of course you'll want to handle this."

"What are you talking about?" Royal was so over this whole thing. He'd tried for her sake, but most of these people didn't care about her enough to even attempt to be careful and he was done watching them tear her up.

"You're the man, I know you'll handle this appropriately now that you know what's happening."

"Okay, this is getting out of hand." James cut in, trying to take control. "Caroline, you're aware of how upset your grandmother gets over this issue."

"Grandpa, I'm not doing this to make anyone feel bad. I'm doing this because it's the right thing to do."

Garrett invaded their conversation again. "The right person died in prison. He should have been put down like a rabid animal. You made the wrong choice and you have to live with that."

"I am not understanding why you're speaking to Caroline, Garrett. Perhaps you can explain that." Royal gave the other man a level look.

"While she ran off with the family of a murderer, her grandparents picked up the pieces and gave Shep and Mindy a home. She turned her back on people, and now she realizes she's never going to get herself on television talking about freeing her daddy the killer. She's back here trying to cause trouble because her grandparents will always protect their daughter's memory. That she's back now actin' this way—"

"That I'm here and acting any way is none of your business, Garrett. Back off and butt out. I don't want your advice. I sure don't need it. This is not your business."

"You're not being fair. He's marrying me. He wants to protect our family." Mindy wrung her hands. *Ugh, fragile.* So totally unlike their mother it made Caroline want to shake her sister and tell her to wise up.

"I'm being *more* than fair. Whatever you let him get away with is your business and your choice. But he's not qualified to give me counsel."

Garrett smiled, smug as he indicated Caroline with a hand. "See? She's just mad."

"She was *my mother.* Is anyone hearing that? I was the first-born child to Bianca and Enrique Mendoza. My mom taught me how to ride a bike and bake cookies. My dad taught me how to roast a chicken and how to change the oil. Am I mad? *Hell yes I'm mad.* I'm mad that my mother was murdered when I was fifteen. I'm mad that my father was put on trial and found guilty of a crime he did not commit. I'm mad that at sixteen I was not even allowed to whisper about my feelings. Regarding my family! So yes, I packed my bags and boxed up my life and I moved across the country. So I could believe what I wanted.

"I didn't run off. *I was run off.*" Caroline looked directly at her grandparents. "And there's no mistaking who did it. So don't ever come at me like I don't care or that my *belief*—backed up by facts—is a betrayal of my mother. You don't know a thing about my relationship with my mother." She stood up and Royal joined her, his arm around her shoulder.

"My investigator will address the police in Millersburg. And anyone else we think might help us. I will continue to do everything I can to find the real murderer and to clear my father's name. I came to have lunch with my family. I didn't start this. Y'all did. But I'm finishing it because I'm going now."

"Wait!" Shep stood. "Haven't we done this enough? Things were just fine before Garrett opened his mouth. Again. Let's everyone calm down and sit and finish up lunch. Everyone has spoken their piece so let's leave it be."

Abigail gave Shep a flinty glare. "Sit. You're going to embarrass us in front of Royal."

Caroline looked at her grandmother, and Shep cleared his throat so she sighed. "I need some air. I'll be back."

Royal followed her out onto the back porch. Once they got away from the house a bit, he wrapped his arms around her and pulled her close. It was damned cold, but he wanted to be there for her right then too, holding her so she knew he'd protect her.

"Whatever you want to do. Tell me and I'll make it happen."

"I just had this realization I can't hide this part of myself from them anymore. I don't want to hurt anyone, but I'm going to include myself this time."

"You should. Damn it. Caro. When you talked about not running off but being run off? Honey, I bleed for you and all this pain. You're their whipping boy. When are you finally going to refuse to bleed for them? Huh?"

"You're right." Her voice was muffled by his chest,

where she had her face pressed. "I don't want to be here anymore."

"Here's what we're going to do. We'll go inside and you can tell them we're leaving. Or I will. Whatever you want. Then we just walk toward the front door. Even if tizzies are being had, we keep going."

"Okay. Let me do the talking. My grandmother might get super shrill. Mindy might weep."

They went back in, and Caroline looked them all over, smiling at Shep. Royal had her hand, holding tight and keeping her grounded.

"I've had enough for today so we're going to go. Grandma, I'll call you this week. Shep, I'll see you Thursday. Mindy, call me when you're free so we can hang out."

Her grandmother shot to her feet. "This is silly. You're throwing a fit."

"I'm so sorry you see it that way." They began to walk out. Shep joined them and they kept moving. Her grandfather called her name, and she paused, turning.

"May I speak with you? Alone?"

Royal looked at her, letting her make that choice. "Royal, can you get everything loaded into the car and wait for me? I'll be out shortly."

"No." Royal shook his head. "It's two light jackets and your purse. I'll carry it all out to the car when you're ready to go. I'm not leaving you alone here."

The relief and gratitude on her face nearly felled him. Royal wanted to punch every person there but Caro and Shep.

She kissed him quickly. "Thank you."

He took her face in his hands. Tipping her up to look

him in the eyes. "Don't let *anyone* make you feel bad for what you know. You hear me?"

She nodded. She did know it. But she needed to hear it again. And from him it mattered so much.

She met her grandfather, and he guided her to his office with a hand at her elbow.

"I apologize for how this has gotten out of hand," he said once he sat next to her on the small couch in the room.

"I appreciate that. But this happens regularly. I feel ambushed and ganged up on. I just wanted to have lunch with my family and my boyfriend. Lunch is over but I'm not staying for a heaping helping of guilt with my pie."

"Now, Caroline, there's no call for rudeness."

"Grandpa, there is. I didn't bring this up. You all did. When she came to me angry about it the first time, I didn't bring it up either. I answered truthfully. And it didn't stop there. Unless I leave it'll keep going and someone will say something they can't take back. I'm trying hard not to be that person."

"You're a mix of your parents. On the outside I mean. Dark hair and eyes, like his. The shape of the eyes and mouth, well that's my baby. Your personality? That's all Bianca. Sometimes when I watch you, I know what you're thinking and feeling because you even emote the same way. Funny how that works. She was headstrong too. Your mother and grandmother used to lock horns. It was impressive. Bianca is one of only a few people who ever took your grandmother on. You can't know what it feels like to lose your child. And in such a way. It changes you. Your grandmother and I made choices.

Some of them were mistakes. But we love you and we love your brother and sister."

His hands shook for a moment, a man brought to his knees by this horrible tragedy that connected them all.

She wished it was her place to comfort him, but she'd been frozen out so long it wasn't something she felt at ease doing. It felt unwelcome, so she kept it to herself.

"No. I don't know what that pain is like. I imagine it's terrible. Probably like losing your mom. I respect your grief. I *share* your grief, for goodness' sake. But I'm not going to allow you to extort me with it. She didn't raise me to give up."

"He's dead, Caroline. What good could it possibly do at this point to keep stirring this up? All you're doing is upsetting people."

"No. All I'm doing is the same thing I'd do for you, or Grandma, or Shep or Mindy. If I thought you were wronged, I'd work until I made it right or couldn't fight anymore. And also? The real killer is out there. He could be here in Petal still. Someone you bump into all the time. That's not safe. It's unjust and it's dangerous."

"So you'd just continue this folly? Knowing your grandmother and sister were so upset they cry over it?"

"Well, at least they're there for one another when they're upset." Caroline winced. "That wasn't nice. I apologize. I'm sorry you think making sure the person who butchered my mother being caught and put on trial is folly. But yes, I will continue this. She was my mother. Do you understand that?"

"I'm afraid I think you're the one who doesn't understand that. You bulldoze through here and tear everything up for him. But you don't do it for her."

It hurt far more than she wished it did. But she would

not give him anything else. She walled it out and managed to sound cold and calm. "You don't know me well enough to say that with any measure of certainty." She stood. "And this is why I'm leaving. I have nothing else to say."

"I wish that was true."

She let out a long sigh. "Bye, Grandpa."

Caroline didn't bother with an *I love you* before leaving.

Garrett, apparently not recognizing the danger in it, approached Royal. "You need to get your woman handled."

"Get away from me, Moseby." Royal kept his gaze on the door at the end of the hall where she'd disappeared with her grandfather.

Shep came over. "Leave him alone."

"She's only going to bring you trouble, Royal. Then again, considering who you've been with before, maybe you like your women with a helping of trouble."

"Do you want to get punched in the nose? You're just making it worse." Shep got right in Garrett's face.

"If anyone in your family tried to rein her in before now, it wouldn't be so hard."

Royal turned to hold Garrett's attention, because he wanted to be sure the other man heard and understood. "Next time I see you in town you better be with your mother or Mindy. Take a step back and shut your mouth, or I'll make you twice as aware of my true feelings when we next meet."

"Garrett, come help Mindy clear up." Abigail came out to where Royal stood with Shep. "Shep, don't you have homework?"

"No, ma'am."

"Shoo." She made a motion with her hands and Shep shook his head.

"I'm waiting for Caroline. I'm going to walk her out."

"Royal, I really must insist you use your powers of persuasion on my granddaughter. Help her to understand how much damage she's doing to her own family. Nothing is going to change. She needs to let it go."

"Mrs. Lassiter, I understand this was a terrible thing you really don't want to think about. But why should Caroline have to hide how she feels? She's making every attempt to not shove it in your face. But she gets to feel grief too. And she has the right to deal with it how she needs to. Caroline has a deep sense of justice. One I do hope you're proud of because it makes her who she is. And she's right. I know you believe her father was guilty, but if he wasn't she'd be right to worry about the real killer don't you think?"

Caroline came out of the office, so much sadness on her face. But her back was straight and her attention was totally on Royal. "Let's go."

He wanted to pull her close and make it better, but now wasn't the time and in front of the very people who made her feel this way wasn't the place either. Instead he nodded to Abigail. "Thank you for having me today." And then held an arm out for Caroline to take, which she did.

"See you Thursday, Shep. Bye, Mindy," Caroline called out. Ignoring Garrett she turned to her grandmother. "Goodbye, Grandma."

Caroline didn't wait for a hug, instead she walked right down the hall to the front door, which Royal opened quickly, and out of the house. Shep jogged next to them.

"I'm sorry."

Caroline smiled sideways at her brother. "Not your fault."

"I hate this. I just got you back and already they're driving you away."

Caroline paused, letting go of Royal so she could hug her brother. "I'm *not* going anywhere. You didn't know Mom, not really, but she taught me to never give up. No matter what, you're my brother, and I'm sorry if I haven't been around enough. I'm trying to make it better."

"Promise?"

She nodded. "Promise."

"I'll see you Thursday."

"You got it. Love you, Shep."

Shep grinned and waited until they got in and started the truck before he turned and walked back to the house.

"We can call off dinner tonight," he said quietly as he drove back to his place.

"No. I chose to come back here. I'm not going to let this run me off again. I'm not that same scared, broken girl who'd lost both parents in such a short time. I'm still sort of shocked at how it went down in there."

"You have so much more self-control than I do. You tried so hard with them just now, and none of them but your brother gave you half a chance. What did your grandfather say?"

"He started off with an apology, but it went way downhill from there. His parting shot was that I wasn't doing this for my parents, but myself. That I didn't really love my mother. I think he meant it. Which, well, sucks. But what can I do? I'm done apologizing. I'm here to get to know them and I guess I have." She snorted. "I came back to be closer with them, but I guess always in the back of my head I knew it was pretty unlikely. I don't want to give up on them, but maybe some space is necessary. I can't be going over there to be ambushed."

"You can't, no. Let them cool down and come to you. Your grandfather had no right to say all that stuff to you. Caroline, you want to build a life here and that includes boundaries that are healthy. Fuck them for trying to beat you up all the time."

"I don't want to talk about it anymore. When are we supposed to be at Lily and Nathan's?"

"In two hours. If I step on it, we have time for a quickie."

She laughed. "I think it's sort of awesome that you consider an hour and forty five minutes or so to be a quickie."

"Well, you know how I like it."

She shivered. "I do."

"We truly can cancel. Lily will understand. She's got her own family difficulties. I know they haven't been the friendliest but they're good people."

"I'm not consumed with rage at what standoffish people your friends have been. I get it. It's fine."

He guffawed. "It's totally not fine. But it's how people are in groups, and I expect you get that part. They'll make it up to you or they won't be in my life. I should have stood up sooner."

"This isn't even an argument we need to have. I'm not mad. I knew what was happening and why."

"I know. But seeing you get threatened the way you do drives me nuts. I want to punch a million people. Garrett better step quickly if he sees me in town. He's been warned."

There was an accident on the road back to his place so they wouldn't have had the time for a quickie, even a truly short one. She had to change and try to screw her head back on right.

Royal pretty much left her alone as she got ready, which she appreciated. But he didn't range far and frequently moved close enough to touch or kiss, which she also appreciated. If he fussed too much, she'd cry and ruin her makeup. She needed to keep herself together and he got that. It was really wonderful to be understood that way.

Truth was, she didn't want to go anywhere. She wanted to snuggle with Royal in his bed, watch movies and have a lot of sex. But Lily had invited them, and it came before she and Anne had made peace so it meant even more.

Caroline stepped into her shoes and gave herself one last look before she freshened her lipstick.

"I think I might be getting a sore throat. I'd hate to leave Lily and Nathan's super early. But man a sore throat? I should probably rest so it gets better."

"Like rest with your cock in me?"

"Best medicine ever." He winked.

Her phone got a text. It was from Melissa. "Damn, one of the windows at Mel's house got hit by a falling tree. Took it out and part of the roof. She wants to know if we're free next weekend instead."

"Yeah, Saturday's fine. Then on Sunday we can stop by Edward and Polly's for a bit. They're having a huge thing over there. A bunch of birthdays happen in April."

"So I'd have to go to that?"

He snorted. "Do you really think Polly would hesitate to come find you herself and bring you over if you didn't come?"

"She is rather spunky." She typed back to Melissa, offering assistance if any was needed and saying they'd see her and Clint the following Saturday. She put the phone in her pocket and looked up to find him grinning at her.

"We don't have time for sex."

He burst out laughing. "I think you'd be surprised at how many things I can do even with a very short amount of time."

"This is most likely very true."

"Since we don't have to go anywhere tomorrow, I vote we don't leave the house at all."

She turned and gave him the eye, but he shrugged, still grinning.

"Sounds like a great plan."

Chapter Fourteen

Caroline had been able to stop by the Millersburg cop shop right as Ron was finishing up. She met several of the officers and then attended a coffee-and-muffin-style debrief with Elliot afterward.

Ron had gotten the name of the person who'd been Chief Dickers's secretary for several years. Dickers, as had been repeated by the cops she'd met, was a "lazy, racist asshole" who routinely lost evidence and half-assed investigations.

There had been missing pages from a call log with tips after the murder. If she could talk with the other woman, maybe she could figure out a possible place to search. There had been a basic search ordered by the judge to find the other pages, but they never were located. It had been ruled during trial and later on appeal that they had no real bearing on the case and it was a paperwork mix-up, not a conspiracy to hide evidence from the defense.

At this point there were no appeals left. This new approach was crafted to find the killer. Something she'd hoped to leave to the cops after she'd freed her dad. But now that was her only choice other than giving up.

She was out of her element with this stuff. She could

argue and write briefs and all that stuff, but her firm in Seattle used investigators. Up until she'd decided to move to Petal, she'd had one perspective on the case, and now she had to switch it up and change her approach.

She was never above asking experts what their opinion was. And so when she did, when she showed the proper respect to them and sought out their advice, they'd given it. Kindly and freely.

On the way out, Elliot walked Caroline and Ron to their cars.

Caroline turned to Elliot. "I'm so grateful for all the information and time you guys provided."

He smiled. "Ron was excellent. You're good with people in general. Listen, one of the guys I know, he produces a radio show. I was talking with him about you. If you're up for it, he can give you five minutes. The station is on the outskirts of Atlanta, but you can hear it out here just fine. If you have a business card, I can give it to him and have him hook you up."

"Wow. That would be awesome. Thank you so much." She pulled out a card and put her cell on the back. "My information."

Elliot tucked it in a pocket. "Keep me updated. If anyone remembers something I'll let you know."

"Thanks. I mean that."

She got in her car and drove away.

"I'm so proud of you. This radio thing will boost the signal. That's going to raise your profile in a big way. If you can't find those lost pages, you can try to get people who are still alive to call in."

She shifted in her bed. Alone. Ugh. That had grown

to suck really fast. But she had an early meeting and hadn't gotten home until after nine so it made sense to sleep at her place.

Sometimes sense sucked.

"I don't like it when you're not next to me. You're warm and I fit right into your side and it makes it easier to sleep."

"Yeah. Me too, baby. I can come over. I'll be there in about fifteen minutes," he said, and it made her smile.

"Nah. You have a long day tomorrow. I have a long day tomorrow. Go to bed. I'll talk with you later and see you Friday."

He paused and then sighed. "You're awfully small to take up such a big part of my heart."

"You say the best things. I love you too."

"Sleep well. Spike is head-butting my hand where I'm holding the phone so he misses you too."

"He's trying to get you to put the phone down so you can pet him."

"Yeah that's more likely. But less romantic."

She laughed. "Good night, Royal and Spike."

"Night. Sweet dreams."

It had been a great day all around but for the absence of Royal in her bed, and as she'd be seeing him soon enough, it could wait a day or two. If anything the time apart from him always made her realize how much she liked hanging out with him.

He was low maintenance except when it came to sex. Then? Well then he was an exacting taskmaster, which was fine with her. If you wanted something done right you had to practice. A lot.

She fell asleep with a smile on her face, thinking of Royal as her fucking coach. Yeah that worked.

* * *

"So, I think you should tell me." Shep put four slices of pizza on his plate. This, along with a giant bucket-like container of soda, and that was just his first go. She had a lot of sympathy for her grandparents. It must cost so much money to feed a teenage boy.

He settled on one corner of her couch, claiming that end table for his cup and plate. She did the same on the other side.

"What do you mean?"

"About him. About why you think what you do."

She paused. It wasn't that she hadn't endlessly thought about how she should deal with this topic. She spent hours just trying to figure it out. Should she tell him? If yes, should she seek her grandparents' permission because they were his guardians? If she did tell him, how much to say?

But the reality of that moment happening after so long got to her, and she needed a bit of time to pull herself back together.

"You want to know about our dad. About why I think he's innocent. Just being super clear."

He nodded.

"I have long wondered if I should ask Grandma and Grandpa for permission to talk about this with you."

"I'm almost eighteen! You're my sister. This is about our parents. Why should you have to ask? You know they'll refuse."

She blew out a breath. "Yeah. That's pretty much what I thought. I think you're a really mature young man. You're off to college in like what, four and a half months?"

He nodded.

"I'm proud of you for that. I know I've said it before, but it bears repeating. You are going to have such great things in your future. Mom and Dad would have been proud. So anyway, you'll be eighteen in three weeks. You're my brother. They were our parents and I knew them better than anyone. Which is why I'm going to tell you. Grandma and Grandpa will be angry when they find out, you know. Are you prepared to deal with that?"

"We got into a big fight after you left. Grandma and Grandpa do not agree at all about what went down Saturday. He feels bad. She's mad at you for embarrassing her in front of Royal and the rest of town with your crusade. Garrett is right up her butt on that. Mindy...well. She wants to support you. She actually argued for you for a while. He doesn't want her seeing you. I just think that's bullshit. You're our sister. This is about our family and our life, and I think we have a right to feel however we damn well feel."

"That was a few curse words there, Shep." She gave him an amused warning.

"It makes me feel like cursing. I don't like secrets. This thing where they want you to shut up about how you feel and what you know about what happened to you? I don't like it at all. That's a damned secret. One of those secrets that tears everyone apart. And you're the one who pays the price. I'm not okay with that. I want you to tell. So I can make up my mind without secrets."

She took a deep breath and she told him.

Over the next few hours she spoke, he asked questions, she answered them. Once they finished eating, she let him see the press kit with all the relevant facts about the case and then handed him a black three-ring binder.

"That's pretty much everything I just went over with

you along with supporting legal documentation and case law. Some of those subjects have articles attached. It's all layers of proof for everything I've just told you."

He dropped onto her couch, an arm thrown over his eyes, and she felt awful for overwhelming him. "Look, let's stop now."

"You keep saying that. But I want to know."

"I know you do. I'm not saying no to giving you the answers, but I think you're tired and you have school tomorrow and I've just told you stuff that you need to find a way to process and deal with. This is enough for the night. I'll tell you more. You can talk to the other attorneys and people I deal with to see what they think. I just want to say to you, Enrique Mendoza would never, ever have hurt Bianca Mendoza. You were two when this happened. You didn't get to know either of them and for that I am so sorry. But I did. I saw them both every single day of my life. He didn't do this. And when, or if, you decide I'm telling you the truth, you're going to struggle. I'm telling you in advance that you need to give yourself permission not to feel guilt. You couldn't have known."

"But I could have! Why didn't you tell me before now?"

"You were two. Mindy was five. It was made clear to me that I could *not* stay here if I continued to hold on to the belief that our dad was innocent. So I went with our dad's family." Jesus, they'd been so anxious to see her brother and sister all these years. Their grandmother would be so thrilled. But she needed to take it slow and not overwhelm him any more.

"And later?"

"It was in my best interests to not speak of it in front of you or Mindy if I wanted to keep seeing you."

"What do you mean?"

"It doesn't matter. The point is, I'm sorry to be dumping all this on you at once. I wanted to tell you, but I wanted you in my life. I wanted to keep on seeing you and Mindy, so I kept my mouth shut. Grandma is going to flip out when she finds out."

"I'm not going to say anything for a while. I want to think on everything you've told me. Read some of these things."

"You should keep that binder to yourself."

"That's more lying. I told you, I hate it."

She nodded. "I get it. I swear I do. So how about you be discreet? Do you think there'll be the peace to think all this over if she sees the stuff in that binder?"

"This is dumb and awful and I hate it."

She hugged him. "I'm sorry. I'm sorry to be giving you this major info dump. I really should have taken it slower."

"I pushed. I want to know. You did the right thing."

They walked to the door. "Text me when you get home, okay?" She kissed his cheek and hugged him before handing over the entire leftover pizza she'd ordered so he'd have breakfast.

"You got it. I'll be discreet." He held up the binder.

"Good. Thank you. Love you."

He'd already been halfway down her steps when he called back that he loved her too.

Her phone rang right after she locked the door.

Chapter Fifteen

Royal raised his glass. "To you, darlin'."

Caroline grinned and took a sip of her beer. "I can't believe they played it during drive time." She'd prerecorded the radio interview *and* played it during drive time.

"Clearly your cop friend likes you to hook you up nicely." He smirked at her.

"He's a nice guy who wants to do the right thing."

"Sure and gaining the trust and affection of the hottest woman to cross his path ever."

"Aw you're jealous?"

He snorted but she blushed and may have giggled a little.

"Well, sir, when you come in to my house and there's a naked man in my bed we can talk."

It was his turn to blush as he nearly choked on his beer.

"Touché," he croaked.

"Anyway. I'll check the tip line tomorrow morning before we go over to Melissa's."

They were nestled in a corner booth up at the front window, a pitcher of beer between them, burgers ordered.

"It's not such a bad way to spend a Friday night. Beautiful woman with great news. There will be some sexing going on when we get to my place. Just in case you were wondering. So that's a good thing. Add beer and a good burger and, really, a man can't ask for much more."

"You're sassy today."

"I'm sassy every day."

She laughed and caught sight of Anne and Beth coming in with Joe. Anne turned, and upon seeing Caroline, she waved and they all started over.

"Hey you," Anne said to Caroline. "If you go over there and sit with him, we can join you."

Caroline rolled her eyes, but it was teasing and taken in that manner. Anne slid in followed by Beth and Joe.

The newcomers ordered food and another pitcher before Anne turned to Caroline. "I heard you on the radio tonight."

"He got a cancellation at nine last night. I went to his studio this morning after court and did the piece. I had no idea it would run during prime drive time. He was going to try for late afternoon."

Anne nodded. "Cool. You made some really great points, by the way. I hope you find answers."

Caroline smiled. "Stop being so nice."

She nearly leered and it made Caroline guffaw. "All part of my plan." Anne looked to Royal. "Doesn't your girlfriend's hair look fantastic?"

Royal's gaze slid from Caroline's mouth up to her hair and them back to her mouth before answering Anne. "She does. She told me she went into the salon, and you did it for her."

"I told you she'd look good with that mahogany." Beth nudged her sister's arm.

Caroline had planned to see Tate but Tate had been called over to the preschool where one of her children had just puked, so in the end, Caroline had gambled on Anne and won. Thank goodness.

And as she walked out of the salon, Caroline sort of had to accept she really liked Anne and her sister Beth. Tate had shown up halfway through the color so Caroline had gotten to know her too.

Caroline gave her hair a flip and felt Royal's attention on her hot and hard for long moments.

The server brought more beer and some food. During all the chaos, Royal leaned over, his lips against her ear. "It makes me so hard when you flip your hair like that."

She kept her eyes on her beer but smiled into the glass.

"Hey, Caroline!"

She looked up to find Elliot Charles standing there.

"Hey, Elliot!" She turned to Royal. "Royal, this is Officer Charles, from Millersburg. Elliot, this is my boyfriend, Royal Watson."

There was some hand shaking.

"This is Joe Harris and Beth Murphy."

"I met Beth and Joe that weekend I chatted with Edward and Polly about you." Elliot grinned at them and then turned his attention to Anne. Anne's eyes went half-lidded and soon enough, Elliot's had done the same.

"But I'd have remembered you," Elliot said to Anne.

"Anne Murphy, Elliot Charles."

Royal stole two of Caroline's rings while she nosily watched Anne and Elliot sniff around one another.

"You should stay for a drink, Elliot. Have a beer," Caroline suggested and Anne threw her a big smile.

Everyone shifted. Interestingly enough it left Elliot sitting across from Anne.

* * *

People came and went over the next hour or two. A pool game got started when a bunch of the Chases showed up. Caroline hung out at the table with Beth. Anne and Elliot had started an earnest debate, Luke Bryan versus Jake Owen.

The place got even more crowded as prime Friday-night social hours hit their peak.

Royal played pool in the back with Trey, Jacob and Nathan. Lily sat with Beth and Caroline. She gave a look at Anne and one to Beth and Caroline.

"Okay then, ladies. How goes it?" Lily leaned back a little, getting comfortable.

"Excellent. Planning the wedding." Beth and Joe were getting married that upcoming August.

"Still considering jetting off to Hawaii and doing it and just having a party when you return?"

Beth looked at Lily. "You have such a big mouth. What if she couldn't be trusted? Joe's mother is so wrapped up in wedding plans, and now Tate is like her partner in crime. If they heard I'd even *joked* about eloping, they'd both have kittens."

Lily waved a hand. "Who's gonna tell? Anne's having hormones over there with officer sweetcheeks. She's not hearing a damn thing we're saying. I'm scared of Tate when she starts planning things so it's not like I'll be running to her with this. Unbunch." Lily turned to Caroline. "Nice radio coverage, by the way."

"You heard it?"

"No, Nathan and I were at the doctor's office. Nothing bad," she added quickly, "just a regular prenatal visit. Everything is fine. Anyway, we heard from Tate when we saw her earlier. All the kids are over at her house watching a movie and having hot chocolate and snacks."

"My sister Tate is like one of those people who loves kids. Oh people say it, but let's be real, kids can be annoying as hell." Beth looked to Lily's growing belly. "Um, not all kids though. Anyway Tate really means it. She's just like so totally alive when she's with her kids, with kids in general."

Caroline smiled. "I've seen her with Matt and their kids. They have happy ending written all over them."

Beth nodded. "Matt Chase might be the one dude on earth who is worthy of her."

"Not that y'all are biased."

Beth laughed. "Where Tate is concerned, I think you'll find all of us are very biased. But back to the radio thing. It's exciting."

Caroline didn't want to get her hopes up, but it was a positive direction at least. "I figure between the people who heard it and people talking about it, maybe it'll get attention."

Anne pulled her attention away from Elliot to speak to Caroline. "Oh, honey, people are going to talk about it. Garrett Moseby is flapping his gums all over town."

Caroline knew her eyes went wide but she was so surprised and yet not surprised she couldn't help it. "He is not!"

Anne nodded. "Totally is. Like a weasel. Thing is, he *is* a weasel so people know that."

"But some will listen." Caroline blew out a breath. "What?" she asked them all. "You think I don't notice when everyone is talking about me? How many people look over here? Just because I hold it down doesn't mean I don't see it."

"Yes, some people will listen to him. Some people think Elvis is alive and tank tops with shelf bras actually hold your boobs up."

There was a moment of silence for how true that last statement was.

"Anyway, all I can do is hope the more people talk about it, the more people remember."

Royal came walking back, and she locked her gaze with his, smiling.

"I just can't seem to step a foot without running into you. You won't be happy until you ruin every place in town."

At first Caroline looked around, trying to figure out what was going on, and then she realized it was Benji and he was talking with her.

"Here she is out drinking and partying while her grandmother weeps herself to sleep." From his place just behind Benji's left shoulder, Garrett sneered.

Caroline glanced at them and then turned back to Lily. "Those are super cute earrings by the way."

"Thanks!" Lily touched the blood-red beads dangling from the vintage-styled chandelier earrings. "Cassie Chase makes them a few times a year and shows up at the farmer's market to sell them at random."

"That's ridiculously cool. Like batman. Only with earrings."

"I'm talking to you. Hey!"

There was movement at the edge of her vision, and she flinched away instinctively, turning to find Royal's hand crushing Benji's fist. "You don't touch her. Ever. You get me?"

Royal shoved Benji back so hard he stumbled, his back hitting a nearby booth.

People began to look as Royal fully inserted himself between where she'd moved, half standing in the booth, and where Benji nearly panted with anger.

"She needs to get out of here. And get out of Petal. This is a town for decent people."

"Like men who'd sucker punch a woman a foot shorter?"

Garrett took Benji's shoulder, not meeting Caroline's astonished gaze. "Come on, Benji. Lay off. You made your point."

"She's a no-good whore who screwed her way into your little group for protection. You lie with dogs you're going to get fleas, Royal."

Time slowed down as Caroline gasped at the whore comment. She noted the bunching of muscles on Royal's neck and the flex of his biceps. She scrambled as all around them, others moved to get out of the way, or to stop it, or to grab their beer before it went flying or whatever.

"What did you just call Caroline?" Royal's voice had gone very cold and sharp.

Oh boy. She'd been a defense attorney a long time. Enough that she recognized this fact pattern. Despite the wall of dudeflesh that sprang up at Royal's side and was apparently set on keeping her back, being short had its benefits.

Squeezing through, Caroline managed to get free of the booth but stayed behind Royal. He was worked up and really angry so if she stayed out of reach of Benji and let Royal protect her, things would be fine and no one would get punched.

She hoped it for no other reason than Benji would love the attention. And Royal could go to jail or something equally stupid. He'd be in there all weekend because there were no bail hearings on the weekends in Petal.

Lily got away from their booth, Beth helping. Which was good because Nathan shot Benji a look that threatened lots of pain. Elliot stood tall and very authoritarian next to Royal, also in between Benji and Caroline.

At this point pretty much the entire restaurant was looking, and Caroline wanted to crawl under their booth. Well, metaphorically because she was sure it was really gross down there.

Elliot spoke calmly, but with that cop voice. "All right, gentlemen. Let's break this up before something bad happens that no one intended."

Benji turned a little with a smile. As if he were leaving and everyone relaxed until he reversed course and threw his entire body behind the fist heading in Royal's direction.

Royal caught Benji's arm, sliding a grip to his wrist before wrenching the arm down and out of the way.

Then. Well then he punched Benji right square in the nose with his free hand like it was his job.

The crowd surged but Nathan reached out to grab her around the waist and keep her standing.

Benji's blood was everywhere as he held his nose in both hands.

Elliot waded in. "Break it up. I mean it." He wasn't in uniform and he worked several towns over, but he carried the authority easily and people obeyed, moving.

"I want to press charges," Benji wailed.

Royal actually growled. "Oh yes, please. And I'll press them against him, and then he and I can be in the same holding cell all weekend long."

Someone handed a bunch of napkins to Benji.

"Fine. He's not that important to me anyway. You better watch yourself." Benji pointed a bloody finger at Caroline, and Royal nearly got loose from the people who'd been holding him back.

Caroline had never seen Royal this angry before. "I told you to leave her alone. You're fucking threatening her now? I'll beat your ass for this."

"That's enough!" Elliot physically pushed them apart, and the three guys restraining Royal got better hold of him.

"This piece of shit just threatened my girlfriend. What the hell, dude?" He strained to get loose, and Benji seemed to finally have figured out how sweet, laid-back, easy, good-natured Royal went fucking nuclear.

"You're his friends, what do we do?" she whispered to Nathan and Trey.

Trey whispered back, "I've only seen Royal this mad twice during the decades I've known him."

Nathan crossed his arms over his chest, standing shoulder to shoulder with Trey to keep her out of the fray.

"That motherfucker tried to hit his woman and then called her a whore. And then he threatened her. Benji is lucky he's got all his teeth left." Trey raised the volume so everyone around them could hear.

"Royal." Caroline pushed her way around Trey and Nathan and approached Royal, reaching out to touch his arm. "Royal," she repeated his name. "Don't let this garbage rob you of what is sure to be a pretty awesome weekend." She reached up, guiding his chin so she could look at him better. "You already punched him once. There's a cop right there. Let it go."

"He tried to hit you."

She nodded. "And you stopped him and defended me. Thank you."

"He called you names and threatened you. I really don't think I can let that go."

"Baby, he's covered in blood. Your hand is all messed up and it's starting to swell. We need to get it on ice. He got the message."

"You need someone to stand up for you. To protect you. Oh I know you can handle yourself. But you need someone who always gets between you and trouble. That's me."

Oh. Everything inside her got sort of gooey for a moment as she smiled, blushing. "I did, yes. And now that's you. Thank you. But now we need to back off because if not you'll go down to the police station and maybe jail."

"I know a great defense attorney."

She laughed. "I'm kind of expensive, so save it up for something really good."

"I could punch him a few more times and that would be really good."

As she spoke with Royal, one of Shane's officers came in and took over from Elliot after hearing what happened. They were smart enough to get Benji out of there.

"Let's go." She kissed him quickly. "I'll show you really good."

"Promise?"

"Every time."

"Okay, everyone. Mind your business and be moving along. Not the first time y'all have seen a fight in a bar," Elliot called out, making a shooing motion with his hands.

Caroline noted Garrett had disappeared. But he'd seen

enough that the entire situation would be reported—with prejudice—to her grandparents.

Out of the corner of her eye, she saw Anne hand Elliot a card and he handed her one.

"Come back to my place so I can clean your knuckles up."

"No to your place. Yes to letting you kiss all my boo-boos at my house. My bed is also bigger," Royal murmured into her ear.

He helped her into her coat as people tried to get him to talk about things until Caroline put herself in between him and the crowd. But he put an arm around her, shifting her so he was between her and any possible trouble.

"You two are really gross." Anne rolled her eyes.

Caroline snorted. "Whatever."

Anne leaned close as they all reached the door. "Thanks for inviting Elliot to have a drink. He's very forceful, isn't he?"

"Um, I guess. He's got a great butt."

"Yes. That too."

Once they got outside of course, Royal spotted Garrett and headed over.

Caroline grabbed his arm.

Royal turned to her, his hand over hers. "He egged that entire scene on. I told him what would happen the next time I saw him."

"He's not worth it. You punched someone for me. Garrett is terrified. Look at him." She pointed and Royal snarled. Garrett caught sight of them making their way closer and got in his car and drove off quickly.

"That wasn't nice," Royal said to Caroline, but he smiled as he said it.

"Oooh. Will you be extra gruff with me? Do I need to be punished for my impudence?"

He swatted her butt but watched Garrett's car until it turned off Main Street.

Royal was quiet on the way back to his place as he tried to process his anger. Not just at Benji and Garrett, but by how people seemed to feel like they could abuse and threaten Caroline at will. Simply because she believed something they didn't. Something they could agree or disagree with her over or basically not give a fuck what she thought one way or the other.

To threaten to physically harm someone because they believed differently than you was bad enough. But this wasn't some random woman. This was *Royal's* woman. All barely five feet of her, and while she was a total bad-ass in many ways, Benji was at least a foot taller and had a hundred pounds on her.

"That was really fucked up," she mumbled. "I'm so sorry."

He pulled into his garage and keyed the car off before closing the garage door. "Sorry for what?"

"That whole scene. So stupid. And your hand. Benji wasn't worth it."

He got out and went around to her side but when he pulled her down, he hauled her close. "No he wasn't worth it. Not one bit. *You're* worth it, Caroline. No one gets to harm you or joke about it or try to scare you with it. No one."

She knew she should have been upset. Or mad or sad. But the way he'd defended her, his eyes sparking, fists balled up just right for punching—well, it made her hot all over and she wanted to rub herself on him. Wanted to kiss and sniff and nuzzle and all those super weird primal things.

This Royal who held her was a man whose territory had been invaded. She was *his* and she realized it was no small matter to belong to a man like Royal Watson.

"You're a sneak alpha." *Damn it.* And it was too late.

One corner of his mouth tipped up as he took her hands and pulled her into the house. "Sit so I can take your boots off," he said, his lips on hers.

She flopped onto his couch and took a long, leisurely look from his toes up to the top of his head. "Damn."

"Is that a good *damn* or a bad damn?"

He pulled one boot off and then the other. "Not only are you a sneak alpha, you smell really good and your body goes all ripply when you take my boots off."

His smile bloomed over his face, and every part of her stood up and cheered. "Wow."

He motioned with a tip of his chin as he helped her to her feet, giving a gentle push toward his bedroom.

"Go on, darlin'." He stalked behind her, all that masculine power flooding through her like a blast of heat.

Still, she needed to give as good as she got.

Caroline looked back over her shoulder, riveted by the sight of his mouth.

"I'm not a sneak anything. Many people mistake being easygoing for being shallow or weak. I don't have any call to go getting all worked up over every little thing, Caro. But some things are worth getting worked up over."

Standing at the foot of his very large bed, he reached out, his hand sliding around the back of her neck and yanking her forward.

"Your hands."

The breathlessness of it made his cock ache. The way

her lips caressed the words and the way her eyes had gotten wide for a moment, her desire banked to focus on his injuries.

"Stay here." She left him in his bedroom. He pulled the shirt, boots and socks off, waiting for her in only his jeans.

He loved the way Caroline skidded to a halt when she came back into the room. She stared at him with that cat-like pleasure of hers as she placed a full ice bucket on the bedside table.

She pulled him into the master bath and washed his hands gently.

"Most of this isn't your blood. You'll be sore, but it doesn't look like you broke the skin anywhere."

"Take your shirt off."

He backed her into the bedroom as he said this.

And then she did, reaching down to grab the hem of her shirt and whipping it up and off exposing all those fucking curves that drove him so wild.

"Damn. Look at you. I want to lick you up one side and down the other."

He reached out, removing her bra. He stepped a little closer, feathering his thumbs over her collarbones. Watched as she swallowed hard and dragged her eyes open.

So confident in his power in that moment, he was felled when she took a cube of ice from her glass between her lips and bent her head over the hand she'd just pulled into hers.

Lower, her head bent over his lap and he let out a shuddering sigh. And then the ice against his sore knuckles.

It was…hot. So fucking hot he shivered from head to

toe three times. And then it was tender. And hot. So hot again when she cut her gaze to him.

"Goddamn," he snarled as she ripped sensation from him with nothing more than her gaze and that mouth. Sucking on an ice cube so her lips were a little swollen, glossy from the melting water.

She spit the cube out at long last and dried his skin gently. "I'm going to tell you you really need to ice your knuckles. And you're going to refuse," she said quickly before he could do just that. "And I'm going to say that you can touch me one-handed while the other is in ice."

Taking his hand, she kissed his knuckles gently before brushing the backs of his fingers against her nipples.

The sexual energy between them sizzled along his skin.

"All right. After."

"After what?"

He grabbed his belt, unbuckling it slowly, fascinated by the way her gaze locked on his hands. Her nipples darkened and hardened. Her mouth had rested in a rather tantalizing O of surprise as she'd shivered and sighed.

Someone liked that very much.

He pulled it from the loops slowly. Once the belt cleared his jeans, he whipped his wrist just right so the leather snapped.

"After I use this belt to restrain you, I'll ice one hand while I use the other on you."

She licked her lips and offered her wrists.

"On the bed. On your back. Hands above your head gripping the headboard."

She got on the bed and lay out like he'd told her to. He straddled her body, using his belt to tie her wrists to the headboard. It wasn't enough to hold her. Not really. Enough that she could struggle though.

He kissed her elbow and then scooted down her body. He unbuttoned and unzipped her jeans, and she writhed as he gripped the pants and pulled them off her legs. Her socks he tossed over his left shoulder.

"Your jeans are still on," she panted.

If he took them off, he'd be inside her before he could remember he had plans. So he left them on.

He eased his injured hand into the ice. "I like it when you take care of me."

With his free hand, he plucked up an ice cube, sliding the edge of it over her nipple. He drew it around and around, watching as it beaded, pleased at the sight of rivulets of water sliding over her breast.

Her eyelids fluttered a little as she arched on a sigh.

Pleased by his life right at that very moment, he tossed the ice back into the bucket. "Tell me something about yourself," he said as he lowered his head to lick over the iced nipple, knowing the change in sensation from cold to hot would make her wet.

"I know it's silly and shallow," she began in a desire-rough voice, "but it makes me all kinds of hot just thinking about what you were like earlier at the bar. No one's ever punched someone for me."

She laughed and the sound drew him close with the need to kiss her. "You taste like something I need a lot of."

With his free hand, he grabbed a piece of ice again to trace the curve of her pussy through the whisper-thin, translucent material of her underpants, and she stilled. He tossed the piece of ice back and changed hands. And icy-cold wetness seized her nipple. One and then the other until his hand started to warm up.

"I don't think this is the spirit of our agreement that you'd ice your hand."

He hooked a finger around the side of her panties and tugged. She lifted up and he pulled them off. "I'm a rebel, Caro. Now would you look at that?" He tickled the tip of a finger against her labia and then brushed it back and forth until he finally got to her clit, and she nearly yelped.

"You're close. Already."

"My body is super easy for you."

"Thank God for it."

Sweat sheened on her skin. There was a light out in the hallway, and the shaft of it bathed a slice of her leg. He rolled off the bed and flipped the light switch, filling the room with a pale yellow glow from the vintage bulbs in the wall sconces.

"There we go. Look at you, darlin'. Luscious."

He dried off his other hand, moving the bucket of ice out of the way before crawling back to straddle her body.

"How is it?" She nodded at his hand.

"Swelling has gone down. Enough for me to touch you all over and punch Garrett when I find him."

"I don't want to talk about him or any of that. Especially right now. You were doing something?"

"Oh that's right." He shimmied from his jeans and shorts fairly quickly before returning to the bed with a condom. His hands slid up the inside of her thighs and paused, looking at her for long moments where he said nothing.

"You have no idea how fucking beautiful you are." He moved his finger faster. "I figure I need to take the edge off and then get down to serious business. You had a rough night. I need to fuck the stress away."

She wanted to laugh but the way the leather of his belt dug into her wrists, the way he'd been so...*elegantly* rough with her, it lay on her heavy and narcotic. She was bound, yes, but in a ritualistic sense more than in reality. One hard yank or the words and he'd free her immediately. Which meant she struggled, but not too much.

The first orgasm washed over her like the tide coming in. Gradually filling her until she burst and it ebbed away.

She sighed happily, sagging against the belt.

"Well I know I feel better. What about you?"

"Definitely. I'd give you a thumbs-up, but you know, tied up."

He grinned. "Yeah, you are. It's really fucking hot." He said this as he rolled a condom on and sidled up to her, pulling one of her thighs up as he dipped into her pussy a few times until he slid all the way in.

"Oh, that's very nice."

He pressed a kiss against her shoulder as he wedged himself halfway beneath her. Having her arms bound above her head meant she was out there on full display for Royal. The way he touched her, kissed her, looked at her, fucked her, talked to her, whatever made her feel so beautiful. Desirable.

She arched and he slid deeper with a grunt. He filled his hands with her breasts. It was nearly too much, being this exposed to him. The covetous way he touched her. It was dirty and raw and she loved it.

He nuzzled her neck and she practically purred. "You still with me?"

She hummed, rousing a little. "I am and I'm pretty

glad about that." She was warm and pliant, and she made his dick hard and made him laugh at the same time.

All his protective instincts had been awakened, and they ran through his bloodstream like adrenaline. She'd known it and had appreciated it. Each beat of his heart was an echo of her name as he thrust into her.

This rhythm was right.

Each time they touched it was like that. That sudden *click* of knowing and of being known settled in.

He was glad his hands had felt well enough to roam all over her body. He moaned as his fingertips found her clit. Still slick and puffy, and when he stroked it, she tightened around him so hard he cursed.

She'd been threatened and he'd been there to help and he was pleased he was there to get in between Caroline and danger. Pleased too she'd allowed it and had sought strength from it as well.

And then he'd tied her up with his belt. She'd been as surprised and aroused by it as he had been.

Not just the belt or the way he'd controlled her, but the way he'd stuck up for her. When she was in Petal, how many people could she count on like that? And yet she'd come back because she loved her family that much, and they didn't all care for her nearly as much in return.

He shoved that from his mind at that point.

Right then it was just Royal and Caroline.

She came violently enough that the clasp of her inner muscles was nearly painful.

"Yes," she sighed out.

"Yes, indeed."

And then he was coming so hard his back teeth tingled.

Loath to leave her, he kept his trip to get rid of the

condom quick and was sliding between the sheets to find her within moments.

This woman owned him.

She'd blown into town, into his life and had turned everything catawampus. But she'd tucked her hand into his and they'd run together. Odd and unexpected, yes. But it was also totally right.

"I don't want to protect you because I think you're weak. It's the opposite. You're more than capable of kicking ass. I've seen it often enough I'm not surprised by it anymore. But you're too kind to the people who deliberately hurt you. And you give them a free pass because you're related to them."

"This topic is messing with my post-orgasm buzz."

"I know. I'm sorry. I just want people to respect you. It doesn't seem like it's worth it that *someday* people will know you were right."

"Once, my *abuela* said to me—we'd just lost a long-shot appeal and I was a mess—anyway, she hugged me, handed me a box of tissues and she said, 'Survive now, cry later.' When I prove he didn't do it. When her real killer is in prison, I plan to take a week off and cry the hell out of it. Retreat to my bedroom with my TV and lots of junk food and alcohol and a case of tissues."

Caroline turned to face him.

"It's not that I feel nothing. But I have to keep a lid on it. That's personal-ego shit. This thing with my dad? That's so much more important than my feelings being hurt because someone likes my sister better than me or whatever."

"Just when I think, oh yeah that's my favorite thing about her. That's the moment when I just totally fell for her! Whatever, you know what I mean. Those moments that are when everything makes sense and you just look at her—or in your case, me—and you're certain. So I've had a few so far. I was thinking, until right now it was the night when you had it out with Anne." He grinned and then kissed her, hard. "You claimed me."

"Of course I did! Did you expect me to be all, *oh no, she had him first and longer, I'll just get out of the way?*" She shook her head and then settled, resting on his biceps as she looked up at his face.

"What *did* you think?"

He'd said it like a tease, but he did want to know. He had entertained in the back of his mind that she could have reacted like that. Bowed to some weird idea of fair play.

"I thought, *fuck that*, she had her chance and she threw him away. This man who is everything and she just let go. That she didn't let go all the way didn't matter to me because *fuck fair*."

Her expression went very serious. "I'm honest. I want you. I wanted you to choose me. Why would I not fight for it? You came into my life well after you ended your thing with her. You've had your affairs and short relationships between she and I. If it was going to happen, it would have. If she'd have really wanted you back, she'd have come and taken you back." He winced and she frowned. "I'm sorry at how that came out. I just meant I wasn't going to toss away this fantastic thing that I love and makes me happy for some dumbass movie idea of honor and fairness. She had her chance. You're mine. I'm not giving you up. End of story."

He drew in a deep breath, snuggling her up to him. "I'm yours. And you're mine. I'd have been a little pissed if you hadn't gone about the thing with Anne the way you had. It's hot when you claim me."

She laughed and he brushed his fingertips through her hair. "Fair warning, if I see Benji or Garrett there will be trouble. I'm saying that up front. I don't care about how your grandparents feel. They're the ones who should have handled this long before now in Garrett's case. I want to be totally sure both men understand they need to keep away from you and not speak to you or about you. And then it's over. If they do what they're supposed to."

She sighed. "I hate this. The problem with a guy like Benji is that the attention only makes him worse."

"Whatever. I don't care to play games with assholes. I most definitely need to underline that he's going to be starting a war he can't win so he needs to back up and keep away. Garrett is a shit stirrer but he's a weasel. Goaded Benji on but kept behind him the whole time. And when it went too far, he panicked. He hadn't even given thought to the possible outcomes of what he'd done. That recklessness makes him dangerous to you. He's going to try to hide behind your grandparents, but that's not going to stop me. They gave him a safe spot to snipe at you. I won't let that continue."

"You know it'll cause some sort of ruckus. He's not worth it. He ran off to call my sister right away. He'll scamper over there first thing and eat at their table while he frames the situation the way that serves him best. If you get in the middle of that, it only makes things more complicated. And pulls you into all that drama."

"First of all, if your objections were like, 'I don't want you to do this. This is my business,' I'd back off. But you aren't saying that. Second, yes he will rush over to Mindy and then to your grandparents. And there's nothing you can do about it. They could ask around and get more information, and if they do they'll know what really happened. But chances are they won't. Shep will defend you. Do some asking himself and come to you. But they'll still have a tendency to ally with Garrett and his version of events. My being involved won't make that any worse. It only creates some boundaries. Caroline, these people can't be allowed to do this to you. This is detrimental to your well-being."

Caroline knew if she just said the words—*I don't want you involved, this is my business*—he'd back off.

Knew too that he was right.

"It just makes me cringe. Knowing you see all this stuff happening."

"It would reflect poorly on you if you ever instigated it. But you don't."

"Jail sucks and you don't have a rich daddy with guilt issues to bail you out."

"You wouldn't part with your ill-begotten defense-attorney gold for me?"

She laughed. "Maybe. But my rates are very dear and my enforcement is very…vigorous."

"Damn. Makes me want to go out and break rules to find out just exactly what that punishment would be. Would you keep me captive only to sexually pleasure you all day long?"

"That sounds like something I need to add to my list." She closed her eyes and sighed happily. "Good night, stud."

He kissed her. "Night, beautiful. Love you."

Caroline smiled, cracking an eye. "Love you too."

Chapter Sixteen

"Oh wait. Can we stop by my place? I borrowed three books from Melissa and I need to take them back to her or I'll forget. Again. Which is why I have three of them."

Royal had gotten up at five, and she'd tagged along with him as he'd worked. Mainly she watched and listened, but a few times she'd jumped in to help.

It made for a much more fun showering process when she had to wash off all the dirt and dust too.

But he was in a damned good mood between how well his crops were doing and having morning shower sex. "Of course." He found a spot to park at the curb on Main a block or two up and walked. Circling back to find a cop car in the alley.

Shane Chase came down the steps and saw them approaching.

"What's going on?"

Royal kept his hand in hers and walked fast enough to stay ahead of her and between her and any trouble.

"Were you here last night?" Shane asked as they reached him.

She shook her head. "No. I was with Royal at his house until about fifteen-twenty minutes ago."

"When was the last time you were here?"

"Last night. After I got off work, I came here to change for dinner with Royal. He arrived to pick me up at six thirty. We drove to his house, dropped my stuff off and then went to dinner. I'm sure you heard the details of *that*. And then at eleven thirty, we went back Royal's place."

Shane wrote a few notes and then spoke, "Your apartment's been broken into and ransacked. Your front door is broken so we know it happened after one when your neighbor came home. He said everything was fine when he got home from his date. But that date left at ten to ten this morning and noticed your door had been broken and only leaned against the jam. She told your neighbor who then called us."

Royal snarled. "Oh great. Sometime between two and ten? Ask Benji or Garrett. Both of those losers came at Caroline last night. I may have punched Benji. In self-defense though. I caught the fist he'd aimed at her head as she'd sat there, unaware he was going to sucker punch her in the temple."

"I've spoken with several people who saw what went down as well as to the officer on the scene and Elliot Charles over in Millersburg. They back up your account. But it wasn't Benji. He went home and promptly got into a knock-down drag-out with his brother, who he'd found in bed with his girlfriend. He ended up in jail. Where he is even now." Shane shrugged.

Impatient, Caroline interrupted. "Can I go in and see what's going on? I mean is this a *buy some new sheets and repaint over graffiti* thing or *oh boy call the dead-body-clean-up specialists* sort of situation?"

Shane smiled at her joke and then got serious again.

"More than the first and less than the last. Just brace yourself."

"What about Garrett?" Royal was satisfied, for the moment, with Benji's alibi, but there was another person who'd be capable of this.

"One of my guys is waiting at the golf course. I gave instructions not to go get him off the green. He'll only make a big deal of it. We'll intercept him as he leaves."

Royal had been about to be angry over that, but Caroline sighed, clearly relieved. "Thank you. He's going to make a big deal no matter what, but I can't even imagine what he'd do if you came up to him during his golf game. That audience is already predisposed to him anyway."

"He's a pain in my ass." Shane rubbed the back of his neck. "Come on and check it out. There's not a lot to find. My crime-scene people left about three minutes before you two came around the corner."

Royal took her hand as they followed Shane up the stairs.

She gasped when she saw her door. It looked like someone had messed with the jamb and wall where the locks were and punched around it. It wasn't on both hinges though, so it leaned drunkenly against the wall.

"Your landlord is out dealing with getting a new door, so someone should be by soon enough to get the old one out and the new one installed," Shane explained.

Inside, the sheer level of destruction was bad enough that even Royal gasped.

All the pictures she'd had on walls and shelves had been pulled down and stomped or crushed with something. Broken glass from the frames was everywhere.

Caroline had her hand pressed up to her belly. Royal took the other one.

"This is personal." She let go of her stomach to wave a hand around the room. "They could have stolen a lot of stuff they broke instead."

Shane nodded. "I won't know for sure until I work through all the facts, but I'm leaning toward that, myself."

She carefully stepped around the remains of the recycled soda bottle glasses she drank her orange juice from every day. "I bought those glasses back in law school. It was a running joke that I have to buy new dishes once a year because I break them so often, but we've never actually broken one of those glasses."

Royal squeezed her hand.

Her bedroom though. Caroline paused, not totally able to stop the sound at the sight of what they'd done.

Her dresser had been emptied. Her panties and bras and shirts and pajamas and those few pieces of sexy lingerie she had lay strewn over every surface. Some of them had been cut to ribbons.

Her pillows had been shredded, though her bedding had fared slightly better. But the antique perfume bottles she'd started collecting about seven years before had all been broken and stomped.

The glitter of blue shards of glass made her heart break. Her favorite. *"Oh."* She swallowed back her tears. "That was art nouveau. I bought it when I was able to pay myself the first time after setting up my firm back in Seattle. Such a silly splurge. But it was so pretty."

Royal heard the tears in her voice, even as she cleared her throat he could see how upset she was. Every few minutes a fine tremor worked through her, and her eyes were wider than they should have been.

He knew she was trying to hold it together so he'd give her something to do. "Did you at least have renter's insurance?"

Caroline nodded, her vision clearing a little. "I do. But some things can't be replaced. There just are fewer of those things left. That's a real shame. Who does that?" Her last words were close to a sob.

Shane stood in front of her, taking her attention from all the devastation. "Caroline. Hey. I'm sorry. This is terrible and I'm sorry it happened to you. But I need you to keep focus so I can figure out if anything is missing. Sometimes this sort of destruction can hide the theft of something small for weeks or months until everything gets cleaned up and it all starts getting replaced. People just don't notice everything. I need your help."

She swallowed and straightened. "You're right. I'm sorry. Um. I don't have much expensive jewelry but I do have a lot of costume stuff." She bent to pick up several bangle bracelets. "Like this. Doesn't look broken so there's that." She stood and looked around. "Royal, can you take pictures, please? The insurance company might like that."

He hated to walk away from her but she had pulled herself together. He knew her motto about surviving first and crying later so he leaned in to kiss her. "All right." This way was better anyway. He'd chronicle the damage, and she would be spared at least having to take pictures of it.

"The few pieces of more expensive stuff, mainly art nouveau, some hair combs, a sapphire brooch and earrings to match. I wear the ring all the time though." She raised her hand to show her right index finger.

"This is my jewelry box, but I keep the valuable stuff

along with my handgun in a safe attached to the underside of my bed." She went to her knees and felt around. "Still here and closed."

"Just check to be sure."

She opened it and put the handgun on the bed along with a box of ammo and the clip, which was stored apart from the weapon. "I have all the necessary paperwork on it too."

"When did you get a gun?"

"I've had it for several years. One of my old cases came complete with a crazy person and death threats. I got it and learned to use it then. This is the same box of ammo I bought like four years ago. I haven't even gone to the range in something like two years." She flipped open the box holding the jewelry. "It's all here. Like I said, it was just a few pieces." She put it back and stood again, dusting off her pants.

In the bathroom, it was a mess of her lotions and creams with soap and shampoo drizzled all over it. Some of her clothes had been tossed in the bathtub and then covered with whatever had been within reach. Her shoes had been tossed everywhere, and she nearly broke down when she saw that the ridiculously high and delicate stilettos she got in Paris had been totally destroyed.

"I cannot even with this guy. He needs to be punched in the butthole a few times."

Shane barked out a surprised laugh.

Royal spoke up from where he took pictures of the ruin in her closet. "She's full of wisdom just like this."

"I'm special." She opened her medicine chest. "Um, stuff missing. I had to get dental surgery and I had leftover pain meds from it. I also had leftovers from something else. They were both probably expired."

Shane wrote on his pad as she walked out into the hallway.

"This whole hall was full of framed photographs," she said, stepping carefully over the piles of broken wood and glass from the frames.

The office was a mass of torn paper.

"Those were strapped to the walls." She looked at the wall where the bookcases had once stood.

Shane looked close. "They've been cut. Hacked at, so probably a knife."

It was like that all over the place.

An hour later after Shane and the rest of the police had left, she called her insurance company and arranged for someone to come over and for the police report and photographs taken to be sent to her agent. The door had been replaced and she had a set of new keys and she still did not feel safe in the slightest.

She also found it interesting that Royal had taken on a hard outer shell over the last half an hour or so. She wasn't sure if it was about her or him or what had happened, but as he was still being sweet to her, she figured it was anger at the situation and she sure empathized. She'd give him the space. Heaven knew she needed it right then as well.

"I need to call Melissa. Jesus."

"You call her and you tell her she and Clint are invited to dinner at my house tonight. That'll give us time to get this mess dealt with. And you can make a list of whatever you'll need and we'll get the important stuff and tomorrow we can hunt down clothes for work and that sort of thing."

"I've got clothes at your house. I just did laundry there. Two suits and some other work stuff. My birth control pills are at your place, along with my makeup. My journal and laptop. Thank goodness for that, I've got work on it."

Royal was glad to see her getting herself together.

"Let's see what we can salvage here. My office is plenty big for you to share with me. Especially when our work is really so different. Or you can use the kitchen table if you prefer. We'll load some stuff into your car too and you can drive it to my place."

"What? Wait, what are you talking about?"

"You calling Melissa and inviting her. That's step one."

Which she did. Melissa was outraged and immediately offered her a place to stay if she wanted, and when Caroline had said thanks but no, she'd also offered to come over and help her clean up.

"You know how when you're all worked up and mad and on the verge of tears? I just need to work it through a bit. I'm not okay right now."

Melissa made a soothing sound. "I got it. We'll see you tonight. I'll bring some of what we have here for the barbecue. Definitely all the makings for margaritas."

"Yes. Thank you."

"Call me if you need anything before I see you later on, okay? I'm glad Royal is there with you."

Caroline hung up, tucking her phone in her pocket.

Royal put down the photograph he'd managed to save from the mangled remains of a frame and took her arms.

She smiled, but she was pale, her pupils still too big. "They'll be at your place tonight. I feel so bad cancelling on her."

"Was she mad?"

"No. Not at all."

"Problem solved. Now as to the second thing. You're

going to move in with me at least until this whole mess is figured out."

She nodded. "All right. Thank you."

When she didn't argue, he truly got how frightened she was. Which made him so angry he had to breathe through his nose several times until he'd gotten himself back under control. "You're not going to argue with me?"

"Hell no. I'm freaked out. In all the time I've been an attorney, I've never had anything like this happen to me. This is scary and awful and I hate it."

"I'm not going to let anything happen to you. You're going to be with me at my house. Spike will be happy to have you so he can ride around on your shoulder all day long."

"He prefers it when I simply accept that he's in charge."

He laughed, kissing her.

"All right, let's make a list. I always feel better when I make lists." She pulled a pad from her bag. "I have multiple copies of all this paperwork. The originals are at my office right now as well. This wasn't all my furniture anyway. I have a storage unit where ninety percent of it is until I buy a house. My bed is destroyed, which sucks because it took me forever to find just exactly the one I wanted."

"It wasn't destroyed. You could salvage it."

She looked at him and her eyes brimmed with tears. "I can't. Someone came in here. Came into my house and touched my things. My underwear! My books and my pictures. I don't even want to think about what makes up that mess all over my clothes in the bathtub."

He ached for her. This wasn't something he could really make better.

"All right. How about we go get some rubber gloves

and garbage bags? We'll throw the clothes away if you like."

"I don't know about the ones in the tub. I just…" She looked at them with a shudder. "Yeah, no I can't. I'll always wonder so it needs to go. I have a bunch of stuff that I took to the cleaner on Wednesday. I'll need to grab some underwear and stuff. I'll order them online from my favorite place back in Seattle. They won't arrive until the end of the week or so, but I've got enough for now at your place. Is it all right if I use your washer and dryer?"

"Baby, I want you to know you're welcome to use anything and everything I have."

She nodded again. "Yes, let's get bags and then we can have throw-away bags, closer-examination bags and keep bags."

They locked up and headed down the street to the hardware store to grab gloves and bags. It was pretty clear the story about the fight the night before at the Pumphouse had spread around town. They received some dirty looks here and there. A thumbs-up several times. Most of it though was just sort of general nosiness and staring.

When they returned after stopping at the Honey Bear and getting some provisions since they hadn't eaten in hours, they began to do what they could to set things to rights again. The throw-away pile was larger than the keep pile. He ran loads down to her car and his truck, packing things that they could keep.

At the end he handed her a pile of photographs. "This is everything. I think many of them can be saved. I know someone who can touch them up, clean up some of them. Others have been ripped."

She'd had three photo albums. One had been thrown

in a sink full of water, but the other two had just been spilled all over the ground with the others.

She looked through the stack of pictures. Some of them she had duplicates for at her office. All the important ones were in Atlanta at a shop that was making albums for her siblings.

"Looks like several of the ones with the worst damage are of my mother like Shane had thought." Which was creepy. Ugh. Caroline looked through again and once more. "This is everything you say?" she asked Royal.

"Yes. I mean there were some that were torn, but in large pieces so you could tell which went where. Why? What's wrong?"

"There are two photographs missing. One of my mom taken about a year before she was killed. We'd been on a camping trip in Tennessee. The other is one taken when I was camping with my aunt, uncle and cousins. My aunt had it framed for me as a gift because I looked so much like my mom. Her hair had been up in a cap and mine was in a bandana."

"You need to call Shane right now with this."

She agreed, calling the number he'd given them before he'd left.

Four hours later they'd done their best, and she was worn thin and needed a shower and a drink and to be away from there. She didn't say anything out loud, but once all this was handled, she was going to find a new place. She couldn't stay there. Not after the break-in. It didn't feel safe or secure. It didn't even feel like it was hers.

"My grandmother has called and left four messages." She looked at her phone and tucked it back into her pants.

"We're going to drive back to my place where you're

going to soak in my tub while I make us a drink and come join you. Don't call her. Not without me around."

"I've been talking to that woman for thirty-one years now."

"Yeah and it cuts you up every time. You're cut up enough for one day. Let me be there to give you some support when you talk to her."

She shouldn't let him take over like this, but it felt good to just nod. "Okay."

She'd reached her car when Edward and Polly rolled up in their Caddy. Polly got out and rushed over, concern on her face. "Oh, honey! We just heard. Are you all right? Do you need a place to stay? Surely it's not safe here now."

Edward had managed to get Polly's door closed and their car parked before he came over.

"Shane mentioned that you'd had a terrible break-in when we dropped Drew off at his and Cassie's place." Edward took her hands, examining her face carefully.

She looked back and forth between Edward and Polly. "Royal has been here with me the whole time. Helped me clean up. The door is replaced and I have a new lock. The landlord also put a new hall light in, this one is a lot brighter."

"This is just terrible."

"It is. But I'll get over it." She shrugged, and this time Royal put an arm around her shoulders. She shouldn't have to *get over it*.

"She's staying with me for the next weeks."

Polly beamed at him, and Edward's brows went up but settled just as quickly. "We were heading back now. I need to wash a lot of clothes, but at least I have them. I was lucky in a lot of ways."

Edward leaned in and kissed her forehead. He spoke quietly to her for a bit until she nodded, mute, and he took Polly's hand and stepped back. "We'll see you tomorrow afternoon. Be careful and let us know if there is one single thing we can do, big or small." Polly winked at Royal and then turned her attention to Caroline again. "I mean it."

Caroline nodded. "Of course." Caro had regained a little color, and for that, he'd be grateful for Polly and Edward coming along right when they did.

Polly's perceptive gaze took Caroline in from head to toe, and she gave Royal a discreet eyebrow raise that said, *take care of this woman.* He nodded back.

Bright smile back in place, Polly looked to Edward, who picked up several tote bags and gestured them in Royal's direction.

"Before you go, I made a little something. Figured you'd appreciate the break from having to cook or go out."

As heavy as they all were—all four of them—he figured they had enough food to last at least three days.

Caroline hugged Polly one more time, thanking her. They all walked back to Royal's truck and Caroline's car and after more hugs and admonishments to rest, they were finally back on the road to Royal's place.

A little something—Royal discovered as he began to unload all the stuff Polly had brought—meant what appeared to be a meatloaf and also fried chicken along with mac and cheese, roasted potatoes, corn, fresh bread and two pies.

All sorts of comfort food he could hopefully tempt his woman into eating. She'd retreated a little, saying she had to put some boxes away and take her shoes off, but he knew she also needed some time and space to get herself under control again.

Caroline wandered in with bare feet. She looked at the fridge, jammed with food. "Plenty of food for dinner tonight. Who keeps spare fried chicken around?" She shook her head. "I bet she just handed over their dinner. Edward said they'd been to Cassie and Shane's and that's where she found out about the break-in. What they didn't say was that they went back home, she finished up the chicken and potatoes and then brought them over."

"Probably. She's sneaky. Come on. You need a bath." He picked up a bottle of red wine and two glasses, following her to the bathroom where he put it all down and got the bath filling.

She allowed it, even when he pulled her clothes off she was a little withdrawn. Which he had every intention of dealing with once they were a little more relaxed.

"No one is expected here for two hours. We will bathe. We will drink some wine and talk about today. Later, I'll watch while you put makeup on and do your hair, and then friends will arrive and we'll have a nice dinner."

She looked dubious but she got in with a hiss and a groan. She sipped her wine while he got his clothes off and then into the bath, settling behind her with her body between his legs.

"I'm really glad I chose the biggest tub they had in this style."

"It's a great tub," she agreed sleepily.

"So, some fucking crappy day, huh?"

She was quiet a long time, gathering herself. "Most people didn't know about my father right away. The older I got and the older the people I met got, the less incidents

I'd have with people who were hostile and never spoke to me again, or more commonly, distanced themselves slowly but surely after they found out and just disappeared from my life."

Her gaze sharpened as she came back from her memories.

"It's a hot button for me. I'm defensive about it."

He scoffed. "I'm consistently amazed at how well you keep your temper. I'd be flipping tables and punching people. But you manage to say *fuck you* by just doing whatever you want anyway."

Pleased at the compliment, she continued. "I've met a lot of different types of people over the last fifteen years or so that this has been in my life. Sometimes it's hostile. Usually it's curious. Open. I've had people yell over me when I was speaking at an event and that sort of thing. But you know before I moved back here, I had a pretty normal life. I had a great job. My coworkers are some of the smartest people I know. I had a fantastic house with a view of downtown Seattle. I had friends. I went out and did stuff.

"This business with Benji and Garrett is distressing. In my life before now, I'd have handled them both. I'd have ignored most of it, but I most definitely would have pressed charges against Benji for nearly hitting me. I'd have told Garrett off so hard his ears would have bled. But this is different. Everything is different, and I'm off balance and freaked."

He tightened his arms around her. "I'm here with you."

"I know and I'm really glad. I gave up all that other stuff, a community, my own firm, a great house, and I came here. Here where people are hostile to me all the time. Here where my family—the ones I moved back here for—are hostile but for one. My apartment got broken into. My panties were handled by some creep! Damn it, that bra I threw away was perfect. Someone broke into my home and touched my stuff and destroyed my things. My memories. My perfume bottles."

She hadn't noticed at first, but survival was over and the tears were coming hard and fast.

"I don't cry in bathtubs! I don't have to deal with the police about anything I ever did. People don't ransack my house. I don't have men trying to punch me in restaurants. This isn't my fucking life."

She'd gotten to that gaspy, hiccuppy crying point where he couldn't understand a word she said, but held her tight and murmured various comforting things anyway.

Finally she ducked under the water completely until the noise died away and then she resurfaced. He held up a bar of soap and a washcloth. "You're dirty."

He started to scrub her back, around each shoulder and down each arm to her hands.

"But I find I like my job. It's not Seattle, I don't have a view and lunch at five-star restaurants weekly, no. But I make a difference. For the most part I like my clients. I really like the people I work with."

She forged ahead, needing him to know how he made her feel.

"And I have you. Which is the biggest and best thing about being in Petal. Everything else I could take or leave, or manage from far away. But you? You're here with your hands in the dirt. And what you do changes lives. I love that. I love that you're doing something so amazing with your land and your life."

Surprised pleasure lit his face. "I'm a simple guy. A farmer."

"Sometimes it's the most simple things that make the biggest difference. Your successful farm is good not only for you and for all the places you sell your produce to, but to the community as a whole. Not just in health benefits, but it brings money to the area. And you've done something to me. To my life. You make me see things differently. And I like your house on this rise with the land spread out like a blanket all around. I feel safe here. With you. I like life when you're in it. When your cat is riding me like I'm his horse and cleaning my head as he does it. I feel very much under siege right now, but less so because of you."

He started to clean some of her better parts, and she gave him one raised brow. He showed her where he thought his dirtiest part was and urged her to get it nice and soapy.

After an hour they hopped in the shower, cleaned up and then got out so they could get ready for dinner. As she walked past him, he stopped her by taking her hand. "You make my life better when you're in it too. I know how much you gave up, but I'm sure glad you've found some of the things here worth the trip."

She kissed him. "Yeah, you'll do."

Chapter Seventeen

Melissa held a bottle of beer Clint's way. "So do you think the guy heard you on the first broadcast or later on one of the syndicated spots?"

Both Royal and Caroline narrowed their gazes as they leaned toward Melissa. "What? Syndicated?" Caroline asked.

"Oh my God, you didn't know?"

"No! I had no idea. I mean, the host guy said they sometimes used the shorter spots to fill out empty air but since my story was more local he wasn't sure."

Clint spoke. "I heard it on my satellite radio when I was working in my office last night at like midnight I think. Melissa heard it during drive time on the local affiliate. The satellite station it was on was one that's sort of statewide legal issues. I bet if you got hold of the guy he'd be able to get you that info. Shane probably needs it for the case."

"Meh, it's a burglary. It's not like anyone is going to make a big deal out of it. People's houses get broken into every day."

"Clint is right, Caro. There's a threat here. The vandalism and theft of the pictures say this is personal. They're going to act to protect you if for no other reason." Royal paused as he ate the rest of the chocolate cream pie Polly Chase had given them earlier. He'd protect her either way.

"I have a friend who produces *Good Day Atlanta*, and I told her about you and your story."

Caroline looked to Melissa and then Clint. "You're full of surprises."

Clint laughed. "She wants to talk with you about maybe doing a spot. A local *if you have any information call this number* sort of segment. She said it's like a three or four minute spot so not huge, but you'd be expanding your audience."

"Wow, that would be incredible."

"I'll get your contact info to her then."

"I really appreciate it. Media is so big and it has the chance of helping. But also, well it's so big I don't know how to get attention focused on it. We made a video and uploaded it to the internet too. Ron, the investigator, he's on the ground doing all this stuff. He's checking the tip line and forwarding relevant things my way. Nothing major so far."

Melissa hugged her as she walked by. "I'm sorry this happened to you. I'm worried about your safety."

"Right now we don't know if it's some jerk who got all bound up because a woman dared to have an opinion in public or if it's the real killer. The first is way more likely."

Royal uncoiled himself from where he'd been pretending to lounge. "She's staying here at least until she finds a new place that's far safer. I know her landlord, the guy likes money, but he won't hold her to that lease. Not after this."

"That means I have to drive in each day. Ugh. I hate that part. But it's really not that far, and it's better than waking up to find a weirdo having broken into my apartment standing over me."

"Not a fan of this type of joke," Royal murmured, and she leaned forward to kiss him.

"Sorry."

"Good. Hopefully that will work in my favor when I explain how I'm going to drive you to work and pick you up every day."

"We'll talk about that later." *Puhleeze.* She didn't need an escort to work for goodness' sake! But when he got all protective, it made her tingly so she'd let it go for a while longer.

"You mean you'll indulge me but eventually think I'll take no for an answer." He grinned at her, totally on to her game.

"Until the sex is done at least," she said in his ear.

"Go ahead on if you think you can withstand all my persuasive ways."

She laughed, hugging him.

They hung out for another hour or two before Melissa and Clint headed out.

Royal turned to Caroline. "Glad they came over. I like them."

"I do too." Melissa was the first real friend she'd made since moving to Petal and they'd become pretty close. "She's smart and funny."

"And a bit of an outsider too."

Caroline nodded. "Yes. She knows what I'm talking about in ways no one else does."

"I'm sorry you feel so alone."

She took his face in her hands, glad they were both sitting so he wasn't towering over her. "I have you."

He smiled. "Yeah, you do. But having other friends is

important. I'd like to hope you also feel that way in the future about my group of friends."

"I like your friends. I mean, we had a rough start, but they're all fine now. And I get it. Their loyalty was to Anne first. In some ways it's nice to see the way you all come together the way you do."

"Nicer when you're part of the us-versus-the-world stuff though."

"Agreed."

He pulled her into his lap. "Now, I believe I have some persuasion to work on."

Shane held up the disc containing the possible worthy tips and the scary calls from the tip line. "I listened to them all. Of the two tips that caught your attention, I think one has merit. I'll have one of my people check in with the county to see if there was a road crew out doing any work around the diner. I'd hope it was addressed then, but—" He shrugged and tried not to appear angry, failing. The sins of the old chief were heavy on his shoulders, Caroline knew.

"The other one I definitely don't think. That dairy drive-through on the corner had been torn down two years before the murder."

She nodded. One usable tip in the few days after the radio interview wasn't bad. Sixteen years after the murder too. She had to hang on to this new way of dealing with the case and hope that she'd find a way to process the lack of control.

"As for the threat. You've got a male who references your radio interview and that he knows where you live. Since you had a break-in following that radio interview and the destruction was quite personal, I don't think it's a stretch to wonder if the two things aren't related or if this is more than one person. These tip lines aren't much help, but I've got someone on it. Right now I don't know much, but I know enough that I don't like it, Caroline."

"I don't like it either. My renter's insurance will write me a decent check. They're replacing my clothes and shoes. But so much was ruined. Books and photographs. A stranger was in my home. I don't like that one bit! He touched my things. Read my notes. Stole a picture of me and one of my mother. 'Cause *that's* not creepy at all."

Shane reached out and patted her hand. "I know this is awful. I'm sorry. I can promise you we'll do all we can."

"I appreciate it. I'll get in touch if we hear anything else. I'm at Royal's for the time being. On the days I don't have to leave town, he even says he'll drive me. Insists. Says. Suggests." She snorted. "I'm going on television next Wednesday. So it may bring a lot of attention or nothing at all. You know how this goes sometimes."

"You're going to need to be extra careful once you do that. This guy who's behind the threats and break-in isn't going to be happy about you taking this stuff out to a wider audience. And if he's the real killer, he's already killed at least one woman and let another person go to death row. That's what we know. What we don't know is far likely worse, and so he's going to be eager to shut you up. Keep aware of your surroundings. If anything looks or feels weird, I want you to call me."

She nodded. "All right."

Justin walked her out. "You hungry? I haven't had lunch and I'm starving."

"I think I'm still allowed to frequent the Honey Bear. It's breakfast for lunch special day."

"Score."

* * *

"Hey you."

Caroline looked up to find Anne Murphy standing there. "Hey, Anne. What are you up to?"

"Decided to come have Belgian waffles for my lunch. With strawberries and whipped cream."

Caroline took a risk and scooted over. "We were just about to order too. Care to join us or are you meeting someone?"

Anne slid into the booth next to Caroline, across from Justin.

Anne and Justin exchanged hellos as their drinks came out. Caroline had ordered her usual, and Anne paused in her chat with Justin to look at Caroline's drink. "What's that?"

"Cherry vanilla coke. Best thing ever. Mrs. Proffit has the hand of God at the fountain, I swear."

"Oh yes, that's it. I need that in my life along with the strawberry waffles." Anne gave her order. Justin and Caroline ordered food as well.

"How are you today anyway? Did you talk to Shane?"

"Yeah. We were just at the police station." She and Royal had gone over to the Chases' home the night before for a freakishly huge and yet oddly intimate gathering. There had to have been at least thirty people there, and yet they all seemed to like each other and have a close relationship.

Edward had come to stand next to her as she looked out over all the kids playing in the backyard.

"I just wanted to tell you how much I admire you. I know things are unpleasant right now. And scary. But I wanted to say this is your home. You are Petal born and raised. That you were elsewhere for fifteen years doesn't

*matter. Petal's in your blood. You think I'm being sen-
timental and old right now, but in about ten years, after
you and Royal have had your wedding and your babies
and you're dropping them off at school, you're going to
remember this moment and you'll understand exactly
what I mean.*

*"It takes courage to believe in something when ev-
eryone else doesn't. You have a steadfastness of spirit
that I am in awe of. It makes you a wonderful attorney.
You have a persistence of affection and loyalty to your
parents. They'd be very proud of you today, I promise
you that."*

*Caroline had blinked back tears, and Edward had
continued to stand there with her. Not saying anything
else or needing her to respond. He knew she was getting
herself back together and he let her do it.*

*Finally she sucked in a breath. "Thank you. I needed
that."*

Shaking that memory, she focused on Anne. "Anyway, they're looking into the threat and one of the tips."

"Why don't you and Melissa come out on Friday? We
thought Margarita Friday needed to be brought back.
So Beth's hosting. Bring something to eat, but we won't
shame you if you bring chips and dip. Accept that Tate
will always make something way better than whatever
you bring or you'll get a complex. Maggie is also a great
cook. I call dibs on dessert."

"Oh you sneaky bitch!"

Anne paused and then laughed, bumping her shoulder against Caroline's. "You just called me a bad name
in an affectionate way. I'm sorry to tell you that we've
become friends."

"I know. You're not too bad once someone gets to know you a little."

Justin choked and Anne winked.

Caroline drizzled berry syrup over her pancakes. "I'll talk to Melissa. I think she'll be up for it. I'll also let her know about the food thing."

Considering how insane her life had gotten this lunch was so remarkably normal and nice. She'd missed that.

After a nice carb immersion they all headed out, Anne going one way with Caroline and Justin going the other.

The rest of her day was awesomely absent any kind of drama, and when she got home it was to find Royal in the kitchen, making dinner.

He smiled at the sight of her. "Thanks for calling to let me know when you were leaving." He put a spoon down and moved to pull her into a hug. "I like it. You being here with me, I mean. Knowing you're on your way to me. When I heard you come in, it made my day."

"You're being very sweet. Did you accidentally leave the door open and Spike got his claws on my boots?"

"A guy makes a mistake once!"

She gave him a raised brow and he snorted. "Whatever. My cat has not ingested any of your items of clothing. It just occurred to me that I was happy and I wanted to tell you."

And then he showed her right after dinner. Twice.

On Friday she'd driven in because she'd needed to attend a deposition held in Riverton. She'd parked a block away from Main so she could come and go quietly. There were spaces out front but the firm liked to leave them for clients. She ran to grab some lunch for later that day before heading in.

Lunch she'd been eating two hours later at her desk when Holly came in. The look on her face brought Caroline to full attention.

"Sit down. What's wrong?"

"Your car was vandalized. I saw it as I was coming back in from lunch. I've called the police too."

Alarm. Fear and dread. Anger. All married in her gut. "Okay. Jesus. What all happened?"

"Paint splashed everywhere. Tires looked trashed. I didn't look a whole lot closer. I called the cops and got back here."

Caroline put her pickle down and wiped her hands. Unflappable Holly was most definitely flapped.

Caroline sat there and knew someone was out there who wanted to scare her, and she was not a fan of that at all. But it had to be dealt with so she got herself together and took a deep breath.

"Of course. You did the right thing. Thank you for calling the police."

She was going to have to tell Edward, Peter and Justin. Was going to have to call the insurance company about her car. Call Royal. Yeah, that was going to suck. He was already pissy that she'd come in on her own. He'd said he'd take her to Riverton and then take her back to Petal. She'd refused but he was going to be extra worked up over it.

First things first.

It was Shane who showed up not even two minutes later. He caught sight of her and shook his head. "I thought you were supposed to stay out of trouble."

"I was eating a turkey sandwich at my desk!"

"Let's go on over to look."

They headed out and then down around the corner

where she'd parked thinking it might be better to keep it low key and come and go quietly. Ha! More like perfect to vandalize during the day.

Her car had had buckets of paint poured over it and the tires were slashed. Nothing that made much noise and so no one had noticed it right away.

She sighed. "Good Lord."

Shane had taken some photographs, helped her get her belongings from it and lugged the stuff she'd had in her car back to the office. On the way she'd even contacted her insurance who then arranged to have the car towed to Joe Harris's shop to be repaired.

She gave a statement, which was easy since she didn't know much other than when she'd arrived.

"I need to run now. I have a hearing."

Shane slid his notebook back into his pocket. "I'll take you over to the courthouse. I have to go that way anyway."

Five minutes later she stood outside the courthouse. She pulled her phone out and got Royal's voice mail. If he was on a tractor or working near machinery, he wouldn't hear it anyway. She let him know that her car had been vandalized and she was having it towed to Joe's shop. She then asked him for a ride and said if he couldn't, she could probably grab one from Justin, and she had her keys to his place so to just call and leave a message because she was getting ready to go into court and that either way she'd see him later.

And she kept her head in her job and went about doing it.

Chapter Eighteen

Royal had come back to the house after being out in the fields all day when he noticed he had a voice mail from Caroline.

He called her back and got her voice mail. "I . . be there," was all he said.

And then he'd changed and was in his truck heading into town, and when she'd walked out of the front doors of the courthouse he waited there.

After a stop by Shane's office. Shane-the-cop didn't say a whole lot but Shane-the-friend told him Caroline had looked a little shell-shocked but left him to go off to court and she'd had her focus on work.

She did seem to thrive on her job. And if it could help keep her mind off as much of this damnable mess as possible, that was a positive.

She wore a suit that day. With trousers and, he knew without a doubt, some sky-high heels. He had no idea how she stood it, especially with all the walking she did, but she seemed immune. Or maybe she was just a good actor.

The charcoal gray of the suit was pretty on her. She didn't have on an overcoat, but the edge of her suit jacket flipped a little in the breeze, and he caught a glimpse of the red silk blouse she wore underneath.

She was put together and really pretty, and then she turned, her attention shifting from her colleague to Royal.

She lit up when she caught sight of him, smiling and saying goodbye to her colleague. He knew he grinned right back at her. Just making another person react the way she had—because of him—meant so much.

In four more steps her hand slid into his as he brought it to his mouth to kiss her fingertips.

"Afternoon, Mizz Mendoza." He tipped his hat and she blushed.

"Hi. Wow you're handsome. I could have met you at the office. I'm sorry you came down here."

"Look at you with your sneaky compliments. Thank you, darlin'. As for the rest? Whatever. You're down here, which is more than enough reason to come this way. Plus I can be with you instead of you haring all over town with a fucking psycho out there who needs a punch to the face with my bumper. Are you all right?"

They started walking back to where he'd parked. "I'm fine. It sucks, don't get me wrong. I just got a new paint job before I came back to Petal. That metallic black was hard to find, damn it. My tires were slit. It needs new tires, to be sanded and primered and repainted. My doors have been keyed and the slot for the key on the door has been bent and there's metal stuck off down inside. The fob for keyless entry works though so at least there's that. Thank God I was paranoid and locked up or he might have gotten inside."

They ran up to her office and grabbed a box of things before loading them into his truck. "I need to work a little this weekend, but I have a thing at Beth's tonight. Melissa is picking me up at six forty-five."

He put her in the cab and dug way, way deep before he got back in on the driver's side. He headed out of town.

"Don't," she finally said, breaking the silence.

"Don't what?" His voice was so ruthlessly careful it just underlined how much he knew exactly what she'd been saying.

"Really?"

He groaned. "Okay, okay. But no, I have to. Don't go tonight. Stay home with me. Where I know you're safe. This whole thing is fucked, and I normally wouldn't ask you to not do something. I respect your independence and that you have friends you hang out with and heaven knows I'm pleased the thing with Anne has worked out."

"But?"

"Look, Caroline this isn't okay. Someone is trying to scare you. Someone *is* scaring you. This is a murderer who sees you as a threat, and I'm sorry you have to change your daily schedule, but it's insane to go out right now. Do you think I could go play pool while you were off with our friends? Exposed. No. Don't ask me to do it."

She sighed, leaning back against the seat. "You're right. Let me call everyone."

But Beth wasn't having it. "No way. We aren't giving in to this guy. If anything happens, he'll be stirring a big hornet's nest."

"No, Royal's right. Some of you have children. Lily is pregnant. I don't want to call any attention to you guys. It's not worth the risk."

"Are you sure?"

"Yes, I really am. I'm a little wobbly right now. It's sort of been a few weeks, you know? You guys have a

good night and a good time. I'm going to call Melissa
and tell her she's still invited though if she feels up to it."

"Yes, please do. And I'll call her too to follow up. Hon,
take a long hot bath and sleep in and just try to forget
this mess for tonight. We'll see you soon."

"Thanks, Beth."

Caroline hung up, called Melissa and reassured her
she was all right. It wasn't like Royal was going to let
her out of his sight anyway. She hung up after promising to call the next day to check in.

He hated that she had to cancel a fun night with
friends just when she was finally starting to build a life
and community there in Petal. "I'm sorry... I know it's
unfair."

She sighed. "You were right. I don't want to be the
cause of anyone getting hurt. But now you're stuck with
me. You're not going to want me at your place alone either. I could go with you to the Pumphouse, but honestly just thinking about going there tonight makes me
a little nauseated."

"I'm not going anywhere. You and I are going home.
We're going to have dinner and I'll let you try to beat
me at Mario Kart again. Then we do lots of sexytimes."

She burst out laughing.

Once they got back to the house, he checked out the
inside, and once he'd done that, he headed out to make
sure all the motion-detector lights were working while
she started making dinner.

Shep texted her that he'd been thinking a lot and
wanted to get together to talk if she had time that weekend, and if not he'd talk to her on Thursday.

It felt positive. He didn't say much one way or the
other but if he didn't believe her, he'd just say so up front.

Or drop the topic. Maybe argue? Certainly not mention a regular get-together if he was mad. Right?

She'd been buttering the bread she was going to pop under the broiler when she heard the front door open up.

"I just got dinner started. We had some chicken so I'm sautéing it now to get a good crust and then I'll pop it into the oven."

"Okay."

He sounded odd so she looked up to find him coming into the room with her grandmother.

Caroline hadn't even been able to tell him about that part of her messed-up day yet. She looked to Royal. "Yeah so when you got back inside I was going to tell you I finally connected with my grandmother today. In the hall. Outside a courtroom." It was a memory she'd cringe over forever.

Her grandmother sniffed. "I don't know what you expected. You've been avoiding me since the vulgar fistfight you got into at a restaurant in town."

"And as I said to you, *I* didn't engage in a fistfight vulgar or otherwise. Garrett and his friend Benji started on us. In front of a crowd, so if you'd like to talk to one of a dozen or so people, let me give you their names. But no. You come down to my place of work, one of the few places in this town when I do not have to worry if I'm measuring up, a place I am respected, and you came in there and started an argument with me in front of the judge I had just argued a motion to. *That* was vulgar."

"You've done nothing but start fights and trouble since you came back to town. I'm really going to have to ask you to stop seeing Shep for a few months. I don't like your influence on him."

"That's not going to happen. He's old enough to decide for himself. And yes, I'm fine thank you. I figure you came out here to check on me after my home was broken into and vandalized and then my car was vandalized today. You must know," Caroline said, cutting off her grandmother's avenue of escape, "since you came out here instead of to my apartment. I'm a little—no actually—a lot shaken up because my mother's real killer is poking around trying to freak me out."

"You stop this right now." Her grandmother's gaze went so hard and sharp Caroline stepped back. "*You will stop.* Your father, Enrique Mendoza, killed your mother, my daughter, Bianca. He died in prison, and I'm sorry I didn't get to see him take his last, tortured breath. Every time you tell someone that monster was innocent, it's a slap to your mother's memory. You don't care about her. You never have. You were a selfish child and you're a selfish adult. At least she's not alive to see what a terrible person you've become. Stay away from my family."

Caroline stood there, utterly stunned into silence. Her grandmother's mouth was set in a hard, angry line on her face. This was a woman who was implacable. There was no talking to her at this point. She'd decided Caroline was the enemy and would slash her as hard as she could to wound her so she could get away.

And leave her shit hanging on Caroline to carry around like always, and Caroline was so done with that.

"Anything to keep from admitting you might be wrong. Oh my God. For so many years I did all I could to make you love me. To make you see that I was still the same Caroline who used to make brownies in your kitchen. But you won't. I can see that now. You will rip me apart to keep me from showing you you might have been wrong all these years. That man is out there right now, and that you would rather be here making me feel bad instead of working with me to catch him says so much about you. You need to be careful too."

"Is that some sort of threat?"

"For heaven's sake! No. It's a warning that a crazy person is out there."

"You're just like his people." Her grandmother put her handbag strap firmly up on her shoulder once more. Arming herself. "Shep and Mindy were spared the contamination of his genes, but you got more of him than they did."

"Mrs. Lassiter, enough!" Royal interrupted. "Stop this. You're saying a lot right now that you can't take back. You need to think about the way you speak before you say it out loud. Furthermore I can't allow you to stand in my kitchen and hurt Caroline."

"Get her out of your life before she wrecks it like she did ours."

Caroline ruthlessly shoved every last emotion down as far as she could.

Royal stalked to the door and yanked it open. "You told me you wanted to make things up with her, and then you used that lie to come into my house and attack your granddaughter. I do think Bianca would be ashamed. But not of Caroline. Now get out of my house and off my land."

Abigail stalked out, and he watched until she got into her car before slamming the door, locking everything and turning to face her.

Caroline was frozen. She felt like if she gave in to any one feeling that it might all go terribly bad. Royal approached her slowly, taking her upper arms. "Oh my

God, sweetheart, I am so sorry. She told me she wanted to make up. I never would have let her in if I'd known."

"Of course you wouldn't." Her tone was faint, but firm.

"Caro? Talk to me. Tell me you hate me or that you want to punch me but don't go all silent."

She shook it off with a deep exhale. "I don't hate you. I love you. I'm just so horrified and embarrassed and angry and hurt and a whole lot of other things, but none of them are pleasant. I don't know how to put it into words."

He pulled her into a hug, rubbing his hands up and down her back, slowly, soothing them both.

Royal didn't know how to make it better. How to fix it or make it right. He swayed with her there, her nose nuzzled in his shirt, head over his heart.

"Just because someone shares your DNA doesn't make them family, Caroline."

"I know." She turned when the kitchen timer went off. "I need to flip the chicken. It feels like a gravy kind of night, what say you?"

"Every night is a gravy kind of night."

He prowled around while she made dinner. Spike trotted along after Royal, making her laugh.

They ate dinner and played Mario Kart and she totally lost. Again.

Back in the bedroom after they'd closed everything down for the night, he'd come in and waggled his brows. "Well, Ms. Mendoza. I see you've lost in my gaming hall tonight. And yet you say you're lacking funds. However will you pay your bill?"

He hopped up onto the bed, and she followed, straddling his body. "I've been told I dust topless really well."

"Ms. Mendoza, everything you do topless you do well."

She started laughing, and he went in for the kill, raining kisses all over her neck and jaw all the while unbuttoning her pajama top.

"I'm so glad you kept the beard." She petted it, loving the way it felt. "It's so sexy."

"Then I'm glad too. I like it when you pet me."

She kissed the top of his head as he continued to kiss her skin. He pushed the sleeves of her shirt down, letting the fabric pool at her wrists.

He slid his palms all over her upper body. From her throat down her chest, circling her nipples and then down to her belly and hips. "Course I like to pet you just as much."

She arched into his touch.

He backed up enough to get his shirt off and returned, pulling her close, all that skin against all that skin. She sighed happily, snuggling into him.

Somehow amidst arms and legs, they managed to get naked and back snuggling. It had started to rain, and the sound of it on the window made her feel better.

He flipped them both onto their sides and kissed her slow. Heat began to tingle in her toes, seeping upward. Caroline gave back as much as he gave her, their tongues sliding against each other.

His taste brought her home. Gave her a stillness inside that allowed her muscles to relax.

"Let me love you, Caro," he spoke, lips against hers.

She relaxed utterly as he kissed her eyelids and her cheeks, her ears and her jaw. Down her neck as he breathed her skin in. Warm and sensual, like a perfume made just for him.

He tasted her, loving her the way he knew she liked best. After he'd made her come, he made his way to the chair across the room and sat. He crooked his finger, and she moved to him, climbing into his lap and sliding her body down his cock.

It was quiet but for the pounding of his pulse in his ears and the sound of ragged breath. Just Royal and Caroline in the dark. He'd know the weight of her, the feel of her mouth on his in the darkest of rooms.

After another orgasm for her and one for him that hit so hard he nearly fell out of the chair, he carried her back to bed.

She turned into his body when he got in with her. "I checked all the locks and the outdoor lights. Everything is secure."

"Thank you." She kissed his chest and snuggled back in tight.

Chapter Nineteen

Royal watched Caroline kill it in her television spot. It was just three minutes, but she'd spent pretty much the entire week going over those one hundred eighty seconds.

She had such a beautiful voice. A little husky in places where she was most emotional. Her Southern had returned in the two months she'd been back, and it worked for her.

Caroline connected with the host and with the camera. She knew her cues, and the whole thing was over in a flash as she was escorted off, replaced by the new guest. The producer gave her some info and thanked her.

"This calls for a fancy breakfast." Melissa gave Caroline a big hug. "You did so well."

"I have many talents," Caroline joked.

Royal put his arm around her shoulders as they headed out.

"I'm starved and in dire need of coffee." Royal had opted for his Charger instead of his truck. He opened the passenger door, and Melissa slid into the back and Caroline got in the front.

Her phone started to beep as they headed out of the main snarl of the city where the studio was located.

"I most definitely vote yes on the Honey Bear." Royal

looked over briefly at his woman, so sexy he really wished they were alone.

Melissa asked, "Do you feel better? I mean that you did this? No matter the outcome, you managed to do this. I'm proud of you and happy and sad too because I know this whole thing is rough, and oh man do I want to punch your grandma. Yes, I know that's disrespectful and all that, but she is a terrible person."

"I'm relieved. Anxious still, but there's only so much I can do and I'm doing it. Everyone has been so kind with all these offers to help." Caroline smiled. "So yes, for this moment, I do feel better. Even if nothing comes of it."

They arrived in Petal, and he found a place to park just a few blocks from the Honey Bear. Melissa made them sit down and headed back to the kitchen to get some breakfast started.

Caroline leaned on him. "Thank you for coming with me today."

"Darlin', there's nowhere else I'd rather be."

She smiled. "Look, I know you have work to do today." He had work to do every day. A farm always had something that needed doing. It was amazing, how much work he did. "You can go back home. I'll just walk to work and get some stuff done."

He frowned at her. "What on earth would ever lead you to think I'd do that? You took the entire day off work."

"Only because I wasn't sure how I'd be afterward. Truly, I'm fine. There's no reason for me to waste a day off."

"With what? Leisure?"

She rolled her eyes. "You have a job to do. A farm

that needs running. You can't spend all your time baby-sitting me."

"In the first place, I can do whatever I want. And in this case, I want to be with you. Yes, the farm needs running. But I'm not the only one who can do it. Everything that needed doing today is taken care of. That's enough. We'll eat and fill up and make sure Melissa is settled, and then you and I are going back to my place and spending the rest of the day in bed. Napping, fucking, reading. We'll stop at the store on the way home for provisions."

How on earth could she refuse?

Which is how she found herself naked in Royal's bed eating ice cream from the carton and reading a novel.

He snuggled up at her back, one of his hands on her hip.

They'd had so much sex she had sore muscles in places she hadn't known there were muscles.

Her skin smelled of him.

"One of my favorite things is how I can smell you on my skin during the day."

He rustled, taking the ice cream and putting it off to the side and pulling her closer. "Yeah?"

"I'll be in court or off doing something, and I'll move or shift and it hits me. Just a wisp of your scent on me." It made her happy. "Like a talisman."

He kissed her neck. "I like that. I love coming back here for lunch, and when I first walk in, I see one of your sweaters on the back of a chair, or I catch a hint of your perfume in the bathroom. I like having you in my life every day."

"Man, you already got it. *Four* times."

He laughed and turned her to her back. "Never enough

where you're concerned. But you're safe for now. I think I need to drink a few gallons of water to rehydrate after the last three hours."

"You make me laugh. Thank you for that."

He kissed her slow, and despite her satiated state, desire still rose when he touched her this way.

"You make me *happy*." He rested his forehead against hers before easing himself back to the bed. "I'm a pretty easygoing guy. My general mood tends toward affable."

She nodded, looking up at the way the late-afternoon sun cast sharp shadows on the ceiling. "It pleases me to be around you, and yes, part of that is this *us* thing that makes me happy, but you're a positive person. It's rarer than it should be."

"Thank you. But there's happy and there's *happy*. You know what I mean?"

"I think so, yes."

"I have a good life. My business is doing well, and that means I've managed to start pulling the farm into the next century. I have nice friends to hang out with. A house that fits me. I dated around and enjoyed things physically when an opportunity arose, and I wanted to accept it."

Caroline growled and he snickered.

"So I had no complaints. I was happy and centered and successful, and then you. I turned my head and I saw you in the grocery store. I watched you contemplate just how you were going to get that box down, and it was like, *wow, there's a whole deeper kind of happy*. Because I thought about you all the time until we finally managed to run into each other again—mainly because I was coming to town daily."

"Thank goodness. I do like a go-getter."

"And there was this connection. I tried to tell myself it was the newness of it. But I've dated before. Enough to know the difference between new-relationship excitement and this fifty-foot-high series of deep ocean waves that came with you. Exhilarating, that's what it is. You're powerful and you have so much energy and it's terrifying and sexy all at once. Knowing you'll be what I see when I wake up each day makes me happy."

He went quiet as she lay there, happiness coursing through her, a smile on her lips.

"You make me *happy*, Caro. In a way that I wasn't craving because I had no idea it even existed until you."

"I'm pretty lucky you love me." She rested her leg on him to touch more, be closer. She *was* lucky.

"You've been having a time of it. You okay?"

She blew out a breath. "This is all so overwhelming, and yet here you are, helping me through, making me believe I can do it."

"You have been doing it. For over a decade before I came into your life."

"Like I said, it's different now. All the stuff I've learned how to do isn't as useful at this point. I'm not a cop or an investigator. Sometimes I feel like I'm drowning in all this. I'm scared I'll mess up. Scared of whoever it is out there who wants to hurt me." That was the worst part. She hated being scared, and she'd gotten used to plowing through the world without fear. And in a matter of months, everything in her life had changed. Some, like the long, tall handsome man next to her, were good changes.

Being scared made her feel helpless.

So many aspects of this new reality with her mother's murder were not only out of her hands, but something she just didn't have enough of a handle on to feel super confident about.

She wasn't a wait-and-see sort of person. But now she had to be, and on top of that, she had this creepy-stalker deal going on.

"Point taken. Things are different, yes. This isn't a legal-system issue. You're a rock star there, so I can understand why the shift is distressing. But you're doing everything you can. Your friends are doing all they can. You have allies here at the Petal PD and over in Millersburg too."

"I'm trying to keep it all copacetic. Trying to remember I can't control everything, and that people who are awesome at their jobs are helping. Most of the time it works. Right now so much is happening, and I'm so glad I took this afternoon off with you because I really needed to let go of all that out there and focus on what's in here. This is the most relaxed I've been in a while. I can't hide forever. I have stuff I really need to think about but not right at this moment."

"Good answer. Do you see how it works out when you just listen to me and do what I say?"

She closed her eyes. "I guess I should listen to you more often. I'd much rather be here than in court. It's way harder to have an orgasm there."

He snorted. "Since I'm nowhere near the courthouse ninety-nine point nine percent of the time, I'm fine with that."

Caroline said, "By the way, we're going bowling tonight."

Royal groaned. "See this was going really well until you brought that up. I thought you liked spending alone time with me."

"Hush you. You know I do. But you have this long-standing thing you do with your friends and that's tonight, and I'm trying to get to know them all too so I'm coming along."

"I want you safe, damn it."

"I can't hide in your house all the time. Not that the constant sex isn't a wonderful way to spend my time, but I have friends and family and so do you. We have lives here in Petal, and we're also building one as a couple. I want to be safe too, believe me. But I'm not just going to stop living because this freak is out there. I'm panicked he'll run for it, so I need to stay somewhat visible so he'll keep trying until we get enough info that we find out who he is and he gets arrested."

He sat straight up. "*You are out of your mind*. No. No, Caroline! Let the authorities handle this. This isn't a television show. This is way out of your area of expertise."

She gave him a look. "The only reason I didn't just punch you in the throat is that you're scared and so am I so you can have some slack. Of course this isn't a television show. I'm not an idiot."

"You need to not take stupid risks. You need to tell Shane what you're doing so he can make you stop this."

"Stop treating me like I'm stupid. I'm not outside wearing a bull's-eye calling out, *you hoooo, mr. murderer* or anything."

"You don't get to be mad at me for being freaked." He narrowed his gaze at her and her anger sort of drained away.

She sat across from him. "I would if I wanted to." She frowned, and he sighed, but there was a smile bubbling up. She took his hands. "I'm sorry for taking for granted

that you were just fine. You're freaked too. I hate that
I've brought this into your life."

He growled and she found herself on her back. "You
didn't bring this. This was just beneath the surface all
that time. All those years your father did time he didn't
deserve, all the time you've been apart from your hometown and your brother and sister. This piece of garbage
needs to be caught and put in jail, yes. I just hate that it
makes you unsafe. Hate it. But this is not your fault except when you think you can act as bait. Not going to be
okay with that, Caro. Not at all."

"Okay, can we just negotiate here a little? I can't be
inside your house all the time I'm not working. It just
isn't feasible, or even really a life I want to live. Plus,
it's been my job all along to put the person who killed
my mother in jail. I have an intense job so being socially
active helps me burn that off. So how about for the time
being I go to things if you'll be there? Otherwise I'm at
work or here."

"What's the situation with your brother and movie
night? I'm obviously not down with you going back to
your place. But if you do, I want to come along. I won't
interfere with your time with him or anything."

"He's coming here instead. That way you can do your
own thing or hang out with us, he's fine with that too.
He likes you. He was told not to come over here, but he's
too old for that sort of control."

Royal had such a goofy look on his face she didn't
know how to take it. "Are you mad? I'm sorry I didn't
run it by you. I figured it would be a good solution for
everyone involved. I can meet him somewhere else too."

Royal shook his head and kissed her quickly to re-
assure her. "Not mad at all. Just the opposite. That you

just did something that indicated you were comfortable enough to invite your brother here? It means a lot to me."

"Oh. Well, carry on then."

"Shep coming over is totally fine with me. I think your proposal is a good one. Not that I like the idea of you out and about at all, but I get it. Thanks for giving in a little. I know it's hard."

"Not like this is something I'm an expert on. I'm feeling my way along here."

Thursday started out on such a high note. There was excellent morning sex, which was just a ruse to get her up afterward and make her run. Running sucked. You'd think a man like Royal would stick with the backbreaking physical nature of his job but no. He exercised too, and he liked to watch her run so who was she to refuse him? Even if she got all sweaty and it was running. She liked to think it was excellent training for the zombie apocalypse.

Then after a nice hot shower, she'd had a great hair day, her skirt made her look taller and they'd had some breakfast and she got to simply watch Royal being Royal.

Royal was a complicated man. The thing was, you first started off thinking he's one thing because he was all slow Southern charm. He seemed mellow and laidback. But that ease only covered the foundations of a very strong and in-charge man. A man who had no hesitation in claiming her, or protecting her. He had opinions, yes, but Royal was a magnetic force. He pulled all sorts of stuff around him like an orbit. He was steady and smart, and he had a certainty she saw in herself.

He moved around his kitchen, handling multiple tasks without breaking a sweat. Pouring this, flipping that.

Caroline sighed at the flex and play of the muscles in his forearms, the stretch of denim at his thighs as he knelt.

All the while he knew she watched. And sometimes he gave her a show, left her breathless.

So she'd ogled his ass and eaten with him, and he'd insisted on driving her to work, which he did, also insisting on coming up and into the office with her.

"Dude," she told him as he came around to her door, "you don't need to come in with me. It's seven so Peter will definitely be here already. Our paralegal comes in early Thursday and Friday so she's there. Secretaries. Holly the goddess. I'm good. You have a farm to run."

He walked next to her. Because this was now part of her workday, he didn't hold her hand. He respected her space and her need to keep her work life and romantic life separate. Which was another thing about him she loved.

He pushed open the outer doors and Holly was at the front desk. Before Caroline could shoo Royal back to work, Holly stood up, and by the look on her face, the news wasn't good.

"I just left a message on your phone."

Caroline dug the phone from her bag. "It wasn't on yet. What's going on?"

Edward Chase came into the reception area. "Ah, you're here. Come on back. I've called the police."

"About what? What's going on?" Caroline followed him, and Royal walked next to her, lending her all that strength. It made her feel better.

Edward indicated a legal-sized envelope on the table in the conference room. "When Holly showed up about ten minutes ago, this envelope had been left."

"She touched it?" Royal asked.

"We get stuff left all the time. Clients leaving papers,

that sort of thing. Sometimes the legal messenger service we use will leave end-of-day reports if we're not here when they finish up," Caroline explained. But that meant there was something about the envelope that upon closer examination meant a call to the cops.

Holly came in with Shane. "Good thing I was in early this morning. What's going on?"

Holly spoke this time. "I like to come in a few minutes before seven to get everything prepared and to have a cup of coffee in peace. When I opened the outer doors, this was on the floor. You know like someone pushed it under the door. There were a few other things with it so I scooped them up and put them down while I made myself some coffee. When it finished I brought everything back to my desk and went through it, putting it all where it went. Mr. Chase came in right then, and when I pointed it out to him, he told me to call the police and then Ms. Mendoza."

"What's it say?" Caroline reached for it but Shane held her wrist a moment to stay her.

"Let me. I have gloves."

"God, if this is just a motion or run of the mill *lawyers are the devil* hate mail I'm going to be so embarrassed," Caroline muttered.

Shane held it so she could see how it was addressed.
Caroline Mary Mendoza.
Deliver to her next of kin.

"Oh sure, not scary at all." Royal groaned. "Why don't you step back, Caroline? Why don't we all step back? Who the heck knows what's in there? It could be someone's will or anthrax."

"Royal is right that you should all get back. It feels like paper. There's no grit that I can sense. But let's be safe."

She let Royal pull her toward the doorway where Peter and Justin now stood.

Shane pulled out what looked to be a photograph, and he paled, covering quickly, but not fast enough for her to miss his initial reaction.

He looked in the envelope and pulled nothing else out. He examined the photo and sighed. "Caroline, I may have to call in some people above my pay grade."

Caroline moved to his side and saw a picture of her. She'd been sitting at a booth with Royal at the Honey Bear. Her eyes had been scratched over with black X marks and a black line was drawn over her throat.

They'd used black ink over Royal's clothes to make it look like a black mourning suit.

She might have fallen over if Royal hadn't put an arm around her waist.

"Call in whoever you have to, Shane. This is fucking not okay." Royal shook his head. He was at the end of his patience with any and all this bull. Nope. "I apologize, Holly."

"This is an F-word situation, Royal," Holly agreed.

"What's going to happen now? How are you going to keep her safe?" Royal didn't want to do anything else until they knew.

"Working on that right now. I've got your statement, Holly." Shane put the envelope and the picture in two different evidence bags. "Caroline, anything you want to add?"

"I came in and I knew something was wrong because Holly had a look on her face and then Edward came out and brought me back here. You came in shortly after that."

"Has anything else happened since the car vandalism on Friday?"

"We've been at home mostly and it's been quiet. There are some new calls on the tip line I haven't heard yet. I checked yesterday but not yet today."

She'd held off after listening to some early on and getting upset. Most were useless. Then there were perverts and weirdos, and some hostility. Royal had encouraged her to let Justin and Ron handle it like she'd agreed to do or at the very least take a break until the following day. He worried this case would consume her, but understood her need to push until she got the job done. It was part of who she was and a big reason why he loved her.

She called Ron and he played the messages over the speakerphone.

Shane got a pad to match the one Caroline had already placed at her right hand along with her pen.

There were four more messages since they'd checked the day before. Nothing pressing but Caroline took notes on one.

Ron told them he'd just checked the email tips, and there wasn't anything connected or even vaguely threatening but he'd contact them both if that changed.

Shane scrubbed a hand over his face. "I'm going to call some people. I'm going to tell you I don't think we'll get much help. This is bad and I take it seriously, but there's not enough for us to operate on the sure knowledge that this is connected to the murder. Which *I believe it is* so don't get that stuck-out chin on my account. I'm on your side. I'm going to have that envelope and the picture printed. One of my younger officers just got back from an eight-week forensics-training program. He's going to wet himself over all this. Pretend that's not weird."

"I have no weird stones to cast." Caroline snorted. She'd been sassy when he brought her in that morning. Happy and chatty. But her spine had slumped a little and there were lines around her eyes.

"What's your plan today?" Shane asked.

"I have three client meetings, some research to do, a few motions on the calendar later at the courthouse. Lunch sometime in there. Then home to Royal's place. My brother is bringing pizza and *28 Days Later* over at six. Then sleep. Or as much as a certain cat will allow because he likes to sit on my chest and lick my hair. Now that is weird."

"Spike's just concerned for your well-being."

"Your cat is weird."

As the cat liked to sit in the corner facing inward and stare at a burl in the hardwood floor, he really couldn't argue. "Whatever. You carry him around on your shoulder."

She snickered.

Shane shook his head. "Go about your business today, Caroline, but be aware. I'll have someone from the police department cruise by regularly during the day. Nothing's happened out at the ranch?"

"Nothing," Royal answered. "The house sits on high ground so it's pretty hard to approach it without being seen. I've got motion-detector lights around the outside. I've been extra careful about locking up too."

Shane stood. "I'm going to get on this immediately. Try not to go out alone if you can help it. Downtown Petal is busy enough during the day I think walking to and from the courthouse or to lunch is fine."

"I'm picking her up after she gets off work." Royal would be doing so from now on, even if he had to drive her to whatever business she might have away from town. There'd be spats, which was fine. It helped her to work through her frustration on him, and it made for super hot make-up sex too.

She shot him a look but didn't say anything. But he knew it would come out later. His lovely Caro was chafing under all these controls in her life.

"You'll keep me apprised?" She rose and they walked with Shane to the outer door.

"Of course." Shane's attention snapped to his father, who walked out to join them. "I need the tape of the footage from the hallway."

"There's a camera here?"

"There is, yes. Actually there are three. However they're offline for a week. Some part or other burned out and it's on order. It's legitimate. It won't be back on until next Tuesday."

"Convenient." Shane looked annoyed.

"These folks have been doing the security cameras here for us for six years now." Edward sighed.

"Doesn't mean it's not on a schedule somewhere. Or someone's brother/boyfriend/neighbor whatever relayed the info without meaning to. You'd be surprised." Shane made a note. "I'll check on that." He looked up at Caroline. "I'm going to get this straight, you got me? I don't like people who threaten women." His expression darkened, and Royal remembered Shane's wife had been repeatedly stalked, attacked and nearly killed by an ex so he had a hot button on this issue.

Caroline blew out a breath. "Okay. Thank you."

Shane said goodbye to his father and left.

"You need to go to work." She looked up at him, her

mouth set in a way that told him she wasn't going to hear any answer but yes.

But he wasn't sure he should give it to her.

"What's your schedule today? Do you have to be out a lot?"

"Come into my office, please."

Holly gave him a sympathetic look as they passed by. She closed her door. "Look, I understand you're feeling worried. *I'm* worried, believe me. I take my life very seriously. But I really can't have you hanging around here all day on the off-chance something will happen and you can stop it or save me or whatever. You have a ranch to run. You took all of yesterday off and it's spring. Go. I mean it. I'll see you at quitting time."

"Caroline…"

"What? Come on, Royal. If I can't walk around in broad daylight in downtown Petal or be in my office, I may as well just give up. I don't want to give up. This guy has stolen enough from me. I'm a badass! I can't be badass with you loping around looking all sexy and wholesome at the same time. I'll be distracted and you'll be distracting just because you're you and then I'll be annoyed and you'll be hurt that I'm annoyed because you're just being nice. Which you are. And I appreciate it. But you have to go. I'll see you at five thirty, and if I need anything, or anything else comes up, I'll contact you immediately. I'm not stupid."

"No of course you're not stupid. But you're fun sized. And this guy could be Shane's size or bigger." He touched her cheek briefly. "You *are* badass. Without a doubt. But you're fragile too. Going to be impossible to get anything done today knowing you're here without me."

"He's a coward. He's not going to put himself in

harm's way. He'll come at me again, but it won't be as I'm walking three blocks up to the courthouse. This isn't over. I know that's not a statement you're comforted by and I understand. But until we figure out who this is, he'll be out there and threatened. We have to hold on until it's finished. I'm sure this isn't the way you imagined falling in love with someone. I come with a metric shitton of baggage."

"You think I care about that? Scratch that. I *do* care but not like you think. It makes you who you are. Since I love who you are, it's just a fact that it's something we'll get through together." He kissed her nose so he wouldn't smudge her lipstick. "I'll go. But, please, if there's a problem and you can't reach me, call my aunt and uncle and they'll come find me. Promise."

"That's fair."

He hugged her and left her to her day, which looked to be incredibly busy, and she supposed that was a good thing because it kept her from obsessing or freaking out.

Chapter Twenty

Shep came in with the pizza and a smile. Caroline led him through the house to the kitchen where Royal was feeding Spike.

"Hey, Royal."

"Shep. How's it going?"

"Well, I would have liked to know you got a death threat today." Shep gave her a face and she sighed.

"You're right. I'm sorry. I should have found a way to tell you. I wanted it to be in person, and I didn't want to go to the high school or the house. Silly when Petal is lightning fast with gossip. I'll tell you everything once we get settled."

Royal washed his hands and pointed at the paper plates. "You two should eat."

"You're not staying?" Shep asked Royal.

"I know this is your time with your sister. I just wanted to be out of the way."

Shep snorted. "She's my annoying sister, but since you're her boyfriend and she's living with you and all, I suppose getting to know you better is a good thing."

Caroline grinned. "See? I told you." She opened the pizza box and hummed happily. "Yay, pizza. I need to drown my troubles in melted cheese and carbs."

They loaded up and moved to the couch. She told Shep about all the threats and what the authorities were doing to help. He shook his head, clearly worried, but she assured him she was fine and everyone was keeping her safe.

"How can anyone deny our mom wasn't killed by our dad at this point? Clearly this is related to the murder and your reaching out for tips in the media. The person who did it is going to do all he can to shut you up. I don't want you to end up like her."

Caroline swallowed hard. "I don't want that either. I'm being as safe as I can without totally up and leaving town or traveling with armed guards. So, you believe me then? About Dad?"

He was clearly upset, but he was also a seventeen-year-old boy so he wolfed down five pieces of pizza before elaborating.

"I read everything you gave me. I did a lot of soul searching. I talked to Mr. Chase. He told me I could if I ever wanted to so I did and he's pretty cool. He thinks you're pretty awesome, you know?"

"Which Mr. Chase?"

"Oh yeah, whoops. Edward. I see them at church pretty often. When you first moved back, he told me if I ever wanted to talk about it he'd be happy to. I think he told Mindy that too. But."

It hurt a great deal to imagine this distance between herself and her sister would last any length of time. She'd come to Petal to get closer and she'd finally managed to totally estrange her grandparents. She still spoke to Mindy but with Garrett crowing all over the place about how horrible Caroline was, it was uncomfortable.

"Well, do you have questions or anything?"

"Just how can I help? I feel…guilty maybe? Bad. Sad. Angry. Resentful. I'm sorry you have done this on your own all this time. I'm sorry Grandma and Grandpa are so blind to this that they've pushed you out of the family. Maybe a little jealous that you had them as parents all those years and I never really did."

Caroline hugged him, kissing his cheek. "You get to feel how you feel. But I'm not mad and they wouldn't have been mad at you either. You know what you're told. And they never told you anything but this one thing. How could you have done anything else?"

"You did."

"I'm fourteen years older than you. You were two when this happened. I was nearly sixteen. There's a world of difference there. And you know, it sucks that Grandma and Grandpa are being closed off right now, but you have so much more family than you really know. They've wanted to see you since the murder."

His chin jutted out just like their mother used to do, and it made her smile even as it made her sad. "Yeah? Well where have they been then?"

"They tried to see you guys, but Grandma and Grandpa fought them so hard they were worried it would hurt you worse."

"Grandma told me they didn't care to see us if we didn't believe in his innocence."

"I'm walking a really fine line, Shep. For all intents and purpose here, you're their son." She wanted him to know, but this was complicated and she needed to step carefully.

"I'm nearly an adult! You're my sister. They were my parents. I deserve to know the whole truth. Why would they lie? Why would they push you and our other family away? I don't get it."

"Our grandparents loved our mother very much. This is a fact and I will never say otherwise. She was their golden light. A homecoming queen. She was prom queen and you know all that. Popular. Beautiful. Super smart. And here comes this guy. Our dad wasn't any of that stuff. Well scratch that, he was really smart. He went to UCLA and graduated near the top of his class. And he came here the summer after he got his degree and ended up working at the railroad depot. He was quiet. He worked really hard and he kept his head down, but when he met Mom, nothing could keep them apart. She brought home not the captain of the football team. Not the nice boy from church. But Enrique Mendoza."

"A common laborer."

"Yes, I've heard our grandmother use that description, though after the last time she said it in front of me, she never has again. Look, I gotta tell you straight, here's this gorgeous blonde girl from small-town Georgia and our dad, half-Mexican and half-Cuban, all dark skin, comes to town. The Lassiters believe people like that belong mowing lawns and nannying kids. Certainly not getting their daughter pregnant and marrying her."

Caroline, of the three Mendoza kids, favored her father the most. Where Shep and Mindy had their mother's fairer complexion and lighter brown hair, Caroline's eyes were deep brown and her hair so brunette it was black. After the funeral, her grandmother had said it was a shame that their mother was gone because everyone would simply assume she was *like her dad* and by that she'd meant the color of Caroline's skin. Abigail had covered it, or had tried to anyway, especially when her grandfather heard it and had reacted to his wife angrily.

But Shep had a lot of other stuff to plow through at

that moment, so he didn't need to know it all right then. And she needed to talk to Royal to get his opinion on how much to let her brother know.

The bottom line was having a relationship with her siblings. That he now saw the truth about their father was wonderful, but she didn't want him to feel like he had to turn his back on anyone either. He had a different relationship than she did with her grandparents for a whole host of reasons. He had enough to deal with right then so she'd be judicious as always.

"Anyway, the Mendozas had not only lost our mother, who they loved a great deal, but their son to death row. And I came out and they took me in and raised me and tried to deal with my anger and my grief and my utter certainty that our father did not kill our mother. They tried to see you. They hired an attorney. But, Shep, you and Mindy were so small and the Lassiters had been a regular part of your life. The Lassiters wanted the Mendozas to make no mention of our father or their belief in his innocence. They didn't want you and Mindy to leave Petal so they did come to visit you here several times. But our *abuela* was getting more and more frail, and it became really hard for her to travel. Danny, that's one of Dad's brothers, he came out here a few times but he and Grandma butted heads a lot. Anyway in the end, they backed off because they were worried about you and Mindy getting caught in the middle."

"You don't think Grandma would stop them from seeing us. She told us they never made an attempt."

"Grandma is a super strong personality, but she's also a fraidy cat. Know what I mean?"

He shook his head.

"She's so afraid of anyone around her believing in

things she doesn't. It's turned her into a person who will stop at nothing to keep her life free of things she doesn't like. Which is why she and I have such a complicated relationship. She truly sees any contact with Dad's family as a threat to her. I'll let them tell you if you decide you want to meet them. Our *abuela* is getting older though. I don't want to pressure you, but I don't know if she'll be around in a year or two."

"Abuela?"

"Spanish for grandmother. Just another kind of *nana* or *gran*. There's so much stuff for you to see and learn and experience with people who love you and Mindy. It's an open wound that they haven't been able to see you. I'm sorry, this is making you feel guilty, and they wouldn't want that and neither do I."

"I've always been curious about them. We don't have all our history. It makes me mad."

Caroline nodded. "I get that, and I can't blame you for that at all. It's been kept from you to protect you. I want to underline that. I don't agree with what Grandma and Grandpa have done, but they did it because they love you and Mindy."

"And what about you?"

"I have plenty of love in my life. I can't beg them for it. I don't even want to. But they loved Mom and they love you guys and somewhere in their hearts they love me too. They're old school. Interracial marriage was hard for them to accept then and I expect it is now too."

"Fuck that." He continued despite the look she gave him at his language. "They don't get to love the fairer kids and pretend the darker one doesn't exist and use your opinion about our father's innocence as a reason to keep you back."

She laughed. "Sure they can. They do. It doesn't mean I have to validate them for it. It's racism, yes. But let's move around this and back to the situation with the case. Yes, it's connected. There's no reason to think otherwise. Which means we need to keep pushing. We have a little momentum after so many years of nothing. My investigator is on it. He monitors the tip lines and all that. He'll follow up on stuff we feel is worth it."

"Can I make calls or anything? Make copies? Go with you when you talk to people?"

"I want you to keep out of this. I'm happy to update you, answer your questions, whatever. But someone is out there trying to hurt me because I'm making noise and drawing attention. He's not going to be the only one out to hurt me."

Royal growled but kept his tongue.

"What do you mean?"

"Shep, I'm taking something people truly believed and I'm ripping it from under them and announcing how wrong they've been. Most people will accept that and be glad the real killer gets caught and put in jail. They'll be sad they thought wrong but in the big picture they'll understand Enrique Mendoza was innocent and move on. It won't cost them anything really. But some people like Grandma and Garrett? They've invested a lot of negative emotion into this and how they believe. It'll seem like an attack to them. Those people are going to feel really defensive and angry at me."

"Nah. I don't think so. People will be fine."

"You have no idea. You're totally outside all the hostility because Grandma's opinion protects you. You're not seen as an outsider so I want you to think carefully about what you say and how you say it. I've had sixteen years to get used to it, but this will be new."

Royal broke in. "I stopped a full-grown man from punching your sister in the temple. In the Pumphouse at prime time. And before that, this same person nearly started a fight at the Tonk. I've seen people treat her badly once they know who she is."

Her brother looked so miserable. She got up to fetch him an ice cream bar and returned with one for herself and Royal too.

Handing it to him, she remained quiet as they got the ice cream unwrapped and got a bite or two.

"People will judge you. Not all of them, which is nice. But if you want to keep it quiet until after this is over, you'll have to deal with a lot less of it. There's no reason to do it now. You might lose friends. If you wait, people don't have to have that moment with you. You can find out with them, which will make them feel better about you."

"No way." Shep pounded his chest over his heart. "My whole fucking life, Caroline! My whole life I *hated* our father for killing our mother. He was near enough I could have visited him. I could have written him. He wouldn't have died knowing I hated him. I can't take that back or make it better. There's no way I'm going to just pretend the truth away because it'll be uncomfortable for a short while. You've handled it *alone* all these years."

She nodded. "Okay well here's another thing, I'm a target because of what I'm doing. I don't want you unsafe."

Royal masterfully managed not to snort, guffaw or roll his eyes as she made the same argument he'd made to her about keeping her head down.

"I don't need to go on television with you to be open about wanting to prove our dad's innocence. I won't write a press release, okay? But I won't pretend anymore or let Grandma try to shut me up."

"All right. But be sure the doors stay locked. Try not to be out alone, okay? If you see anything weird, tell Shane Chase." She went to her bag, found one of Shane's cards and brought it back to her brother. "This is his info. He's working on the case. He's a really good guy and you can trust him. Or you can call me. Whatever. Just don't ignore something you feel weird about."

Shep finished up his ice cream bar, had two more slices of pizza and quizzed her for a long time after that.

It was ten when she called a halt to the evening. "You need to get home. You have school tomorrow and your grandmother is already unhappy. Call me tomorrow or text me, whatever. You know where I am." She stood. "I have something for you. I've been arguing with myself about when and if to give them to you. But now, well, hang on."

Caroline went to the closet in the spare room she'd sort of taken over and grabbed the wooden chest.

"So," she said as she came back out, "every two weeks for every year Dad was in prison he wrote me a letter. I wrote him back all the time too, of course. It's very difficult to see people on death row, you know. It's not really geared at keeping connections with their lives outside. But later I got in to see him because we were working on his case. Anyway, I'm rambling. When he died, the prison sent his stuff to me." She handed the box over. "He wrote you every two weeks too. But he wasn't allowed to contact you guys. So he wrote them and put them in envelopes and addressed them and he never got to send them. I don't think Mindy is ready for hers. He was your dad, Shep, and he loved you. If you don't take anything else with you the whole of your life, know that. He would not want your guilt."

Shep's eyes brimmed with tears. "He wrote me?" He opened the box and pulled out a packet of mail.

"He did. I didn't open anything, but I bundled them by year just to give you somewhere to start. If you want."

Shep turned the bundle in his hands over. He pulled out a few larger envelopes. "Cards?"

"Every year for Christmas, your birthday and Easter. He loved Easter."

"Jesus. I don't know what to say."

"Then don't say anything. You don't have to read any of them if you don't want to. You can leave them here until you're ready. I don't want you to do anything you don't want to."

"No, I want to read them. Thank you for this."

She hugged him tight.

"And Shep? Grandma probably doesn't need to know about those letters. Just saying. She might not respond so well." She would burn them or throw them away or something equally horrible.

"Yeah. Got it. I'll talk to you later. You be safe."

"You too. Text me when you get home and then when you're safely inside."

He sighed. "Fine. God. Worrywart."

"That's what big sisters are for. I love you."

"I love you too, Caroline. Thank you. For understanding and for being patient and for these letters."

They didn't see the movie, but she and her brother were in an entirely new relationship and it was something she wanted to last.

Chapter Twenty-One

Tuesday of the following week she'd been standing at her desk, preparing to head out to lunch. A new email came in, and she reminded herself to turn that sound off because she was unable not to bend to look at her screen to see who it was from.

Then there was a crack and a slam and shattering glass and the thunk as the bullet hit the far wall.

She screamed and hit the ground. Adrenaline made her hands shake as she got her shit together with a mental slap. Now was not the time to lose it. She double-timed her crawl to the door, nearly arriving when it jerked open with Edward standing there.

"Get back!" she yelled at him. The last thing she needed was to get her boss shot on the job. She'd be lucky to keep her job after this as it was.

"I called the police," Holly called out.

Edward reached down, grabbed her under her arms, pulled her up and out of the room. Behind him, Peter yanked the door to her office closed.

"Are you all right?" Edward set her on the couch.

"Uh?" Caroline looked down at herself, still shaking. Her clothes had been ripped in a few places from the glass. There was a lot of blood though. "I think so. Someone shot into my office."

He knelt in front of her as Holly brought over the first aid kit. "Caroline, I need you to focus. Can you do that? Just give all your attention to what I'm saying." Edward's voice was emotionless but also sharp enough to keep her on track. Vaguely she realized he was talking to her like she was in shock.

"The bullet hit the far wall."

"Caroline, you have a lot of blood all over you." He and Holly brushed over her hair and her upper body and glass went everywhere. "I just want to be sure you haven't been really hurt."

"You're going to get glass all over the place."

He smiled. "I think we can let it go this one time."

The door burst open as police officers came in. Caroline recognized Matt Chase in his handsome blue uniform. He had one of those tackle-box things with a red cross on it, and she figured he probably did some sort of double duty as a paramedic when needed.

Holly took over as Edward got up and went to speak to the police.

"Will you call Royal, please?" Caroline asked Holly. "If this gets to him before I can tell him, he'll be worried sick and also mad."

"As soon as Matt takes over I will. I promise."

Which happened two breaths later.

"You're a troublemaker, Caroline Mendoza." But Matt Chase grinned as he said it. "I have an awful lot of troublesome females in my life as it is, so how about you stop getting shot at?"

He looked into her face, latching her gaze. "I need to

be sure you didn't get shot or injured from the glass in places I haven't seen. Can you stand?"

"Yes. I'm freaked and shaky and really mad, but I don't feel like I've been shot." He helped her to her feet, and Holly stayed close, a steadying hand on her waist. "Not that I know what being shot feels like. I imagine it would not be fun. And probably that it would hurt enough to feel."

Matt chuckled and touched her carefully as he looked her over. "You managed to miss getting shot."

"Achievement unlocked." She managed a thumbs-up.

"If your attitude is any indication, I think you're going to be okay. I'd like to take you to the hospital. You've got a pretty nasty gash on your back and it might need stitches, but it certainly could stand getting cleaned up either way. I can only do so much here."

"Holly, can you tell Royal they're taking me to the hospital but underline that I'm not dying or anything," she called out weakly. Holly was apparently already speaking to Royal, and Caroline didn't want to interrupt. Plus if she heard his voice right then she might cry. And badasses didn't cry in public.

"I'll take her right now." Edward stepped closer. "Good thing your insurance kicked in already." He winked and she groaned. "Matt will help us out to the car. The police have cordoned off your office but I managed to grab your bag for you."

Holly came back over as they waited for the elevator. Justin had run down to bring Edward's car around. "Royal will meet you at the hospital. Peter is going to cover your hearing this afternoon. He'll get you rescheduled. Now go."

* * *

Royal made it to the hospital in one piece and that was sort of a miracle given how fast he drove. The ranch was about equidistant to the hospital as downtown Petal so he figured he'd get there pretty soon after they did.

He'd come back to his house, grabbed his truck keys and rushed over. After parking, he ran from the parking lot into the main building, heading to emergency.

He saw Edward as he rounded a corner.

"They just took her in. Matt's with her. He said she'd most likely need stitches in at least one place."

"Thanks, Edward." Royal held up a bag. "I brought her a change of clothes and some shoes. I thought she might appreciate it. Holly said her stuff got torn and bloodied. She likes to look neat. Caroline, I mean."

Edward's smile deepened. "Yes, the glass tore her up. She'll appreciate it. You truly do love her, don't you?"

"Huh? Well sure I do. There's doubt?"

"I knew you when you were with Anne. And Anne is like one of our family so when you and Caroline got so close so fast, I admit I wondered. But every time I see you and see the way you look at her, I'm more and more convinced you two have something truly special and lasting. That you thought to bring her clothes, well that's just proof to me, I guess, that you care about her."

Edward pointed to a room. "They're in room B."

Royal knocked and Matt opened. There was a drape pulled around where the exam table was. Because he needed to say something, to hear her voice and know she was all right, he spoke. "I brought clothes for Caroline."

"Royal?" He heard the relief in her voice and he felt better too.

Matt held a hand up to stay Royal's progress into the room. "Let us get her cleaned up and then I'll call you. Okay?"

The room they were in was quite small so he stepped back. "I'll be right out here, darlin'."

"Okay." Her voice was a little thready. Fighting off tears, he knew. Holding back the fear. Because that's who she was.

He needed to keep it together. She had to lean on him so he put all his own panic and fear as far aside as he could as he walked back to join Edward. "They're stitching her up now. Thanks for bringing her here. And for being so good to her, in general."

Edward nodded. "In her I see a girl who got a pretty raw deal. A woman who turned all that insanity and lack of control over her circumstances into a hugely promising career. Polly and I, well, we want to scoop her up and mother and father her because heaven knows the Lassiters are useless fools. I have children myself. Love them more than is reasonable sometimes. But you do because you created them and raised them and they're your babies even when they're well over six feet tall and have babies themselves. Caroline is brave and she stands up for what she believes in and for people who need her to defend them." He shrugged a shoulder.

Royal was so glad Caroline had Edward and Polly in her life. "She's going to apologize for this you know. *I'm so sorry some freak shot through the window and I know it's causing trouble and I understand if you need to fire me.*"

"It's good you understand her. Yes, she will and I'll tell her exactly what I think of that. But this means we need to work even harder and faster to find this man before he truly hurts her."

Matt came out, and about two minutes later, the doctor followed with Caroline. Royal hadn't realized he'd come to stand until he was at her side.

"If you have any problems give us a call. Watch out for infection. Careful using this arm for a while. The stitches in your back will pull and that's no fun. Come back in three days and we'll get the stitches out."

Shane rolled up as they were heading toward the parking lot. Royal waved. "I'm going to get Caroline back to my place. Can you get her statement there?"

"Oh for God's sake." Caroline managed to get herself into a seat in a waiting room. "He's here. I'm here. He's got other stuff to do. Let's do this now."

Royal held back a snarl. Barely. "Caroline, Jesus, you were just shot at. Can you ease back if for no other reason than my heart?"

She took his hand, and she was so cold he put his around hers to warm them. "Can you please just let me do this? I'm still mad and that helps."

He got it then. She needed her anger to help her get through this. So he sighed, sitting next to her, keeping her hands in his. She leaned against him as she told Shane everything that had happened.

"I'll keep this short since you need to get some rest. We found a bullet from a high-powered rifle lodged in the far wall in your office. Given the general angle, it looks like the shooter was up in a tree just beyond the back parking lot for the building next door."

"Was it an easy shot or a complicated shot?" Caroline asked.

"The rifle was one used by someone who wanted to

kill something. A deer, a nosy attorney, whatever. That says he's serious. That he's been camping and watching you is also an indicator that he's focused on getting rid of you. The angle? Are you asking if I think the guy is military or law-enforcement level trained? If so, I don't know yet. It wasn't from a long way and through a bunch of crazy obstacles or anything like that. You'd need that sort of aim and concentration for deer hunting too."

She nodded.

"We're on it. Asking around. Some of the nearby businesses have video so we're trying to piece something together now. I'll let you know what else I hear. Now go home and be safe."

Caroline faced Edward, who shook his head before she could say a word. "No you don't, Caroline. You *aren't* responsible for what this person did, so no we're not firing you and no one is mad at you. We have your schedule handled today. Also, head's up but I'm fairly sure my wife will be knocking on your door in about half an hour. I told her you'd been hurt and were here."

Caroline smiled. "All right. We won't sick Spike on her because she'll probably have pie."

"We definitely won't then." Royal helped her to stand and they walked out.

Once they were on the road, after she'd called Shep's phone and left a message, she tipped her head back and rested it against the back of the seat.

He knew she was on the verge of losing it, so he waited until he'd gotten her into the house and changed into pajamas.

"You want me to set you up on the couch or in bed?"

"You need to go back to work. It's still daylight. I'm just going to take some pain relievers and sleep awhile."

"Do you really think I'd just tip my hat and let you be here alone? You're out of your mind. Bed or couch?"

"Why are you mad at me?"

He pointed to the bed and she got in. He kicked off his shoes and followed. "I'm not mad at you. I'm scared something is going to happen to you. I'm worried for your emotional and mental well-being with all this stress. I hate that your grandparents weren't there. I hate that I can hear the tears in your voice that you won't just share."

She burst into tears and he felt bad for a moment. "I didn't mean to make you cry! Well I wanted you to let go but not because I made you upset."

Caroline snuggled into his body, and he held her, mindful of the stitches on her back and forearm.

After a few minutes she'd calmed to an occasional hiccup. "I hate being shot at."

He grinned, unable to stop himself. "Fancy that. I hate it when you get shot at too. Let's never do it again."

"I can't even with this. And by the way I trust you enough to cry. I was just trying to hold on until you were out of here. I hate that my stuff keeps interrupting your work. I don't want you to have to be my babysitter."

"Maybe you could play babysitter. I think I'd like that."

"You're a deviant."

He kissed the top of her head. "Totally. Now, take a nap. I'm not leaving the house so don't even suggest it. But I'll do some work in my office. The door will be open so yell and I'll hear you. Polly should be here in a bit anyway."

"Thank you for coming for me."

"Oh, baby, I will *always* come for you. As long as I draw breath I will come for you."

Her smile was wobbly, but genuine. He stacked pillows so she wouldn't roll back and hurt her back, and then he headed down the hall.

"You're aging me prematurely," Royal told her as she finished applying her lipstick. "Can't you just take one more day?"

"No. I have so much stuff today it's not funny. I can't expect Peter, Edward and Justin to pick up all the slack all the time. Plus I like my job, Royal. I like it and this shithead is not going to steal that from me either."

He groaned.

"I'm going to work. And you will go to work too and that is that. I'm allowing you to drive me in. No one is going to let me do anything alone anyway. Plus the investigator is coming to my office at four. Shep is coming over to hear the update. Then you'll be there at five thirty to pick me up."

"I'll be there at four to hear the update from the investigator and then we'll go home from there."

"Really?"

He nodded. "Of course. I want to know too. Your struggle is my struggle, silly. This has been a long road for you. I just want it all to be positive. And safe. So I'll see you at four. At the office?"

"Yes, okay. I'd like that. Thank you for being interested in this, or at the very least faking it well."

It wasn't like she actually got shot or anything. She got some stitches in non-important places. There was no reason for her to be anxious or sore or freaked out.

Royal told her about his plans for the day, and she turned slightly in the seat so she could look at him as they drove.

A song started, one that made her sigh wistfully. "I forgot my iPod was still in your car." Kate Nash's "Nicest Thing" sounded between them. She looked at his hands on the steering wheel. Capable. Strong. The hands of a man who used them to work hard. They were work rough and sometimes he'd apologize when he'd stroke up her thighs.

But she liked it. Liked the slight burr. Liked the contrast between using his hands to haul and pick and throw and all that, and the way he touched her.

"I love that song. It used to make me a little melancholy. I mean, who hasn't felt that way toward someone? The words are so wistful and full of yearning. But now I hear it differently."

She'd shifted her gaze from his hands back up to his face. He was smiling. "And how's that, then?"

"I was that person, the one in the song. Only not really about anyone, just that dreaming of having someone who knows you so well. I wanted that connection. And now when I hear it, I know I've found him. It's like reading back through journal entries from a year ago, or from a time in your life when things were very bad. You appreciate it all the more now that you've weathered that storm. You're different because of whatever that moment is. *You're* that moment, that person. You're my nicest thing."

Royal took a deep breath. "I don't think we've really talked a whole lot about me and Anne because it's weird. I know it's unusual that she and I are such close friends. But you seem to deal with it in stride and I love you for it and I also love that you're secure in my feelings for you."

"Pffft. Listen, mister, if she ever steps over the line again I will take her out. However, she seems to be a total idiot and gave you up. Her loss is my gain and I will not tolerate any nonsense."

"You are a zero-tolerance-for-nonsense sort of person. At last with your grandparents even. Anyway I've touched on most of it, but not what finally drove me away."

She waited, not wanting to spook him.

"You were talking about that song, and I hadn't heard it before but I heard it in two ways too. The obvious one is that you're that special and important to me. All the time I was with Anne, she was settling. And part of me knew it. And part of her knew it. But I loved her and kept hoping she'd love me, and she was comfortable with me so she never really made a move to go. So I took whatever she gave me and lied to myself that the closeness we had was enough. That it was love in its own way. And it was. It is.

"I don't even know if the last year or so we were together that I actually believed it. But she and I just let ourselves get comfortable. And I watched another one of my friends truly fall in love with someone who deserved them, and it just hit me that I could not live that way another day. She came to my house, the old one, before this one was finished, anyway, and I'd packed up her stuff that she'd left around and I ended it once and for all. I got some coverage here at the ranch and I took off. I was in San Diego for a month. I just needed to be gone."

And, if Caroline wasn't wrong, to try to fuck himself into happiness. But he wasn't that type. Oh sure fucking felt good, but fucking to fill up some empty space in your life never worked.

"I came back, and there was a time when I think she waited to see how it was going to go. We'd always gotten together in the past. But I was done. Being gone it just allowed me to really own my shit. I told myself the day I came back to Petal that I would never settle for someone who didn't love me as much as I loved her. It's lonely and fucked up even when both people truly care about one another. I look at you, or I hear your laugh, smell you on my sheets, and I *know* not only how I feel but how you feel. I see it reflected on your face, or in the tone you use when you talk about me. I never feel like I'm not quite enough when I'm with you. That means *everything*. Despite being shot at and broken into and vandalized and threatened, I wouldn't trade this. I never expected what you've given me."

"Yep. We're awesome all right." He took her hand and squeezed briefly.

Of course he insisted on escorting her inside where her window had been replaced and a special film put over it to make it impossible to see in. She also had new curtains and her desk had been moved.

"Wow. Thanks."

Holly grinned, handed her a mug of coffee, a stack of messages and welcomed her back.

She worked her way through her day steadily until she looked up to find Anne Murphy in her doorway.

"It's lunchtime and I'm starving. And I bet William will be extra nice to you if I take you along with me to the Honey Bear. You know, he'll ply you with treats and because you have good manners you'll share. Also you've had a pretty craptastic time of it lately, and I think you could probably use a break."

"Thanks. Yeah I'm hungry." She stood and carefully reached to grab her wallet from her bag.

"You're okay to walk a few blocks? Tate said you had to get stitches in two places."

"I'm fine. The stitches are in my back and arm. Thanks for asking." She checked in with Holly, sure to tell her where they were headed, and they made their way out and down to the sidewalk.

"So Tate told you? How'd she…oh! Matt. I forgot for a moment."

"This time next year you'll be saying *how's your momma* and *that's so precious* like an expert again. First you need to remember that *nothing* is a secret in this town very long. A friend of Beth's saw Royal in the hospital with you yesterday and was telling everyone how gone he is for you. So don't touch your stomach in public or everyone will start timing your cycles to see if you're knocked up."

"Joy. I mean, toe to toe with getting shot at, I'll choose everyone in town knowing when I'm on the dot."

When they went into the front doors of the Honey Bear, Maryellen saw her and came over to gently hug her. "Honey, how are you? Melissa told us all about that whole mess yesterday. Come on back and have a seat. Get off your feet. Hey, Anne, I really do love that new hair color. Looks so pretty on you."

Maryellen grabbed menus and took them to an open table. She looked at Anne. "You're an orange soda and you're cherry vanilla coke, right?"

Both women nodded and looked over the menu before ordering. William sent out orange sticky buns as a treat for Caroline, who shared them with Anne.

They'd gotten through lunch and were drinking coffee and waiting for the check when Polly Chase came in. She saw them and came over.

"Don't you dare stand up." Polly bent to hug Caroline gently. "How are you feeling, honey?"

"I'm all right, thanks. Would you like to sit? We're having some coffee and have also been talked into a brownie fresh from the oven."

Polly sat after giving Anne a hug. "Thank you. I'm glad I saw you in here. I ran into your grandmother today."

Caroline sighed and turned to face Polly better so she wasn't stretching her back muscles. "That couldn't have gone well."

"I was at the police station dropping canned food off. They're having a food drive. Anyway, on my way back to the car I saw Abigail and she waved me over and I said how sorry I was that you'd been having such a rough time but how I was so happy to have you back in Petal after you'd been away from us so long."

Caroline could only imagine how that went.

"She asked me about you, you know. I understand your grandmother has done and said some pretty unforgivable things and I'm not advocating for you to do anything but keep away from her. But I just wanted you to know that. Anyway I told her about the stitches and I urged her to look into her heart to find a way back to you because you're not only a piece of their daughter, but you're their oldest grandchild and you were so special. In the middle of that, Garrett Moseby comes sidling up all sneaky like. He dutifully reported that you'd merely done all this to yourself to make it look like your father was innocent and the real killer was out there still. And I said, 'Abigail, are you going to take a chance that this is some silly ploy? You don't know that girl at all if you think she'd do something along those lines.' She told him to hush up. I gave him a look. I should have boxed his ears but Shane says he can't protect me from assault charges if I do it. Really the men in my life all conspire to keep me from having fun."

Caroline and Anne laughed. "I'm sad to hear it, but not surprised I guess. Thanks for letting me know." She balled up her napkin. "I need to get back to the office. I have about a million calls and emails to return, and I have a meeting at four too. Mrs. Chase, I appreciate that you'd defend me. It means a lot. You and your husband have both been so welcoming and kind to me."

"Garrett Moseby is a creep who likes to tell your sister what to do, and with her big sister back in town, she's got a good example of strong womanhood. You're a threat to him and that's why he's acting like a jerk. He doesn't believe any of this nonsense about the case or you faking things. He doesn't want to lose Mindy to some sense and good advice. As for Abigail, I hope she comes around. I'd hate for her to lose out on you for stupid pride. Tell my handsome husband I said hello and I'm making him stroganoff for dinner, please."

"Will do."

They walked back to her building. "You didn't have to walk me back here, you know," Caroline said to Anne.

"We started out on a bad note, but I like you. Not just as my friend's girlfriend, but on your own you're pretty cool. I'm just keeping an eye on you."

"And what about you?"

"No one's trying to kill me. Probably because I'm nicer." Anne winked and Caroline scoffed. "Go on back inside. I'll talk to you later. Thanks for lunch and don't forget to tell Edward about stroganoff!"

"Are you kidding me?" Caroline asked her investigator. "I have three decent enough leads. I followed each one. One person might have some journals about that time in his shed. He lived catty corner from your parents, and he said he always kept detailed notes about the day's events. He offered them to the police at the time but they weren't interested. The other was a bust and the last one—"

He passed out a sheet of paper.

"Her name is Joyce Marie Petitbone, and she's eighty-seven years old and quite honestly the sharpest person over fifty I've ever met. She talked to me on the phone today for a few minutes. She lives in Riverton in a back house at her daughter's home. She saw the television spot you did and wrote down the information and then forgot about it until day before yesterday. She lived here in Petal sixteen years ago, and she's got something I think might be pretty major. But I want you to hear it and she only told me a tiny bit. I think she'd like the company, and she's agreed to see you and one other person tomorrow at nine in the morning. She doesn't truck with lateness, clothing that shows your lady business like a floozy or bad manners. She wanted me to underline all that." He grinned. "She also wanted me to tell you she was partial to old-fashioned doughnuts."

"Okay we'll go meet her. But you can't just not say what it is she knows." Caroline might have to jump over this table and punch him in the face if he didn't. She wisely kept that to herself though. For the moment.

"She may have seen the murderer clean up." Ron, her investigator, leaned in close. "Caroline, she's old and she likes attention but she's sharp and her memory is strong. She has a story to tell and my gut tells me you need to listen."

There was a ruckus then because everyone started talking and asking questions at the same time.

Ron held his hand up. "I've told you pretty much all I know. She's a little cagey because she wants to tell you herself. She lived in Petal until a year after the murder and then went to live in Riverton in the small house on her daughter's property. She says she called the police about it, but they told her over the phone not to worry because they'd caught the killer." He raised a shoulder and looked to Shane, who groaned.

Edward patted his son's shoulder. "You've made it better. That's all you can do at this point."

"Why don't I go over there? I'm pretty good with elderly women." Shane had that voice people in charge used when they were trying to get the women out of the way.

Ron shook his head. "She's not going to talk to you, Shane. She wants to talk to Caroline. I did a records search on her. She's exactly who she says she is. Her daughter and son-in-law have owned the house for nineteen years. He manages a flooring business, you know, sells carpet and laminate stuff. Wife is an administrator at the school district. Joyce Marie was a lunch lady at the cafeteria at Petal Middle School for twenty years. She's going to like Caroline. She's going to talk to Caroline. She'll let you flatter her, but she's not going to give you that story."

"I'll go. I want to hear what she has to say." Caroline refused to get her hopes up. She'd had her heart broken enough times with horrible disappointment that she'd learned to not get invested. She'd treat whatever it was like a very unlikely-maybe thing until she learned for sure.

"I'm coming too." Royal gave her a look, daring her to argue.

But she didn't have to.

Shane interrupted. "I'll go with Caroline. Royal, I appreciate that you want to be with her and it's probably not even a problem. But I'm a cop and you're not. Hell, I'd rather *none* of you be involved in this. But after Caroline literally dodged a bullet yesterday, I have a feeling she's quite capable of hitting the deck and letting me handle any funny business if it comes up."

"You can be assured that I would definitely hit the floor first and ask questions later at any sound resembling a gunshot."

Royal's mouth was set. She knew he was pissed that he wasn't going. But Caroline also knew he understood the reasons for it. In the end she was safer with Shane and that's what mattered.

Caroline thanked Ron and promised to keep him updated, and Shane made arrangements to pick her up at eight fifteen. He promised to stop and get doughnuts for Mrs. Petitbone. She wrapped her day up, turning off her computer and getting her bag and some work she'd do at home.

Home.

She'd begun to think of Royal's place as home. Every time they pulled up the long drive leading to the little rise the house sat on, she relaxed. It was like a weight being lifted. That house was solace and safety, and it had Royal in it, which made it even better.

Two months and she felt like she'd known him forever. He held the door for her and then took her hand. That too had simply become a natural thing. Touching him like he was hers. And as totally crazy as it seemed, he was.

Shep waited in the outer room for them.

Royal patted him on the shoulder. "Want to grab a

bite? I was just about to take your sister out for burgers and rings because I'm a party animal like that."

"Are you sure we're, you know, welcome at the Pump-house after the fight with Benji?" Caroline asked quietly. "We can go to the Sands or El Cid." The Honey Bear closed at six so their usual spot wasn't available.

Royal shrugged. "I guess we'll see, won't we?"

"Aren't you sick of drama?"

"You know, I sat in that room while you tossed your-self into a stranger's house willy-nilly. But I kept my mouth shut because right is right and with Shane going it's fine. He's better with shooting someone in the face if they try to hurt you. You live in Petal, and I will *not* have you hiding because of what other people did. I'm with you. We'll sit away from the windows. But we're going to the Pumphouse, and we're having a burger and rings and if anyone gets in my way when I'm trying to give that to you, God help them."

She smiled up at him. "Wow."

The deep lines of anger faded into a surprised—but pleased—smile. "I was inspired."

Shep sighed. "Can you two just not with all that? Jeez. You're worse than tenth graders."

"I'm sorry to be such a trial." Caroline winked, happy to be with both of them. "So you coming with us to have burgers and possibly a fight that ends with Grandmother having to pick you up from jail? I can pay your bail, but she's your legal guardian."

"Wouldn't miss it."

She hadn't told either of them what Garrett had said to Polly, and it lay heavy on her mind as they had a rela-tively trouble-free dinner. Their server had asked after her, saying she'd heard about all the attacks. She'd received several smiles and a few waves.

Of course she also got a few dark looks, and she couldn't stop wondering if they'd heard from Garrett or his gossip and thought she'd actually be capable of faking all the horrible stuff that had happened to her.

"You okay?" Royal asked her quietly when Shep headed to the bathroom. "I know this is a tense time, but you seem preoccupied, or more preoccupied than usual. People have seemed pretty okay tonight, did I miss something?"

"No, everyone is fine. I just… I had lunch with Anne today. I think I forgot to say that. But anyway, it was fine so get that look off your face. Jeez. Polly came in right before we left, and she told me about this rumor Garrett is spreading. I don't know if I should tell Shep, and I'm paranoid and wondering if people believe what he's been saying. Oh and I may actually connect with the evidence that could clear my father's name and send the real killer of my mother to prison. It's a little overwhelming in my head right now."

"I know. I shouldn't have suggested dinner out. I just don't want you to hide. Fuck that asshole trying to make you hide in shame for something *happening* to you."

"No, it was good. I should be out and about. I should be hanging out with my brother. I should be sitting with you in a back booth pretending I didn't see you steal those rings from my plate."

"As for telling Shep—because you will of course tell *me* on the way home—will it affect him somehow? Will he hear it eventually because all gossip gets around, it's impossible to avoid it? And when he does, will it hurt him that you didn't tell him first?"

"Garrett is telling people I faked all this stuff to happen to me to make it look like my father is innocent."

"He what? I told him. I warned him what would happen if he kept this up."

Jesus.

"Okay. Whoa. While it would be incredibly satisfying to let you punch him, it's a little busy just now. Also, if you punch him it involves you yet again in this bullshit."

Shep came back out and took a look at the two of them as he slid into the booth across from them. "What?"

So she told them both the whole story, and at the end she held up both hands. "Shep, you have to go back home and you'll be seeing Garrett and that's why I told you." Royal's point about how he'd hear it eventually anyway was spot on. But she didn't want any more of this to spill over into anyone else's life if she could help it.

"Yeah I'm going to see him. I'm going to see him and then I'm going to punch him."

"Well I'm so glad I told you then." She leaned over the table. "Enrique Shepard Mendoza, be smart. You have a bright future ahead of you. Don't screw it up by getting into some dick-measuring contest with a man with no dick and no spine. You got me? Our revenge for this is proving Dad innocent and putting Mom's killer away. Garrett doesn't matter. Not in the big picture."

"How can Mindy and Grandma let him do the stuff he does?"

"Oh, honey, I don't know what to tell you. I was raised by our mom. She taught me to respect myself and demand a partner who respected me too. But Mom didn't raise Mindy. Not for long enough to make an impact. Abigail Lassiter raised her. And look, she didn't have to.

They stepped in and did what they were supposed to, I never fault them for that. But her vision of marriage and relationships is distinctly old school. I want you to understand something really important. Abigail Lassiter has her own opinions. No one tells her how to think. If she wanted to shut Garrett down, she could. She's the true alpha there. Just keep your head down. Finish school. Spread your wings and go off to college."

Her brother's expression darkened. "He's not just insulting you with this. He's insulting me too. And anyone else who knows the truth."

She nodded at her brother. "Yep. But he's irrelevant, and he'll use you, me, whoever, to *be* relevant. He's a small, weak man who thinks he's far stronger and tougher than he is. He'll get his. But *you* are relevant. Do you see? You have a future full of options. In the end, you're worth ten of him. And he knows it. So fuck him. Unless he comes at you, just avoid him and do your thing."

"I don't know. Honestly I'm seriously pissed. She's on my case about seeing you and hanging out with you. Wants to know what we talk about. I'd have told her if she hadn't been so dictatorial about it. Garrett is at the house with Mindy. He now calls them Grandma and Grandpa. Grandpa is mad a lot. I think he and Grandma are fighting. I hate that Garrett comes into my house and is trying to poison them. I don't like that he'd say that about you when you're being terrorized."

"It's your life and your fists. I get that you're mad. I do. I'm mad too. I'm just used to triage and to keeping my eye on the big picture. He's nothing and no one."

He didn't make promises and she didn't make him. He was nearly grown and would do what he wanted anyway.

* * *

"You know, it's the fact that Garrett is irrelevant and nothing that makes me want to punch him most." Royal had been pretty quiet on the way home but once he'd started to change his clothes, he began speaking.

She put lotion on her hands as she looked up from where she'd been reading something for work.

"See, I told him. I told him nearly two months ago that if he could not slow his tongue and quit bringing you up, he and I would have a problem. Then he started that shit at the Pumphouse and egged Benji on, and now he's telling everyone that you're a liar who faked attacks on herself to make it look like her dad was innocent. I have a big problem here, Caro."

She blew out a breath.

"I told him. And he ran off after the thing at the Pumphouse. I need to make it my mission to bump into him so we can talk this out."

"If you do that you could get arrested. He's not worth that."

"No, Caroline, I am respectful of what you need to do with this. I stand back even when my brain is screaming at me to duct tape you and keep you in bed until this guy is picked up. But I know you need to do it. And I know you make big allowances for how I feel about stuff as it is. I appreciate it. You don't have to but you do anyway."

"Because I love you."

He smiled, bending down to kiss her. "Good. Another thing I appreciate. I love you too."

"But you're going to punch him anyway."

He nodded. "Yes. More than once. I'm sorry my choices are hurting your feelings. But yes."

"My feelings aren't hurt. To be totally honest, I'm flattered and it makes me feel all giggly and tingly when you want to punch someone to protect or avenge me. But I hate it anyway because while I am absolutely sure you're capable of winning with one arm tied behind your back, I don't like anyone trying to hurt you. I don't like a big fuss being made and everyone looking at me. More than they already do. You push and it opens you up to negative attention." It mattered to him because he was deeply woven into Petal. Far more than she was, and she didn't want him estranging himself from everything he'd ever known to avenge her.

But when she said that he just turned and sighed. "Caroline, do you think I'd want people in my life who'd think it was okay for a grown man to run all over town and tell stories out of school about my woman? I have friends who are worthy of that friendship. I don't care about anyone else other than you. Got me?"

She nodded, giving a wobbly smile. "I've cried a lot in the last few months. I'm a wimp."

He rolled his eyes. "Oh yes, you're such a wimp for crying three times in the midst of someone trying to kill you to shut you up, of being on the outs with your mom's people, all this change in your life."

"Are you mocking me?"

He took the files from her hands. "I'd rather fuck you. Carefully of course so we don't pull your stitches."

"Other than onion rings, this is the best offer I've had all night."

He knelt on the floor between her thighs as he reached out to cup the back of her neck and pull her closer.

"Am I helping you work through some of your aggression?" she murmured into his mouth during their kiss.

He gripped her neck a little tighter. "You up for that?"

She pulled back. "I'm not going to break."

He must have understood because he grabbed her pajama shirt and spread it wide, a button flying off to the side.

Whoa.

"Yeah, I liked that too." He kissed her again as he brushed his thumbs back and forth over her nipples before sliding down to push her pajama pants and her underwear from her legs.

"Perfect access." He licked the back of her knee and then put her calf on his shoulder. "Scoot down a little, make sure you're okay when you lean back." He stroked up her thighs, and she moved quickly to find an angle that wouldn't put pressure on her stitches.

And once she had, his mouth was on her, his tongue licking and swirling, fingers pressing up and inside. Sensation slowly filled her. Starting at her toes, it seemed to build and build until it engulfed her when she came way faster and far harder than she'd been expecting.

"There we go." He kissed her belly and then got to his feet, helping Caroline to hers as well. "I think you need to bend over the bed. Arms above your head. I don't have my belt to keep you in place so you'll have to imagine it binding your wrists together."

On slightly wobbly knees, she walked to the bed and did as he'd told her.

"This is the perfect reason to keep my bed this height."

He put a step stool under her feet so it was more comfortable and lined up once he'd gotten a condom on.

"Christ. You're so beautiful this way. All your curves." He caressed her hips as he slowly thrust into her until he was seated fully. "Your hair is spread all over your back and shoulders. So pretty. Your skin, damn. You're just swoops and swirls and curves. It does me in."

She closed her eyes. He *saw* her. He looked at her and he saw beauty and worth and she felt it. Royal was not only exciting and sexy, he was her safe place.

"I love you," she said right as he made her come again, reaching around her body as he continued to stroke deep and steady.

He groaned. "Feels so good when you come around my cock like this." The hand he'd had at her hip tightened, his fingers digging into her flesh, holding her exactly how he wanted as he sped, keeping deep, and came.

He bent, brushed a kiss over her uninjured shoulder and bit. "Love you too."

Chapter Twenty-Two

The drive over to Riverton was pleasant enough. It wasn't overly far, and Joyce Marie lived in one of the more established subdivisions just about a mile from the courthouse. She drove down this stretch of road at least once every two weeks on her way into town.

They parked at the curb, and Caroline carried the box of doughnuts past the main house and up to Joyce Marie's front door. Shane knocked and shortly thereafter the door opened to reveal a wildly barking dachshund and a very tall elderly woman with a crown of pale, white hair she'd braided down her back.

"Hello, Mrs. Petitbone? I'm Caroline Mendoza and this is Shane Chase. Shane is the chief of police in Petal. I believe you spoke with Ron Rogers yesterday?"

"Snickers, if you don't hush up I'm going to lock you in the bedroom and then you won't have any company." The dog seemed rather unimpressed but he lowered his volume and gave his owner side-eye. Joyce Marie turned her attention back to Caroline. "I see you brought a bakery box. What's in it?"

"A dozen old-fashioned doughnuts from the Honey Bear. Freshly baked at six this morning."

Joyce Marie nodded and then opened her screen door.

"All right then. Come on in. You, big shoulders, just sit right there in the chair and look pretty while I talk to Caroline. You can eat doughnuts and drink some coffee though."

Caroline hid her grin as Shane withheld a sigh. "Thank you, Mrs. Petitbone. We sure do appreciate your time." He sat and she poured him some coffee and handed the cup his way.

"Milk and sugar right there. Plates for the doughnuts too." Then she turned to Caroline. "Sit down. My goodness you have your daddy's hair and eyes, but you sure do favor your mother. I used to go out to their diner every Sunday after church. Your father made such great roasted chicken. Funny the things we remember all these years later. So let me tell you the story. I'm sure you have a busy life. Mr. Rogers said you're an attorney?"

Caroline nodded.

"Your parents would have been proud."

"My father was still alive when I got my degree. He was very proud."

Joyce Marie sighed. "I surely am sorry for all the loss you've seen."

Caroline got Joyce Marie a cup of coffee, which earned a smile and a compliment about her manners.

"Sixteen years ago. And I can remember it really clearly because it was early November, near Halloween, and so numbnuts all over the neighborhood had firecrackers and kept lighting them off like it was brain surgery." Joyce Marie shook her head. "My sweet PBC—short for peanut butter cup—hated the noise. So I'd been keeping him inside but he got out as cats are sometimes bound and determined to do. PBC was a mutt of a housecat. Brown all over but he had these orange-ginger spots.

Like peanut butter and chocolate. My husband brought him home as a kitten. He's gone now. The husband and the cat. But anyway, I'd been keeping an eye out for that cat to get him back inside. He hadn't come back all day. I was dead tired and wanted to go to sleep, but I was too nervous with the darned cat still out. Finally I heard meowing at the back so I went to let him in. And that's when I saw my neighbor hosing himself off in the side yard that abutted his house and mine.

"I thought it was odd. It was early November, like I said, so it was chilly that night. Way too cold to be using the hose outside. But being strange isn't any of my business. I brought the cat in, and about five minutes later I saw he'd left a bloody paw print in the kitchen. I cleaned him up, thinking he must have cut himself. I didn't find anything. But cats, you see? They get up to all sorts of great adventures when they're not around so he could have done anything. I was relieved he wasn't hurt and I went to bed."

She sipped her coffee and ate some more of her doughnut before continuing.

"The next morning I was up early and went out to fill the hummingbird feeder. Another reason I remember this is that the days were so warm and clear the hummingbirds were still around. But it had been dry so there was dust everywhere. Anyway. I had a multiple bird feeder hanging on the tree to the side of the house, and when I went up on the ladder, I saw a puddle over on the concrete pad running next to my neighbor's house. The sun hadn't reached the patch between the houses or it would have dried up. There was a stain on the grass too. I could make up a story about how I saw it so clearly from my yard, but the truth is I'm a nosy old lady and I went over to get a closer look and it sure as shootin' looked like blood on the grass and on a corner of that concrete. I went back inside but it niggled at me all that day, and then when I went into town the following day, I heard about your mother's death and I called the police that afternoon." Joyce Marie looked to Shane.

"What did they say, ma'am?"

He didn't add anything like *can you remember*, which would have insulted Joyce Marie. Smart.

"They told me they had the murderer and that my tip was a dead-end."

Caroline had been through the call logs and had never seen Joyce Marie's name. Then again, there were missing pages so it could have been logged. They just had no way of knowing.

"I saw you on television and I listened to your story. I never believed your daddy was capable of such a thing. I was talking to my daughter about this whole thing, and she urged me to call the tip line."

"Mrs. Petitbone, thank you so much. I most certainly appreciate that you called. Back then and now. People don't like to get involved. I'm just grateful you did." Caroline tried to bat the hope back, but it grew anyway. She needed not to count on this information meaning a damned thing. But her heart raced as her palms sweated just a little.

"Did I help?"

"You took a risk and you said what you knew and that helps no matter what. I don't know if we'll find anything. But it's more than we knew before we came here."

"You'll tell me what happens?"

"As much as we can." Shane smiled at her. "Do you know his name by any chance? Your neighbor?"

"Vernon Hicks. He owned the place for several years. Don't know when exactly he moved away, but it was after I came here. Probably ten years ago or so."

They stayed awhile longer, thanking Joyce Marie and promising to let her know if anything came of her information.

On the road back to Petal, she called in and had flowers sent to Joyce Marie. She'd go over to the Honey Bear to see about maybe sending her doughnuts regularly too. She had kids and grandkids and a busy life, but it was always nice to be remembered.

Shane took her back to her building. "I'm going straight to work on finding who this Vernon Hicks is. I have a vague memory of him, but let me dig and I'll get back in contact. You did great today. You're good with people."

She wanted to ask if he thought it was a good tip. Wanted to ask what he thought. But so much had happened. Everything could change because of what she'd just heard. It was so exciting and terrifying all at once that she just needed to lock it down.

"Thank you for going with me. I'm going to have Ron look into Vernon Hicks too. Two sets of eyes might help." Plus Ron would have access to sources Shane might not, or might not want to use.

"Yes, that's good. Have him get with me if he finds anything."

Her smile was wobbly but she held on to it like armor as they went inside.

Shane went off to work and she filled everyone in. The mood was cautiously hopeful, and after everyone had wandered off and she'd left a message for Shep, she looked up at Royal.

"You okay?"

She shook her head. "Nope. But I will be. I will work today and stay busy, and then I won't be checking my messages every five minutes. I'll be here all day. Client meetings and some research and writing. And when I get home, I'll let it all go. But you need to scamper that fantastic butt of yours back home."

"You trying to get rid of me, sweetheart?"

"Listen, I ride that stalker line enough as it is. I could be with you all the time and be totally content. But I *hate* how much time this takes away from all the stuff you need to take care of."

He kissed her quickly. "Hush with that. I like being around you too. I want to be here to help. The farm will always need me but you're important to me."

"Enough. You're going to make me cry."

"All right, Caro. I'll see you tonight. Maybe I'll make you cry my name instead. Once we're alone I mean." He gave her a roguish look and with a little wave he left and she got on the line with Ron to get him working on Vernon Hicks.

Shep showed up after he got out of school, and she filled him in on everything they'd found out so far.

"Are you okay? You must be, wow, blown away."

"I'm working on being okay. I mean, I'm held together by duct tape, paperclips and some gum, but so far so good. You have to manage your expectations. I've gone through this before. If you get your hopes up too high and it doesn't work out, the fall is worse. Each time we got news back that our appeal had been denied or we'd lost on something that was so stupid and technical that it weighed more than his innocence. That one took me a month. I was an undergraduate. My junior year. I had a job and a full schedule so I would go to work or class and pretty much cry the whole time I was at home. I learned after that to just treat everything like a probably won't happen so that if it doesn't, I'll be sad but not so devastated my whole life falls apart."

"Falls apart? You carried a full load and worked. You cried in carefully defined times. Jeez, Caroline. If that's your idea of falling apart, you're an even bigger control freak than I thought. This is all new to me. You've been alone with all this before and now I can help. We can lean on each other. I don't know what to think. I get it, keep your expectations low. Dad's dead, Caroline. I hate that. But he's not depending on you. This is something else. We'll clear his name. You can count on that. But I sure as hell do hope this is our guy so they can arrest him and get him off the streets for good. I want you safe, and that's not going to happen until he's been arrested. I know this is old hat to you, but I hate it. I hate that you're exposed and unsafe. I'm working on it, but you're so strong and you never get scared. I'm not there yet."

She blew out a breath. "Hah! It's an act. I feel like…" She shook her head and took a different tack. "One of the friends I made once I delved into the Innocence Project stuff, he's an attorney in a small former Soviet country and things are horrible for him. He defends people the government picks up and tosses into jail for months or years at a time. Sometimes without ever even charging them. So people disappear off the street in the middle of the day, and six years later that same person, only forty pounds lighter and near death, gets tossed back on a front step. Sometimes they never come back at all. And my friend, he gets death threats all the time. Like on a monthly basis. He's been kidnapped twice. Picked up and arrested. Beaten and interrogated. And he gets up every day he's not in jail, he packs his case and he goes to work. I admired that before, but now? Now that I'm scared out of my skin all day long every day from some *threats*? Now that I know just a small slice of what he must deal with I guess I'm having a learning moment. This shit is crazy scary, Shep. I'm freaked out all the time. And I can't stop living, but at the same time, I want to hide. I'm not perfect. I save all my strong for when people are looking at me." She smiled at him. "I hope this is different. I want it to be different. It might even feel different. Shane will hopefully have at least part of an answer soon enough."

Shep nodded as he put his hands in his pockets. She thought of him at two, toddling around, laughing and giggling as their father had teased that he was going to eat him up.

"I've read six years of letters so far," he said quietly and quickly.

She hugged him.

"I couldn't decide to start at the beginning or the end. But then I felt like I needed to start at the beginning and get to know him that way. Who he was at that time. I spend hours every day just reading them. I'm paranoid Grandma will find them and take them away so I have them in my trunk."

"If you like, you can keep them here. Or at Royal's house."

"Maybe. I don't know. I just know I'm so sad." His bottom lip wobbled, and she scooted next to him on her couch, her arm around his shoulder. "He loved me. Oh my God, Caroline, he loved me and they always told us he didn't. It hurts to read his words. It hurts to know how alone he was. I didn't know him two weeks ago. And now I know him a little bit. Did he write you little stories?"

She smiled at that memory. "He did. For like three years he'd send me a paragraph here and there until he finished one of them. Sometimes poems. A memory he had that he wanted to pass on to me. He did love you. Don't be sad about it."

"I feel so guilty for not helping him."

"Sweetie, you're not even a legal adult yet. There wasn't a damned thing you could have done. Anyway, I'm just saying, be sad. Feel bad and miss him. Be angry or curious. But don't be guilty."

She went home, and then got dragged out to bowling where she was thoroughly trounced by Beth and consoled herself with a five-gallon jug of sugary sweet icy stuff and a giant pretzel.

She'd been busy trying not to recoil from the bag of fresh crackling handed her way when her phone rang.

"Give those to Royal. He loves them." And that she still allowed him to kiss her after knowing he ate them was a true testament to her love for him.

She answered.

"Caroline? It's Shane." Pressing a hand against her other ear, she moved away from the lanes to hear better.

"What's going on?"

"I've found out quite a bit about Vernon Hicks. I wanted to talk to you about it. It sounds like you're out, though. We can talk about it tomorrow too."

"Are you kidding? I'm at the bowling alley with our goofy friends, or as they're also known, your family and extended family."

He chuckled. "That's right. I forgot it was moved to Thursday this month. I'm not too far away."

Royal came into her line of sight, and he moved to her, concern on his face.

"We can meet you at the station or the office or whatever. I'm really interested to hear what you've got."

"I'll meet you at the bowling alley in ten minutes. I can give you the rundown then."

"Thank you, Shane."

And ten minutes later, she and Royal were sitting in the back of the café area that no one ever used.

"Vernon Hicks moved away from Petal six years after the murder to Porter, a city just outside Macon. He's been arrested seven times for domestic violence, including violating protection orders. He did a two-year stint for nearly killing someone in a bar fight. I have calls into the cops on the DV stuff for more detail, but it looks like Vernon has himself a stalking problem. Those seven arrests were for four different women."

"Four? And this guy is free to stalk Caroline? After he did all that? You tell me how that makes a lick of sense." Royal was pissed and she sure didn't blame him.

"I don't make the laws. I don't handle the trials or the sentences. I just uphold the laws other people create. And I don't think his history started the moment he moved away from Petal either. But I didn't find much about him here. Our recordkeeping sixteen years ago wasn't always as thorough as it could have been. But I spoke to a few old-timers. They routinely had to haul him to the drunk tank. He liked to hang out near the old beauty college that used to be out where the big-box hardware store is between here and Millersburg. I also think he might have changed his name when he got here. I can't find anything on him before he arrived."

People like Hicks drifted around and frequently changed names to dodge debt collectors or the cops. Of course he had to drift because he appeared to have a problem with his temper and self-control.

"Ron is on it too. He'll call me tomorrow to check in and I'll let you know. So he's in Porter which means you'll go talk to him? Or?"

"I need to find out all I can and then start putting together a case. I don't have probable cause right now for a warrant. I can't search his house either. Hell, you and I know he can tell me to eat shit and slam the door in my face when I go. And yes, I will go to Porter and talk to him, yes."

"We need a connection. I never knew him so he wasn't a friend of our family. I worked out at the diner every weekday afternoon so he wasn't a server or a cook. Do you have pictures?"

Shane opened a file folder and showed her a few of his mug shots.

She shook her head. "He wasn't a regular. At least not in the afternoon, evening and weekends. I was there enough to know the regulars. I was at school in the mornings until three so maybe it could have been then.

"I've been through all the papers I could salvage. Before the trial, early on, my grandmother went through our house, put every one of my dad's belongings in plastic bags. She told the police to come get it. They'd already searched the house so they didn't care. One of my friends kept those bags for me in her back shed until my uncle could get it. I had all those papers and ledgers. I've never seen that name. She had journals, my mom I mean."

Shane froze. "I've been over that case file three dozen times. There were no journals admitted into evidence."

"No there weren't. We brought that up on appeal. I personally called the police department to say I had them, and they weren't interested. Even his original attorney didn't care. But *I'd* have tried to use them, for God's sake. Anyway, she mentions silly fights they had, or when he left his beard hairs in the sink. But there were no affairs. No violence in their home or in their relationship. No mentions of Vernon Hicks."

She needed to figure out that connection. Once she knew how Vernon Hicks came into their lives, she'd have everything they needed to send him to prison forever.

"Can I see them? The journals I mean." He paused at the look on her face. "I'll respect them. I know these journals are about her inner life. But if *anything* in them can help me nail Hicks and clear your father, I think it's worth it."

She nodded. He was right.

They left after she promised to bring him the journals to the police station the following day. They were in her storage unit so thankfully they weren't destroyed when her apartment had been broken into.

"You know, I think we should go to the storage unit now. I'm just skeeved out by this Hicks guy, and I don't want to go there if he can watch you. It's dark, we'll know if anyone is around by their lights."

She agreed, and they headed out of town and toward Riverton, where her stuff was. No one was behind them on the road the whole drive over so Royal breathed a lot easier once they'd retrieved those journals and were on the way home again.

She was quiet, he knew she was anxious and worried and scared and too freaked out to hope. In the dark, mouths fused into a kiss, he loved her until she was too tired to do anything but fall asleep in his arms.

Chapter Twenty-Three

Ron had shown up and had briefed Caroline, Edward, Justin and Shane. He'd found Vernon Hicks's trail from before he'd come to Petal. He'd been born Vernon Pickerell in Amarillo. He had a sealed juvenile file and had enlisted in the army at eighteen and had been dishonorably discharged eighteen months later. He'd lived in Sacramento for a few years until he skipped four months' back rent, some department-store credit and an assault charge against a nineteen-year-old who worked weekends at the feed store who'd dared to say no when he'd asked her out. As Bob Vernon he'd bounced around, never staying anywhere for long. Indiana, Kentucky, Tennessee, all for a few months. He'd done six years for manslaughter in Missouri as Bob Vernon. And he'd come to Petal not even a week after he'd been released.

Shane took over at that point, talking about Vernon's life since he'd left Petal. The DV stuff he'd found along with the assault charges and the time he did for that.

"He's still in Porter. He's got a part-time job at a print shop. Which we think might be his connection to the information about the security outage for the cameras at your office."

"It's pretty clear he's got some issues with the ladies." Caroline shook her head.

"Given the types of crimes he tends to commit over and over, yes, I think women are his favorite target. And in my gut I am convinced this man killed your mother. We're going to nail him. I'm going to Porter tomorrow. I have a call in to the PD there. I have a few friends so one of them will come with me out to Vernon's apartment. You will not be coming so don't even think about asking, Caroline."

"I'll wait in the car."

Royal put his face in his hands.

"What? I want to know! I want to see him. I want to hear him when he lies. I need to."

Shane took her hands. "Caroline, I know you do, and in your place I would too. Hell, I'm not in your place, and I gotta tell you it will be my pleasure to take this piece of garbage down for you. But this has to be done right. Step by step. You're a defense attorney, you know this better than anyone else in this room. I want this done absolutely to the letter. You didn't wait this whole time, suffering all those defeats to screw it up by rushing at the very end."

Everyone left, Shane promising to let her know how the visit went when he returned from Porter the following afternoon. Ron headed out to Vernon's old neighborhood to do a canvas, and she tried to work.

At five she called Royal and left him a voice mail that she was going to her grandparents' house to talk with Shep and also see if her grandparents knew Vernon Hicks.

He called her back as she was riding over there in Shep's car.

She saw it was him and answered with an apology. "I know. I wanted to see if they have any info about Vernon Hicks, but Garrett might be there and I didn't want anyone to get punched."

"Too bad. I'm waiting in front of your grandparents' right now, and I will be coming in with you. And if you ever pull this sort of thing again, we're going to have a big problem, Caroline."

He was right to be mad. She'd have been in his place too. "Okay. I'm sorry, I should have let you know and included you from the start. I'm glad you're here, and I'll see you in a minute or two."

Shep looked at her briefly. "Told you."

"Yes, yes you did. The thing is, I sort of want him to punch Garrett and that's really bad of me. I'm trying to protect him. Not that I think he'd get beaten up. But from all this drama and emotion."

"If the situations were reversed, how you would you feel? He loves you and he wants to be there with you when you face something difficult. Wouldn't you want the same in his place?"

"Gah. I hate it when everyone but me is right."

They pulled up the driveway, and Royal got out of his truck and met them.

"I'm sorry. I should have waited and included you. I just want to protect you from all this gross stuff. But I know you want to be with me and I value that so I'm sorry."

"I didn't even have an hour to be mad." He kissed her.

"The night is young."

Shep went up the steps and unlocked the door, bringing them inside. "Hey, everyone, I've got Caroline and Royal with me," he called out as they went into the family room.

"Why?" Garrett asked as he looked up.

Caroline sneered at him, and Royal gave him a look that promised blood.

Garrett paled and winced. *Message received.*

"I need to talk with you all about the case."

Abigail shook her head. "No. I told you long ago not to bring that into my house."

"You did. I was twenty years old, and Mindy asked me about the Mendozas. It was a silly question, but the end of it was about where our dad had been born. And you shoved me into the den, slapped my face and said if I ever spoke about any of my father's family in front of Mindy or Shep, you'd make sure I never saw them again. Good times."

Heavy silence fell as her grandfather looked over at her grandmother, anger on his features.

"Moving right along. As you know, though we pretend you don't, I've been working for years and years to free our father from prison because he'd been falsely convicted of our mom's murder."

Her grandmother stood, back ramrod straight. "I told you never to mention his name."

"I didn't mention his name. In any case, as you're also aware, my father, Enrique, died in prison. There was no more chance to get him freed but that still meant the real killer was out and needed to be found and apprehended."

"Enrique Mendoza killed your mother!" Abigail reached out to slap Caroline, but it was Royal who halted her hand halfway there.

"No." Royal shook his head. "I will not allow that."

"Abigail, let's settle down and hear what Caroline has to say," James said to his wife.

Garrett stood and Royal stepped between him and

Caroline. "You and I have business. Don't think I've forgotten that."

"Are you threatening me?"

"I told you there'd be consequences. You stirred that fight at the Pumphouse. A man twice Caroline's size nearly sucker punched her and you were part of that. And now I hear you're spreading your special knowledge all over town that Caroline, who got *shot* at, had her car vandalized, her apartment broken into and her belongings destroyed and received a death threat is somehow faking that. You put her in more danger and that makes me very unhappy."

"What are you talking about?" Mindy asked.

Royal faced Mindy. "He's been spreading rumors."

"I have not."

Caroline pulled a phone out of her pocket. "Shall I call Polly Chase and let her know you're calling her a liar? Or maybe we can just ask Grandmother since she was there when he said it."

"I don't recall that." Her grandmother's lie wasn't very convincing.

"You're going to say that to a defense attorney?" Caroline looked at her sister. "Garrett has been stirring trouble for me for two months now. But back to what I was saying."

"No! You leave Shep and Mindy alone! I forbid this whole thing."

Shep shook his head. "I'm so bummed you're acting this way, Grandma. I've read the files. I've read articles and essays and the trial briefs and motions, all that stuff. I know what was missing, what was never followed up on."

"That's lies! She has an agenda. Defense attorneys hate the police. All his people do."

Caroline pretended it didn't hurt and sort of succeeded. "*His* people? You mean *my* people? *Mindy's* people? *Shep's* people? Or they get a pass because they look whiter? Grandma, I really don't know how my mother turned out the way she did hearing this sort of dog-whistle racism all the time. In any case, Shane Chase, the chief of police here, is working the case. The chief of police back when our mother was killed wasn't so very attentive to details when he had an easy target instead. Of course I've tried to tell you about all the missing things going into the trial, and you refused to listen."

"I've been sitting in on these meetings. I've heard Officer Chase talk. I've heard the other police and the investigator too. Grandma, you've been hating the wrong person all these years, but you can make it right now and listen to what Caroline is saying."

"She can't be here. Caroline, please leave our home now."

Caroline's grandfather shook his head, placing a hand on Abigail's forearm. "No. That's enough. Come in, let's all sit down. Garrett, you should be going."

"What? No. James, I'm here to back you up in this."

"Have you been going around town stirring enmity toward my granddaughter?"

"Not the way they say!"

James picked up the receiver of the phone in the hallway and dialed. "Hello, Polly, it's James Lassiter. I have a question. Did Garrett Moseby tell you the attacks on Caroline were faked to make Enrique Mendoza look innocent?"

He was quiet as Polly spoke. Most likely lecturing him, or so Caroline hoped. Garrett paled but James had him nailed with a stare so he stood there.

"I see. Yes, yes, you're right. I understand. Thank you, Polly."

James turned to Garrett. "Get out of this house, and do not return to it."

Mindy's hands went to her mouth and she rounded on Caroline. "Why do you have to ruin everything? We were just fine before you came here."

Caroline ignored her sister and the pain in her belly at her words. Instead she addressed her grandfather. "A man named Vernon Hicks has been identified as a possible suspect in my mother's murder. He lived over on Teller Avenue, next door to Joyce Marie Petitbone."

Her grandfather paused. "Vernon Hicks." He tapped his chin. "That name sounds familiar."

"It was sixteen years ago." But her grandmother also paused. "I'll be right back. Shep, I need you to pull something down from the attic."

Shep looked Caroline's way and she felt awful for him. But he hadn't wavered in his support or in his belief of their father's innocence so there was that.

Royal put an arm around her shoulder, holding her close. Reassuring her.

"Garrett, I told you to leave."

"Sir, don't you see how she's ruining your family? Just like her father did. Blood will tell. You know that."

"Blood will tell? Are you kidding me?" Royal's gaze went sharp and venomous. "So are you one of the pure who will save us all?"

"Purer than her." Garrett jerked his chin at Caroline.

"I think you're looking for inbred, not pure," Royal said.

Caroline couldn't stop her surprised cough of laughter.

"You shut your mouth, whore."

One moment Royal was next to her, and the next he'd sprung from the couch to his feet, using his momentum to carry him to Garrett, who let out a surprised shriek and ran for the front door.

Mindy flipped out, but their grandfather held her as Caroline leapt up to follow.

"I told you what was going to happen and that was before you called my woman a whore, you piece of shit." Royal stalked Garrett in the front yard. Garrett's nose was bleeding.

"You punched me!"

"I winged you as you ran past me shrieking. But I *will* punch you so don't worry about missing anything," Royal snarled.

"Someone is going to call the cops," Caroline called out.

"Don't care. He called you a whore."

She smiled. "You're so sweet, Royal. I appreciate the punch but we talked about this and the whole jail thing."

Royal made a face and shrugged. Then he took two fast steps Garrett hadn't expected, cocked back his fist and plowed it straight into Garrett's face. Hard enough to knock the other man back a few feet before his eyes rolled up and he hit the grass.

"And once again I find myself cleaning your knuckles." Caroline pulled him back inside to the hall bath where she left him for a moment to go out to the living room. "Let her go, Grandpa. Mindy needs to pick him up off the grass once he's awake." Caroline turned and went back to Royal.

"I should apologize, but I can't. He's lucky I didn't beat him to death. That piece of trash calling you a whore? After his racist purity bullshit and everything else he's done, he deserved a two broken ribs beat down."

She looked his hand over. Once she'd cleaned it up, she realized all the blood had been Garrett's.

Royal opened and closed his fist, and then she bent to kiss his hand. "Thank you. I hope you don't get arrested, and if you do, I'll bail you out and defend you."

He grinned and kissed her. "Let's get your info and go. This place is not for you anymore, if it ever was to start with."

They headed back out to the living room when her grandmother came in. "Vernon Hicks used to do odd jobs for all the businesses on that stretch of road where the diner was."

Caroline had to sit down because hope had broken free and was running riot. "Jesus. After all these years." She looked up at her grandmother. "How did you know?"

"I keep all my date books. They're stored in the attic in case we ever need them. I pulled the one from the year your mother was killed down and the year before it too and flipped through. I made a note. He worked on the diner a few months prior. I'd asked her his name when a friend of ours needed some work done on his property. I probably wouldn't have found it, but it was written on one of the tabbed pages. I'd been flipping through them from tab to tab just looking." Caroline flinched as her grandmother looked up at her. Always waiting for whatever venom would come her way.

Caroline kept her voice level. The flinch had been involuntary but she wouldn't give anything else. "May I have that?" She indicated the date book in her grandmother's hand. "They're going to question Vernon Hicks tomorrow in Porter. I'd like Shane to know about this before he goes. So he understands the connection."

Her grandmother handed it over.

"Thank you. I'll be sure Shane gets it back to you when he's done with it. Excuse me a moment, please." She took several steps away and called Shane. She stared at the name of her mother's killer on the page. It seemed so immense for what should have been a small thing. Not the information, no that was huge. If they could make a connection tonight, they could serve an arrest warrant and a search warrant at Vernon's apartment.

That was a whole different kind of immense.

It was the simplicity of a jotted note. A bunch of letters in her grandmother's date book that spelled out the name of a person who had destroyed her family. Right next to *paint for entry powder room*.

Shane answered and she forced herself to focus. "I have the connection between Vernon Hicks and my mother."

He rushed over to the Lassiters' to take their statements and take the datebook to enter into evidence.

Mindy came back in at some point but their grandfather had made her be quiet.

"Okay, so before I call in my favors to get warrants for Hicks, run it through with me," Shane said to Caroline. "We have a murder. We have a suspect who was seen washing blood off the night of the murder, and there's a connection between that man and the murder victim."

"And we have a suspect who has a history of violence. A man who has done time for manslaughter and assault. He has a history of stalking and hurting women. The murder bore really personal hallmarks. The kind a man Hicks might be. Angry at women. Obsessive. He's got major anger problems."

"I need some more, here, Caroline. What's his motive?"

"I know. Damn it. Okay. He did time in the system in

several places. Did he submit DNA on any of them? We could get it to the lab to see if it's a match. You'd have a physical tie to the scene."

"That's a good idea. There's a backlog but this is exigent. You're being threatened. He's tried to kill you. He took photos of you and the victim from your apartment. My concern is that he's now stalking you, Caroline. We found evidence of a little sniper's blind in a tree. The one the rifle appears to have been fired from."

Royal cursed under his breath and took her hand.

"Well isn't that comforting? Okay so he's obviously stalking me. But, you don't know that Hicks has any connection to me at all. You absolutely do need to arrest him, don't get me wrong. But you need to run this by the prosecutor to see what he thinks. Order the DNA if it's in the system. But if you arrest him without enough and you have to let him go before he gets charged, he might bolt. He's changed his name multiple times, he's moved around a lot, creating new identities."

"Okay, defense attorney, knock holes in it," Shane said.

"This is all totally circumstantial. So Vernon Hicks knew Bianca Mendoza when she was murdered. That's not a crime. A nearly ninety-year-old woman who remembers blood from sixteen years ago? There's no evidence she came forward at all with this information. You have nothing to tie Hicks to that murder but acquaintance."

She blew out a breath and realized her sister was crying, her head on their grandfather's shoulder. He looked absolutely wrecked as he stared at her. She tore her attention from however much they hated her for this and got back into the right headspace.

"Maybe your father would have better advice. You

have probable cause to arrest, but arrest him on a stalking charge. I'm being stalked and threatened. He's a stalker and threatener with a history of being locked up for violence and obsessive harassment of women. The current victim is the daughter of a murder victim Vernon Hicks is also a person of interest in. If you arrest him for that, you have him in while you serve the search warrant. He seems the type to trophy collect. Some of my mother's hair was taken. The pictures from my house. He's a collector. If he really did do it and he hasn't had to dump it when he ran or went inside, proof should be there."

"And while he's in interrogation and we're in his house, he'll go crazy imagining us going through his stuff. Touching his trophies can probably use that fear to get him talking if he doesn't lawyer up."

Caroline snorted. "He's a career criminal. He's going to lawyer up ten minutes after you get him in a room. If you don't find anything at his house, you're screwed. You'll have to let him go." She continued to pace as she thought. "So assuming *that* doesn't happen, we have ten minutes. All right. We've both dealt with his type before. He thinks he's way smarter than he is. He's got a hair trigger. Poor control means if you hit the right buttons in interrogation you can get enough to make a dent on holding him before he realizes he's screwed up and asks for a lawyer. Especially if you find something at his apartment."

"All right. I'm calling now. I'll have to run this all by the prosecutor and then a judge to get those warrants. I'd like to hit him as soon as we can. We'll need to coordinate with Porter on this obviously. I'll let you know when I can." Shane hugged Caroline. "It's nearly over."

Caroline smiled. "Thanks, Shane."

They walked him out and she went back in to grab her purse. She hugged Shep. "It's gonna be okay. Call me if you need me."

Shep looked between Caroline and Royal. "I hate this."

"If I'm right, this will be the beginning of the end of this whole thing."

"No not that. Though yeah, that's bad too. I mean the family. I mean the way this has gone down and you've been dumped on."

She hugged him again. "It was worth it. And I have you back in my life. You gotta take your victories where you can."

She turned her back on her grandparents, and Royal escorted her out.

Chapter Twenty-Four

"Are you all right?" Royal asked her as he helped her into the car.

"Not really, no."

"You mad that I punched Garrett?"

"Nope. He needed punching. Thank you for punching him."

"I'm sorry your grandparents are horrible people and your sister is a useless whiner."

That made her laugh.

She reached out and he took her hand.

"I can't think about it right now. Okay? I can't think about it or talk about it. Warrants being argued over. They could say no. If they do, he can bring him in to talk. But a career criminal knows his rights, trust me on that, so even if they bring him in, he'll talk but he won't tell them anything. And then he knows we're on to him. We lose our edge. He can run."

"Do you want to keep not talking about it? Like how it doesn't matter, because you have literally shed blood for this. This is going to happen. I can feel it. You have put so much into this. Years and years of your life. If anyone has the will and the persistence to make something like this happen successfully, you do."

He took her home and they had sweaty sex and she pushed all the stuff she needed to deal with really far away because she just couldn't do it that night.

He slept, and she got herself snuggled into him and closed her eyes.

And when she woke up again, it was to the sound of her phone ringing. A bleary look at the phone told her it was four in the morning. She grabbed it quickly; the ID told her it was Petal PD.

"Caroline Mendoza."

Royal turned one of the bedside lamps on.

"I just got back from Porter. I desperately need to sleep but before I do that, I wanted to call to let you know what happened. Hicks is in custody. For first-degree murder."

"What?"

"It took a few hours to get the warrants, but we got them and my friend in Porter served them with me. Hicks opened the door bitching about being woken up, and then he saw it was us and he ran for it. We chased him six blocks and took him down. We took him back to his place, and we walked inside where some of Porter PD were executing the search warrant. Anyway, there was enough there that we tossed him in the back of a cruiser and down to the station for processing. We charged him on stalking and got him in a room and my God. He just opened his mouth and started talking. First about you and then about your mother. *He confessed.* Without any prompting on our part."

"I don't… What the hell is going on? He confessed to killing my mother?"

"Caroline, I have seen a lot tonight, and I know you're eager to know all the details, but I want to come out there to you and tell you everything face-to-face. I want to shower, sleep for a few hours and then hug my wife and son. Can I come out to the ranch at ten?"

"Yes, yes. Come on out then. Thank you." She put her phone down and turned to Royal. "They arrested Hicks on the stalking charge, but they also charged him with first-degree murder. Shane says he confessed after whatever they found in his apartment but wouldn't say what it was. Now I'm freaked and imagining things like heads in aquariums or zombies on leashes. He didn't tell me the whole story but he's going to sleep a few hours, he just got back. And then he's coming out here at ten so I'll let Shep know when it's a more appropriate time to call a seventeen-year-old."

"Come back to bed. Rest for a bit."

She cuddled with him awhile but couldn't go back to sleep. He couldn't either so he headed out to work. She'd work from home until Shane came by.

Before she got started though, she made all the calls she needed to make and ended up spending an hour on the phone with her uncle.

She didn't have as much time to work before she had to stop and get ready for Shane to come over, but it was worth it. She'd missed her uncle more than she'd thought she did. Hearing his voice made her smile, and after she'd briefed him about the situation with Hicks, she ended up spending far more time telling him about Royal and her growing feelings for him.

It had kept her busy, and prevented her from thinking too deeply on anything but putting one foot in front of the other.

Royal came looking handsome and all cleaned up while she'd been making a fresh pot of coffee, and they'd just poured two cups when there was the sound of a car approaching the house.

Royal stilled. "We'll both go to the door."

Nodding, she took his hand, and they walked to the front and peeked out before opening up and stepping onto the porch.

It wasn't Shane, but Shep who'd approached and parked. The words sending him back to school were on her tongue until her grandfather got out as well.

Fuck. She didn't have the reserves to deal with another fight with her grandparents.

James raised a hand in a wave as they came up the steps to the doorway where Caroline and Royal stood. "I let Shep leave school for this meeting on the promise that I'd get to come along."

"Why is that?"

"You and I have some things to work though. I'm sorry, Caroline. I failed you in a lot of ways, and I don't know if you can get past it. But I hope so. I'd like you to give me a chance, and I'd also like to come in and hear what Shane Chase has to say."

Caroline took a deep breath and stepped from the way, motioning them into the house. "There's coffee in the kitchen. Shep, show him where it's at. Shane's pulling up to the house now." She waved his way and they all went inside.

Royal watched her. His usually confident Caroline was nervous. There were chinks in her normally self-assured armor of confidence. He wanted to comfort her, but it was clear she was holding on by her fingernails.

They all settled around the kitchen table.

"We served the warrant, like I said." Shane sipped his

coffee. "And he freaking ran. We chased him and brought his butt back to his apartment where they were doing the search. Hicks didn't want to go back inside, and when we got into the living room, I knew why."

"Why do I want to cringe before I even know?"

"The whole room was papered with pictures of you, Caroline. Newspaper articles you wrote going back as far as your first year in college. And the pictures he took from your apartment were up on the wall too."

"There's your link."

Royal's stomach bottomed out. He leaned a little closer, bumping his thigh to hers.

"Yes, there's our link on the stalking, and as we're all standing there in his living room, he knows it. So we take him back to the station in Porter and, I shit you not, I turn on the recorder, introduce myself and the other officer in the room and he just starts talking. He starts *confessing*. He'd been obsessed with your mother. In the search they found some of what we think is the hair taken from her at the scene. He had pictures of her too. Polaroids usually shot from what looks like a dumpster at the back of the diner. Stacks of them he had in a box with a locket necklace that had pictures of Enrique and you guys in it."

"My mother had a locket. It had their wedding picture and then a tiny department-store picture of me and Mindy holding baby Shep. It was white gold with rose-gold accents. I think it had little diamond chips in it. Nothing flashy."

"That's what we found. Anyway she was nice to him, he said, but she always turned him down. So he waited for your father to make a run to the bank as the diner cleaned up and readied for the next day. Hicks came in when your mother was alone and he killed her. He described the kind of knife. It's what killed her. He never knew Joyce Marie saw him. But he heard you on the radio, and then he saw you on television because he keeps up on you, what you're doing, where you're going. So he listened to that radio show, and it enraged him. And then the television. He knew you had to go and he had plans to kill you. He wrote them down in a notebook and he also told them to us."

"Why? Why would he tell you all this? This guy should be savvy. He's done some time. He should know the drill."

"Right? So there I am, I can't figure that out. I'm poking around, asking him questions trying to figure it out when he tries to make a deal to keep us from putting him back inside. Turns out he's ripped off a local drug dealer who has a lot of *associates* doing time. Hicks panicked, and then he lost his control and confessed to try to save himself. He's seriously scared of this dealer he screwed over. So much he didn't even make a fuss about moving to Petal. Figured his attorney would fight it just to slow things down. Guess Petal's lack of drug lords in the cells was a better option than fighting because once he got himself a lawyer, no one said a thing about it."

"Pity."

Shane sighed. "So there you go. He confessed. On tape. There's so much evidence in his apartment I had nightmares. He definitely needs to be off the streets. We have his journals, which he stashed in a friend's garage with all his boxes of trophies, while he did time. There are other victims. I'm sure of it. The state folks are already looking at it, and since he's moved around across several states, the federal people are too. Your father, Enrique Mendoza, did not kill your mother, Bianca

Mendoza. Please count on my help when you go through the process to clear him posthumously. I'm deeply sorry that shoddy investigation by a racist incompetent let the man who killed walk free, and an innocent man spent fourteen years in prison on death row. I'm sorry Petal PD had any part of it."

"You helped solve it. You can't own what the other guy did, as people tell me so often. You made it right because your department has the integrity his lacked. Thank you."

"The prosecutor will call you about interviewing you and getting evidence from you. He's interested in seeing your files that you put together."

She got up and brought him out a huge three-ring binder and then a smaller one. "I have them copied in bulk."

They walked Shane to the door and he drove away.

Shep sat at the table, his hands clasped tightly. "You did it."

"I'm not even sure how to put it all into words." She smiled at Shep and he got up to hug her. "But I'm glad you were here to hear it with me."

Shep sat again as uncertainty rose from where her grandfather sat.

"I had a lot of help. So much help. There's still a ways to go though, so it's best to brace yourself for a long process. But I'm hopeful and I'm going to allow myself that hope. And now people can see Dad didn't do it."

She turned to her grandfather. Royal stood close enough that the heat of him blanketed her back as she faced one of her demons. "He's innocent."

James cocked his head. "It appears that way."

"He's innocent," she repeated. Because it was important. If they ever were to get to a place where she could work things out with her grandparents, they needed to admit it.

Her grandfather understood and took a deep breath. "Yes. He's innocent. I misjudged you and your father. Now that we've got all this proof, your grandmother will come around. Mindy too. We really had no idea you'd been threatened and harmed to that degree. If we'd have known…"

"You *did* know. You *knew* someone shot at me and you never called to check on me. Not once. You *knew* my apartment had been broken into. You *knew* my car had been vandalized. And you never called. Now that you know the truth and it's been proven by another person, you want to just what? Pretend none of that happened? She slapped me. And she threatened me to never see my brother and sister again. It was bad enough you threw me out, thank goodness for the Mendozas. Because *they* finished raising me. They dealt with my grief and pain, and they sent me off to college and law school. They came to my graduations too. For a long time I pretended it didn't matter. I pretended that I could make this better if I was just more of this or less of that. But it never worked, and it won't because I can't be anything but what I am. And I don't even want to. So I accept your apology from earlier. But I don't know how I'm going to be taking any new steps back toward you all."

"That's fair. She was wrong to have hurt you. Wrong to have threatened you. She and I had a very bitter disagreement once I found out. We love you. All three of you. We did what we thought was best but we messed up. People make mistakes."

"I love you too. But I need some time and some space away from you and Abigail. I'm sorry your daughter died. You didn't deserve that." Caroline hugged him.

"Thank you for finding her killer," he whispered before kissing her cheek and leaving with Shep.

Shep came back inside. He hugged Caroline tight. He was so lost, her baby brother.

She hugged him back. "It's okay. He's behind bars. At last. He'll pay, Shep. He'll pay for what he's done to our family."

"I can't quite believe it. I want us all to meet. You, me and Mindy. She needs to think this through. Especially now. We need to stick together. All three of us for Mom and Dad. She needs her letters."

"What if we misjudge, and she destroys them or tells Grandma about them? My heart breaks to imagine how she'll feel later when she realizes she was wrong."

"Don't baby her. Everyone babies her. She needs to accept what is true. She's a grown woman, and she has to choose her freaking future. Garrett, whose anger will turn on her some day? Or us? The truth? And we need to be a united front to make sure everything happens the way it should and Vernon Hicks is the one behind bars. This is a big job and you've done it alone long enough. The three of us can do the job together."

"You're an admirable young man, Quique."

"Did he really call me that?"

"Everyone called you that. Mom did, Mindy and I did."

"Where did Shep come from? That's all I ever remember."

"Grandma used to call you that. She felt Quique and Enrique were too hard to pronounce. She said she liked it because Shepard was her paternal grandmother's name."

"I'm going back to Mendoza. I've thought about it for a while."

She looked at her brother. "You don't need to decide

right now. Baby steps and we'll get through this just fine. It's your name if you want it. If you don't, that's not a thing either. Understand?"

He hugged Caroline again. "I do. I love you. I have a final in my last period so I gotta get back to school. I'll call you."

She watched them drive away as she leaned into Royal. "I can't quite believe it."

Royal brought her back inside, closing the door and locking it.

"You're afraid to believe it."

"Yeah, that too."

He turned off lights and the coffeemaker and drew her back to the bedroom. "No way, buster. I have to go to work. I can't be taking fuck breaks."

He laughed but after he stole a kiss, he sobered. "You're not going in."

"Am so."

"Oooh, will you say that and stomp so your boobs jiggle? It'd be even better if you pouted a little."

Her brows flew up, and Royal knew he was on the right track. Ever since he'd met her, she'd kept a tight rein on her feelings about the whole mess she'd pretty much dragged single-handedly over the finish line. In the end people helped her, yes, but it was her dogged persever-ance that won out.

But he knew she pushed her emotions—vulnerability, doubts and fears, her survivor's guilt, her grief and her anger—out of her mind. To examine them would have been to pull her foundations down when she needed to keep strong.

But she paid a price for it. A big one and he was over watching her bear everyone else's weight and never thinking about dropping her burdens every once in a while.

And you needed to. It was a safety valve that prevented you from exploding.

"So here's a thing, the police just arrested the man responsible for killing your mother when you were just fifteen years old. The same guy who let your dad go to prison. The one who tore your family apart. He's why Quique is Shep now and why Mindy is with a dingus like Garrett. And then he stalked you and hurt you and made you scared all the time. The man who did all that damage to you is finally known and in jail."

"Yes." She was aiming at bland, he could tell, but she missed that by a mile. "But I still have to go to work."

"There'll be work tomorrow and Sunday and Monday and beyond, now that the piece of human garbage who has terrorized you for sixteen years is finally fucking dealt with."

"I can't do this right now."

"Just another week. Or another month. Just until we figure out who the guy is. Just until he's arrested. Now it's what? Just until trial? Just until he's sentenced? Goes to prison? How long, Caroline, are you going to push fifty percent of what you should feel away, and when is it going to break through? Vernon Hicks killed your mother. She would have been scared and in pain. And alone on that floor as Hicks walked away like she was nothing. Your poor father. Walking in on that? Of course he was incoherent for a while. And then he got railroaded and sent off to death row. And your entire life continued to just plummet as you refused to believe your father was guilty, and your grandparents, grief laden and selfish, pushed you away for it instead of trying to deal with it head-on. And then, you had to leave here. Leave everything you ever knew, and while the Mendozas love you, you had this whole side of your life you needed so badly and it just wasn't there." He pushed her to the mattress where she watched him through exhausted, wary eyes.

He slid her shoes off. "You're driven though. And they love you and support you, and you get yourself into UCLA and then off to law school because sure it'll be a good career, you'll have way more expertise to use to aid your father. It wasn't until later that you discovered you loved the law, but at the start you just did it for him. And you went through appeals that didn't go anywhere. Disappointment after disappointment made all the worse because there was evidence that no one even freaking *looked* at. And then your father, who should have been here with you all along but for Vernon Hicks, well, he gets cancer and dies and you can't hug him again or hear his voice or walk with him out those prison gates, though you imagined that moment thousands of times.

"You alone get it in a way that estranges you. So you bottle it all up and pretend it doesn't matter, all while carrying everyone else's shit and then this fucker turns up again and he stalks you, terrorizes you and hurts you. Your grandparents are assholes. And yet you keep going."

He pulled his shirt off, and when her attention was on his chest, he unbuttoned her blouse and exposed the pretty camisole she wore underneath.

"That guy is *finally* in jail. And he confessed. And there's all sorts of evidence. It is okay to be proud of all you've done. And it's okay to let yourself weep for the mother you lost. For her pain and her fear and for every day since that you've lost some new memory you should have made with her. And it's okay to let yourself weep for the father who loved you so damned much and died in prison no matter how hard you tried to free him. It is bittersweet. It is sad and unfair and good and all those things. Don't let feeling all those things about this continue to be taboo. Let it go. I'm here and I have you."

Her eyes had widened, and her mouth trembled at the edges as they slid down. She made a gasping hiccupping sound and then a ragged sob tore through her as she crumpled. Royal got on the bed and pulled her close.

This was a person who had held in such deep sorrow for so long it seemed to rip from her with each exhale. He held her tight as she clung to him like he was the only thing keeping her from drowning.

Her sobs and the aftershock of hiccups and phantom gasps began to slow and then ease as she relaxed, her breathing going very deep.

He kissed her forehead. "Close your eyes, Caro, and let it all go. Sleep a bit and we'll face the rest."

Caroline snuffled, snuggling into his body as close as she could before she fell into sleep, and once he knew she'd made it safely, he closed his eyes and joined her, his heart aching for all the pain she had to suffer.

An hour or so later, Caroline and Royal woke up, and she shifted to look up at the ceiling.

"It's so unfair. There is no way to make it better." Her voice was scratchy from sleep and crying.

"Nope. All you can do is honor their memory, which you already do."

Royal Watson was her *one*. She didn't want to go back to what their relationship had been like before. It was nice dating him, but living with him had been wonderful. Not just safe, but she loved the house, the view, the kitchen, his kooky shoulder-riding cat. This place had become one that felt hers.

"I don't want to move back to my apartment," she said quietly.

He stilled. "You're moving back to Seattle?"

"What? No! I'm not moving away from Petal. I just… I like it here. With you."

He hugged her tight. "Oh. Well yes, of course. I want you here too. I was planning on always being busy when you wanted to go back to your apartment, and you'd just give up and stay. Or maybe I was going to come out and ask you to live with me."

"I asked you instead."

"We'll go through your storage unit to find things you want to bring here. We can get your photos reframed and hang them. I want this to be our place. I love you. I want to build a future with you that does not include you being in danger all the time."

She fist bumped him. "You and me both. There's more to go, you know. The trial, all that. The craziness with my grandparents, I don't know how that's going to work out. I'm giving you one last chance to bolt. After this I'm clinging to you like a barnacle."

He laughed. "I'm all yours to cling on to. I know your life has had a lot of upheaval, so let me be your steady ground, your safe space. Where you know you can be and be loved and cherished. You can count on me."

She smiled, turning into his hold to hug him and bury her face in his neck, breathing him in. "I love you for that."

"Love you too, darlin'."

Epilogue

Eight months later

Caroline stood up after brushing off the marbled face of the new headstone they'd put next to Bianca's. Their father at her side as he was meant to be all these years.

Royal stood with her, handing over the flowers. Caroline put the creamy white calla lilies on the marker and lilacs on her mother's.

Mindy put white roses on his stone and yellow ones on their mother's. Shep laid lilies on both markers.

The siblings stood back for their father's family to come forward. Each brother, sister and their *abuela* left things or said a few quiet words. It had been a way to put closure on the situation. Enrique finally buried with his wife as their wills had called for. He was home.

First Shep had traveled to Los Angeles with Caroline to meet his father's family, and then Mindy had. Both had been taken in with a lot of love, which made Caroline happy.

The trial had closed three days prior with a guilty verdict. The sentencing was the following week. Vernon Hicks would likely die in prison. Which was just fine with Caroline.

There was an FBI task force that had added Hicks to its list. They had found at least three female murder victims they believed carried a connection to Hicks. Caroline tried not to dwell on any what-ifs when it came to Hicks and his fascination with her. He was gone.

"Come on back to the house for lunch, everyone," Caroline called out to the crowd that had gathered in the cemetery.

Edward hugged Caroline. "I'm so proud of you."

"Me?"

"Of course. Look at this. Just take a moment and look over this crowd."

She did. There were at least ten Mendozas who'd come to Petal. Her brother and his new girlfriend he'd met at college. Mindy, who'd finally broken off with Garrett and was focused on finishing school before deciding to date again. A whole passel of Chases, including Shane. Justin was there, as was Peter. Murphys abounded as well. Newly married Beth and Joe. Anne, who'd grown to be one of Caroline's closest friends. Melissa was there, but she and Clint had broken up the summer before.

Friends, her intentional family, really. And they had come to put a period at the end of this long life sentence.

And there was Royal. In a suit. Lordy. Handsome and in charge. People paused to speak with him often, but his attention was on Caroline. Worried about her, she knew. She hadn't been feeling well on top of an already difficult situation.

She had indeed counted on him. And he'd never broken his promise to be there.

"This is because of you, Caroline. It's easy to give up. It's easy to give in when things get really hard. But you never gave up. You made this happen. That's phenomenal."

"Thank you. And thank you for being a mentor to me and opening your family the way you have."

Over the year she'd been in Petal she'd done her part to make the firm even healthier. She loved her job. Edward encouraged her, challenged her, and he and Polly had adopted her into their huge brood. He was far less like a boss and far more like a father. Which had worked out because she dug having a father, and certainly Edward Chase was a spiffy dad.

"Did you see them?" Edward pointed to her grandparents who stood a ways off.

Most of the time she loved Petal. She and her siblings had a real relationship. Though making up with Mindy had been emotional, it had been worth the pain. Caroline and her grandfather had started playing online chess six months back. After a while, they agreed to coffee. They met once every few weeks for an afternoon cinnamon roll and some hot chocolate.

Her grandmother though hadn't spoken a word to her since that night when Shane had come over. The night they'd identified Vernon Hicks.

"I didn't. Are you and Polly coming out to the house?"

"We are, definitely. I'll see you over there." Edward kissed her cheek, and then Polly hugged her and they headed off to their car.

Royal approached. "The Lassiters are here." He took her hands. "You want to go over there? I can come with you or wait here."

In other words *I'm not leaving you here to do this on your own*. She was so lucky.

"Come on."

Hand in hand they approached her grandparents.

"Hey, Grandpa." She looked to her grandmother and nodded.

Abigail spoke. "It's a nice stone. I saw it yesterday. We were here as they installed it. She'd have liked that."

"Thank you."

"Would you come to dinner sometime?" her grandmother asked. "Both of you, I mean."

"Yes."

Her grandmother licked her lips and gave a tip of her chin to indicate she was pleased. In the background Caroline heard people moving back to their cars and realized they needed to head back to the house. She thought about inviting them but she didn't know that the Mendozas were ready for that yet. Caroline was pretty sure she wasn't ready for that yet either.

So she didn't. She and Royal stepped back. "Thank you for coming."

"I'll be in touch about dinner."

Caroline nodded. "Okay."

And then it was over, and she and Royal were on the way back to their house to be with all their loved ones.

"You all right?" Royal asked.

"You know, I think I am."

"Good. Because I think you need to marry me."

She nearly choked on the lifesaver she'd been sucking on. "How did you know? I don't want you to marry me just because I'm pregnant."

"You're *pregnant*?"

"You didn't know?"

"What the hell?" He pulled off the road and shifted to face her. "You're pregnant?"

"I've been sick for three weeks. I've been stressed. But when Melissa came over this morning, she made me take a pregnancy test."

He unbuckled his seat belt and she was in his arms as he kissed her. "I can't believe you didn't tell me!"

"I just found out four hours ago! I have a houseful of people. I was going to tell you when we were alone."

"Well now I'm doubly asking you to marry me."

"You really wanted to before you knew I was pregnant?"

"Didn't I just ask you before I knew? I've wanted to ask you for four months but I figured it would be best to wait until after the trial, and then just now it felt like I had to ask or burst."

"Yeah. I'll marry you. And have your babies who will ride around on your four-wheeler and get muddy with you."

"Awesome."

People began to honk and slow down, wondering why the trip to the house had been interrupted. Laughing, Royal kissed her one last time before he pulled back onto the road. And this time when she passed that piece of empty lot, she wished they were there to celebrate, but she didn't feel like she'd break anymore.

She had a life and a future with this man she'd fallen for when he'd reached a high shelf for her. And the next generation they would build together.

* * * * *

Acknowledgments

Thanks goes to Angela James and her amazing team at Carina for giving these books a home (and spiffy new covers!). Back in the day when the books originally came out, Angie was my editor and I'm so happy to say she still is well over a decade later. She's a unicorn and I adore her.

I can't forget to shout out to Anne Scott, my original editor for *Lost in You* and *Count on Me*. She's fabulous and did a great job and I loved working with her.

As the heart of both series is family and connection— I'd be remiss not to thank my own family. My husband who has supported me and my writing from day one. The guy who picks up the slack even though he's got his own busy work schedule. The model for all my heroes.

About the Author

Lauren Dane is a *New York Times* and *USA TODAY* bestselling author of over fifty novels and novellas across several genres. She lives in the Northwest with her patient husband and three wild children.

Visit Lauren on the web at www.laurendane.com.

E-mail: laurendane@laurendane.com

Twitter: @laurendane

You can write to her at: PO BOX 45175, Seattle, WA 98145

Meet the Hurley Brothers:
Paddy, Ezra and Vaughan.
Sexy, loyal and a little bit of trouble.
Available now from HQN and Lauren Dane

Read on for an excerpt from
The Best Kind of Trouble
and then pick up all three books in digital,
audio or paperback!

Even after years of the rock-and-roll lifestyle, Paddy
never forgot the two wickedly hot weeks he once shared
with Natalie. Now he wants more...even if it means
tempting Natalie and her iron-grip control. But there's
a fine line between well-behaved and misbehaved—and
the only compromise is between the sheets!

CHAPTER ONE

I⊤ REALLY DIDN'T matter that the day was sure to be hot enough to melt asphalt; coffee was a necessity if she was expected to work all day at the library and not maim anyone.

Public safety was important, after all. That and her terrible addiction to things that were bad for her like caffeine and sugary baked goods.

Common Grounds was a daily stop on her way to work or other errands in town.

Bobbi was behind the counter, and when she caught sight of Natalie coming through the doors, she grinned. "Morning!" *So. Perky.*

Perky was not in Natalie's wheelhouse, so she aimed for amiable because Bobbi the barista was Natalie's pimp. "Morning. Hit me with something awesome."

Another luminous smile from Natalie's favorite barista as she got to work. "I have a new something to try. Are you game?"

"My vices are few, so I like to enjoy what I've got." She looked over the stuff in the case. There were no doughnuts, sadly, so a scone would have to do. "I'd like to enter into a relationship with that cinnamon scone there to go with my something new."

"It's early for you, isn't it? I thought the library didn't open until ten today?"

"It doesn't, but I'm doing story time for some pre-schoolers."

"Aw, that's nice of you."

Natalie had the financial ability to volunteer in her free time and a strong commitment to giving back, so reading to preschoolers once or twice a week was pretty fun as such things went.

Bobbi handed over the bag with the scone and her drink. "Latte with orange essence and a little shaved chocolate. Tell me what you think."

"Sounds fantastic." As for nice for reading books to kids? "It's a good thing when children like to read. Plus, they're adorable when they're three and four. They blurt out the best stuff. Usually shit about their parents. Last week, right as I finished up *Fancy Nancy*, one of them pipes up and says, 'my dad doesn't wear pants on week-ends.' It was awesome."

Bobbi laughed. "My nephew's like that. My sister says she and her husband have to be careful about stuff they say now because he told his kindergarten class that he walked in on mom and dad *naked wrestling*."

That made Natalie guffaw. "It's pretty hilarious when it's *other people's* kids ratting them out."

"Yeah. Our time will…oh…*my*." Bobbi's gaze seemed to blur as she gaped in the direction of the front door, and that was when Natalie heard *his* voice.

Not for the first time.

"Care to help out a man in dire need of some caffeine?"

She couldn't help it. Natalie turned to take in the ridic-ulous male glory that was Paddy Hurley. In jeans and a T-shirt, he still looked like a rock star. Though she'd seen him naked, and he looked like a rock star then, too. His dark brown hair had lightened up, probably from being out in the sunshine. He'd put his sunglasses on top of his head, so those big hazel eyes fringed by gorgeous, thick, sooty lashes had extra impact.

Impact that made Natalie's heart beat faster and her face warm as she remembered some of the things they'd done together. *To each other.* Dirty, filthy, naked things. Really good things the mere memory of had her libido sitting up and panting over.

Bobbi was entranced by him as she stood at the counter, blinking slowly, clearly caught up in her admiration. He kept smiling, as if he was totally used to that sort of attention. Of course he was.

"Can I get an iced coffee and a slice of that blueberry loaf for here?" He changed his tone a little from that flirty drawl to something more direct, and it seemed to do the trick.

Bobbi stood a little taller and cleared her throat. "Uh. Yeah. Sorry. Yes, of course."

"Thanks." He grinned, all white teeth and work-in-the-sun glow. *Good God*, he was beautiful.

"I'll bring it out when I'm done." Bobbi got to work but waggled her brows at Natalie, mouthing *holy shit, it's Paddy Hurley.*

Natalie tried to turn quickly and make an exit, but he'd caught the direction of Bobbi's look, and she saw the moment he recognized her, too.

"Hey, there. *Wow*." He searched for her name, which is what allowed her to pull her mask on and pretend she had no idea who he was.

"Hello." She turned to Bobbi. "See you tomorrow!" Natalie put the lid back on her cup and gathered her things, but Paddy stepped closer.

"Natalie, right? You worked at that dive bar attached to the bowling alley near Portland."

A lifetime before.

"Sorry?" She cocked her head like she had no idea he was talking about the two weeks they'd spent nailing each other like sex was going to be outlawed any moment.

"It's Paddy Hurley. I'd know that mouth anywhere." He said it quietly. Enough that she appreciated his discretion.

That Natalie stayed in the dive bar. The Natalie she was now had risen from the ashes while she was in college, and she rarely looked back if she could help it. Paddy Hurley and those two weeks they'd shared were a great memory, especially the naked part. But she'd spent too many years and a whole lot of effort to be *more* and had no desire to go digging up that lifetime again.

"Nice to meet you, Paddy. I enjoy your music. I need to be on my way." She reached for the door, and he searched her features and shook his head as if he couldn't believe what was happening. Which was sort of charming, and she had to remind her hormones sternly to back off and let her brain do the work.

But he rallied. "I know it's you. Stay and have coffee with me so we can catch up."

"I have to get to work." She opened the door, nudging him out of the way a little as she did. The heat of the day greeted her, and she stepped out, covered her eyes with her shades and walked away.

The past was the past. She had a life now. One she'd spent a lot of time and energy building, and she needed to keep the door on who she'd once been firmly closed.

Even if it left a tasty bit like Paddy Hurley on the other side.

PADDY WATCHED HER retreat down the sidewalk, the hem of her skirt swishing back and forth, exposing the backs of her thighs. Thighs that had been wrapped around his hips more than once.

She had tattoos, matching ones, at the top of each thigh, right under each ass cheek. Pretty red bows like at the top of stockings. He smiled at that memory.

"Her name is Natalie, right?" he asked the barista when she brought him the coffee and pastry.

"Yeah. You know her?"

"She lives here in town?" He sipped his drink. He and his brothers had gone out for an early ride so he was hot and a little sleepy. The iced coffee helped with both.

"Sure. Works at the library. Comes in every morning before work to get coffee. Well, except Monday because the library is closed on Mondays. She's single. You know, if you were asking because you thought she was pretty."

He gave the barista a smile. He did indeed think Natalie was pretty. Her hair was short now where it had been long years before. He normally loved a woman with long hair, but on her that pixie thing worked. She had a great neck.

A great everything. She'd kept up with him on every level. They partied hard, fucked hard, worked hard. He and the band his brothers had formed, Sweet Hollow Ranch, had had a series of gigs at dives all over Portland and Southwest Washington. They'd managed to get two crappy hotel rooms included as part of their pay.

The motel had been right behind a bowling alley and the shithole of a bar attached to it. Natalie had been a waitress there, slinging drinks and dodging overeager hands when he'd met her.

It had been a matter of hours after meeting—the

chemistry so instant and thick between them—until they'd stumbled into her studio apartment and into her bed.

She'd been underage, as had he, but they'd spent the next two weeks together around her shifts at the bar and his gigs.

And then he'd gone on the road, and she'd gone off to college. He'd thought of her over the years. One of their songs, "Dive Bar," had been about her and those two weeks.

Turns out she lived in the same town. Which meant it was fate. He continued to smile after he'd thanked the barista.

Why she'd pretended not to know him was the question. She had her reasons, and he aimed to know them, too. The woman behind the counter said Natalie was single, so it wasn't a boyfriend.

Paddy hadn't achieved the success he had because he gave up when things got hard.

He'd simply keep at it.

He leaned back in his chair and watched the street outside as he drank his coffee. A new challenge was always fun. Especially when it concerned a pretty blonde with long legs and a smile that invited a man to sin and not repent.

CHAPTER TWO

"You remember that shithole of a bar we hung out in just outside Portland?" Paddy handed a coil of rope to his oldest brother, Ezra.

"Dude, you've got to be more specific than that. There are dozens upon dozens of shithole bars I remember. More I don't." Ezra snorted as he hung the rope up on a hook just inside the stable door.

Paddy laughed. It had been fifteen years since they'd started out, and that particular shithole bar had been at least a dozen years before. "Back at the beginning. Right before we headed to L.A. and made the first record with the label. The bar was next to a bowling alley. We had two rooms in that rat trap of a motel that was behind it."

"Ah! Yes, I do remember that one. Damien got his ass jumped by those cowboys who heckled us and waited for him after the show."

"Then we all jumped in, and you got arrested."

"Wasn't the last time."

"And now you have pigs and dogs, and you only beat on your brothers."

"I'm too old to beat anyone up but you people. Plus, I have great hands. Why you taking me down memory lane?"

"There was a girl."

Ezra barked a laugh. "Yeah, well, you'll have to be

more specific with that, too. Even more of them than shithole dive bars."

"Natalie. Long blond hair. Big blue eyes. Dimples. Juicy mouth. She worked in the bar. We had a thing. Hot, hard, fast, for two weeks before we left for L.A."

"Hmm, sounds familiar, but Paddy, you have a thing for blondes. There are stories like that from coast to coast and across Europe. They all run together after a time."

"I do have a really fucking awesome life."

Ezra rolled his eyes. "Does this story have a point?"

"She's here. In town, I mean. This morning after our ride, I went down to get some coffee. She was there. At the counter. Hair is short now, but it exposes her neck."

Ezra hummed his approval as he put things away.

"She's a librarian."

Ezra's brows rose appreciatively. *Well, now.*

"Right? But she pretended she didn't remember me."

Ezra turned and then laughed so hard he had to brace his hands on his knees. "Man, I wish I'd have seen your face when that happened," Ezra choked out in between fits of laughter. "I love how your ego paints it like she pretended not to know you instead of her just not remembering."

"Har har. She remembered me. There's no way she forgot it. It wasn't a night or two. It was two really intense weeks. Plus, asshole, I'm unforgettable. Anyway, she didn't deny knowing me. She just stepped around admitting knowing me. I know the difference."

Ezra stood up, wiping his eyes and settling down a little. "Thanks for that. Totally made my day."

"I'm asking you for advice. You give Damien advice all the time."

"He's an idiot. He needs it more than you do," Ezra

said, referring to one of their brothers, the drummer of Sweet Hollow Ranch.

"Yeah, there is that."

"Okay, so hit me. What advice do you want? How to deal with the blow to your ego? Suck it up and move on. So what? There have to be dozens upon dozens of women who feel the same way about you, Paddy. You dumped her, and she does not have fond memories. You're lucky she didn't knee you in the gooch."

"I didn't dump her! It was fall, she was heading off to college and we were on the road. It was fine. No tears. No drama." He ran a hand through his hair. "I liked her. I liked her then, and I want to know if I'd like her now."

Ezra looked him over carefully as they left the stables. "So you want to what? Be this woman's friend? See if she wants another turn in the sheets with you? This is your hometown, Paddy. Don't shit where you sleep. If you charm her out of her panties and then it goes bad, then what? Do you really want some pissed off ex-girlfriend who knows where you live?"

Paddy made a face. "It's not like that. I can't believe I haven't bumped into her before now. It's not like Hood River is a bustling metropolis."

"Yeah, well, you've been out on multiple tours in a row and traveling in between."

"True. Anyway, I don't just want to nail her, though she's gorgeous and all. Like I said, I want to see if we still click."

"Cut the shit. You're into it because it's a challenge."

Paddy sucked in a breath. "Okay, so maybe that's part of it. But not all of it."

"For whatever reason, you have an unhealthy level of self-confidence. You're okay-looking and all. Chicks dig you, and you hate to lose. So go for it, but don't be a dick."

Which, come to think of it, was pretty good advice.

NATALIE WALKED INTO Common Grounds with a spring in her step. She'd had a really great dinner with her housemate and best friend the night before. They'd watched a movie, and she'd gotten eight solid hours of really good sleep.

It was sunny, a breeze came in off the Columbia and she was well and truly prepared for an excellent Friday.

She waved a hello at Bobbi. "Good morning! I think I'd like an Americano today with lots of room. What sorts of delicious, calorie-packed goodness do you have left in the case?"

Bobbi looked over to her left. "See, like clockwork."

Natalie followed her gaze and nearly jumped when she saw Paddy Hurley sitting there with a grin on his face. The muted sunlight from the window he sat next to danced over his skin. Jesus H, he looked fantastic, his long legs stretched out, the denim straining at the thighs and over his crotch.

He packed quite a treat behind his zipper. Her belly and regions south tightened at that memory.

She snapped her gaze from his cock and tried not to blush.

"Have a seat." He pushed the chair across from him away from the table with one booted foot. Not cowboy boots, worn work boots she figured cost more than she made in a month.

She wanted to go over and sit. Wanted to flirt and chat and let it lead right back to her place. Something about the man had gotten under her skin right from go. He was dangerous. Wanting too much was dangerous.

"I have to go to work." With sheer force of will, Natalie turned her attention back to the bakery case.

Bobbi gave her a single raised brow but then got started on the Americano. The sounds and scent of the coffee-laden steam settled Natalie a little. "Ooh, I want one of those banana-chocolate chip muffin things."

"Here's the thing, Natalie." Suddenly, Paddy was standing very close. How had he done that? "*That* muffin is on hold. I'm a nice guy, though, so I'll happily let you have it if you'll sit and have coffee with me while we catch up."

In her head, her sigh was wistful, but on the outside, she added a little annoyance to keep him back. Natalie had a weak spot for charming men, and boy, did Paddy have that in spades.

She was careful not to turn to look at him. He was so close, she probably couldn't have kept her little resolution and stay on her Paddy Hurley–free diet. "I'll have the blueberry one instead, then."

Bobbi, clearly confused about the entire situation shrugged and handed over the Americano and the muffin. Natalie thanked her and paid before heading toward the door.

Paddy caught up to her before she'd gotten more than a few steps. "Natalie? I was under the impression that when we parted ways before, things were okay between us. I guess I got it wrong. I'm sorry for whatever I did."

Natalie paused. She might know it was best to keep him at a distance, but she didn't want him feeling guilty or to come off looking disgruntled. "It was fine. There's no need to apologize."

His expression was smug for a moment, and then he caught himself with an easy smile. "So you *do* remember me."

There was no way she could stop her smile in response. "Yes. You're pretty memorable."

"So what's the deal?" He leaned a little closer. "You like being chased?"

With an annoyed hiss, Natalie stepped away. "*No.* I'm not interested in this…whatever it is. I don't want to play games. I'm not being coy. I have a nice, *quiet* life. I like it that way."

"There's no *whatever it is.* Not yet. We already had that. I just think we could get to know one another again. I promise not to trash your living room or put a guitar through your television or anything."

The charisma flowed off him in waves. It wasn't something he put on. It wasn't an affectation. It was impossible *not* to be attracted to him. They'd clicked all those years before, and it was still there, that chemical pull that made her a little sweaty and dizzy.

She stood a little straighter. "I have to go to work. I'm glad things are going well for you and your career. Have a good life, Paddy."

He grabbed her hand, twining his fingers with hers, and a shock of connection rang through her. She could *not* want this.

The heat of him sort of caressed her skin, and it wasn't even gross and sweaty because it was a thousand degrees outside. Was he some sort of sorcerer or something?

His attention shifted from where their hands were together to her face. "Wait. Let me walk you over. You're at the library, right?"

Using all her will, she slowly pulled her hand free, their fingers still connected until the very last.

"No. Really. I can't. I don't have room in my life for you and all that comes with you."

He flinched a little, but she had to give him credit for doggedness. "You don't even know me now. How can you know what comes with me?"

"I'm truly happy to see your success. You worked for it. But come on, I'm no dummy. I know what comes with a life like yours." She took a step away and then another until she was far enough to get a breath that wasn't laden with him. "Enjoy your Friday."

She left him there on the sidewalk as she kept going until finally, after she'd turned the corner, the squeezing pressure in her belly eased, and she could breathe again.

She'd made the right choice.

She liked him. It wasn't like she could lie about that. But she'd spent years of struggle to make herself a life she wanted, too many to let her ladybits take over. Truth was, she let that fear remain. The fear that his wild life would be one cringeworthy experience after the next; the fear of all that chaos and insanity kept her steadfast.

The library beckoned, and she kept moving toward it. She had a direction, and it was forward, not back. There was room for pleasure; she certainly hadn't left sex behind, after all. But fleeting pleasure wasn't stable or strong. That's what he offered, and so she needed to pass on it.

BUT WHEN SHE walked into the coffee shop on Tuesday, he was there. Natalie ignored him and once she got out to the street—and man, was she glad she'd driven that day so she could put a closed door and a bunch of steel between them—she saw he waited just on the other side of her car.

"*What?* God, I told you, I'm not interested."

His smile was slow, easy and effortlessly sexy. "You're not interested in Paddy the rock star."

Natalie frowned. "Is that so hard to believe? Not everyone wants to latch on to you for your fame, you know. I'm happy for you and your brothers. I like your music. But I don't party like that anymore." Hell, she didn't *live* like that anymore. "I'm not that girl."

He leaned against her car like a cat. "Darlin', none of us are those people anymore. If I drank like that now, I'd be seriously fucked up the next day. When I'm not on tour, I'm here in Hood River. Not exactly known as a place to do blow off a hooker's ass now, is it?"

She groaned. "I have no idea. It could be, and there could be a huge hooker/cocaine thing going on, and I wouldn't know it. This is my point. Why are you so set on me, anyway?"

"You're so suspicious. It's sort of sexy. I'm set on you because I like you. Let me take you to dinner. Somewhere low key. Hell, I'll make you dinner at my house. No photographers. No keg stands. Just Paddy and Natalie."

"Patrick, just leave it be. There are a million women who would be happy to have dinner with you. I'm a librarian living in a small town. I don't have dinner with rock stars."

"I won't be a rock star at dinner. I'll be Paddy. Anyway, I love books. Come on. Give me a chance. While I'm impressed you'd think a million women would be interested in me, *I'm* only interested in one woman. You."

She got in and closed the door. After she'd started the

car, she opened her passenger window a little. "Look, I'm flattered, I really am. But I'm not the woman for you."

She pulled away, and he gave her a cheeky wave.

In retrospect, it was right then that she knew she was in very big trouble when it came to Patrick Hurley.

Don't miss all three books in the
Hurley Brothers trilogy:
The Best Kind of Trouble, Broken Open, *and*
Back to You

Available now from Lauren Dane and HQN